STAY

NICOLA GRIFFITH

ALSO BY

The Blue Place

Slow River

Ammonite

STAY

NICOLA GRIFFITH

A NOVEL

STAY

d o u b l e d a y

New York
London
Toronto
Sydney
Auckland

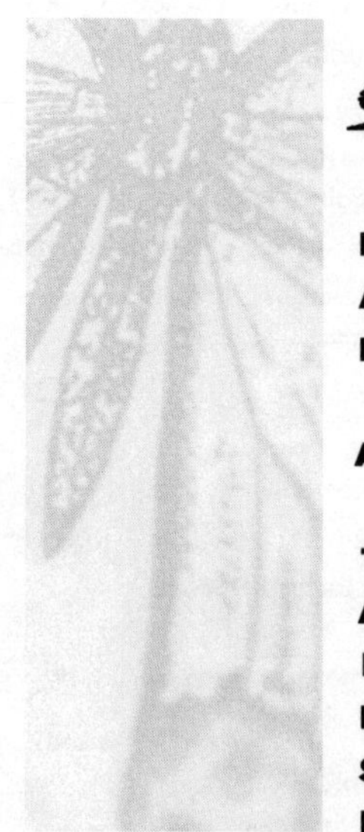

N A N A. T A L E S E

Published by Nan A. Talese
an imprint of Doubleday
a division of Random House, Inc.
1540 Broadway, New York, New York 10036

Doubleday is a trademark of Doubleday,
a division of Random House, Inc.

Book design by Terry Karydes

This novel is a work of fiction. Names, characters, places, and incidents either are the product of the author's imagination or are used fictitiously. Any resemblance to actual persons, living or dead, events, or locales is entirely coincidental.

Library of Congress
Cataloging-in-Publication Data
Griffith, Nicola.
Stay : a novel / Nicola Griffith.—1st ed.
p. cm.
1. Police—Georgia—Atlanta—Fiction. 2. Atlanta (Ga.)—Fiction. 3. Policewomen—Fiction.
4. Lesbians—Fiction. I. Title.
PS3557.R48935 S73 2002
813'.54—dc21 2001052474

ISBN 0-385-50300-8

PRINTED IN THE UNITED STATES OF AMERICA

April 2002
First Edition
10 9 8 7 6 5 4 3 2 1

FOR KELLEY, MY HOME

STAY

ONE

l
a
r
v
a

larva (from *larva,* L. for ghost, or mask)

1. a disembodied spirit, or ghost (obs.)

2. immature insect, such as a caterpillar

. . . in the grub or larval stage the insect is wingless, designed for environments and purposes that are quite different from those of the adult form . . .

CHAPTER ONE

From the roof of my cabin I can see only forest, an endless canopy of pecan and hickory, ash and beech and sugar maple. Wind flows through the trees and down the mountain, and the clearing seems like nothing but a step in a great green waterfall. Even the freshly split shingles make me think of water. Cedar is an aromatic wood; warmed by the autumn sunlight of a late North Carolina afternoon, it smells ancient and exotic, like the spice-laden hold of a quinquereme of Nineveh. It would be easy to close my eyes and imagine a long ago ocean cut by oars—water whispering along the hull, the taste of spray—but there's no point. There's no one to tell, no longer a Julia to listen.

Grief changes everything. It's a brutal metamorphosis. A caterpillar at least gets the time to spin a cocoon before its internal organs dissolve and its skin sloughs off. I had no warning: one minute Julia was walking down the street, sun shining on black hair and blue dress, the next she lay mewling in her own blood. The bullet wound was bigger than my fist. Then she was on a white bed in a white room, surrounded by rhythmically pumping machines. She lasted six days. Then she had a massive stroke. They turned the machines off. The technician stripped off his gloves, and grief stripped me raw.

I set the point of a roofing nail against a shingle, lifted my hammer, and swang. The steel bit through the cedar right on a hidden imperfection, and the shingle split. The hammer shook in my fist. I put it down and laid my hands on my thighs. The shaking got worse.

A plane droned over the forest, out of sight even though the sky was clear, a hard October blue. Birds sang; a squirrel shrieked. The droning note deepened abruptly, grew louder, and resolved into a laboring car engine. There was only one road. I didn't want anything to do with visitors.

The ladder creaked under my boots, but once on the turf I moved silently. Truck and trailer were locked, and the cabin did not yet have windows to break. I collected the most valuable of the hand tools—the froe and drawing knife by the sawhorse, the foot adze and broadaxe by the sections of split cedar—stowed them in the old hogpen, and walked into the forest.

Parts of the southern Appalachian forests have been growing uninterrupted for two hundred million years. Unlike the north, this area has never been scoured to its rock bones by glaciers. It has been a haven for every species, plant and animal, that has fled the tides of ice which creep across the continent every few thousand years: the ark from which the rest of the East is reseeded after the ice melts. A refuge, my refuge.

On my right, brilliant white-spotted orange puffballs bloomed from the horizontal trunk of some huge tree that had fallen so long ago it was impossible to identify. It was being absorbed back into the forest: carpenter ants and fungi broke down the cellulose; raccoons and possums lived in the cavities and salamanders in the shade; deer and wild pigs ate the mushrooms. When the whole thing collapsed into rotted punk, more microbes would turn it into rich soil from which a new tree would grow. I touched its mossy bark as I passed. This was the world I belonged to now, this one, where when a living thing died it fed others, where the scents were of mouse droppings and sap, not exhaust fumes and cordite, and the air hummed with insects rather than screams and the roar of flame.

Ninety feet over my head the canopy of ash and white basswood shivered in the constant mountain breeze; it was never quiet, not even at night. I stood for a while and just listened.

The sudden, rapid drumming of a pileated woodpecker echoed from the dense growth ahead. I pushed through fetterbush and fern and skirted a tangle of dogwoods, trying to pin down the source. It drummed again. North.

I found it forty feet up a huge yellow buckeye on a stream bank orange with jewelweed: big as a crow, clamped onto the bark by its strange backward-and-forward claws, and braced against the tree with its tail. Its scarlet head crest flashed forward and back in an eight-inch arc, over and over, a black-and-red jackhammer, and almost as noisy. Wood chips and plates of bark as big as my hand showered the weeds. When it reached softer wood, its tongue went to work, probing for carpenter ants, licking them up like a child dipping her tongue in sugar. Perhaps woodpeckers developed an instinct for which trees were rotten with ants, the way a police officer can spot the criminal in a crowd. It was efficient and brutal. When it was done, it launched itself from the tree and disappeared downstream, leaving the remaining ants wandering about in the wreckage of their shattered community. I wondered if the bird ever gave any thought to those left behind. I never had.

I emerged from the jewelweed and sat on a boulder by the rushing stream. Damselflies hummed; a chipmunk chup-chup-chupped next to a fallen pecan; birds began their evening song. Tree shadow crept to the edge of the far bank, then across the water. I let it all pour through my head, emptying it.

When I stirred, it was twilight under the trees; in the valleys it would be full dark. If my visitors had been smart, they would have turned their lights on to drive back down the mountain. I stretched, then walked along the stream bank, savoring the cool scent of moss and mud, following its curve north until it met the trail that led south and west to my cabin.

Three hundred yards from the clearing there were no birds singing, no squirrels scuttling through the undergrowth. The long muscles in my arms and legs and down my back plumped and warmed as adrenaline dilated blood vessels. I flexed my hands, moved silently to the tree line.

Woods surround three quarters of the clearing, but the southern quarter falls down the mountain as a heath bald and, unhindered by trees, the last of the evening sun slanted over the grass and splashed gold on the windscreen of a dark blue Isuzu Trooper parked by the trailer. A man sat on the log by the fire pit, one leg crossed over the other, an unlabeled bottle by his foot. He was slight, with black hair long enough to hint at ringlets where it touched his collar, and although I couldn't see his eyes I knew what color they would be: Irish blue. He was whistling "Kevin Barry" through his teeth as though he might sit there forever.

I know how to look after myself; I have the money to buy whatever I need. Neither of these things is any protection for the raw wound that is grief, and this man sat like a sack of sharp salt in the middle of the only safe place I knew.

He didn't hear me step from the trees, didn't hear me cross the turf. It would be easy to break his neck, or pull the hatchet from its stump and chop through his spine at the sixth vertebra. But he had met Julia, once.

I stood behind him for nearly a minute—close enough to smell the familiar bitter hint of coffee grounds—before he jerked around and whipped off his shades.

"Aud!"

Aud rhymes with shroud. After a moment I said, "Dornan."

"I was beginning to think . . . But here you are."

There were dark circles around his usually bright eyes but I didn't want to see them. "What do you want?"

"Would you sit down at least? I brought a drink." He held up the bottle.

"Say what you have to say."

"For the love of god, Aud, just sit for one minute and have a drink. Please."

I didn't move. "It's almost dark."

"We'd best make a fire then." He stood, tried to look cheerful. "Well, now, hmm, I'm no expert but that looks like a fire pit, and this, over here, is no doubt firewood. If I put this in here, then—"

I took the hickory log from him. "Kindling first."

"And where would I find that?"

"You make it."

"I see. And how do I go about doing that?"

His forehead glistened. He knew me, what I might do if he pushed too hard. Something was so important to him that he thought it worth the risk; I would have to hurt him or listen. Briefly, I hated him. "Bring the bottle."

Inside the trailer, I turned on lights and opened cupboards.

"Well, would you look at this! You do yourself proud." He ventured in, patted the oak cabinets and admired the Italian leather upholstery, then stepped through the galley to the dining area. "A satellite television!" He pushed buttons. "It doesn't work." I had never bothered to connect it. "And a real bathroom." The trailer, a fifth-wheel rig, was a treasure trove of hidden, high-tech delights. I let him wander about while I assembled plates, bowls, cutlery. "I had no idea these things could be such little palaces," he said when he came back. "There's even a queen bed."

After five months of solitude, his prattle was almost unbearable. I handed him a chopping board and knife, and he frowned.

"So where's the food?"

I picked up a cast-iron pot. "Bring that flashlight."

"There's no electricity?"

Only when I ran the generator, and I preferred the peace and quiet. He followed me to the water pump, where I handed him the pot. "Fill this. Less than a third."

While he pumped inexpertly I jerked the hatchet from the chopping stump, split the hickory into kindling, and carried it to the fire pit. Beneath the ash, the embers were sluggish. I blew them to a glow. When the kindling caught I added a couple of logs and went to the bearproof hogpen to get the food. The sky was now bloody, the trees behind us to the north and east a soft black wall.

Dornan handed me the pot and I hung it over the fire.

"Pumping's thirsty work," he said, and uncorked the bottle. He drank and gave it to me. The poteen smoked in my mouth and burned my gullet. I shuddered. We passed the bottle back and forth until the water came to a boil. My forebrain felt strange, as though someone were squeezing it. I added rice, and opened plastic tubs of sun-dried tomatoes, green olives, olive oil, and cashew nuts.

"No meat I see."

"You're the café owner. Next time call ahead."

"I tried. Do you even know where your phone is?"

It was around somewhere, battery long dead. The fire burned hotter. I drank more whiskey. When the rice was done I handed him the slotted spoon. "Scoop the rice into the big bowl. Don't throw away the water. It's good to drink cold."

He gave me a sideways look but spooned in silence. Sudden squealing from under the trees made him jump. "Mother of god!"

"Wild pigs," I said. The rice he had spilt in the fire hissed and popped.

"Would they be dangerous?"

"Not to us."

He handed me a bowl of rice. I added the dried ingredients and olives, a little oil, and salt and pepper.

We sat on the log side by side and ate quietly while the sky darkened from dull red to indigo. Firelight gleamed on my fork and, later, when we set the plates aside, on the bottle as we passed it back and forth. I rubbed the scar that ran from my left shoulder blade and along the underside of my arm to the elbow.

"Still hurt?"

Only inside. "Tell me why you came, Dornan."

He turned the bottle in his hands, around and around. "It's Tammy. She's missing. I want you to find her."

He had disturbed me for this. "Maybe she doesn't want to be found."

"I think she's in trouble."

Overhead, the first star popped out, as though someone had poked a hole in a screen.

"Now, look, I'm not a fool. I know you're hiding up here, eating this, this rabbit food, because you want to be left alone. But I've tried everything, phoned everyone: police, family, her friends"—Tammy didn't have friends, only male lovers and female competition—"and I've nowhere else to turn."

His face was drawn, with deep lines etched on either side of his mouth, but I turned away. I didn't want to know, didn't want to care. *Stay in the world, Aud,* Julia had said from that metal bed in that white room.

"It started in July. Tammy changed jobs, left those engineers she was doing business development for and joined some new outfit. Something to do with shopping complexes."

Stay alive inside. Promise me. And I had promised, but I didn't know how.

"So off she goes down to Naples, Florida, to talk to some people who are putting in a new mall. Said she'd be gone a week or ten days. Then I get a phone call saying no, it'll be another three weeks, or four. But just when she should have been coming home, she calls again. From New York. She's learning a lot, she says, and she's decided to spend a bit of time in New York learning firsthand from the consultant who was advising the

Naples group. His name is Geordie Karp. He's one of those psychologists that study shoppers and shopping. You know: how to design the front display to get shoppers inside, where to put what so they'll buy it."

He waited. When I said nothing, he sighed.

"She called at the beginning of August, and she sounded happy. So now you're probably thinking: Tammy met someone and decided to leave me. After all, it wouldn't be the first time she's seen other men, would it? No, you don't have to answer that."

The bottle in his hands turned round and round.

"The thing is, you see, I know Tammy; I know who she is, what she's like. I know you don't like her, and you're not the only one. But I love her anyway. Maybe I'm a foolish man, but there it is. So I gave her the ring. I can't help hoping that one day she'll look at that ring, she'll recall I have money in the bank and I've promised to take care of her, and love her, and she'll think, You know, maybe Dornan isn't so bad, and she'll come home and marry me."

He drank, wiped his mouth, remembered me and passed the bottle.

"She was so happy when she called. Do you know what that's like? That she was happy with someone else? But I've been through it before—she drops them as quickly as she picks them up, and she always comes home. But it's different this time—never lasted as long before, for one thing. For another, she didn't give me an address, or a phone number. And she hasn't called again. It's been two months. That's not like her."

Dornan's voice was an irritant. The need to push him away was becoming harder to ignore.

"I tried directory assistance. Unlisted, they said. So I went to the police. They wouldn't help me: they don't have the time to go chasing down every woman who leaves her boyfriend."

I drank some more. Irish whiskey, even the illegal kind, has a rough beginning but a smooth end, quite unlike most Scotch whiskeys. Which would Julia have preferred?

"Those first few weeks in Florida she couldn't stop talking about this Geordie Karp and his bloody mall. 'Geordie this, Geordie that.' You'd have thought he was god himself. On and on, then nothing."

I should really put some more wood on the fire.

"This silence isn't like her. Something's happened. I just don't know what." He ran a hand through his hair. Waited. "Well, say something."

I added a log, pinewood that spat as the resin ignited. The flames burned more yellow.

"Aud, listen. Please. Julia is dead, yes, and I'm sorry for it. Sorry you had to see her shot, and sorry you had to watch her linger. Probably you think you should have been able to protect her, but—don't you see? That's how I feel about Tammy."

If I closed my eyes, I could pretend he wasn't there.

"Will you help?"

All my filters were gone. Everything was too big, too loud, too sharp. The squeal of brakes, a bright shirt, the stink of plastic: everything got in and I could sort none of it out.

"I can't," I said. "I'm not—I can't."

"Ah, Aud . . ." He scrambled unsteadily to his feet, arms open.

"Don't. Don't come near me."

I didn't want his friendship. I didn't want to be connected. Never again. Stay in the world, Aud. Before I met her, everything had been so clear, so simple, but she had made me aware how alive and complex the world and the people in it were. And then she died, and now I couldn't shut that awareness out again, couldn't make it go away, and nothing made sense apart from this cabin. I could look at the wood I had hewn, the shingles I'd split and the pegs I'd hammered, and know what they meant and that they were real.

Stay alive inside. Promise me.

"If you could just—"

"No."

A log broke open in a spume of orange sparks, and flames began to gnaw at the tilted remnants.

I upended the bottle, swallowed the last of the whiskey, and dropped the empty on the grass. The silence lasted a long time. The flames ate their way inch by inch to both ends of the broken log, and began to die.

"It'll be winter soon," he said, finally. "You won't be able to work on the house in the snow."

"Once the roof's finished and the windows are in, it's all indoor work."

"Look, I know you hurt, but you'll hurt for years. You can't stay up here that long."

"I could stay here forever."

He studied me; his eyes reflected black, with tiny orange flames. "But you won't?"

I didn't say anything.

"We all worry."

I looked at him.

He nodded. "Helen and Mick, Beatriz, Eddie, Annie."

Annie, weeping by her daughter's bed as the words echoed around that white room: cerebral hemorrhage, massive brain trauma, we'll give you a moment with her. All because of one bullet, a piece of metal an inch long. And now I was here, and she was dead, and Dornan was alive, and Tammy: alive and walking around, laughing, breathing while Julia was dead.

All I had left of her were the promises she had asked of me. The promises I had given.

"I'll find her for you."

He turned away and poked vigorously at the fire with a stick. "Good," he said after a while. "We'll go back to the city in the morning."

"You go. Bring back everything that might help us find out

where Tammy is. Bring the mail from her apartment. Bring anything she sent you in the last few months: phone messages, cards, letters, photos. All of it." The lovesick fool would have kept everything, just as I would have kept Julia's letters, if I'd had any. "I'll need other things, too. I'll give you a list."

I didn't want to go back to Atlanta, to the house with the unfinished chair I had worked on while thinking of Julia, to the rug where she had curled up one evening, and the laundry on the floor that smelled of her: of sunshine and musk and dusty violets, of her rich skin, and her hair, oh dear god her hair . . .

"What?" Dornan said.

"There's a sofa bed in the trailer," I said harshly. "Go inside and leave me alone."

I watched the rest of the stars come out, one by one, and tried to catch back that fleeting sense memory, her scent before she ended up wired to those machines, smelling of pain and medication and death.

An owl screamed in the wood and I wanted to ride behind its eyes when it plunged its talons into living flesh, wanted to tear something warm and soft to pieces while it squealed; wanted something else to hurt.

I dreamt of the phone ringing, the answering machine in Atlanta blinking red as messages piled up.

Beep.

A tremulous southern voice: "Aud, this is Annie. Why did you leave? You killed my daughter. She would be alive if she hadn't gone to Norway. If she hadn't loved you. You killed her and I want her back."

Beep.

A cold, Norway-accented voice: "Hold for Her Excellency." A pause. "On reflection, Her Excellency does not wish to speak to you. She no longer considers herself your mother. Not that she ever did, deep down."

Beep.

Another voice, a woman's, as warm and familiar as my own knuckles. "Love? You promised me. You promised."

Dornan got up two hours after dawn. A raft of cloud had just floated over the sun and there was a breeze. He shivered as he climbed down from the trailer. I had water boiling over a fire.

"Morning," he said. "Been up long?"

If he used his eyes he would see the pile of fresh shavings and newly stacked shingles by the shaving horse at the south end of the clearing. "There's coffee in the pot but I'm boiling more water if you want fresh. I have some apples, and what's left of yesterday's rice, but if you want eggs or bread, then you'd be better off eating on the road."

"Not too subtle, as hints go."

"I put a list of the clothes and other things I'll need in the glove compartment of your car."

He nodded, but frowned. I waited. "I won't, ah, I won't bring any guns. Not across state lines."

"I don't need a gun. Here." I handed him a cup of scalding black coffee.

"Ah, bless you." He sipped, seemed to enjoy it as much as a fresh latte from one of his Borealis cafés.

"The day after tomorrow, then."

"Aud . . ."

"Drive carefully."

He smiled at me oddly, and carried his coffee to the Isuzu. The engine caught with a metallic shudder. He waved. I nodded. He turned in a circle and went back the way he'd come, leaving me to the wind and the birds and the smell of sawdust.

CHAPTER TWO

It was nearly midday and the clouds long gone by the time I hammered the last shingle into place and sat back. The birds were quiet, the sun streamed down, and for a moment the valley felt like a place out of time, secret and silent and still, where no one intruded and nothing ever happened. Then I saw that the gilding on the trees up the mountain wasn't just sun but the first tints of autumn which would seep downhill until all was copper and russet and gold and, not long after that, bare.

I climbed down the ladder and rattled the extension down after me; this afternoon I wanted to work on the ground-floor window framing. Once they were glazed, the cabin would be weatherproof.

It would have been easy to buy precut framing, just as it would to get already-made roof shingles, but the fine details kept me anchored. I'd already split out the boards from good pine, and dressed them with what was probably the same drawing knife that had been used on the original. I'd found it with a stack of other tools in the falling-down hogpen years ago, when my father's will had cleared probate and I first saw the place. Many of them had been too rusted to be saved but some I'd taken back to Atlanta, where I had sanded off the rust, sharpened the blades, and fitted new handles of smooth hickory. Then I'd oiled and wrapped them, and forgotten them, until grief drove me from the city and I made my way here, somehow, with everything I needed, without even knowing how or why, except that I had to rescue something from ruin.

That meant no shortcuts. The original framing had been fastened to the logs with locust wood pegs. I'd destroyed those pegs pulling the rotting frames out, so I would have to make more. Metal pegs rot wood; it takes several decades, but every day I would imagine the deterioration eating at the logs and pine uprights.

The pile of seasoning lumber smelled of sunshine and brittle beetle wings. I had to unstack several pieces before I found the plank of yellow locust I'd split out when I'd first arrived. I hefted it onto my shoulder, careful of its rough edges, then realized I should have worn gloves. Both hands were a mess of splinter scars, new, healing, and half faded. I should have been wearing gloves for months.

The sawhorse stood in the sun. There was still no breeze, and cutting can be heavy work, so I picked it up with my left hand and carried it and the plank into the shade. There was no pain now in the injured arm and shoulder, not even a twinge.

I marked the plank at inch intervals with a blue pencil, picked up the saw, and braced the plank on the horse with my left knee. Yellow locust is dense and hard, but the bright steel teeth ripped through the plank in three easy pushes, and a finger of wood, an inch square and five inches long, dropped onto the grass. I shifted the plank an inch, set the saw, pushed forward and down, and ripped off another, then another, until it was a mindless, mechanical rhythm, and after a while there was nothing left of the plank but a nine-inch board I could use for something else, and dozens of wooden bars in a pile. When I scooped them onto a square of canvas, they sounded like a disordered xylophone. I sat on the turf and poured them through my hands and listened, imagining a mobile strung with different woods that made soft, wooden sounds in the breeze among the trees.

After a while I simply sat. Sometime later, I realized I hadn't eaten.

The hogpen smelled of wood, and dirt on cool stone. The sealed painter's bucket sat on the right-hand shelf. I swang it down, opened it, and took out the airtight tub of rice salad. I carried it to the log by the cold fire pit, and ate mechanically with my fingers. The woods were still quiet. The tomatoes seemed unnaturally red, the olives too pungent.

Somewhere in Atlanta Dornan would be sorting through piles of precious keepsakes, wondering whether to trust me with embarrassing love notes or the fact that he had kept phone messages from Tammy from the last eighteen months. In the end, he would; he wanted her back. To want someone back and know it might be possible . . .

A familiar shuddering started deep deep down in a place I couldn't even name. "No," I said aloud to any bears who might be listening. "Not now. I have things to do."

Then do them. Concentrate on the details and everything will be all right.

No birds nested in the engine block, no rat snakes curled around the battery. It took a moment to loosen the dipstick, but when it came free it glistened with clear, pungent oil. I wiped it on the cloth, redipped it, and pulled it out again. The smell was stronger now, thick and sullen and artificial, and, as though some spell had been broken, a cool breeze set the foliage whispering. The oil looked fine.

The cab was hot—I'd kept the windows closed to prevent spiders and squirrels from nesting in the upholstery during the summer—but the fuel gauge looked healthy. When I turned the key the truck started with a deep, authoritative rumble. It was strange to feel artificial fabric on my bare legs and the vibration of manufactured power under my feet. The Chevy was a big truck, an extended bed rear-drive V10, fitted with a second gas tank and compression brakes. The dashboard was a complicated affair, with extra displays to support the cooling system, the trailer's lights, the brake controller, and all the other extras a driver needs to haul thirteen thousand pounds up a steep incline and control it on the way back down. The side and rearview mirrors were big, and minutely adjustable. I looked in the rearview. An oil smudge split my forehead between my brows, like war paint. It should have made me look fierce, but it didn't. I hadn't realized how much my hair had grown, how startling my eyes were against a tan, but the real difference was my expression: the shock of seeing myself had been written across it clearly, just as now it registered intent interest. I had forgotten how to wear a mask.

I turned the engine off and climbed back down to the turf, checked the tires on the dual back wheels, and the muffler and lights. The gas can, jack, tools, fire extinguisher, jump cables, and flashlight were in the trunk; the spare tire felt firm. No mask. How odd. Under its protective tarp in the truck bed, the fifth-wheel coupling looked fine.

When I couldn't think of anything else to check, I went into the trailer, to the sink in the tiny bathroom. I turned on the tap and let the water run over my hand, endlessly. My hand got cold. I stared at it, then turned the water off. I'd been waiting for it to run hot. It wouldn't; the point heater was set on OFF to conserve the battery. I stood gazing at the wet sink for five minutes before I lifted my head.

My face lay on the glass like a picture of someone else. I turned this way and that. No, more like a picture of a rock after some vandal has ripped off its decades-old layer of moss and soil, and the bare stone is revealed. I touched my reflected eyes. *Wolf eyes,* Julia had said, not long after we met, *so pale and hungry.*

For a moment I saw her behind me, leaning in the doorway, arms folded, smiling at my reflection but serious as she said, "More like a blasted heath, now, Aud," and she was so clear, the words so exactly what she might have said, that I almost turned around.

Run, I thought, run and run and run, and when Dornan comes back, don't be here. Hide.

Sunshine warmed the middle of the clearing. I stripped, knelt, hands palm up on my naked thighs, and began the measured breathing of zazen. At first I was aware of the dry grass poking at my shins and instep, the ruffle of breeze stirring the tiny hairs in the small of my back, the scent of my body, and I still wanted to run, but as I breathed steadily, in and out, and in and out, everything faded but the rhythm of air. My eyelids half closed. My heart beat steadily, relentlessly, like a machine. "You are not a machine." Julia's voice in my head. I smiled. A tear ran down my cheek. I didn't move to brush it away. Not a machine, then. A living, breathing being. Alive. Julia was dead, but I was alive. Skinless, and half mutated, but alive. In and out. Stay alive, Aud. Promise me. Had she known how hard it would be?

In and out. In and out. Nothing else.

A bluejay shrieked. I blinked. The sun was well past its meridian. Midafternoon. The need to run was buried, for a while. I stood, stretched, walked naked to the hogpen, and pulled the tarp off the generator.

The Onan Microlite 4000 is essentially a lawn mower motor that drives a tiny electrical generating plant to produce 115 volts. Like a lawn mower, it can be cranky. I changed the oil, put in new spark plugs, and topped up the fuel reservoir from the red plastic can, then pressed the starter button. The clearing filled with its shattering roar and a plume of blue hydrocarbon smoke. I watched it for a few minutes until it burned clean, then climbed up into the trailer to take a look at the converter and smart charger. The flickering LEDs all said what I wanted to see:

the deep-cycle marine battery was charging swiftly. I tested the electrical appliances one by one, turning them on and then off in careful sequence. Everything seemed to work.

I hadn't run any of the propane kitchen appliances for a long time so I checked and rechecked the fridge and stove and air conditioner to make sure the gas lines were closed and the pilot lights off before I went back outside and detached the regulator. The two tanks on the tongue of the trailer were more than half empty. I hefted them into the truck bed.

Still naked, I walked into the trailer, turned the water heater on, found my cell phone and started it charging, then took paper and pen to the captain's table and wrote a list. The pen felt strange in my hand. When the list was done, I found my wallet and put it on the bed. Next to it went clean clothes, suitable for going into Asheville. Then I dug out a towel and fresh soap, and had a shower.

I drove through the toylike downtown to carefully streetscaped Wall Street, with its new old-fashioned lights and neatly ordered trees. Everything was very clean, very open. Healthy-looking people smiled. It was like moving through the set of a 1960s TV show of the utopian future. There was a parking space in front of the Heads Up Salon. Someone had even left time on the meter.

A young woman was cutting a man's hair in the brightly lit interior. "Be right with you," she called, looking up from her work, beginning to smile. The smile went out and she stepped forward a pace. "Ma'am? Are you all right?"

"Yes. Fine, thank you."

"You just sit right down and let me bring you some water."

She was the first stranger I had seen without metal and glass between us in months. I experimented with a smile. "No, really. I just . . . It was a little warm out there."

"Well then, if you're sure? I'll just finish up here. Won't take but five minutes."

I feigned an overwhelming interest in the rows of hair care products lining the shelves above the large plants near the cash register, and she went back to work. After a minute or two, I could breathe normally. I didn't want to flinch every time the hairdresser or her customer laughed at something the other said. I tried to remember how small talk worked. The weather. The news. I didn't know any news. What a lovely town this is . . . ? Yes, and What a nice little salon . . . I could do this.

The customer admired his cut in two mirrors, stood, paid, left.

"Your turn," the woman announced. I sat in the swiveling chair. We looked at ourselves in the mirror. She ran her fingers casually through my hair. I made myself sit still. "It looks as though it's been a while."

"Yes."

She fingered a few inches thoughtfully. "You'd look great in one of those new, sleek cuts that you just wash and go. But they're very short." She cupped both hands around my face, looked at me in the mirror, got suddenly enthusiastic. "I think we should do it! With your eyes and height you could carry it off!"

"I'm game," I said, and tried a grin, and just like that I went from stranger to conspirator. It was easier than I remembered. A chameleon, Julia had called me. *Don't you ever get lost, pretending to be so many people?* I hadn't understood, then.

"I'm Aud," I said abruptly. "This is my first trip into Asheville."

"Oh." She blinked. "Well, I'm Dree. I've lived here since I was two."

"Dree isn't a name I've heard before," I said as she led me over to the sinks.

"It's from India or Pakistan or something. My mom wasn't sure. Maybe it's short for something. I tried looking it up once, but couldn't find it. Lean forward." She wrapped a thick, soft towel around my shoulders. "My mom was one of those old feminists, you know, who came out here to live on the land in a women's community." Slush of water from the tap. Squirt of liquid. "This is chamomile mint." She held her hand under my nose. It smelled light and young, like Dree. "Lean back."

The water was warm, the shampoo cold. For some reason it wasn't as hard to have her touch me, now that she knew my name. Her fingers were very strong and brisk. I wondered who she went home to, whether she washed their hair for them in the shower or bath, if she knew how easy it would be to hit me across the larynx with a shampoo bottle and watch me choke to death. I almost sat up.

"I'm going to use an intensifying conditioner. Like all our products, it's made from all-natural extracts and not chemicals."

"Everything is made with chemicals," I said at random. "Water is a chemical molecule: made of hydrogen and oxygen. The air we breathe, even the food we eat: carbon, nitrogen—"

Her hands had stilled, so I made myself stop, but then I felt her shrug and she laughed. "Okay. So it's made with naturally occurring stuff, from plants, not things made with a giant chemistry set. Better?"

"Better."

She finished rinsing my hair, wrapped it efficiently in the towel. "Come over to my station."

I sat in the chair before the mirror and she combed my hair through and picked up her scissors. "Last chance to say no."

"Go ahead."

She pulled wet hair up between her index and middle fingers, like a ribbon, and cut. "Will you be in town for a while?"

"I've inherited some property a few miles from here. I'm renovating it."

Pull, snip. Pull, snip. "To live, or just a vacation home?"

"I haven't decided."

"It used to be that you couldn't get a job around here unless it was as a forest ranger in the park service, or working at Biltmore. At least not year-round. Summer jobs, waiting tables, selling crafts, during tourist season. But then people started to live here."

"Seems like a nice town."

She shrugged without missing a beat in her cutting rhythm. "I suppose. People are moving here all the time from Atlanta and other big cities." Snip, pull, snip. "Tilt your head sideways for me, please. Ken—that's my brother—works for McCann construction, and he's never been so busy. They're building houses as fast as they can nail together two planks. Not just itty-bitty things, either, but monsters with pools and party decks, the whole nine yards." Snip, pull, snip. "Oh, this is going to look good. Such lovely hair. Bet you've never wanted to color it."

"Can't say I have."

"And there's a bunch of— Hold on while I just lower you a bit. How tall are you, anyway? —bunch of businesses that moved close to town a while ago that just keep getting bigger and bigger. There's Sonopress, ITT, BASF, all those high-tech places. They're even going to expand the airport."

"I didn't know Asheville had an airport."

"It's about as big as my left toe. But like I said, that's going to change. My mom's always moaning about how fast everything's growing."

Her mother's opinions carried us until she exchanged the scissors for a hair dryer, which roared to life like an old Norton Commando and effectively put a stop to all conversation.

"There." She turned it off, spun my chair this way and that, nodding to herself. "Take a look." She turned me back to face the mirror.

"It looks great."

"I think it works," she said complacently, and hummed to herself as she pulled off my towel and brushed a few stray hairs from my collar.

She went behind the cash register. "Would you like some product—some of that conditioner? Then that'll be just thirty-five dollars."

She zipped my card through the magnetic reader and the receipt churned silently from its machine. I added in a good tip and signed.

"That cut should be trimmed every six to eight weeks, so I'll expect you back before too long."

"I'll be here." And then I was outside, with the sun warm on my newly exposed neck, and feeling hungry. I started walking.

The heart of downtown Asheville looks as though some mad city planner scooped up half the art deco buildings in Miami, dumped them at random points around a small town square, then stuck in a fountain for pretty, along with a few postmodern structures whose only apparent aesthetic purpose was to reflect in their green glass the older, more substantial buildings. Everything was achingly clean.

As I moved more or less east through the streets, the character of the passersby gradually changed from individual people striding purposefully on everyday errands to that amble, stop, gawk-while-we-hold-hands-and-block-the-street pattern of the tourist.

I turned around and marched down a street called Biltmore Avenue, looking for a place real people might belong.

I found two pubs, practically side by side. I avoided the one with the aggressively shiny brew kegs, wine list, and perky logo, and chose the one that boasted Forty Beers on Tap!

It was like stepping back in time to being a teenager in England; the place smelled of smoke and beer and felt utterly peaceful. Patrons talked in low murmurs, minding their own business over tall glasses half filled with dark, murky brew and streaked with white foam. Smoke curled bluely through the occasional slant of sunlight; dark wood gleamed. I found a table in a corner, facing the door, and ordered pizza and a pint of Greenman ale, which turned out to be more like a bitter than anything else and slipped down beautifully. The pizza, when it came, had everything on it. The sausage was chewy and tough and I savored every bite. I ordered another beer, and half drowsed in the snug warmth, until I felt the light touch of Julia's hand on my hair, and her whisper, *My anti-Samson.* The room fractured and shimmered.

She sat next to me in the truck all the way back, her hand resting on my thigh.

"Something's changed," she said. We drove west. The sun, low on the horizon, shone straight into the cab. She wore the same coat as on the night we'd met. A raincoat. Today it was dry.

"I still love you."

"Bed linens, bread, orange juice . . ."

In the rearview mirror, my face was gold in the sunlight. Hers wasn't, and when she turned to look at me, she didn't squint against the glare.

". . . beer, milk, fruit and vegetables and fish. And a newspaper."

"Dornan will need a decent place to sleep tomorrow night, and breakfast. And I want something for dinner that's not rice." I couldn't explain the newspaper.

The raincoat had disappeared. Now she wore jeans and a white, low-cut button T that exposed her tight belly. When had she worn those?

"You didn't mention the other things," I said. The tarps, the cash, the liquid propane gas, the double tanks full of diesel fuel. She didn't seem to hear. After a while, I realized why: they were going-away things.

CHAPTER THREE

The Isuzu bumped into the clearing just after midday, and Dornan poked his head through the open window. His face had more lines, or maybe it was the light. He climbed out and stretched. "Mountain roads . . ." He looked around, looked at me. "Something's different."

"Yes."

"Ah. Well, I brought everything you asked for, plus a few extras." He went round to the back of the Isuzu, opened the rear door, and pulled out a cooler. "There's steak, and beer, and potatoes. Some decent coffee. And just in case you get the power on . . ."—he balanced the cooler against the rim of the trunk, reached in, and pulled out an espresso machine—"this."

"Good," I said, then ran out of polite conversation. "Bring the records, and my clothes." I lifted the cooler from him and carried it into the trailer. He followed with my hanging bag.

"Where should I put it?"

I jerked my chin forward, towards the bedroom, "On the bed," and started transferring the cooler contents to the fridge.

By the time he came back with the two cardboard file boxes,

the food was in the fridge and I was wiping down the inside of the cooler. "On the table. I've almost finished."

He leaned against the table for a moment, considering. "The power is on," he said, "and you've had your hair cut." It wasn't a question, so I didn't respond. "I'll make coffee."

He hummed to himself while he ground and measured, but he moved more slowly than usual, and there was more shadow than there had been around the bones of his wrists and nose.

"You've lost weight."

He didn't turn around, but said after a moment, "So have you."

"I'm sorry," I said, and now he did turn around, but I wasn't sure how to explain what I meant: that I knew I'd been selfish; that I hadn't cared about his worry, about Tammy; that there just wasn't much room inside me for anything but my grief.

"I just want you to find her for me, and bring her back," he said.

"I'll find her."

"And bring . . . Oh, god. You think she's dead."

"No." The espresso machine hissed and spat. "Make the coffee and come and sit."

He made the coffee mechanically and brought it to the table.

"I'm going to find Tammy," I said. "I'll talk to her. If she wants to come back, I'll bring her. If."

"You'll tell me where she is?"

"If she wants me to."

He could have said a lot of things then, but he didn't. He forced himself to smile. "You'll let me know she's safe at least?"

"Yes." If she was.

He sipped at his coffee for a while, as though I weren't there. "It's a nice afternoon," he said at last. "I think I'll take a walk."

"There's a trailhead on the west side of the clearing. If you follow that, it'll bring you to the creek. If you're not back by four, I'll come find you."

I sat for five minutes after he'd gone, then took the lid off both boxes. One held a collection of opened and unopened mail—junk and bills mainly—going back at least three months, plus the other information I'd asked for: insurance documents, 401(k) and bank statements, birth certificate, apartment lease. The other was Dornan's private shrine to Tammy. He had saved everything, in no particular order: printouts of e-mails were bundled with birthday cards and Post-it notes; snapshots poked out from cassette cases; there were plane tickets and hotel bills and dinner receipts. On top lay a shopping list. *Slim-Fast,* it said forlornly, *toothpaste, water, dishwasher soap.* I imagined Tammy loading a dishwasher, and the only picture I could get was her playing to an audience: stretching so that her pants pulled tight across thigh and buttock. But her handwriting was not what I'd expected: no circles over the *i,* no fat loops; it was strong and clear and angular, and she had preferred black ink.

I didn't want to know what Tammy had said to Dornan via e-mail, what she had whispered late at night to his phone machine; I doubted I'd need to.

I started with the mail, sorting it quickly into bills, junk, and personal. The junk I put back in the box, the personal—all unopened—I set aside, and the bills I sorted further by date and type, discarding anything before the first of the year. Tammy had not canceled the lease on her apartment, so there was ten months' worth. All had been paid by Dornan; his notation of check number and date and amount was scrawled in the upper right corner of each. The Visa card pile was significantly smaller than the others; it contained nothing since August. Her other credit card, an American Express, was there in full, though the last three months showed no spending activity. I pulled an example from each pile. The AmEx listed plane tickets, hotel bills, out-of-town restaurant meals. Business expenses. Probably referred immediately to the company she worked—used to work—for. The Visa was billed from a variety of Atlanta restaurants, two different hair salons, Macy's, Saks, auto repair, pharmacy: purely personal. The conclusions were obvious.

I found the 800 number on the bill and, while it rang, assembled a few things from the box. A bored, beaten voice answered. "ParkBanc this is Cindy how may I be of service."

"Yes, hello. I'm calling about my Visa bill."

"Name please."

"Tammy Foster."

"Account number please."

I read off the number. I heard her fingernails ticking on the keyboard even on the cellular phone. "Tammy J. Foster," she read back to me like a robot. "Last four numbers of your social security number for security purposes."

I read them from the bank statement. More plastic ticking. As my partner, Frank King, had said when I was a uniformed rookie in Atlanta, *Finding people's not rocket science, Torvingen. They got a social security number, it's easy—*

"Address please ma'am."

"Yes, well that's why I'm calling. I haven't had a bill since July, so you probably still have my old Atlanta address."

"No ma'am we have a New York City address."

"Well, it's probably the wrong one because, like I said, I haven't seen a bill since July."

"Your account is current ma'am."

"Well, that can't be right. Like I said, you haven't sent me a bill for months. What address do you have there?"

"One moment."

—It's your illegals that are hard to track. Otherwise, hell, just follow the money. Frank had been right, mostly. The exceptions were dead people, and smart people with no scruples and enough money to pay for both active and passive concealment. Unless Tammy was dead, I could probably do it just from the bits of

paper I had here. Dornan could easily have hired a private investigator to do the job for a hundred dollars: all they had to do was run her name through their subscription databases. No doubt he hadn't gone that route because—

"Your mother's maiden name please ma'am."

I read it from the birth certificate. "Acklin."

"Yes ma'am. We have you listed at Apartment C 95 Seventh Avenue South New York New York 10012."

Greenwich Village. What was she doing in Greenwich Village? "Well, that's the right place, all right. But I don't get it. Why aren't I getting my bills? It doesn't make any— Oh, shoot," I said, doing my best to sound embarrassed. "I think I'm calling about the wrong account here. I was looking at my American Express and my Visa at the same time and I guess I just mixed them up and called the wrong one. It says here I paid the last few bills, so I guess I got them."

"Yes ma'am. Your account shows your last payment of $354.89 paid September 29th. That was billed to the New York address."

"God, I'm sorry."

"Yes ma'am," she said, still bored. "Have a good day." She disconnected with a click.

New York. Blaring horns, shrieking sirens, the sour stink of ten million people, all streaming by at a thousand frames per second. New York. And I would have to go there. That's why Dornan had asked me to find her, not some faceless agency, so that I would go to her on his behalf and ask her to come home.

I put each item back in the box one at a time, carefully squaring envelopes and aligning stamps, concentrating on arranging the bills in chronological order, deliberately not thinking, because if I thought about all the basic groundwork I should do, the phone calls I ought to make, I would walk away, walk into the woods and not come back, and I had promised.

I heard Dornan emerge from the trees just before four, but

he didn't come in. I got two Coronas from the fridge, opened them, and took them outside. He stood at the southern edge, looking down and out over the heath bald. I let the bottles clink as I walked, and held his out when he turned.

He nodded and drank. "Nice woods you've got here."

"About two hundred acres."

He nodded some more. "So why do you have that strip of AstroTurf in front of the trailer when there's all this natural stuff?"

"It doesn't get muddy. Works as a doormat."

"Ah." He wouldn't meet my eyes.

"I didn't look at the private papers. I didn't need to."

Now he looked at me. "You know where she is?"

"Yes." Her, or someone pretending to be her. "I'll be ready to leave tomorrow. It might take a few days." He rubbed his eyes with his free hand. It shook slightly. "I haven't shown you what I'm doing with the cabin. Bring your beer. Then we'll cook that steak."

His smile told me he knew I was doing it to help him, but he followed me to the cabin anyway.

"It faces south and west, and the long side measures thirty-six feet. The logs are oak, hand hewn. They're a hundred years old and there's no reason for them not to last another century." I laid my palm against the solid wood. It was still warm from the sun. New York. "This is a craftsman cabin, built for my great-grandfather by masters, not one of the more usual settler's shacks made from whatever came to hand and which have long since rotted away, and good riddance."

His smile was real this time. "You always have been a snob, Torvingen."

"I like well-made things." I squatted and patted the corner of the building. Ten million people. "See how the sill and first end log are quarter-notched? If you could rip up the floor you'd see that the sleepers it rests on are all lap-jointed and middle-notched, and then pegged."

He nodded seriously. He hadn't a clue what I was talking about. It was suddenly necessary that he understand.

"Everything here was done by hand. You couldn't just drive to Home Depot and load up your truck a hundred years ago. They had to cut the tree—and remember they didn't have chain saws. Then they had to hew the logs: make the round sides flat. Even the chalk they used in their chalk boxes was made from local stuff, like pokeberry juice and lime."

"What's a chalk box?"

"What you use to snap out a line, so you know you're cutting straight. You make the line, then score the log every two or three inches with a poleaxe. Then you use a broadaxe to slice off the chips."

"Which you could probably use as kindling, to start a fire."

"What?" My throat felt very tight.

"Don't look at me like that. I'm doing my best. I only know two things about wood: it grows on trees and you can burn it, and I only learned the second thing two days ago. But go on, I'm listening."

"This door—"

"There isn't a door."

"—doorframe. It's pine that I split out myself, and it's pegged with yellow locust."

"Locust? Strange name for—"

I talked right over him. "Do you know how rare yellow locust is now? Do you know how long it takes to cut it, season it, then slice it into bars, then whittle it? Then you have to auger out the frame holes and get the wood braced properly against the logs. It's hard to do that on your own, to get it vertical, to get a ninety-degree plane this way, too, and then to hold it there while you hammer in the pegs when you only have two hands and I don't know how I'm going to hang the door itself, to make it all fit seamlessly so no one can tell I was— You have to never give up, never stop, because then you have to *see*—"

"Aud . . ."

"You have to see she's not there, that there's this great *hole* inside instead, nothing there—"

"Aud."

My fists were balled and the veins on my wrists and the back of my hands thick blue worms.

"Aud!"

I panted. My face felt cold.

"I'll help you hang the door."

"The door?"

"I'll help you hang it." He put down his beer. "Right now. Where is it?"

"Inside."

"Then let's get it."

My body belonged to someone else. I led him inside, over the wide, heart-of-pine floors that would be refinished once the door and windows were in, past the hearth I had already rebuilt, right through the wall that would be—between the studs I would cover with pine board one day soon—to the oak door. I had to put my own beer down before I could pick up the far end. He picked up the near. We walked it outside and leaned it on its end to the right of the doorway. He followed me to the hogpen, silently accepted hammer and nails and spirit level while I lifted down the massive wrought-iron hinge pieces and candy-cane-shaped drop pintles, then followed me back.

I watched myself lift half the hinge and put it against the logs at shoulder height and measure with the eyes, move it up slightly, hold it with the left hand, and with the right lay the spirit level along its top. Hinge a little low on the left. Move it slightly. Nod at Dornan, at the hammer in his hand, swap left hand for right and step to one side to watch while he puts in the big nail, don't flinch even slightly as he swings, don't move as what should be three swift blows for each of the three nails becomes a dozen swings, fourteen, then a pause, and on to the other hinge, at knee level this time. Bang bang bang, bang bang bang, bang bang bang. See Dornan's pleasure: he can do this. Nod. Lift other hinge pieces, position, drop in steel spindle, move assembled hinge back and forth, remove. Measure door. Nail on upper hinge. Pause. Let Dornan nail on second. Pointing. Lifting the door. Holding, maneuvering, dropping in spindles. Done.

And with a snap I smell my own sweat, feel utterly weary, realize Dornan is watching me carefully.

"We hung a door," he said.

"I'm sorry," I said, for the second time that day. He waited. "Going off like that. You must have— It's . . ." I had never bled on someone before. I didn't know how to apologize for it.

He didn't seem to know what to say, either. He pushed the door gently, watched me and the door both as it swung smoothly backwards. "It works."

"It's not quite finished." All I wanted to do was walk into the woods and stop thinking, but if I left the job half done it would drive me mad. "The top of the pintle needs securing, nailing down."

He bent and picked up his beer, deliberately casual. "You'd have to show me how."

"No."

"Many hands make light work."

"No."

"Why not?" he asked softly.

I didn't know.

"You're helping me with Tammy. I'd like to help you."

The sun shone warmly, the birds sang, and my cabin was more whole than it had been. I began to pant again, felt my heart accelerating, and this time it wasn't a smooth machine, a turbine beginning to whine as it reached redline, it was a panicking, soft muscle. Accepting help would be like levering open my rib cage with a crowbar and giving him a knife.

Dornan's face was tired, but the harsh lines bracketing his mouth had gentled. I don't know what my face must have looked like, but he nodded as though I'd said something. "I'm your friend. I have been for a long time, even if sometimes I wonder if you know what that means."

I was the one who helped, the competent one, armored and invulnerable. Aud rhymes with proud.

"You saved my life once, and I know you'll find Tammy for me, but I know that none of that really means anything to you. You're helping me the way you'd help a hurt dog. Which doesn't exactly make me feel good. I'm a person, not a dog. But you don't know that because you won't let anyone in. I've been banging on that particular door for eight years. Mostly it's been a waste of time. Even just six months ago, if I'd said all this you would have smiled and ignored me because you'd have had no idea what I meant."

But now I knew, because Julia had turned me inside out like a sock, and there was no going back.

"So, will you show me? About the hinges?"

Children in the schoolyard ask, Will you be my friend? and they mean it, but this was the adult version, loaded with traps and consequences.

"And then you can show me the other stuff. The cabin. All the things you've done on the inside."

"You're not really interested."

"I admit I don't know a piece of pine from a piña colada, but I want to hear all about what you've done with the place, because it was you who did it."

"Why?"

"Because we're friends. That's how it works."

That's how it works. He seemed so sure.

So I showed him how to take a picture nail, hammer it part of the way into the doorframe just below the handle of the pintle's candy cane, then use the hammer to tap it into a U-shape arching up over the pintle and back into the frame so the pintle couldn't fall out. He did the second. Two small picture nails. Two friends. We stood and looked at our handiwork for a while.

"Now we can look inside, and you can tell me every single thing there is to know about how to make a log cabin from scratch."

"Everything?"

"Everything. Though if there's a lot to say—and I can't imagine it being otherwise—then perhaps we should wait until we've eaten. There's steak. What would you like with it?"

"You're the cook. I'll sit out here and think." Not think. "About finding Tammy." About being in the world.

"And you'll be wanting another beer brought out to you, I suppose?"

"I'll be down there." I pointed to a boulder fifteen yards down the heath bald.

He headed back to the trailer and I walked sideways down the slope. From the boulder, blackberries, azalea, and rhododendron stretched all the way down to maple and cherry and other successional trees. Julia appeared about ten feet away, her back towards me. She said nothing for a moment, and when she turned round she was frowning. "You're blaming *me* for this?"

"You made me make that promise."

"You could have said no."

"Not to you."

She laughed then, that rich, fuming laugh, like Armagnac, and knelt next to me. "It was your choice, Aud. You were ready. I just came along at the right time."

"Beer," Dornan said from behind me, and handed me a frosted bottle. "Does that miniature stove work the same way as a real one?"

I turned back to look at Julia, but she was gone.

"Aud? The stove?"

"Yes. It takes a bit longer, that's all."

"Dinner in half an hour, then." He turned to head back up the slope.

"Dornan?"

"Yeah?"

"Nothing."

He shrugged and climbed back up, those long wiry muscles working under his jeans. He rarely wore anything but jeans, even though he made a lot of money from Borealis, his string of cafés. The closet in his midtown home was full of good clothes; he had shown me them years ago, complaining that his girlfriends always bought him suits, as if he couldn't afford them for himself, if he'd wanted. I knew what clothes he had, what films he enjoyed, what books he read; his favorite color, his hopes and fears and dreams. I knew that his front tooth was blue not as the result of a barroom brawl, as he liked to pretend, but because he had hit the metal bar with his mouth when trying to beat the Trinity College, Dublin, pole vault record. I knew that his first wife had died of leukemia six months after they had both graduated, before he and I had met.

In the time I'd known him I had driven him home when he was drunk, held his head while he puked, put him to bed. I listened on the nights his pre-Tammy girlfriends had left him. He had been to my house once, the night he drove me home from Borealis, the day he thought I'd been in a car accident, the day Julia died. I had not even let him through the door. And now he was here, and I had let him help.

The steak smelled good, rich and red and strong. Muscle. Cooked muscle. I flexed my left hand, the one holding the beer, and watched the muscles in my forearm swell, then relax. What had Dornan's muscle felt like when he swang that hammer? Everyone's muscle attaches differently, to a bone that's thicker or thinner, under skin that is sensitive or not.

Everyone is different, I thought. Everyone is different. I stood. "Dornan, I'm hungry."

"Then get up here and eat. It's more or less done."

We ate outside. The steak was so big there was barely room on the plate for the red potatoes tossed in butter and marjoram.

We had to eat the corn first. It was succulent and buttery and very hot. Dornan admired the wood-and-steel prongs jammed into each end of his corn.

"Halfway up a bloody mountain, half mad, no food, but you remembered to bring these— What are they called, anyway?"

"No idea." The corn was the best thing I'd tasted in months.

"Come to think of it, there are a hundred things I don't know the name of, usually fiddly little things. These, for one. And those things they use to nail cable and wire to the baseboard in your house—you know, those double-spiked U-shaped thumbtack things—for another. And where do they all come from, who thinks them up?"

"Um," I said, around my corn.

"Rubber bands. Toothpaste caps." He touched the ruby stud in his left ear. "Those little metal things that go on the back of earrings. I've had this since I was twenty, never lost the stone, but I've probably sent the sons and daughters of the devil who makes earring backs to college."

That was something Julia might have said. I felt my mouth twist. Dornan tilted his head and waited.

"Julia . . ." I tried to swallow past a closed throat.

He understood. He went back to eating his corn. After a moment he said, "I liked what I saw of her, that once, in the café."

I set my corn aside. "Tell me what she looked like to you." I was hungry for another viewpoint, to see Julia again for the first time.

"Tall, taller than she really was, anyway, because of the way she held herself, like a ballet dancer. When I saw her come in that night with you, I said to myself, Now there's a handful, because I thought she'd be snooty, you see. It was the way she carried her head. But she wasn't." He picked up his steak plate and knife and fork. "Until Tammy came in. Though I don't blame her for it—I expect she took her cue from you." He looked up. "Your face is a study."

I just stared.

"You think Tammy's body blinds me to her faults?" He shrugged comfortably, then started cutting his steak. "Bit more well done than I like. No, I think I see her very clearly. You, now, you were the one who was blinded. You couldn't see her good points for her bad. Ah, now your face is closing up. I haven't seen that face for a while. No doubt you're thinking, He doesn't know the half of it and I'm not going to ruin his image of his fiancée by telling him. Tell me, did she try to seduce you? Yes, I thought so. She tried it with all my other friends who didn't like her."

"I—"

"Oh, I know, you turned her down." He speared a piece of steak, put it in his mouth, chewed, swallowed. "So, you turned her down, not your type, but the point is, Torvingen, the point is, she is my type. She might use sex like subway tokens but I trust her in my own way." He forked up more steak. "Eat, eat, while it's still hot."

I did. My teeth sank into the juicy muscle. Everyone is different. "Different people want different things."

"Yes. And Tammy was the one for me."

"I'll find her."

"No doubt." He looked at his steak sadly. I reached out and touched his arm.

"I'll find her," I said again. We ate for a while without saying anything. I drank my beer.

"She pretends she's tough," he said, "but she's not. She's smart, and pretty as a picture, and she knows her way around the world, but sometimes I'd look at her and just want to hold her, protect her from everything. She wouldn't let me."

"No," I said. I hadn't been able to protect Julia. I hadn't been able to protect myself from her. Dornan got up, disappeared into the trailer, came back with a box of tissues.

"Every luxury," he said with a crooked grin that showed the blue tooth. "Even halfway up a mountain."

I wiped my face. The tears kept welling, I kept wiping. "I can't bear it."

"You will, eventually."

"Tell me about it, Dornan, about grief."

"It never goes away. After a while, though, after a long, long while, life starts to sand it down and take the sharp edges off. Over the years it gets smaller, until you don't notice it so much. Sometimes some jagged bit will catch you off guard, but that happens less and less."

I thought of Julia weeping on the boat in Norway, so many years after her brother died. "I don't think I can live for years feeling like this."

"You don't have much of a choice."

"There are always choices."

"Oh, you won't kill yourself, you're too self-centered, and you're too stubborn to go mad. So that means you'll have to cope."

Cope. A small word for a terrible task.

"Building this house is one way of doing it, of course." He put his plate down and twisted to look past me at the cabin. "It looks almost finished."

"The outside, maybe. The inside needs a lot of work. That interior wall needs finishing, some of the floor pulling and re-laying. The handrails up to the loft have to come out. I have some lovely walnut I want to put up there, really fine grain. I also want to turn the board gable into one of half logs, so it matches everything else."

He stood, dusted off his jeans. "Show me."

I did. I showed him each joint, discussed every decision on materials and design, and explained how I'd cut the walnut for the railings myself, from the sixty acres of mature black walnut plantation that was part of the reason my great-grandfather had bought this land in the first place. As the evening wound on, I took the flashlight down from the nail near the door and kept talking. He listened patiently for hours, as friends do.

Outside, it was almost dark.

"Espresso, I think," Dornan said, and went into the trailer. I sat on the log, stoked the fire back to life.

He brought two cups and a carafe outside, sat next to me on the log, and poured for us both. We stared at the fire. Far away, wild turkeys gobbled.

"I've told you what happened my first night in this country," I said.

He nodded. "The man who broke into your apartment. That you killed."

"Yes." Fourteen years ago. "I never told you how it felt." A hot night in a new country. I'd fallen asleep naked and woken with a gun in my face. "It was like a dream—how could it be real to wake up with someone pointing a gun at you?—but I knew it wasn't. Under my pillow I had my father's flashlight." Old. Heavy. Polished steel. "I hit him with it. It was easy. I just stood up and hit him with it, and his neck broke. I didn't have to think, because the adrenaline took me to a place where—" I couldn't tell him, after all. "It took me to a place where you don't think. And that's what happened in Oslo. I didn't think."

Julia walking down the street to my Aunt Hjordis's house, oblivious to the two men right behind her, lifting their guns. Me leaping from the car, smiling, almost floating, getting one before he could shoot—crushing his spine where it met the skull—but reaching the other a split second too late. If I had been five seconds earlier, if I had not forgotten I had a gun . . .

"I could have saved her."

"Drink your coffee," he said eventually. We sipped for a while. "That night you brought her to the café, you and she hadn't, you weren't yet—"

"No."

"But I knew you would. It was as plain as day."

I remembered. Julia had excused herself at one point, and when she walked to the bathroom we both watched, and Dornan said *Very nice, Torvingen,* and I said—I believed—*It's all business, Dornan,* because I hadn't understood. Not then.

"Just six months ago," he said. "All four of us under one roof." He shook his head.

"How tired are you?" I asked.

"It depends what you have in mind."

"Before I leave, this cabin has to be weatherproof. That means getting tarps up at the windows. I could do it tomorrow, but if we both worked tonight for an hour or two, I could leave early in the morning."

"Just a bit of hammering?"

"We'd have to fire up the generator and hang a few lights, but, yes, just a bit of hammering."

We split the night open with noise and light and the stink of diesel and it felt good, it felt human, and although the tarps were heavy and the nails awkward, although Dornan hit the knuckle of my left index finger once and his own thumb twice, I think we both had the most fun either of us had enjoyed for months. It was a single, simple, discrete task, and we did it well.

When the generator had been turned off and the tools stowed in the hogpen, we went into the trailer. In the steady, yellow-white fluorescent light, Dornan's shoulders were no longer hunched; the lines at the corner of his eyes were not as deep. I felt tired, and peaceful.

"Time for bed," I said. "Tomorrow I want an early start."

I did not sleep for a while. From the woods to the west, a screech owl hooted. Another answered from the north. Calling to each other in the dark.

CHAPTER FOUR

I shook Dornan awake just before six. "I have a long drive today. I want to be out of here in an hour. Clean the shower after you've finished."

While he blundered about getting showered and dressed, I poured coffee, then unplugged and cleaned his espresso machine. I unloaded the fridge and put the perishables in a cardboard box.

Dornan peered into the box over his coffee. "Eggs. Green peppers. Seems like an odd choice to eat on the road."

"This is for you to take with you. No point it all going to waste."

"You expect to be gone a while, then?"

"A few days. I'll call, when I find her. That's all you need to know. Now drink your coffee and load your car. I want to leave before seven."

I wiped down the inside of the fridge and propped the door open, shut down the appliances one by one, turned off the propane and water lines, checked locks, latches, and bolts on the cabin, hogpen, and trailer, put my bag and phone in the truck. The light in the clearing was like cool green tea, and dozens of birds sang. Dornan leaned against his Isuzu, sipping coffee and looking forlorn.

"Got everything?"

He nodded.

"Then I'll call you in a few days."

He nodded again, turned and slid into his seat, put his coffee in the cup holder and the key in the ignition, but didn't shut the door. "Which way are you heading?"

"Go home, Dornan. Go home and take care of your business. Don't come back here. I'll call you."

I stood there for a long time after he bumped his way over the turf and down the track, until the smell of his exhaust had faded into the trees and soil, and I could hear nothing but the birds. The air smelled like rain.

By seven-thirty I was on I-26 heading north and west for Tennessee. If I ignored the weather, ignored the scenery, and just drove, I could hold the clearing in my mind; I could imagine the soft patter of rain on the leaves—a flatter sound, now that the leaves were drier and getting ready to fall—building to a harsh rattling, the gush of rain runneling over the rich forest loam. In my truck, I could pretend I was not heading for a place hard with machine hum and concrete and seething with people who stank of fear and need. Once on I-81 I crossed Tennessee and Virginia at a steady seventy-five miles an hour, tires thrumming rhythmically over the concrete and whining on the asphalt, stopping only to refill the truck's huge twin tanks. At about one in the afternoon, just before Roanoke, I took a twenty-minute break to eat, drink, and use the bathroom. I didn't stop again until seven in the evening, not far outside Harrisburg. Both times I chose seedy, ill-lit fast food shacks where the colors would be dim and the noise low—no children screaming and running up and down, no canned music—and I wouldn't have to smile or talk. In the rest room I didn't look in the mirror. When I got back into the truck near

Harrisburg, the wind was blowing pewter clouds into an already darkening sky.

"It won't work," Julia said.

"What won't?"

"Pretending. The world's out there. You have to move through it at some point."

I changed gears unnecessarily and didn't reply.

"And why do you need a truck in New York?"

She gave me that smug smile she always used when she was being Socratic, and disappeared.

Rain hissed against my windscreen, washing it to silver and mercury. I hadn't thought further than the fact that I didn't want to fly. The truck was familiar, a piece of my refuge. I should have rented a car in Asheville.

I drove grimly through the rain. Pennsylvania became New Jersey. I took the Newark Airport exit, and the streaming windscreen yellowed to cadmium and sodium as I approached the long-term parking lot, which turned out to be full of cars but empty of people. The rain was steady, and when I looked up as I got out of the truck, falling drops seemed to stretch and streak until they were golden needles. It seemed I had not thought to bring a coat.

The shuttle bus was driven by a woman with drooping eyelids and swollen knuckles. One of the pair of doors wouldn't open fully; I had to hold my bag in front of me to squeeze through. The driver watched noncommittally. "Which airline?" Jamaican accent.

"American." It made no difference. The bus jerked into motion.

Inside it was too hot and too bright, the air swollen with rain evaporating from wet passengers, bulky with coats and hats and umbrellas. I couldn't breathe. I shut my eyes. Grass, trees, pigs rooting by the remains of a fallen tulip tree. Fish finning idly in the dark, deep water near the bank. The bus jerked again, and I heard "Which airline?" delivered in exactly the same tone, as though the driver were a machine, except the designers of such a thing would have made it pretty and white and young, with an insanely cheerful smile and large breasts.

The bus stopped again. "United," the voice announced, and I stood up with a couple who studiously ignored each other, even though their matching rings said they were married. The driver didn't seem to care that I was getting out at the wrong stop.

The terminal was a madhouse of flashing blue-and-white screens, security personnel in red-piped uniforms waving people through lines, green exit signs, arrows pointing this way and that at eye height and overhead, labels on bathroom doors, logos on storefronts, and flashing Bureau de Change icons, and it roared with voices and trundling luggage wheels, childish screams and the beeps of video games and cellular phones. I walked into the nearest rest room, into a stall, and shut the door. Grass, trees, pigs rooting by the remains of a fallen tulip tree. Grass, trees, pigs. Breathe. The place stank of disinfectant and dirty water. My heart rate slowed.

I changed from my wet traveling clothes into an Eileen Fisher tunic and trousers, swapped my boots for shoes, added earrings, and left the stall. The sinks were slimed with violently green liquid soap, scummy with old lather, and dripping with dirty water. I reached for the paper towel dispenser and stopped. The mirror showed a face with wild eyes and skinned-back lips, the face of a fox gone mad. I closed my eyes and rubbed my cheeks and forehead with the heels of my hands, stretched the muscles wide then pulled them tight, pulled and relaxed, until they let go. I practiced until my expression was bland, then went to find a cab.

I said, "Midtown, the Hilton. Fifty-third and Sixth."

The cab was hot and reeked of air freshener. My window wouldn't work. Halfway through the Holland Tunnel my knuckles began to ache; I wanted to punch the glass from the doors and escape.

The city sucked the cab north with terrifying ease, as though we were falling downhill, as if the whole island had tilted north. I closed my eyes against the momentary vertigo. When I opened them again, I kept my gaze focused forwards. Even at ten-thirty, traffic blared, lights flashed, and pedestrians gesticulated as they walked swiftly. Radio City Music Hall was already advertising the annual Christmas Rockettes show; there must have been some special event at MoMA because women in elegant dresses and men in casually expensive clothes streamed onto the wet sidewalk, whose slick black surface sizzled with reflected electric blue and neon pink. A sea of people, all distinct, all with dreams and fears, bank accounts and health problems, family and enemies. Too many, far too many.

The cab pulled into the semicircular driveway in front of the hotel. Big and busy and anonymous. A uniformed doorman opened my door and took my bag, another waved the cab forward to join the line waiting to take some of the perfume- and cologne-drenched passengers queuing behind a red velvet rope. I followed my bag through the lobby to the registration desk. The woman spoke, and my answers must have made sense because I handed her my credit card and she handed me a pen, and then a key card, but it was like watching a silent film. Then I was following the bellman and his gilded bag trolley to the elevators.

The elevators stood near the bar, which was full of burly-voiced conventioneers, several of whom decided at that moment to return to their rooms. When a door tinged and opened, they bulled forward, and although the bellman gestured that he would follow me onto the elevator, I shook my head. The bellman, unlike the usual cheerful kind, merely ducked in assent.

When the next elevator came, he again waited for me to get in first, and pushed the button for the twenty-second floor with a powerful finger. His nails were ragged and chewed, but there were no tattoos on his hands. Curious. His body language—his excessive, almost cringing politeness, his careful button pressing, lack of swagger—was something I associated with time spent in prison, where assertiveness is beaten out of you in a matter of weeks and replaced by a nervous need to please. But there were no jailhouse tattoos.

He knew I was watching him. He didn't know what it meant. It made him anxious. "Good flight I hope. Well, my name's Bob, and I'll be happy to help you with anything you might need during your stay. I'll just get these bags, this bag, to your room and get you settled. The ice machine is just a few doors down from your room—which faces north, so you should have a view of Central—"

He shut up abruptly. I wondered if my lips were skinning back again. I smiled and forced the bland expression back into place, but he still tried unobtrusively to put the trolley between us. Bad haircut, cheap watch, new shoes, nervous eyes. He hadn't been doing this long, and it was probably his first steady paying job for a while. What kind of family waited for him when he got home after his shift? Probably divorced, maybe with two kids he was allowed to see every other weekend. The hotel might not even know he had been in trouble with the law. The lack of tattoos meant he'd done his time somewhere soft, and not for too long, so whatever he'd done was probably crime against property rather than person; forged checks, boosting truckloads of cigarettes, something like that. I could do or say almost anything in this elevator and he wouldn't retaliate: he needed this job, and it would be his word against a guest's. I tracked the way the muscles in his shoulders moved as he kept his balance in the elevator: not easy, not supple.

The door opened, I stepped off first, he followed cautiously. My room was halfway down a long corridor. I opened it myself, lifted the bag from the trolley, and gave him a ten because it occurred to me that even timid guests probably sensed they could undertip him, and because I felt soiled, having imagined the things I could do to him if I wanted. I knew he had sensed my understanding of his vulnerability, might have bad dreams tonight in his fifth-floor walkup with the bath in the middle of the kitchen. "Thank you," I said, and shut the door. I opened it again when he was gone, put out the DO NOT DISTURB sign, then locked and chained it.

It took less than a minute to unpack: I had forgotten almost everything. No toiletries, no underwear, not even a comb. Just the clothes I had worn for most of the drive, the clothes I stood up in, three pairs of socks, two books, my phone, and a can of half-frozen concentrated orange juice. How strange.

It was an anonymous room, done in the artificial pinks and grays popular for public spaces five years ago, with two beds. I couldn't remember the last time I'd been in a hotel room with two beds. The furniture was all fake-mahogany-veneered particleboard, and the window would only open three inches, barely enough to let in the greasy, hydrocarbon air. Room service was open until midnight: another ten minutes. The desk phone felt large and unnatural in my hand. I told the woman who answered that I wanted tomato soup, chicken teriyaki, a bottle of Samuel Adams, and three bottles of Evian. I had to repeat myself because even up on the twenty-second floor and even at night the ululation of sirens and honking of angry drivers on Sixth drowned me out. That done, I stripped off the Eileen Fisher and hung it up.

The only space big enough to lie on the carpet was in front of the dresser. I sat and stretched my tendons one by one. I wondered when Bob got off shift, whether or not he had friends to go for a drink with, or whether he crept home to a microwaved dinner and reruns and infomercials on TV. I stood, began the slow swelling inhalation of an aikido warm-up. Maybe he had a cat who would curl up on his stomach and knead his chest, digging its claws through the cheap cotton and into his skin, reminding him that love hurts. I moved in the blending exercise, soften, step, exhale, turn, slide. There wasn't room for a kata, or a tai chi form.

There was a mirror above the dresser. I touched my reflection with a fingertip. My reflection felt nothing. That's what I wanted from the world, to feel nothing. To feel nothing and not be involved, for everything to stay comfortably outside myself and not get in. How did people survive all this knowledge of suffering in the world? How did they carry it around, day after day, and not go mad? And what would I wear tomorrow?

The food came. I didn't let the man push the table into the room, refused to look at him; I didn't want to know what he looked like or how he felt or anything about him. I didn't care, I didn't want to care. It wasn't until I shut the door again that I realized I'd answered it in my underwear.

I dreamt of the woman I had found on patrol nine years ago drowned in her tub, eyes turning to glue, the water so still I knew her heart hadn't beaten in days. Once again I felt the slow, inevitable realization that the air in my lungs was still and stale, that I was dead, too. I woke at three in the morning and thought of how Julia had shaken me fiercely from the same dream six months ago and put her hand on my beating heart and my hand on hers, and told me I was alive, alive.

I had breakfast in my room, then called information. They had no Tammy Foster listed, no Geordie Karp. No Tammy Karp or Geordie Foster. Not in Greenwich Village or anywhere else in Manhattan. It would have been convenient to call ahead and make sure she was there.

At nine in the morning, the concession shops were deserted but none of them sold underwear. Guests might forget toothbrushes, they might forget a pen, their vitamins, a comb, but they didn't usually forget underwear. I had remembered the perfect change of clothes, down to jewelry, brought credit card and money and socks and shoes, but had not thought of a coat or underpants. We only recognize we have an autopilot when it goes horribly wrong.

Even in dirty clothes it was a pleasant walk to Saks in the kind of sunlight New York specializes in at the beginning of autumn: too warm in the sun, too cold in the shade without a coat. There was never quite enough space on the sidewalk to stride, and after I bought underwear and toiletries I walked back along Fifth all the way to East Fifty-seventh, just so that I could swing my arms. St. Patrick's Cathedral, St. Thomas's Church, the Fifth Avenue Church: a similar concentration of churches per square mile as the poor Baptist South, though probably not as well attended. Central Park beckoned briefly, but I resolutely turned left and kept walking. Move, don't think.

After I'd changed I didn't pause to talk to the concierge or to get a map but walked back out again, to the subway at Fifth and Fifty-third, and down into the stink of diesel fume and stale urine to catch the F train. If I could get to Washington Square Park, all I had to do was walk west to find Seventh Avenue. On the platform I tried to shut down my senses, close out the noise, the carbon-slippery air, the three middle-aged businessmen in expensive coats talking in tight voices about some deal that had gone south. A redheaded boy on crutches who couldn't have been more than fifteen stood next to the men, whose discussion had now escalated to the kind of argument people have when they're looking for someone else to blame. The boy stood too close. Any of those men could lash out in frustration and the boy would tumble off the platform onto enough electricity to hard-boil his eyes in four seconds. Anyone could push any of us off. I looked behind me. No one. I stepped back several feet and tried to breathe normally. There could have been someone there. I should not have had to look. I should have known. Be present, stay alert: the first rule of self-defense. But then I wouldn't be able to shut out the noise and stink and tension around me.

The train was not full. No one paid attention to anyone else as we racketed past signs for Rockefeller Center, Forty-second Street, Herald Square. The same tunnels, different signs. It could have been an episode of *The Twilight Zone:* dead people traveling in Charon's twenty-first-century barge. When I got off at Fourth Street, the steps were too steep, and the higher I climbed the less oxygen I seemed able to pull into my lungs, but at the top, outside, the sun still shone. Again, I had that brief sense of vertigo. I walked without thinking, without direction, just to be walking, to be not trapped among the women with cross-slung purses and men with messenger bags who radiated aggression and fear, and eventually the press thinned and I could breathe, I could begin to separate out different packets of information—a smell from a shout from a flash of color—and I found I was heading south on La Guardia Place. At the next cross street, Bleecker, I turned right and headed west.

I passed the Bitter End, "New York's Oldest Rock Club," and two or three blocks later the Greenwich Village Funeral Home. Old rock stars never die. Right again, north on Sixth, because it was wider, and there was less information per square foot, but before I could head north and west on West Fourth I was caught by the flash and thud of a ball and the slip and play of tree shadow on the sweat-sheened arms of two men rising to the basket, and I had to stop because the information made no sense: taxi honk, thump of ball, back-and-forth flash of green, then white, as money and drugs change hands, fence around a paved court, crunch of fallen leaves, screech of tire on asphalt. And then it was clear: pickup basketball on an urban court around which rip-off-the-tourist drug deals met gentrified neighborhood in early autumn sunshine. I leaned on the wire fence around the court, let it dig into my back, breathed until my heart slowed. I knew where I was. I started to walk. I knew why I was there. I swang my arms. I knew where I was going.

My arms would not swing properly. The tension in my shoulders would not let go.

The last time I had had to consciously relax as I walked a city street was nearly eleven years ago, during my first weeks on patrol with the Atlanta PD. Then, I had reared at every shadow, flooded with adrenaline at every human voice, wondering if this was the situation that would get away from me, if that might be the man who would be bigger or faster or stronger. I had learned after a while to recalibrate my sense settings, to distinguish the shout from a bar doorway that meant I am about to shove this shank in your kidney from the one that said Damn, I feel good today!, to differentiate the flash of movement on a sunlit downtown street that signaled the sudden attack from the one that meant someone had just realized he was late for his meeting and had to run. You had to trust your unconscious mind to understand the whole picture; it can process faster than thought. It will let you know if the charging man has bared teeth and mismatched socks, or whether he is wearing a silk and cashmere suit. It will add that information to whether he is growling or merely cursing his own idiocy under his breath, and whether his smell is Mogen David or something by Calvin Klein, and then flash a red or green light to your adrenal glands, all between one heartbeat and the next. If you adjust your conscious filters to the appropriate setting, you can relax and let your subconscious take care of things. It's something I used to be good at.

I kept walking north and west on West Fourth, swinging my arms, telling myself I was relaxed. If you walk as though your mind is easy, your mind believes your body and becomes easy. If your mind is easy, your body believes it and becomes easy: a basic feedback loop. I half closed my eyes, ignored the noise around me, imagined my wrists loose and my fingers relaxed. Breathe, stride, swing. By the time I turned north on Seventh I didn't have to think about it anymore.

The ground floor of 95 Seventh Avenue South turned out to be a pizzeria, but there was a doorway to the left, and three neat black bell pushes and an intercom grille. No mailboxes. I took thin leather gloves from my jacket pocket and put them on. I tried the door: locked. None of the buttons were identified by apartment number, but two of them had names, Jhaing and Donato. I pushed each button in turn. The grille crackled.

"Yeah?" A man's voice, young.

"Package," I said.

"Uh, so you could put it in the mailbox."

"Won't fit the mailbox."

"Then leave it in the lobby. Jeez . . ."

New York, I reminded myself. "I can't get in to get to the lobby, asshole, because I'm not from the goddamn post office, okay? If you don't want the package, then fuck you and have a nice day."

"Whoa! Okay, okay. Jeez. You'd think—" Whatever I was supposed to think was drowned out by the buzzer and I pushed the door open. The mailboxes were on the right, three of them, and all were labeled: Apt. A: Jhiang, Apt. B: Dutourd, Apt. C: Donato, Karp, Foster. They were locked.

The stairs were made of a glittery stone composite and didn't creak. I stopped halfway up the first flight and sniffed: something summery and old-fashioned. Lavender. My face tightened as adrenaline nudged up my blood pressure: this was not the kind of place I would expect to find Tammy, or the darling of retail sales, Mr. Karp.

The first floor was carpeted in neutral beige. The green-painted door said it was Apt. A. The second floor was a well-finished hardwood, with a cheerful rag rug and a vase of dried flowers on a Chippendale hall table. Probably the source of the lavender scent. I kept going, and hadn't quite reached the third floor when a door banged open above me and a slightly built man hurried along the hallway to the stairs. I went perfectly still. He literally jumped when he saw me.

"Who the fuck are you?"

Early twenties, black hair, black eyes, left ear pierced twice, and the kind of clothes that didn't fit with the probable rent of his apartment.

"I said, who the—"

My heart was pumping smoothly. "I'm looking for Tammy Foster."

"She doesn't live here."

"I'm still looking for her."

He tensed and backed up. "You the police?"

"No."

"My mom send you?"

"No." Oxygen-rich blood coursed through dilated blood vessels. "Where is Tammy?"

He frowned but his shoulders came down a fraction. "Why do you care?"

My muscles were relaxed and my voice, when I spoke, sounded almost gentle. "I don't care, particularly, but you will tell me—"

"I don't—"

"—where she is and why her name is on your mailbox."

"There's no law against that. Is there?"

"We'll talk about it inside, Mr. Donato." I mounted another step, lightly, easily, walking right at him, and he blinked, then gave in.

The hall smelled of old dishwater and uncleaned toilet and there were boot marks on the paintwork. He led me into the living room, where he hurriedly cleared takeout cartons, and a stack of what appeared to be bad charcoal sketches, from a love seat, looking embarrassed and about seventeen years old. I ignored the couch and stepped back into the hallway, stuck my head in the kitchen, then the filthy bathroom and the mess and disorder of the bedroom. A nice apartment, clearly beyond this boy's apparent means, both economic and psychological. It was also clear that only one person lived here.

"Give me her forwarding address."

"What?"

"Tammy Foster's forwarding address."

"I don't have that!" He sounded genuinely surprised.

"Tell me where you send her mail."

"But I don't."

He began to shift from foot to foot. He wasn't lying. "Explain."

"It's like, you know, an arrangement." I waited. "They pay me. This is Mom's apartment. I mean she pays the rent but I live here. She doesn't pay for, you know, food or clothes because she says if I want to waste my time on— Right, okay. So this dude pays me a few bucks a week to collect their mail, and that's about, you know, it." He shrugged with his thin arms, inarticulately.

"Does Karp or Foster come and get it?"

"No. I just toss it in the garbage."

"You throw their mail in the garbage."

"Well, yeah."

It would be so easy—my right hand on his right wrist, pull and step, left arm across his throat, whirl and spread my arms, like a dance, and he would drop spine-down over my thigh, snap: less than three seconds, start to finish—but a broken boy would help nothing. The adrenaline ebbed.

"Do you have any mail addressed to them that you haven't thrown away yet?"

"Yeah."

"Give it to me." In the absence of adrenaline I felt mounting irritation.

"Uh, isn't opening other people's mail like a federal offense?"

"It's exactly like a federal offense. So is aggravated assault." I reached slowly into my inside pocket, giving him time to register the fact that I wore gloves.

"Whoa! I was just—"

"Bring me the mail." He scuttled off into the kitchen and came back with five envelopes and two catalogues, all obviously junk apart from one white envelope with a familiar blue logo. "Give me the one from American Express." It was addressed to George G. Karp. I opened it. A bill. Not a solicitation, but a regular bill. I scanned the list of charges. It seemed genuine. I put it in my pocket. "What else do they get?"

"Stuff. I don't keep track, you know?"

"Visa? Utility bills?"

"Yeah, like that."

Why would someone go to the trouble of setting up a mail drop and getting bills and other correspondence mailed to it, only to have those bills thrown away? "How much does he pay?"

"It used to be twenty-five a week, but when he added the Foster chick's name, I told him, man, I can't do it for less than forty."

"Cash?"

"Well, duh. Every other Thursday, in the mail. Paid last week."

I reached into my jacket again. Before he had backed up more than two steps I pulled out my wallet. He bobbed his head: a combination of relief and greed. I extracted five crisp twenties. "I want to know everything you know about Karp and Foster."

I put my gloves in my pocket and walked around the Village for a while. Donato had not been able to remember what bills had come or what the cycle was, and he couldn't describe Karp except that he had, you know, maybe sort of blondish hair? He'd only met him, like, once. Tammy he had never seen. I had taken back four of the twenties.

Tammy had to be here. She'd told Dornan this was where she was going after Naples. Her credit card confirmed it. I had followed the money and it led nowhere except back to Tammy's Atlanta apartment and to a mail drop. But if she hadn't lied to Dornan, then she was here with Karp. Find Karp, find Tammy. I knew Karp was somewhere close: his American Express showed dozens of charges to Manhattan restaurants, mainly in midtown, SoHo, and the Village, with a few in Brooklyn.

I wandered past endless coffeehouses on MacDougal

Street. It was only eleven o'clock, not yet lunchtime, but the crowds were growing, the air starting to feel used. A double-decker bus stuffed with tourists rumbled past.

Inside the café, there was one spare table and a line at the counter. Most of the people sitting and sipping were talking—half to friends, the other half to their phones. One woman tapped diligently on her tiny keypad and frowned at the display. The web. Of course. You had to have an official billing address for a credit card or utility, but you could pay by phone or online.

Somewhere, Karp would have an e-mail address, maybe even a business website. I didn't have my laptop and my phone screen was tiny, its processing power more suited to instant text than a web search.

A hard-eyed young thing behind the counter asked me what she could get me. I ordered latte, and dropped two ones in the tip jar. "Where's the nearest library?" I asked.

"Library? Public library?"

"Yes. Where is it?"

"Hold on." She called back over her shoulder to the man behind the espresso machine. "Hal, the library's at Sixth and Tenth, right?"

"Around there, yeah."

She turned back to the counter and spoke to the customer behind me. "Get you something?"

The library was an imposing brown-and-white building that looked like a cross between a Gothic cathedral and the Doge's Palace. There were two Macs on the second floor, one, on the right, already taken by a woman in her fifties, who froze when I came into her peripheral vision, and stared rigidly at her screen until I sat.

A Google search brought me eight hundred hits, none of which seemed to be a home page. There was a profile from *Talk* a year ago, a *Business Week* cover spread, and literally dozens of features in obscure trade journals, both print and web-based. Interestingly, there was no photo: both the *Talk* and *Business Week* articles were accompanied by the cover illustration for his book, *Hostage Exchange: Their Money for Your Goods,* which had been reprinted in a paperback edition last month.

The woman next to me had relaxed enough to resume her tapping. Every now and again she sighed loudly.

There were several links relating to recent and forthcoming appearances; he was doing a reading and signing at the Citicorp Center Barnes and Noble in four days. I skimmed half a dozen interviews: repeated citations of design awards, recycled plaudits from a variety of retail executives, including a glowing but utterly impersonal quote from the Nordstrom VP of Full Service Stores, some number-dense analyses of retail sales from various stores pre- and post-consultation with Karp, and one snippet in an article written almost five years ago about how Karp worked from his SoHo loft "with a cell phone and a laptop."

The articles shared a sameness that hinted at very, very careful information management by Karp. It wasn't easy to control the editorial content of magazines. I wondered how he had done it. Then I laughed, aloud, which made the sighing woman look at me sharply—funny how tiny infractions made people bold. I gave her a smile with a lot of teeth.

Most magazines rely on advertising revenue; many advertisers are retailers; Karp had great contacts in the retail world. A discreet word here, a favor called in there would bend a few rules. But favors were usually costly in any profession. What did he have to hide?

I went to Switchboard.com and tried Karp, and G. Karp, and George Karp, and Geordie Karp, in the state, then the city. Hundreds of Karps in New York State, too many to trace one by one. No George Karps in the city. One G. Karp in Brooklyn. I wrote down the number and address but knew it wouldn't be him. An initial was a flimsy hiding place. I repeated the exercise for Tammy, and found nothing promising. I tried again on Bigfoot with the same results.

I followed a few more links. Nothing. Why was he so careful? What was he afraid of?

On my way past the woman at the other computer I stopped. Her shoulders hunched but she didn't turn around. "You should always look," I told the back of her head. "Not looking never kept anyone safe."

Outside, I called the Brooklyn number. A machine picked up after four rings. "Hi, this is Gina Karp. Leave a number. You know the drill."

I closed the phone. A loft in SoHo, but five years ago. Not much else. Just the book, and the bookstore signing in four days. If all else failed, I could go to that and follow him home, or go to the restaurants and bars listed most frequently on his statement and hope he showed up. Either alternative meant staying in New York, talking to people, interacting. I didn't think I could stand one more day of concrete and braying voices.

Washington Square Park was crowded with dog walkers, mime artists, skateboarders, street musicians, jugglers, and chess players; tourists seethed so thickly around the fountains that I could only see the top of the water spout and couldn't hear it at all; people sat in ones and twos at the foot of every tree, reading.

Maybe Karp's book would tell me something about him.

The Village is full of bookstores. I bought a copy, carried it back to the park, and folded myself onto the grass to read.

Several case studies, complete with photos. A hint of smugness, perhaps, gleaming cold and hard through the personable prose. Again that boast: he needed no office but his cell phone and his laptop. No other scrap of information about where he was born, where he lived, who he was.

A pair of police officers strolled down the bike path, a white man and Hispanic woman, nodding occasionally to passersby, smiling at a toddler being dragged along by his parents. Obviously officers specially trained to be nice to tourists. Their eyes remained watchful.

I turned the book over and over in my hand, front and back, back and forth, feeling its weight, taking its measure, the way an antique dealer might handle a jade carving, or a sculptor her wood. I put it on the grass in front of me, turned my face up to the hazy sun. In North Carolina, the sun would be yellow as an egg yolk on a blue plate, and leaves would be drifting down onto the cabin roof.

I picked the book up again, riffled through the pages from back to front, and there it was, the copyright notice: © Koi Productions. Hiding behind his own cleverness.

I had to walk a few yards before my phone got a decent signal. Information gave me the address: Koi Productions, 393 West Broadway. The SoHo loft.

I took three cabs, getting in and out after random intervals, before I found a driver who spoke English and who spent just a second too long looking in the rearview mirror at the roll of money I took from my pocket. His ID said his name was Joe Czerna; he had a red nose and gray hair. Late fifties, maybe. I made my body language younger, more excited. I smiled a lot, as though nervous.

"So, Joe, what's it like driving a cab in New York?"

He shrugged. "It's okay."

"Bet you get some real wackos to deal with sometimes."

"Sometimes."

"You ever see anyone get shot?"

"Maybe."

"Did you call the cops?"

"Nobody shot me. I just drive. I got money to earn."

"You want to earn some money for helping me?"

Pause. "How much?"

"A hundred, plus fare and tip."

"You gonna shoot anybody?"

I laughed. "No, no. No shooting, but some people might be upset. It's my sister, y'know? She's, like, a bit crazy. I'm gonna go get her, from where she's staying with her boyfriend. But she might not want to come, y'know?"

"No drugs, nothing like that? I don't want no throwing up in my car."

"Nothing like that. Just some yelling, maybe. Okay?"

"Your sister?"

"My sister."

"My family shout alla time. Where you want to go?"

"West Broadway."

It didn't take long. I got out, tore a hundred-dollar bill in half, gave one piece to him, and put the other in my pocket. "Wait for me. I shouldn't be longer than half an hour maybe."

He tapped the meter. "Gonna keep this running, too."

"Okay, whatever. But wait."

I was beginning to wake up. I had been too long in the woods. I had forgotten, for a while, to be cautious. Bears and bobcats could be dangerous, but they didn't feel the need to hide, and they weren't smart enough to hide their addresses. If I needed to get Tammy away against her will or anyone else's, I wanted a cabbie with a vested interest in taking what would look like a risky fare. Of course, she might not even be there, in which case I'd just wasted a hundred dollars.

Number 393 was a brick-faced building, a shop front, Anderly Flowers, and six steps with no railing leading up to a metal door, with a keyhole beside it. It took me a moment to recognize it as an elevator door, the kind that goes straight up to a loft. My scalp felt tight. I put my gloves on and pushed the buzzer. No response. I waited a minute, then pushed it again. Nothing. Again. Just like fishing. I had all day.

"Who is it?" A woman's voice. Tammy's, though it was hard to be sure over the hiss of the intercom.

"Mr. Karp?"

"He's not here." Definitely Tammy's.

I made my accent warm and Hispanic. "No, no. I'm *from* Mr. Karp. I have a delivery."

Silence, then: "I'm not expecting anything." Her voice sounded thick, as though she'd been crying, and with a questioning lilt, oddly hopeful, like a child's.

"Well, I have a special delivery here for someone called Tammy. From Prada. They're paid for. I'm just dropping them off." Silence. "A present maybe, I don't know."

"A present?" Her voice was uncharacteristically tentative. "You could just put everything in the elevator."

"No, no, I have to come up. You have to sign."

"Wait, two minutes."

I waited. After a while the doors opened. There were two old-fashioned Perspex buttons, UP and DOWN. No key slot to override instructions from upstairs. A perfect trap. But I knew Tammy. She would never cry or sound childish in front of a man. I stepped in and pushed UP. The doors closed and the cage rose.

The doors opened to brick and blond wood, soaring spaces lit by bright halogen light, and there was Tammy, elevator key dangling from the thin chain she'd wrapped around her wrist, standing straight, and well dressed, but looking destroyed, torn up by the roots. She had just washed her face, but the lids were still puffy and she breathed through her mouth because her sinuses were still blocked from weeping.

I stepped from the cage. "Hello, Tammy."

"Aud?"

She looked behind me, as though expecting to see a young Hispanic woman dead on a pile of Prada couture on the elevator floor. The elevator doors closed. "Aud?" Then her hand went to her heart, as though someone had punched her, and her face turned a dirty gray. "Is Dornan here too?"

"No."

I'm not sure she heard me. She seemed about to topple with fear.

I took her by the elbow and considered. To the right, the stainless steel of a chef's kitchen; ahead, a short corridor with three closed doors; to the left, a vast living room with ivory leather furniture, a brilliant kilim worth more than a luxury car, and a minimalist audiovisual system flanked by two large plinths that supported what looked like nineteenth-century French bronzes. I steered her towards the living room. "Dornan doesn't know where you are. I didn't tell him. No one knows except me. Come and sit down."

She moved like an ill person, not drugged but docile, and unconfidently, as though the world were a dangerous place. Perhaps it was, or at least this part of it. I led her around a brick support pillar to a couch.

"Sit." She sat. The features were the same as Tammy's but this wasn't the Tammy I'd known. "Dornan is worried—" She began to blink rapidly. She couldn't be afraid of Dornan. Afraid of him seeing her like this? "He doesn't know where you are, and I won't tell him unless you want me to. He doesn't have to know about—" Distinct pallor. What had she done? "—any of this. But he's worried, so he asked me to find you and make sure you're all right. Are you? All right?"

Her eyes filled with tears but she made no move to reply. It was clear that she was very far from all right.

"I have a cab waiting downstairs. We can go to my hotel. We can talk. We'll drink tea. You can tell me what's going on. After that, you can come back here if you—"

"No!"

That seemed clear enough, so I stood, took her hand, helped her to her feet, and headed for the elevator.

"No!" she said again.

"You don't want to leave?"

"I mean . . ." She made a vague gesture towards a closed door. "My things . . ."

Her things. "Where is Karp—Geordie—when is he coming back?" But she had closed her eyes; she wasn't listening. "Give me the key. The elevator key."

Without the key, she couldn't leave, or let anyone else up. I had no idea what was going on, but I knew she was afraid. I didn't want to be surprised. She handed it over without protest, and I put it in my pocket. Behind the first closed door was a windowless office, almost bare but for a utilitarian desk on which stood a printer and small photocopier, and, against the wall, a self-contained video playback unit and a stack of tapes. A lateral filing cabinet, freestanding supply drawers. No fax, no phone, no computer. The second door hid a half bath. The third led to the bedroom, which appeared ordinary enough—king-size bed with crimson-covered duvet, two dressers, a lovely eighteenth-century beechwood armoire, thick cream rug, reading lamps, long, heavy crimson curtains—but felt strange. I stood there for a moment, trying to work out where the oddness lay, then dismissed it. Tammy's purse sat on the bed. I tipped out the contents to make sure that keys, wallet with credit cards, Georgia driver's license, health insurance—all the personal essentials—were there, then shoveled everything back in. The master bath yielded two bottles of prescription pills and one cream, and contact lens paraphernalia. No watch. I took a toothbrush for good measure, and a comb, and added them to her bag. On the way back through the bedroom, I opened the dresser drawer and scooped out a handful of hose and underwear. Glasses from the bedside table. Was that everything she'd need for twenty-four hours? I didn't want to have to take my eyes off her for a while. Something else, something else . . . Ring. She hadn't been wearing Dornan's ring. An antique jewelry chest, also eighteenth-century, but made of some dense tropical wood I wasn't familiar with, sat on the second dresser, but I couldn't find the ring. I tipped everything out, stirred it with my finger. No ring. Back to the bedside table. Nothing. Bathroom: no jewelry case. I went through the medicine cabinet more carefully. Nothing. I paused. This was Karp's apartment; his ownership was apparent everywhere, from the precisely placed bronzes to the orderly kitchen to the matching leather furniture. Tammy had not made a single impression: she didn't feel safe here. An engagement ring was personal, perhaps even precious, something to keep private, hidden. I went back to the underwear drawer, pulled it out, tipped it onto the bed. Nothing. Dornan still meant something to her or she wouldn't be so afraid of him seeing her like this; she would have kept the ring. I shook out each pair of underpants, one at a time, put them back in the drawer. Opened the packets of hose. Began unfolding the sock pairs. I found it in the third pair, tucked down near the toe.

Back in the hallway, Tammy still stood by the elevator. I held out the bag but she took no notice of it. I used the key, and when the elevator opened she stepped in without a word.

She didn't say anything when I gave her the bag and opened the cab door, nor when Joe turned to look at her black hair, chocolate brown eyes and full figure, then at my height and light blue eyes, and said, "Sister, huh?"

I gave him the other half of the hundred-dollar bill. "Different fathers."

"Uh-huh."

I gave him another fifty. He drove.

"We're going to the Hilton," I told Tammy. She stared through me as though I were talking in algebra. Her pupils looked normal, she wasn't flushed or overly pale, and her breath came smoothly; she was not drugged; she had removed herself somehow, as though she had given up all responsibility for herself, or hope. Dornan had said she was smarter than I gave her credit for. What would he make of this?

We pulled up outside the hotel. "We're getting out here," I told her. She climbed out obediently. I sighed and reached back into the cab for her bag. Joe drove off without a backward glance. I held the bag out; she took it. "This way." She followed me through the lobby, crowded now with guests checking their watches and exuding stress and impatience. "We'll be in my room soon," but she didn't seem bothered by so many bodies all trying to breathe the same air, the same molecules that had just slithered down one red throat, then back up, to be snatched by the phlegmy lungs of a passing bellboy, who exhaled near the mouth of an old woman whose heart was probably as weak as her watery eyes. My clothes felt too tight. I wanted to punch my way to the street and not stop running until I reached Central Park and could lean against a maple trunk and look up into the leaves and believe I was not in the middle of ten million people; but here was Tammy, standing by the elevators, empty as a gourd, and Dornan, my friend, needed me to make sure she was safe.

The elevator opened and Tammy just stood there. I began to shake. I lifted my hand, but turned it instead into a light touch on her elbow and a gesture. "In. We have to go up."

Halfway up she began to weep silently, but her expression didn't change.

"You're safe," I said, wondering if I was lying. "We're almost there."

A couple was waiting at the twenty-second floor to go down. The younger of the two noticed Tammy's tears and gave me a sharp look, but neither of them said anything.

Housekeeping had already tidied and cleaned the room; with my personal things hidden behind doors, it felt as comforting as an autoclave. I sat Tammy down on the edge of the nearest bed and went round turning on all the lights. The dim yellow glow added some warmth to the room. I closed the curtains to make her feel safer. "I'm going to run you a bath, and I'll order some food while you're relaxing." Tammy just sat there. I took her hand and tugged her gently towards the bathroom. Her hand was cold. "The bath will get you warm." The water gushed into the tub. I made sure there was soap, that the bath mat was on the floor. The chlorinated water frothed on itself, water so clean it was dead. I tried to ignore the automaton breathing behind me. The tub filled. As though she were a child, I tested the temperature of the water with the back of my hand. I turned off the taps. "I'll shut the door, but I'm just out here if you need me."

I listened outside the door. There was no snick of the lock, but after a moment I heard the soft plash of flesh meeting water, and moved away.

I called room service, ordered tea and coffee, sandwiches, water, juice.

No matter how many lights you turn on, hotel rooms are always too dark and always too small, and when you press your face up against the glass, all the people so many stories below always seem to have more freedom than you do. Even the people in the building opposite, harshly lit by fluorescents in their office cubicles, seemed to have fuller lives. One man wearing a shirt and suspenders kept scratching at his sandy-haired head with a pencil. He held a phone in his right hand and the pencil in his left, talk talk scratch scratch, then he swapped hands, scratch scratch talk talk. If the pencil was sharp, he would have tiny rips all over his scalp.

Stationary cabs lined up like golden beetles down the center of Fifth, glittering in the strange New York sunshine. In any other city on earth the drivers would have been standing by their cars, arms folded, leaning against hoods and gossiping.

No noise from the bathroom. To the left of the office building, a huge sign spelled out ESSEX HOUSE backwards. Sandy Hair put down his pencil and scratched fiercely at his temple with his fingernails, exactly the way a squirrel would, only much more slowly. Cabs opened their doors, closed them, and drove off with fares. Other cabs took their place.

Someone rapped on the door and announced that they were room service. When I opened the door, a rotund woman, crisp as a freshly baked dinner roll in her white jacket, pushed the cart briskly into the room. I stepped in front of her before she could go any further. "I'll take it." I signed the tab and herded her out.

Sandy Hair was still scratching his scalp. I set the table up so one chair faced the corner and the other the door. "Room service is here," I called to Tammy. I lifted plate rings, poured tea, divided sandwiches. I ate one. Tuna salad. No sound from the bathroom. I sipped tea. Not made with boiling water. Tammy was probably sitting in the bath with her mouth hanging open. She hardly knew me, yet here she was, depending on my goodwill, like a child. Selfish, like a child. What gave her the right to assume I'd just take care of everything? There was no way to know what to do with her. It was obvious she didn't want to see or be seen by Dornan, but I couldn't leave her on her own in this state; I didn't trust her to look after herself. I didn't trust her, full stop. If I got her in my truck and drove to Atlanta, or anywhere else for that matter, I wouldn't put it past her to cry kidnap when she recovered her wits.

"Tammy. Food," I called again. Nothing. The bathwater was probably getting cold. Maybe that would prompt some movement.

I will find her, I had told Dornan, but all I'd found was a shell. I had no idea how to go about finding the rest.

I poured myself more tea and took it over to the bed nearest the door where Tammy's bag lay on its side next to the pillows. Cup in one hand, I opened the bag with the other and tipped it upside down, stirred the spilled contents with one finger. The two plastic bottles both held the same thing, Ambien, a prescription sleeping pill. I put them on the bedside table, along with the ring, the contact lens case and its solutions, and the glasses. I stuffed everything else back in except for the underwear, which I put in the drawer next to the one that held mine. No clues.

I put my empty cup back on the room service trolley. That bathwater would be really uncomfortable by now.

"Tammy?" I knocked on the door, listened. Nothing. "Tammy?"

Memory of my dream about the woman dead in the bath made my knees sag as though I were in a high-speed elevator braking to a halt. I hammered on the door. "Tammy!" I turned the handle and slammed into the door, forgetting it wasn't locked.

Tammy wasn't sitting in her own blood, her eyes weren't rolled up, she wasn't floating facedown. She was hunched, knees under her chin, at one end of the bath, weeping silently, great fat tears falling like fruit onto her thighs. The ends of her hair were wet. Eight hundred miles for this.

"Get up," I said. She was alive, and she didn't care, didn't understand how precious that was. "Get up!" Her face was quite still and calm. If it were not for the body language and the tears, I might have thought she was meditating. She was removed, no longer caring; life wasn't worth living but there wasn't enough of her left for her to bother killing herself. Maybe she wanted me to do it for her.

"Let's get you out of there. Come on now, Tammy, come on." I took one of the towels from the rack and held it out encouragingly. "It's lovely and soft and warm. Come along now." She blinked slowly. I slung the towel around my neck and leaned down. "I'm going to put my hands under your arms, that's it, just like that, and lift you out, that's it, move your legs, that's right. And now you have to step over the rim, onto the mat." Her skin felt firm and cold, meat waiting to be cut. "Put this towel around you. Yes, yes, come on now." She made no move to pull the towel closed about her. I left it draped over her shoulders and got another one. "A good, brisk rub and you'll be fine. And when you're dry, I'll put you to bed. There's tea, and food if you want it. And perhaps a bit of television. The door's locked, no one can come in or out. You can sleep. You're safe." I opened the bathroom door, put my right arm around her waist, and took her left hand in mine to lead her forward. "Here we go. Here.

This bed. You sit right there. I'll turn on the television." She sat obediently, unconscious of her seminakedness, while I flipped through channels until I found a soothing natural history program about domestic cats. "Stand up just a minute while I pull back the covers. There we go. Sit down. Now swing your legs up." Flash of skin, smooth now, warmer. She smelled of towel. "Lie down, that's right. Here, let me take the towel. What you need right now is some sleep." The food could wait. I tucked the bedclothes around her shoulders and under her chin. She closed her eyes obediently. I sat next to her on the bed. "You're safe. I'll be sitting near the window, right here. You sleep." Maybe I should give her a sleeping pill. Her breathing deepened. Just as I eased off the bed her eyes flicked open, and they were frightened.

"What time is it?"

I glanced at the bedside clock. "Two fifty-three. In the afternoon."

She followed my glance to the clock, wouldn't take her eyes off it.

"Here." I moved it so it was closer, and facing her. She looked at me, back at the clock, at the curtains.

"Open the curtains."

"You'll sleep better if they're—" Her eyes started to go dead again. "Okay. Hold on."

I opened them. She looked at the concrete building, the blue sky, back at the clock. "Afternoon?"

"Yes."

"Two fifty-three?"

"Two fifty-four, now."

She nodded slightly to herself and fell asleep as though someone had pulled the plug.

I settled myself in the armchair near the window. Taxis honked; sirens grew, dopplered, faded. On the TV, an orange kitten chased floating dandelion seeds through the sunlight of a summer garden. I did not know what to make of Tammy's behavior. Fear might explain some of it, but fear of what? She had had a key, she could have left anytime, or if she was scared of something outside the apartment, she could just have picked up the phone. Except, of course, there hadn't been a phone.

The kittens were replaced by some woman with a Canadian accent demonstrating the art of stenciling in home decor.

Tammy woke after an hour. She didn't sit up or say anything, just gasped, and her respiration rate went up. Then she started turning her head very, very slowly towards the clock, as though her life depended on me not knowing she was awake.

"I'm here," I said. She froze. After a moment she turned her head to look at me. "Are you hungry yet? The sandwiches are still here. The drinks have gone cold, though, so if you want tea or coffee, we'd have to order more."

"Where are we?"

"The Hilton."

She looked at the clock. It seemed to reassure her.

"The tuna salad sandwiches aren't bad." I put one on a small plate, added a napkin and the saltshaker, and brought it over to the bed. She looked at it as though it were a snake. I put it down near the clock. "Food is almost always a good idea." She reached for it without sitting up, careful not to let the covers slide off her shoulders. Well, well. "I'll bring you a robe." I put it on the bed and withdrew to the bathroom for a couple of minutes, where I folded her corduroys and cashmere, and when I came back she had taken a bite and was chewing. I poured her some water and brought that over, too. She was still chewing the same bite. "Swallowing comes next."

She swallowed obediently. I sighed, and she flinched and dropped the sandwich, which made me sigh harder with irritation, and she shrank back against the headboard.

"What's the matter with you?"

"I don't know what you want," she said in a small voice.

I stared at her. The Tammy I had first met nearly two years

ago would have walked naked down Peachtree Street before it occurred to her to wonder what anyone but herself wanted. She studied her sandwich fixedly. "I want you to eat that sandwich, if you can, and drink some water. Then I want you to sleep again. I want you to know you're safe. And then tonight we'll decide what to do."

She looked at the clock again, and picked up the sandwich.

As I'd thought, the carbohydrates combined with whatever shock she'd had sent her off to sleep again within a few minutes. I got up and turned the heat down, then went back to alternately looking out of the window and watching the television. The Canadian woman was now demonstrating color glazing. Every time the camera pulled back, the word "cheap" hovered brassily in the corners of the small, flimsy set; the wall wobbled as she leaned on it. To the English, cheap is not a pejorative word, simply descriptive, and usually delivered with an air of triumph: "I got these jeans cheap at the market!" In the United States, of course, cheap means shoddy, tacky, gimcrack; I didn't know a single American who would boast of buying something cheaply. Where were the Canadians on the cheap scale? Perhaps they followed the same cultural and geographic axis as the country in general: more European in Quebec, more American in Vancouver.

The chattering Canadian came to an abrupt end, and was replaced by an earnest magazine program dealing with health care for the mentally disabled. A while later I began learning more than anyone needed to know of the reproductive cycle of emperor penguins.

Sandy Hair and his coworkers had just begun to pack up to leave when I realized Tammy was awake and watching me. When I looked at her, she lowered her gaze in the universal primate gesture of submission. I should have noticed her wake, but, like a prey animal, she had learned to move quietly. Interesting. She seemed to have her wits about her, now.

"Good evening. It's pretty dark outside. You're not wearing much and this room is lit up like a stage. I'm going to close the curtains."

No protest this time. She sat up, touched her bare shoulder with her left hand. "You undressed me."

"Yes."

Silence, then: "Have you told Dornan anything?"

"No."

Another silence. "I want to leave."

"The door's right there. You have money in your purse."

"No. I mean, I want us to leave New York."

"Us?"

She didn't say anything.

"Is someone looking for you?"

"I have to leave now," she said.

"I'll be driving back south, but—"

"I don't want to go to Atlanta!"

"I'm not going to Atlanta, and I'm not leaving until tomorrow—unless you want to talk to me, tell me why you need to leave right now."

"Where are my glasses?"

"Right there next to the water."

She found the case, put on the steel-rims. I expected the gaze she turned on me to be sharper, but it was as blank as before. "Why can't we leave now?"

We. The I-can't-cope-by-myself ploy was something I had seen her use before, but not like this. This time there was no glint in her eye, no upthrust breast or canted hip, just a frightening brokenness.

I didn't want to stay in this hotel, in this city, another night anyway. "I'll pack while you dress."

CHAPTER FIVE

Midnight, and a black autumn wind was trying to push the truck this way and that as we crossed the southern edge of Maryland. Tammy slept in the passenger seat, right hand curled around her left wrist and the cheap watch we'd bought her at the airport. All she'd done since I'd taken her from that apartment this morning was sleep.

"It's a shock reaction," Julia said. She sat sideways on Tammy's lap, facing me. "A way to hide. You hide in the woods, Tammy hides in her dreams." She stroked Tammy's face gently, moving the back of one finger up her cheek, as if catching a tear. The muscles in my legs tensed and the truck jumped forward. "Where's the fire?" she said.

"I want to be in West Virginia before we stop."

She studied Tammy, whose eyes were darting from side to side beneath closed lids. "Did you take away those sleeping pills?"

"No."

"Might be an idea. At some point she's going to crawl far enough out of her pit to get her self-will back. That's when she's liable to do something stupid."

Tammy umphed and turned in her seat, moving Julia, who said, "Bony hips. I think she's lost weight," and I suddenly couldn't stand the idea of Julia touching another woman, not touching me, never touching me again.

"Please," I said.

Julia raised her eyebrows.

"This—I can't—" I braked and started to pull over.

"What?" Tammy sat up.

Julia vanished. I yanked on the parking brake before we quite stopped moving and Tammy jerked forward against her seat belt. The engine rumbled. The wind howled. Her gaze slid this way and that but she kept her head down.

"Get out."

She put her hand on the door lock and prepared to get out, in the middle of nowhere, in the middle of the night, without even looking at me. It was as though she had expected all along to be abandoned, as though she accepted it, even deserved it.

Shame raised prickles on my skin from knees to neck. "I mean get in the backseat. There's more room, you can stretch out."

She climbed out and into the back without another word.

"Are you warm enough?" She nodded, eyes huge. "Good, that's good." The truck started up again smoothly and I pressed the accelerator down and down until it wouldn't go any further. Lane marker studs streamed under my wheels. The engine began to whine. Annoying.

"It's all right," I said, to myself, to Tammy, to Julia, wherever she was, and eased my foot off the gas. The stream flowed more sedately. "We'll take the next exit and stop for the night."

The Days Inn was plain and comfortable; spending the night with Tammy was neither. She didn't take off her underwear or her watch and lay rigid on her tautly made bed like a knife from the wrong set of silverware set out on its napkin by mistake. She didn't talk, she barely breathed, and her eyes glimmered slightly: wide open and empty even of fright.

I woke at six the next morning, and opened my eyes just in time to see Tammy's flick open and watch me. Back to square one. I got up, ignored her, and went and had my shower. There was no packing or unpacking to do.

"I'll be back in an hour," I said. "Be ready to leave. Assuming you still want to come with me." It took most of that hour to get a copy of the elevator key made, to find and buy an envelope, to persuade the desk clerk to run it through their stamp machine, for a fee. I put the original key in the envelope, addressed it to Geordie Karp at his loft address, and dropped it in the mailbox. The duplicate went back in my pocket; you never knew.

When I got back I walked around the parking lot for the remaining minutes, saw license plates from sixteen different states, almost all on American cars, and wondered what the percentage of foreign to American vehicles would be at a hotel as opposed to a motel. Probably some ethnologist has done a study.

Tammy was washed, brushed, and standing by the bed like a cadet in a military academy when I got back. So she could at least make sense of what I was saying.

"Hungry?" I asked. She waited a fraction to see if I'd give her a hint about what I'd prefer her answer to be, and when I gave her no clue, she shrugged very slightly. Apart from that single "What?" when she woke in the truck, she hadn't said a word since we'd left New York. "I need to eat before I drive." She picked up her purse. She was connecting at least some of the dots. I drove us through a quiet, gray morning and, when I could find nothing else, to the violence of light and plastic and noise that is Denny's.

Our server's eyes were overbright, as though he were in the middle of a speed jag, but it could just have been the light. "What'll you have?"

I ordered pancakes and eggs and bacon, with coffee. Tammy refused to look up from the menu. I smiled blandly at the server, offering no help at all. He shifted from foot to foot.

"Regular breakfast is pretty good," he said finally. Tammy nodded. "With coffee?" She nodded again.

We ate in silence. When the bill came, I stood up. "I'm going to the bathroom. I'll see you outside." She made a panicked, abortive movement, but no sound. "Your wallet should be in your purse."

"She's not ready to do things for herself," Julia said from behind me as I washed my hands.

"I think she is." I pulled a paper towel from the dispenser, lifted my gaze to her reflection in the mirror, and the floor seemed to drop six inches: Julia's indigo eyes had darkened to chocolate brown, like Tammy's.

"Imagine if it were me out there," she said.

The bathroom door swang back and forth behind me as I walked rapidly back to the restaurant.

Tammy, pale-cheeked, was still at the table, but she had her credit card out, sitting on top of the bill.

"You—we should probably take that up front."

After a moment's hesitation, she picked up the bill and card and followed me to the cash register. She handed it over to the server without a word. He handed her a slip and a pen. She looked at me with those empty brown eyes.

"Sign," I said. She wrote slowly. "And add five dollars, for a tip." The faster she came back to the real world, the faster I'd be rid of her.

In the parking lot, I went to the driver's side, unlocked it, then climbed in the passenger seat. Tammy looked at me, looked back over her shoulder at Denny's, then up at the sky when a solitary raindrop hit her shoulder.

"Better get in before you get wet."

She got in. I handed her the keys.

"I've done too much driving lately, I'm tired. Wake me in a couple of hours." I curled up and closed my eyes. We sat there for nearly thirty minutes before she put the keys in and turned the ignition. I kept my eyes shut while the engine idled.

"I can't," she said at last. I waited some more. "I don't know where we're going."

"No," I agreed.

Another long, long wait.

"Where are we going?"

"North Carolina, near Asheville." I sat up and turned to face her. "Unless you'd rather go somewhere else. I'll travel with you wherever you want, get you settled somewhere."

"Not Atlanta," she said.

"All right."

"North Carolina?" I nodded. She nodded back and steered us carefully out of the parking lot, onto I-81 South. Her driving was bad at first, but improved rapidly. She stayed slightly under the speed limit. I was starting to go to sleep for real when she spoke again. "What's in North Carolina?"

"Woods, birds, a house. There's room enough for two, for a little while." Until Dornan can come and get you. She didn't say anything but the engine hit a higher note.

I didn't sleep but drifted in a theta-wave state for a while until she began to brake too hard and make abrupt lane changes.

"Take the next exit," I said. "I'll take over."

When she sat in the passenger seat it was obvious that returning to the world had taken its toll; her shoulders were hunched around her ears, and she picked endlessly at her thigh where the corduroy had worn thin. A person who is new in the world—a child, or an adult in a foreign country or just out of hospital—needs safety, first of all, but then they need to know that they matter, that their opinions are considered, that there are choices. The trick is not to offer too many options at once.

I turned on the radio and skimmed through channels: the blandly perfect smile of fusion jazz, a huge-voiced country music diva belting out about how her dawg done left her, an apoplectic talk show host ranting about tax reform, a commercial for wireless phone service that degenerated into the low-toned gabble of federally regulated footnotes. I kept trying, and eventually plumped for some college station that sounded as though it was broadcasting from the bottom of a disused well. "Not exactly to my taste. Feel free to change the station." The thigh-picking slowed, but we listened to well-bottom music until the weak signal started to fade. "Find something else, will you?"

She found something that called itself adult contemporary and sounded as though its artists, mostly women with little-girl voices, lived on Prozac. Still, it was a decision.

"Maybe we should stop at the next town and buy some CDs." I couldn't remember the last time I'd shopped for something unnecessary.

I drove for another hour. Tammy napped. When the adult contemporary signal faded, she sat up and changed the station without prompting. Mommy's little helper.

At Wytheville, just north of the North Carolina border, I left the interstate and took us onto the Blue Ridge Parkway: more than two hundred miles without a single traffic light or fast food franchise. With a speed limit of forty-five miles per hour—less on some of the hairpin bends—leaving the interstate meant adding at least two hours to our journey, but it was an essential buffer zone between where Tammy had been and where she was going. I turned off the radio and opened both windows.

"Breathe," I said. Valleys ran long and deep to either side, and cows grazed in pastures framed by split-log fences. The air was rich and cool and edged with life.

"It's cold."

"Put your sweatshirt on. We're two thousand feet up a mountain."

"You live up a mountain?"

"A valley halfway up a mountain, but we've a couple of hundred miles to go." Somehow, in four or five hours, I had to show her how much there was here to appreciate. She had to know before she got there how special this place was. It had to become special to her, too, otherwise she would trample all over the fragile peace of my refuge. She squirmed into her sweatshirt and we drove for a while in silence.

"These are the Blue Ridge Mountains."

She nodded, but didn't say anything.

"Part of the Appalachians, one of the oldest mountain ranges on earth. They're so old that they appeared before most animal and plant life existed."

"No fossils," she said after a moment.

"Right. Lots of gemstones, though." Smarter than she looks, Dornan had said. "Some of the rivers are even older than the mountains."

She didn't seem interested in the apparent paradox. Mountains form in geological time, in slow motion. A river that exists before the mountain forms will cut through the new, soft rock to get to the sea. Most of those seas were long gone, but the rivers remain. We passed a sign for Blowing Rock, the head of the New River. Stupid name for the oldest river on the continent.

"It's about time for lunch. We could stop and eat and take a look at the river."

She nodded, though I'm not sure whether it was the food or the river that appealed.

Blowing Rock is a small town with a lot of money whose inhabitants had managed to keep the ugly face of tourism from their doors. We ate fettucini in a café under a bright awning, surrounded by window boxes spilling flowers; sun warmed those wood and fieldstone houses not sheltered by maple and poplar.

Tammy spent more time watching relaxed, clean, happy people walk past the window than eating.

"Is this real?" she asked eventually.

I nodded, and for a moment I thought she would burst into tears, but she just shook her head.

When we got back in the car, she watched the scenery more intently, and once pointed to a speck hanging high over the canopy. "What's that?"

"Hawk," I said. "I can't tell what kind."

She was silent the rest of the drive, and I left her to her thoughts, because now we were driving through the beginnings of Pisgah, and the air began to smell like home.

An hour later we drove into Asheville and I parked in more or less the same place I'd parked when I got my hair cut, and when I climbed out of the truck into the slanting afternoon sun, I had the absurd urge to drop into the Heads Up Salon and see if Dree was there.

Tammy was trying to get out of the truck and pull off her sweatshirt at the same time. She managed both, then just stood there holding the sweatshirt in a bundle in front of her, as though it were something dirty.

"Is your house near here?"

"No. It's . . . some distance outside Asheville. We're here to pick up food, and clothes for you." She might be staying with me, but she wasn't going to wear my clothes. "Bring your money." She rooted around in her purse, then hesitated, still clutching the sweatshirt. "You won't need that. It'll stay warm for another hour or so."

Somewhere between the sidewalk and the first hanging garments, Tammy's body language changed; her brows arched disdainfully; she sighed and shook her head dramatically at the offerings, then fingered a slippery rayon dress.

"T-shirts and shorts and boots would be more appropriate for where we'll be; some jeans; a sweater for the cool nights."

She swung the hair back from her face and eyed me sullenly, now the perfect teenager. Infant to child to teen in one day. With any luck she'd be dead of old age before we reached the clearing.

"Your money, your choice." It would only be for a day or two, anyway. And if she bought all the wrong things she could either suffer or drive herself back here. Nursemaid was not part of the job description.

Tammy remained in teenage mode as we drove north and west along secondary roads which narrowed to gravel, and then took an abrupt turn left and hit the unpaved track up the mountain.

"Where are we going?"

"My cabin."

She sighed heavily and pulled her sweatshirt back on. After another ten minutes she rolled up the window.

I took the last half a mile in second gear. Judging by the mess alongside the road, hogs had been through recently, and tree debris indicated high winds sometime in the last couple of days. For some reason my heart was beating high as we pulled into the clearing.

It was all there, as I'd left it, cabin roof still on, tarps snug and tight across windows, trailer fast shut, but different. Forest litter from the wind or storm lay everywhere, and foliage that had been green had faded to yellow, what had already been yellowing was now gold, and the elder and dogwood and maple leaves had deepened to rich, winelike hues. I parked and just sat there for a moment, drinking in the smell, which was loamier, wilder.

"This is it?"

"Yes." Even I heard the smile in my voice.

"What happened?"

"A storm. The wind must have really ripped through here while I was gone. We can use the deadfall for firewood."

"No. I mean the house. It looks . . . scabby."

"I'm rebuilding it," I said shortly, and climbed out of the truck, but I looked at the cabin again, at the different colors of the old and new wood—that could, I supposed, look leprous to the uneducated eye—and the messy tarps, the gables. "It will look better when the windows are in and the new wood's had a chance to weather." But I wondered, which made me angry. "Did you pull the wings off flies, too, when you were little?"

Her face changed abruptly, the same look a child gets when she breaks a parent's favorite ornament and looks up, too frightened to even cry out that it was an accident.

"This place means a lot to me. If you don't have anything good to say about it, keep quiet."

"I'm sorry, I'm sorry, I—"

"You weren't to know. Let's get unpacked. We'll be sleeping in the trailer."

We unloaded the food, then her things. I showed her where to stow her clothes, handed her sheets, which she accepted wordlessly, and pointed out the sofa bed. I left her to it, and went to start up the systems. There was enough propane for a while, but after Dornan's visits and with Tammy here, I'd have to take the trailer out in a few days and pump out the gray and black water tanks. Refilling with fresh from the pump was no problem, but there was no point if the sewage tanks were full. That would be another new thing; I hadn't had to pump the tanks since I'd arrived here, shell-shocked and more than half mad, not wanting to shower or wash dishes or use the toilet, not wanting to have anything to do with civilization at all.

I went back into the trailer. "Tammy." She was sitting hunched on the couch that was the sofa bed, as though she had been given permission to use only that piece of furniture.

"Come sit at the table." She did, cautiously. "I'm going to show you how everything works. Most of it's simple, but if you have questions, ask. Tonight I'll cook dinner, but from tomorrow you'll take your turn."

She watched me as a crippled deer does a hunter.

"Do you understand?" She nodded. "Good. But first I'm going to take the phone outside and call Dornan." No reaction. "I won't tell him where you are now, but I will say I found you, that you're all right, but that you don't want to talk to him at the moment. Would that be a fair statement?"

She started to nod again, then said, "Yes."

"I will also tell him that either you or I will get in touch with him again within a week." With luck, she wouldn't be here that long.

Outside, late evening sun pooled on the canopy like syrup and the air felt slow and thick. Somewhere a wildcat would be crouching on a maple limb, waiting for a turkey to strut by; newly fallen leaves would rustle with the beetling of shrews and chipmunks; flycatchers would start swooping through the invisible insect towers hovering above the leaves, snipping up their dinner. It was just after six o'clock, a busy time at the coffeehouses. I called his home phone; this would be easier for everyone if I talked to his machine.

"It's Aud. I found her and have her somewhere I can keep an eye on her. She won't be running off anywhere anytime soon. She's fine but doesn't want to talk to anyone at the moment. We've agreed she'll call you in a week, if not before." I lowered the phone, not ringing off but not knowing what else to say. For months, Dornan had been having god knows what nightmares about Tammy maybe sitting in seven separate garbage bags in a ditch alongside some dirt road in Alabama, or getting married to a red-haired, pompous psychologist, or wandering New York in an amnesiac daze. And he had helped me. I lifted the phone again. "Dornan, she was glad to leave. I think she's been through a bad time, emotionally, but I think she's going to be just fine. I'll make sure she talks to you soon. And Dornan—she hasn't thrown away your ring."

I closed the phone up and resisted the urge to walk into the trees.

Inside, I set about showing Tammy the dos and don'ts of trailer living. I began with the stove and refrigerator, then took her outside to show her the propane hookups. I didn't want to get blown up in the middle of the night just because she wanted a cup of coffee and the pilot light was out. "The fridge operates on propane, too. Here's the shower. Gray water capacity is only sixty gallons, so you won't be using it often. You turn the hot water on here, like so, but again, you won't be using that much. The toilet is pretty self-explanatory and I'm expecting you to use it as little as possible." Black water capacity was only forty gallons, and there were plenty of trees to use as screens. "We'll get most of our freshwater from the pump, and there's a stream we can use while the weather is good." Ah, but how much longer would that be? "When you use the stream, use only the shampoo, soap, and toothpaste on this shelf. I don't want you killing the trout. Over here is the TV. Music. Again, use sparingly. We can prime the batteries anytime, but it's noisy, and I like my peace and quiet. Tomorrow I'll show you how to use the generator. Crockery down here, bigger utensils up here, tins in the pantry. Dry food and other staples in the hogpen. No open food to be stored in this trailer except in the fridge." Which was airtight. Telling her about the bears could wait for tomorrow. "Beer in here." I took two bottles from the fridge and opened them, but didn't hand her one. "Which reminds me. You have a decision to make: you can drink, or you can take sleeping pills. It's reasonably safe out here, but not if you mix and match your poisons."

She nodded. I sipped my beer with obvious appreciation but didn't hand hers over.

"You're saying I have to decide right now?"

"Right now."

"Jesus. You're not my mother."

My mother wouldn't have cared. "My land, my rules."

"I'll take the beer."

I took another sip from my bottle.

"Jesus!" She rooted around in her bag, handed me both bottles of pills.

I handed her the beer. "What do you want for dinner?"

I lay in bed and watched moonlight inch its way down the wall by my side. Tammy had been asleep for over an hour; the whole trailer hummed with her presence.

After giving me the pills, she had eaten her dinner quietly and cleaned up without being asked. Even after she was in bed I felt her cowering, quivering, afraid to make a noise in case I disapproved and did to her whatever had been done to her in New York.

When someone cowers, their body language says, essentially, Hit me. The permission is there, they are telling you they will not retaliate, and I could feel this terrible urge to throw aside my duvet, stride down past the galley, and drag her outside by her hair into the moonlight. Her shirt would ruck up around her waist, her eyes would be black in the silver light, she would look up into my face and see hard bone and shadow, wet strong teeth, and she would tell me everything. Then I could take her somewhere else, get rid of her, tell Dornan, I found her, here's what happened to her in New York, and I would finally be alone again, and safe and quiet. It was tempting, and I resented the temptation.

CHAPTER SIX

I surged upright, then realized it was morning, and that the noise that had woken me was Tammy leaving the trailer. I knelt on the bed and watched through the window as she took a pan to the pump and filled it, then studied the pile of firewood by the pit. She stood there for a while, then looked around. I'd put the hatchet away before leaving for New York. She went to the hogpen, hauled open the door, and disappeared inside. I imagined her studying the different axes. She reemerged with the hatchet.

"Promising beginning," Julia said, joining me at the window.

Tammy glanced around again, as though she thought someone was watching from the trees, then lifted a log onto the chopping stump. The swing needed improvement, but she got the hang of it after a while and soon had a small pile of kindling at her feet. She took off her sweatshirt.

"Interesting. Oh, don't look at me like that. I meant the fact that she has a clue how to build a fire."

"She hasn't built the fire yet," I pointed out.

"She has lost weight, though."

Tammy was about five foot six. When I first met her, I would have guessed her weight at a lush hundred and forty-five pounds. With her dark hair and eyes and golden skin she had been as sleek as a seal. Now some of the luster was gone, and about fifteen pounds of fat. On another woman it would have looked fine, but on Tammy it was all wrong. Her breasts no longer plumped out her T-shirt with soft weight; the seams of her jeans did not strain over hip and buttock as she knelt on the turf by the fire pit; the bones of her face, once softened with subcutaneous fat, stood out sharply.

She had her back to the trailer, face to the woods, but I could see enough of what she was doing to know that her first attempt to light the fire would be a failure. The kindling sputtered and went out. She looked around again. Perhaps it was some kind of tic. She pulled the pile apart, rebuilt it along much the same lines as the first, and tried again with the same result. This time she took everything apart and thought about it for a while, then carefully made a pyramid of twigs and dry grass surrounded by the seasoned kindling. It caught at the first try and she watched it with quiet pleasure. Too late she realized she should have brought more fuel, and the brave little blaze died to nothing.

Julia lay down and stretched luxuriantly in the pool of sunshine on the bed. "Are you going to let that poor girl struggle out there for hours to get a fire going?"

"Let her do her learning in private." Even as I watched, Tammy assembled what she would need: grass, twigs, seasoned kindling, green wood as fuel.

This time it worked. I watched long enough to see the fire blaze up merrily and Tammy carefully hang the water over the flames, then turned back to Julia. She was gone.

I dressed in boots, shorts, and tank. The soap and toothpaste and towels in the bathroom were undisturbed. I thought about that for a while, then brushed my teeth at the sink, used the toilet and flushed it, and went outside. The air was cool and still, and my boots left tracks in the dew.

"That looks like a good fire."

She scrambled to her feet. "I thought you might want some coffee when you woke. Or some cooked breakfast."

"Thank you." The fire wouldn't be much good for cooking until it had been burning long enough to produce coals, but there was no point in spoiling her triumph. "Don't make my coffee too strong."

We sat in the sun and sipped while the dew burned off and the fire snapped. She held her mug in her left hand and the right hung empty and relaxed from the wrist resting on her knee. It was the first time I had seen her neither tense nor posed.

"I've decided to take the trailer into town today and get the wastewater tanks drained and the freshwater filled. That way you'll have showers and other indoor plumbing conveniences for the few days that you're here." And I wouldn't have to live in a small space with the smell of an unwashed, unbrushed guest. I finished my coffee, which wasn't bad. "I shouldn't be longer than four or five hours. Don't play with any of the edged tools while I'm gone."

"You're going to leave me here?" Both hands were now wrapped around her mug so tightly that her fingertips were white.

"I had planned on that, yes."

"What will I do?"

"Whatever you want. Go for a walk. Take a nap."

"Where?"

I wasn't sure what she was getting at. "Well, right here. The grass is comfortable, and it'll be warm all day."

"But—out in the open, all exposed?"

She was genuinely frightened. I opened my mouth to tell her she could always lock herself in the hogpen if she was afraid of bears, but I doubted she had even considered that possibility. I shrugged. "Well, come with me if you'd rather, but don't expect to be an idle passenger. There'll be time for you to take a shower."

I banked the fire and cut more firewood but was still done before Tammy emerged, hair wet, smelling clean and young.

"Come help me get the rig ready for traveling. I don't want a single loose item by the time we leave. Start with your bed."

It always took longer than I thought. Everything that was on an open shelf or countertop had to be stowed and secured, a rubber band snapped around the roll of toilet paper, the water heater turned off, food in the fridge and cupboards cushioned against breakage, rugs rolled and furniture moved to pull in the living area and wardrobe slide-outs, awning stowed, and all the carefully reconnected propane appliances disconnected again.

I used a hitch with an adjustable quick-slide base, so it didn't take too long to hook up the truck, but then there was the rig's tire pressure check, a last check to make sure all doors, interior and exterior, were dogged and/or locked, and, finally, unchocking the rig's wheels. I threw the chocks onto the rear seat of the truck and Tammy got into the passenger seat. I looked around the clearing.

I had no memory of getting here, all those months ago, and it was a minor miracle I hadn't ended up in the natural ditch that ran along the northern edge of the track. I'd have to fill that ditch sometime soon. Meanwhile, I wasn't alone.

I leaned in to the open window. "How are you at guiding drivers?"

"I don't know," she said. "Why?"

"I need the truck and trailer to be lined up dead straight before I hit the top of the track, otherwise the trailer wheels might cut across and end up in the ditch. And I'd rather not flatten the well pump while I'm backing and filling."

"I could try, I guess."

She did an excellent job, and after ten minutes we were

creeping down the mountain. I kept an eye on the dash readouts; engine compression holdback was excellent, even on the steeper grade halfway down, and I began to relax. It's a forty-minute drive down Highway 25 to Naples. We kept our thoughts to ourselves.

The service station was empty except for two coverall-clad workers: a tall, soft-faced boy who could not have been more than eighteen, and a wizened, bowlegged man who came up to his shoulder and had probably been born before cars were invented.

I pulled in and leaned out of the window. "Hey there."

A nod and "Ma'am" from Bowlegs, just a blush and a bob of the head from the boy. In my peripheral vision Tammy began to rearrange herself subtly in her seat, sitting up straight, tilting her face so her dimples showed, pulling back her shoulders to push her breasts up tight against her shirt—and then her pupils irised down to points and her focus turned inward and something in her sagged. She slumped and pulled herself in and down.

"I need to empty her out, hose her down. If you'd point me in the right direction I'd be grateful."

"Empty her out, is it?" *Eee*-yut. He cocked his head at the RV bay. "Just had everything topped up Thursday." *Thur*-us-day. "Should suit. Need some help?"

Tammy slid a bit further down in her seat.

"Just about got it covered."

"You sing out now if you change your mind."

I parked, got out, and chocked the wheels, just in case. Then I showed Tammy how to hook the power cable up to the converter so the batteries could start charging. "There should be two pairs of rubber gloves in the undercarriage storage bay. Get them."

We drained with the red hose and rinsed with the green, opened and closed, connected and disconnected for a while, then washed the whole place down—including the truck and trailer—before rinsing and filling the freshwater tanks a final time. It was tedious, messy, and foul-smelling, but once all the hoses were stowed and all the valves, cocks, and caps firmly closed, I felt the usual satisfaction of an unpleasant job well done. I told her to check the tires while I squeegeed the windows. She finished first. When I'd dried the windscreen wipers and snapped them back in place, I walked slowly past the glistening tires. They looked fine and fat and all the dust caps were in place.

"You're dying to check, aren't you?" Julia said, sitting cross-legged on the roof of the truck.

I was.

"Don't do it."

"Aud?"

I hadn't heard Tammy approach.

"Aud?" A curious glance at the truck, then at me. "Are we done?"

"Yes. We'll fill up on gas and pay on the way out." I remembered her reaction to the men. "Or I can walk over and pay while you stay here."

She steeled herself. "On the way out works."

She sat stiff as a ramrod as I chatted to Bowlegs and he scratched his chin and wrote a few smudged figures on an invoice while his young assistant filled the gas tanks and money changed hands. She didn't say anything as I pulled out, or as we drove back up Highway 25.

"New York," I said, and her head made a slow, unwilling turn. "You don't have to talk to me about it if you don't want to, but if you do, I don't have to tell Dornan."

She said nothing for a while and I thought she was going to go back to that unnatural, unreachable place, but then she breathed in and out, fast, twice, the way you do before you dive through a doorway not knowing who or what is on the other side, and said, "It's not a pretty story."

"No."

"I mean, it doesn't make me look good."

We didn't say any more for five miles, but she began to fiddle with her window button, then her air vent, then the seam of her pants. She tucked her hair behind one ear, then the other, then pulled it forward again.

"I want to tell someone."

"Yes."

"It— I just can't."

"Okay."

"Stop being so fucking agreeable!" Her face worked as she tried not to cry, paling at the creases like a stretched and twisted pencil eraser.

"Tissues in the glove box," I said.

After she had finished, and had wiped her swollen face clean of mucus, she stared out of the window. "This is the road back to the cabin," she said suddenly.

"Just about there," I agreed.

"Maybe we should get everything set up and back in place, first."

"If you like."

We worked for two hours putting everything back together, and when that was done it was time for a late lunch. In the clearing, Tammy talked brightly of the food, of the road, of the rig, and her eyes shone like spinning coins. When she stopped talking, the clearing was silent but for the wind hissing in the treetops. A blood red maple leaf spiraled down from a branch and landed tip first in the grass.

"Aud?"

"Mmm?"

"What was it like, being here on your own, with everything so quiet?"

"Peaceful."

"You didn't get . . . nervous?"

"No."

"This morning, when I was making the fire, I felt jumpy, exposed."

Exposed. Second time she'd used that word. "But you don't feel that way now."

"No. Because you're here. And there's the trailer, somewhere I can go."

I looked at the massive tulip tree, the trillium growing at its base, at the maple leaf. This made no sense whatsoever to me. "But it doesn't worry you if I'm here?"

"No."

"If you were downtown on your own in"—I nearly said New York—"some big city, at this time in the afternoon, would that worry you?"

"Jesus, look, I know cities. I know how they work, what the rules are. This outdoors stuff, it's . . . It just doesn't feel safe."

Nothing was ever safe, not the way she meant it. But she had said *exposed,* and I knew that word. Exposed meant going back to live in Norway when you were ten years old, speaking English with more facility than Norwegian, and already being two inches taller than your classmates. Exposed meant conspicuous, different, not fitting in, not feeling at home, at least not until you learn that your self is your home and no one can take it away—until you fall in love and are led partway down a path that disappears as abruptly as your lover and leaves you stranded, lost in the mist.

Tammy's eyes were bright again, and her mouth twisted at one corner. "You have no idea what I'm talking about, do you?"

"Why don't you tell me."

After a pause she said, "I grew up in Connecticut."

Either she'd get to the point or she wouldn't.

"I grew up knowing the woods weren't a place I should go. No one ever said anything straight out, but the woods were where little girls got raped and trees got hacked down and Bambi got shot. You read about it in the papers." She shredded a blade of grass with great concentration. "It was like someone stuck big labels on everything: the woods, all the outdoors, was theirs, and if we went there, we'd end up like the deer or the trees. So, before, when you were still in bed and I was building the fire, it was like there were people in the woods watching, or animals, or whatever. They knew I was out here on my own. But it wasn't so bad because I knew I could run into the trailer. And you being out here, now, makes it safe. Or something. And the trailer's safe because I slept there."

Forest can be dangerous if you don't treat it with respect, but it's just trees and birds and bears and beetles. I tried to think of a way to explain that. "A forest is just like a city. It can be dangerous, but if you learn what to expect and how to deal with it, you're fine. Once you know how to read traffic signals and use a crosswalk, you're pretty safe crossing a road. It's the same with the woods."

"Right."

"You just have to get to know it, neighborhood by neighborhood, except you have streams instead of avenues. The places a stream runs through can feel like different worlds, the way, say, Park Avenue runs through both the Upper East Side and Harlem. I can show you one little neighborhood, if you like."

A week ago, this part of the river, where trees on each side of the bank touch and merge overhead to form a living tunnel, had been a green-and-black oil painting of dark water and moss-backed boulders. Now it was as though some vandal had hurled cheap emulsion at the canvas: the arterial red leaves of a low-lying maple branch streaked violently from one bank to another, and on the far side, little poplar leaves the exact color of twenty-four carat gold lay strewn over the boulders like pirate treasure. Autumn, like grief, changes everything.

The air smelled the same, though, rich and slow and secret.

"The best times of day to see wildlife are dusk and dawn." The sun would go down in half an hour or so. "Sit quietly, and keep still. Even blinking can be enough to scare a bird off. Watch the falling leaves—they all fall at the same speed. When something moves at a different speed, you'll notice. Use your peripheral vision." It was like adjusting to the rhythms of an urban beat: learn the patterns, tune them out, and the unusual is instantly apparent.

We sat still and quiet, and gradually the ever-present rush of water faded into the background and I could hear Tammy's breath. Ten yards south, a jumble of boulders and two fallen trees helped form a quiet backwater where the black, gleaming surface barely moved.

A bright *chur-wee* cut through the wood, and a little bird with powder blue wings flashed out then back into the trees. Tammy jumped.

"There'll be more. Wait."

Then it seemed the woods were full of bluebirds with their *chur-wee* and *tur-a-wee* and rusty-colored breasts. Two females flew at each other like kamikaze pilots playing chicken and Tammy smiled, but the battle was in earnest. Everywhere at this time of year, female bluebirds fought female, and males fought male, defending territory with the snuggest nesting hollows. When winter came, the winners would survive; the losers might not. The battle gradually retreated back into the trees and the calls faded.

Something plopped in the backwater. "Turtle," I murmured, though I hadn't seen it. Nothing else made quite the same sound, like a dinner plate falling flat into a full sink. The light began to change, thinning from rich afternoon mead to a more sophisticated predusk Chablis which slanted in through the trees and picked up the wings of insects dancing over the surface. Far fewer than there had been two weeks ago. Seasons are like economic change: cycles of plenty and dearth.

A flash of blue and white feathers and yellow feet caught

my eye for a split second, then a kingfisher was rising up out of the water with a silvery fish in its beak. It alighted upstream on the blood red maple branch over the water and looked this way and that before maneuvering the fish so that it could swallow it headfirst. Then it was off again, sturdy body and mohawk haircut disappearing as it followed its river road to wherever.

We sat for a while, until the light began to drain away in earnest. "Time to go." When you are visiting any strange place for the first time, short visits are best.

It was darker under the trees, and I walked behind Tammy so that she could see ahead instead of looking at my back, and so that she wouldn't have to worry about an unnameable something creeping up behind her in the glimmering dusk.

It rained on and off for two days. Tammy didn't seem inclined to talk and it was impossible to sit for hour after hour in the trailer with rain drumming on the roof, so I took her into the cabin and showed her how to use a drawknife and a saw. We started on the interior wall. Most of the studs were up; it just needed pine board hung, and pine is an easy wood to work with. That first morning Tammy, although she tried hard, was a real hindrance; she had no idea how to hold anything, how to steady a board on a sawhorse, how to plane smoothly with a drawing knife. I demonstrated, over and over. We were both glad to break for lunch. After lunch, I gave her the task of cutting the boards to size and nailing them to the studs.

"Don't worry about making mistakes," I said. "That's how you learn. If you saw something short, we put it aside and cut another. If you nail a board in the wrong place, we pull the nails and do it again. The worst thing you could do is mash your fingers flat with that hammer." Or slice open your femoral artery if the saw skids. A sudden image of me kneeling before her, arterial blood gouting over the unfinished floor while I ran my hands up her smooth thigh and into her crotch, seeking the pressure point, made me turn away abruptly.

I worked in my corner on a piece of walnut that would become part of the stair rail, and pretended not to watch as she tucked her hair behind her ears, took a deep breath, measured once, measured twice, then cut.

She went to bed at eight o'clock that night and slept like the dead for twelve hours. I didn't. The noises she made while she dreamt kept me awake. Her face was drawn when she woke.

"Okay?" I asked over coffee.

"My muscles ache."

I let it pass. "Ibuprofen's in the bathroom. And a hot shower will help."

The drip and runnel of rain ran counterpoint all day to the rasp of steel on wood. I worked steadily, but she kept stopping and staring off into the distance, then looking at her saw as though it had appeared in her hand as unexpectedly as a dinosaur bone.

The next day was beautiful, hotter than it had been for a while, and Tammy, whose sawhorse stood in the sunlight streaming through the door, sweated while she worked. Her scent—earthy and light, like the smell of crisp baby carrots when you first pull them from the ground—mixed with that of sawdust and leaf mold. She pulled a handkerchief from her pocket, wiped her face, and bent once again to the board she was recutting. Muscle flexed in her thigh as she steadied the wood against the sharp rip of the saw. The shorts were mine and fit snugly. I turned away and drank some water, then contemplated the walnut I'd been working.

Walnut is a hardwood that cuts and splits almost as easily as pine, but its real value is its beauty. The grain of the three pieces I had cut and polished for the handrail up to the loft could have been painted by a long-ago Chinese artist. Imagine porous paper stretched tight under a silkscreen, healthy dollops of gold and saffron ink, smaller ones of chestnut, tiny, tiny pinpricks of some color paler than the winter sun, the sudden back-and-forth of the wedge, and while the wavy lines bleed into each other, the artist dips his fine brush in umber ink and paints on careful rosettes which spread like the ripples in a pond. Then, while the ink still glistens, he sprays everything with lacquer and the surface is liquid-looking but hard, and complex as a natural fractal.

"You look like you've seen god," Tammy said from right beside me.

I smoothed the wood with my palm, then looked at her. She was grinning.

"I'm done," she said, and stepped aside so I could see the interior wall. It was finished, or one side of it was, at least. I stepped up to take a look, trying not to think about the hammer handle shoved down the front of her shorts. It was suddenly obvious that she wasn't wearing underwear.

"Looks good," I said. "Now help me with this stair rail."

Two hours later, still sweating, muscles aching pleasantly, we stood admiring the finished railing and one-sided wall.

"It's starting to look like a house," Tammy said.

"Long way to go."

"Jesus. Would it do any harm to pat yourself on the back, just kick back and drink a few beers?"

Julia had said the same sort of thing, more than once. "A few beers it is, then."

We built a fire in the pit while we drank our first, and opened a second while we waited for the coals to get hot. It was about six o'clock, and the sky glowed like stained glass.

"It'll cool fast tonight," I said. "I'm going to put on some warmer clothes."

In the trailer I changed into old corduroys and sweater, and tried to remember what clothes she had bought in Asheville. I took fresh beers outside.

"I laid some spare sweats on the bed, in case you needed them." She took the empties back in with her.

Icy beer, hot fire, fading sun and total quiet. Lovely. I lay on the turf and stretched. When Tammy reemerged I propped myself on one elbow and pointed to where I'd put her beer on the log, away from the heat. She took a swallow, then squatted down opposite me to examine the fire.

I shouldn't have lent her the sweats. She still wasn't wearing any underwear, and the cloth was old and thin and contour-hugging. I could see, clearly, the swell of her vulva, the bone of her hip, the curve where inner thigh becomes groin. When I looked up at her face, she was watching me watch her. She bent to poke the logs, then sat, and the moment passed.

"You did a good job today. You learn fast."

"Oh, I learn fast all right." It sounded bitter.

I didn't understand that. "Dornan helped me, too, when he was here. Though I think he hit more fingers than nails." She didn't smile. "You should call him."

She shook her head. "I can't. I just can't." Without looking at me she said, "Anyhow, I'd have thought you'd be happy to keep me away from him. You never liked me when we were together."

There was no point denying it.

"So why'd you come find me? How'd he get you to do that?"

Because we're friends. That's how it works. "He knew you were in trouble—he just didn't know what kind."

"Neither did I," she said. "Not at first." Now she looked at me. "You know what my job is, right?"

"Business development."

"And you probably think it's a nothing job that any zero brain can do as long as she's pretty and smiles and flirts." I don't like being told what I think, but this was her therapy session, not mine. "It was kind of true, at least it used to be. But then I went down to Florida, to that mall development in Naples, and met Geordie Karp.

"Geordie was . . . he was like a dream, you know? Famous, kind of, and good-looking and rich and great at his job. He's probably, I don't know, in his late forties, but he looked a lot younger. And he singled me out, and told me I had lots of talent, people talent. Then he offered to mentor me."

I nodded.

"It was like he'd looked inside me and seen exactly what I wanted; he understood. He saw me, the real me, not the southern party girl who was fun to have around at the business meetings so you sometimes threw her a bone."

A time-honored southern strategy.

"He was going to help me, give me the tools to be professional, he said. Then I could get what I wanted without having to flirt and smile. He'd been looking for someone like me, he said, someone worth his time. And I believed him. But it was more than that. Geordie was . . . Look, just don't judge me, okay? Geordie was gorgeous. Tall, maybe two inches taller than you, and fit, sort of whippy, with curly golden hair and a red-brown beard. Soft, not like most men's facial hair. And he knew all the best restaurants, and the people there always knew him, and he was generous, and funny, and well dressed."

"He dazzled you."

"Yes. And I thought I dazzled him, too, especially when the Naples project was done and he said did I want to go back to New York with him and help him in his new project. Did I tell you he's a psychologist?"

"No." Present tense at last. I was beginning to think she'd killed him.

"He's a clever son of a bitch. He knows how people work inside, really knows. That's how he got me." That bitterness again. "Geordie earns seven figures a year telling Nordstrom and Tiffany's and the Gap how wide to make the aisles, where to site their stores, what product should be where in relation to the door, so that consumers spend more. It's a science. He's got all these charts and graphs and programs—can quote numbers like a TV guy doing sports stats. The time per visit that the average American spends in a shopping mall is fifty-nine minutes, he says to his customers, down from sixty-six in 1996 and seventy-two in 1992. Then he tells them how he can make each minute worth more to them, how to maximize each square foot of retail space."

"And can he?"

"Oh yeah. Like I said, he's good. The best. I learned a lot from him: the downshift period, the decompression zone, the invariant right. Think about a street in New York, people walking fast to get someplace. When you walk fast, your peripheral vision narrows, so you don't pick up visual cues well, and it takes you a while to slow down if something catches your interest—depending on how fast you're going, you need up to twenty-five feet. So the best place to be is next to a store with a cool window display, because by the time the shopper begins to slow to shopping speed, he's outside your place, and the things in your window will really catch his eye, and he's more likely to come inside. So then he goes inside, but he's still in street mode for the first ten or fifteen steps, so it's useless putting anything near the door because he just won't see it. That space is where the potential shopper decompresses. Once he's begun to do that, he always—invariably, Geordie says—turns to the right. Why? Who cares, he just does. So that's where you put the stuff you want him to notice: twelve paces in and to the right. You do that and sales go up more than thirty percent. It's like a guarantee. And that's just getting them inside. Geordie told me that after one retailer talked to him and redesigned their stores, gross sales climbed sixty-one percent. Since then, his contracts always include a bonus clause."

"So you learned a lot. Was this in Naples?" Beneath the burning logs the coals were beginning to glow, and I was hungry.

"Some. We were there—I was there—six weeks; he'd been there a few weeks before me. Then we went to New York."

"And you stayed in his loft in SoHo."

She wrapped her arms around her and nodded. I waited. Her gaze stayed internal.

"How about another beer?"

She nodded again. I brought two back, put one on the grass beside her, and settled down again. "So, you moved to SoHo."

In what seemed like an irrelevant aside, she asked, "Did you know that half the grocery stores in the country have these tiny cameras inside their frozen food cases, or even inside cans of peas sitting on a high shelf? It's illegal to have video surveillance of changing rooms, but they're wired for audio. Half the mirrors in a department store have cameras behind them—and hundreds on the ceilings. Geordie's apartment was like that, except I didn't find out until later."

Cameras. I hadn't thought of that.

"Man, I loved that loft: so urban and cool. Those halogen lights, high ceiling, bare beams, antiques in the bedroom. An elevator right from the street! And Geordie took me with him to his first job on Fifth Avenue, told everyone I was his associate, even consulted me on where to set up our cameras—though even then I knew it was more his way of teaching me than real consultation. Jesus, the things I learned. Unbelievable. And it was all real."

"But other things weren't." I didn't like the idea that I might be on tape.

"No. Only Geordie kept my mind on other things so it was hard to tell. He flattered me, he treated me like a peer. He was kind. He . . . the sex was great, exciting—he was generous there, too. It was great, everything was perfect." She had begun to circle; we were coming to it. "He talked a lot. Sometimes it was hard to tell when he was joking. He talked about all his cameras and his charts and statistics and how he could train anyone to be his slave if he wanted. As long as they were young enough when he started. A woman my age was too old to train, he said, it would be easier to break me than train me. But he talked as well about training shoppers so they were like lemmings, and he'd laugh—I would, too—and it would be a joke, so I thought it was all a joke. Life was one huge joke, a big party, and I was the guest of honor, and I deserved it."

"But then something happened."

"Yes. He . . . the first time, it . . ." She took a swallow of beer, then a deep breath. "We were having sex. I was on top. He suddenly said, Stop, and his voice was all cold, so I stopped, and he pushed me off and got off the bed, and I thought maybe he was ill—was going to the bathroom or something—but then he suddenly grabbed me from behind, shoved me on my face, and got on top of me, and I could feel that he wanted me up my ass, so I said, No, stop, wait, let's get some lube, but he just . . . he didn't, he wouldn't, he just fucked me anyway, and it hurt, and I yelled, but he kept on and on until he came, and then he laughed and climbed off."

"Why didn't you hit him?"

"Hit him?" She looked as though she had no idea what I was talking about.

We stared at each other: the alien across the fire.

"Anyhow, I cried. And when he saw I was crying, he smiled, but then his face fell and he said, Sorry, sorry, oh god, sorry, I forgot, and the change was so quick I thought maybe I'd imagined it, especially when he started crying, too. He stroked my hair, he just kept saying sorry. Then he brought me some tissues, and he held me, and he said that his last girlfriend—he'd talked about her before, they'd been together about a year—had liked that, liked being fucked up the ass and taken by force, pretending to say no, and he'd just been confused. And then he ran me a bath, and washed me—he was sweet—and said sorry again, and made me cocoa. And the next day he took me out for a great dinner at Le Cirque, and gave me a diamond bracelet."

The clearing was silent but for the hiss and pop of the fire. "And the second time, what did he give you for that?"

"Stock. But that makes it sound so easy, so simple. It wasn't."

I waited, but she didn't seem to want to say any more. I drank some beer, savored its bite. "Did you know," I said, "that fizz isn't just the feeling of bubbles of carbon dioxide bursting on your tongue, it's mostly a chemical reaction detected by your taste buds?"

She took a sip. "It feels like bubbles."

We both silently contemplated the enzymatic breakdown of carbon dioxide to carbonic acid. After a while, I sighed. "Finish the story, Tammy. You may as well just get it all out."

After a long moment she bowed her head, and began again.

The second time, she said, was not until after she had finally come to believe that she had been wrong about that cruel smile, that it had just been a mistake, a slip akin to crying out an ex-lover's name just as your muscles begin to squeeze and shudder. Geordie was letting her analyze his data on the shopping traffic at the boutique he was consulting for, and was paying her well for it. Their sex was good, and everything else, especially for a southern girl who had spent most of her adult life in Atlanta. They went to MoMA, and off-Broadway plays, to a New York premiere of some film directed by a colleague's brother. She'd been out to lunch at one of the galleries, then bought a few things at Saks, then come back to the loft to find Geordie on the phone. She'd put her shopping down near the elevator door, tip-toed up behind him, and kissed him on the back of the neck. He turned and punched her in the stomach.

"He didn't hesitate, he didn't change expression, he didn't even check to see where I'd landed, just kept talking. Didn't miss a beat. I lay half on and half off the rug, thinking, Oh, I have a run in my hose, and trying to figure out why I couldn't get my breath, and he just kept talking. And when he put the phone down, he smiled and said, Hi honey, what are you doing down there? It was so . . . so confusing, and he seemed so concerned, that I couldn't put it together. His reality and mine."

When she'd got her breath back, she told him he'd hit her—but she was hesitant about it—and he said, Oh, I must have caught you in the stomach with my elbow—you should never sneak up on me that way, honey—I'm really sorry I hurt you. And a portfolio of biotech stock appeared in her name the next day. She was bewildered: was it possible he really believed he hadn't punched her? Had he? Was she mistaken?

He started to talk about her joining him in business partnership in a few months, about her bringing her things from Atlanta. Their sex became more adventurous; lots of fantasy role-play. Their schedule—all in the analysis stage, now, and done in the loft—was hectic, and sometimes they didn't sleep for thirty hours at a time, and even when they did sleep it was at odd times of the day; their meals were ordered in, and erratic.

"I didn't know, sometimes, what time of day or night it was, or even what day of the week. There's no windows in that place, except the bedroom, and he's got those covered in this slippery gray plastic stuff. The outside world started to feel weird. My watch had disappeared that first week, so I only ever knew what time it was when I asked Geordie, and sometimes what he told me didn't make any sense. What?"

"Nothing." I understood, now, what had been so odd about that loft: no clocks. Even the VCR and microwave displays read 88:88. And there had been no radio tuner on the music system, heavy drapes closed in the daytime bedroom, no phones. "Go on."

"It was surreal. He'd sometimes stop in the middle of talking about foot traffic patterns and shopper penetration zones and say . . . weird stuff, like 'Women are lesser beings,' and he sounded so, I don't know, so earnest and reasonable, that I just . . . I ended up agreeing with him."

That, she said, was when their sex play went from make-believe bondage to using silk scarves, which became rope, and then chains. One time he chained her up and teased her sexually for hours until she was crying out, screaming, begging him to give her an orgasm, and he just goaded her into saying more and more humiliating things, explicit things, until he finally let her come and come again. "And I liked it," she said, half defiant, half ashamed.

I kept my expression vaguely concerned.

"What I didn't know was that he had the whole thing on tape. He played it for me one day—it could have been morning, it could have been the middle of the night—when we were eating breakfast. Have you ever watched yourself having sex? It's . . ." She closed her eyes for a moment. Her head was almost wholly in shadow, black against the stained sky. Uncertain firelight, a softer orange, made the shadows dance and sway, so that her face looked hollowed and old. She opened her eyes. "You don't look like a person, you look like a thing, a wiggling white thing, dripping with sweat, drooling, face all swollen. The audio makes it worse. I looked at that video and hated myself. And Geordie smiled, and said something like, Imagine if your family and friends got their hands on this! And then he went back to eating his scrambled eggs and asked me to pour him some more tomato juice. And I did."

After that, things got worse. He acted as though they were still partners, equals. She didn't know up from down. He even began to seem sort of fatherly. "That's when he told me about the girl in Arkansas. He called her his wife-in-training."

She played with the cheap watch we'd bought in New Jersey, the one she never took off. My bottle was empty, hers barely touched. It would only delay her, and my dinner, if I asked if I could have it, so I lay down again on the grass and breathed its scent, green and vital and unspoilt. The fire burned cleanly now, bright in the gathering dusk, and the wind in the trees whispered back and forth. The whispering grew, and was suddenly shot through with myriad tweets and twitters. I sat up.

"Oh," Tammy said, as a thousand red-breasted grosbeaks settled like feathery locusts in the trees surrounding the clearing. The air shivered with their flutter and preen, and their calls sounded like the metallic squeaks of a thousand rusty water pump handles. After a while the noise died to an occasional squeak or flutter as they settled for the night.

"Where did they come from?"

"The north. They're migrating. Tomorrow they'll be on their way again, after they eat all the high-lipid berries and unwary insects in sight." Asset strippers. But she wasn't interested in the birds, just in avoiding talking. "So," I said.

She pretended to be busy watching the trees.

"You were talking about his wife-in-training. That's an odd phrase."

She muttered something.

"What?"

"I said, he meant it literally. Her name is Luz. She's nine years old."

I knew I didn't want to hear this.

"He bought her in Mexico City two years ago. She was seven. Her mother was a prostitute, and her brother and sister. Or maybe they were dead. Geordie said she'd still be on the street if he hadn't . . . if he hadn't rescued her. He said they flock like birds, the kids there. Gangs of them, running around wild on the streets. He adopted her but she's being fostered by someone else. That was the hardest part, he said, finding just the right family. He seemed so proud of it, the way people talk about the dream house they're having built. You know: they tell you when they first got the idea for something, what sparked it, even where they were; they go on and on about how they picked the architect and the builder, how they found the land and beat all the obstacles, the building permits, getting the utilities connected, what they did when they found out that what they'd figured was bedrock wasn't. Jesus, I hate people like that. Anyhow, he found a couple in the Bible Belt, an hour's drive from Little Rock, and he paid them a lot of money—a lot in their terms, he said—to school her at home in traditional values, to teach her to cook and sew and obey her future husband, to keep her away from the influence of TV and video and the web, even books. She had enough English now, he said, to read from the Bible. He pays the couple to keep their mouths shut. She's nine now. Very pretty, very sweet, he said; he's been to see her twice. Real healthy, and smart. When she gets to be fourteen—a well-trained, brainwashed fourteen—he'll take her to Georgia or someplace and marry her. And she'll belong to him totally. She's already trained to think he can do what he wants with her, he said. If she even squeaks, all he has to do is divorce her and she'll be kicked back to Mexico, still a teenager. No family, no money, no job, nothing. She'd probably be dead in a few years. And you know what? It's true, pretty much. He can do all that. It's legal. He liked telling me that part. He didn't apply for citizenship, and because she's a minor she wouldn't even really be a legal resident. If he divorced her at fifteen, she'd be shipped off and no one would care."

No one cared now.

I stared up and back at the trees behind me. Here was a smart, good-looking woman who had grown up in the last quarter of the twentieth century, yet she had been reduced to nothing more than a shell in just three months. She had allowed herself to be raped, and beaten, and humiliated. She had let him convince her she was crazy. Three months. And even after learning what this man was doing to a child, she had stayed. She had had a key, and money, and Dornan, who loved her, and she had stayed. I didn't understand at all.

"Why did you leave with me? What made things different? Karp still has that tape."

Tammy laughed, and it was one of the saddest sounds I had

ever heard. "You have no idea what you're like, do you? There I was, floating in this loft like . . . like a goddamn orange bobbing in space, tethered to nothing, no up, no down, no idea how I got there, no air to breathe, no way home, everything so unreal I wondered if I even existed, and you walked through the door. You're like concrete. Completely real. Even just standing there, before you said anything, you made everything else real: the walls, the floors, what he'd done to me."

Me, real. It was my turn to laugh, but it didn't sound sad, and now that I'd started I couldn't seem to stop.

You're frightening her, Julia observed.

"I know," I said. "Dornan was wrong. I think maybe I'll go mad after all."

Tammy sat back on her heels, and I suddenly saw her as she must have looked when she was thirteen, with new breasts, and the realization that she was never going to be allowed to do things boys did, never just be herself, and I was filled with a horrible, insidious tenderness. She was fighting hard. It wasn't her fault that she didn't have any of the tools.

"What do you mean about Dornan?" she said.

"What? Oh. He told me I wouldn't go mad with grief, that I'm too stubborn."

"Grief?"

I stared at her. How could she not know? "Julia," I said carefully.

She took the kind of short breath people do when they remember something they know they shouldn't have forgotten. But it had been back in May, and I had only been her fiancé's friend who didn't like her, and then I'd just disappeared, and so much had happened to her since then that it wasn't surprising. Except, of course, it was.

"Don't." I held up my hand. "Don't apologize."

She didn't. She just studied my face for a while, then rocked back on her heels and up onto her feet, and walked into the trailer. She came back with a fresh beer for me.

I felt tired and sick and didn't really want it.

Let the woman apologize. Take the beer, Julia said, and for the first time, I wished she would go away. I tried to call the wish back, but it was too late. She disappeared.

"Aud?"

I shook my head, and accepted the beer. I took one swallow and set it aside. "Dornan," I said. "What are you going to do about that?"

"I don't know."

"Well, think about it."

"Sure." Her eyes cut sideways, the way a street dealer's would if you rousted him on the street with a dime bag in his pocket.

"I mean think about it now. At some point you're going to have to face him, face yourself. At some point you'll have to leave here."

"Oh, right. I'll just leave, go back to Atlanta, and pick up where I left off. No problem. Only I can't. Not while that prick is out there with that tape. He could send it to anyone, anytime. He could already have sent it to Dornan. All he has to do is threaten to do that, to make me do anything he wants."

"Only if you let him. If you call Dornan, tell him everything, Karp has no power over you."

"Could you do that?" Her voice was intense. "Could you have picked up the phone and told your girlfriend, 'Sorry, honey, yes that's me screwing some guy, but why don't we pretend it didn't happen? Why don't you just never, ever let it cross your mind again?' "

I wanted to smash her lush, filthy mouth with my bottle.

She changed tack. "I have some money. I could give it to you, if you helped me, if you fixed him for me. Geordie."

It was an effort to speak politely. "I'm not in the revenge business." But I remembered what I had done after Julia's death.

"Please, Aud."

"No." If I hit her I wouldn't feel any better. I breathed as evenly as I could. "We could both do with some food."

This time we ate inside, and neither of us spoke.

I woke when Tammy slid naked into my bed. It felt good, her mouth at my throat, her hand on my breast then my stomach then my thigh, and my breath went ragged, the muscles in my belly tight, and I got hot and swollen and wet, before I realized what was happening and held her away from me.

"Please, Aud. I need this. Please, please. I need someone to hold, someone." And her waist was so warm and soft under my arm, her thigh so smooth, and it had been so long I wanted to let her.

She kissed my cheek. "I saw you looking at me tonight, the way your eyes followed me. Here." She took my right hand, put it on her breast, where the nipple puckered and tightened under my palm, and despite myself I groaned. "Yes, you want me, don't you?" and she rolled on top of me, belly against my vulva, face between my breasts, "Oh, yes, come on, come on," and it would have been the easiest thing in the world to just give in, push myself wet and slick against the warm rounded skin, I wanted to, but I heaved her off and raised myself up on one elbow. It took a moment of groping to find the light switch.

She lay on her back, hair tousled, cheeks touched with sharp red. Her eyes glittered. "Turn it off." Her voice quavered. "What's the matter? What did I do wrong?"

"Nothing."

"Is it because you don't like me? Not even enough to fuck? How hard would it be, Aud? A half hour of your life. Is it so much to ask? " Short, angry movements as she wiped her cheeks with her hands.

I wanted to turn to her, cradle her head against my shoulder, let her feel her tears dropping on another human being's skin, not a sheet, but I knew if my body came close enough to touch hers I might not be able to stop a second time. "It's not me you want."

"Everyone is always telling me what I want! Like my own opinion doesn't count!" She grabbed my hand, thrust it between her legs. "There, does that feel like I don't want you? Does it? Does it matter, does it really matter what else is real except that we could have sex here, just two people, giving each other back something good? But it does to you." She thrust my hand away. My fingers were wet and sticky. The small trailer was thick with the smell of sex. "Well, maybe you're right, maybe I wouldn't fuck you if you were the last person on earth, except that I want something. That's what you think, isn't it? Well, I do want something. I want you to get that man for me. Fix him. That's something you're good at, isn't it? Hurting people. It would be easy for you. Fix him. Oh god, Aud, please! Get the tape. Please."

"He won't use the tape now." I didn't know why my voice didn't shake, didn't know how I kept it so flat, why I didn't just kiss her and tear her apart. "Think about it. There's no point. It was to control you, but you've already left. He doesn't sound like the type to waste time on a lost cause. There's nothing to worry about."

"Nothing to worry about." Her voice was thick with anger. "You have no fucking idea, do you? Look at you. You've always done what you want, got what you want—you just reach out and take it. You have no fucking idea. You've never been paralyzed with fear, never had to wonder if you did the right thing, or wish you were different. Always so self-confident, so fucking controlled. You have no idea even what it's like to make a mistake."

I had made bigger mistakes than this woman even knew existed. To her a mistake was something that made you feel bad, something embarrassing on tape. My mistakes had led to that white room, to those machines, that dead husk. Tammy's mistakes were her own. Mine had dug a hole in two lives and annihilated a third. And here Tammy lay, so smug in her assumptions, still healthy, still breathing, still alive.

I put my hand on her throat. She went very still. It wasn't a small throat, it was smoothly muscled, young and strong, but I could rip out her trachea or crush her larynx in a second, or I could just squeeze. Some harsh noise began to irritate me, and I realized it was my breath, tearing in and out, and Tammy was terrified, and I lifted my hand. "Go away," I said. "Just go away."

She scuttled away to her own bed at the other end of the trailer and I turned off the light.

Rage and sex and grief bubbled like magma below my breastbone. I wanted to fuck, to kill, to hurl myself from a cliff. Julia was dead, she'd gone away and left me, naked and raw and uncertain in a world where people who called themselves my friend kept pulling off the scab and making me do things for them. Dornan had assumed I could just go find Tammy. Tammy assumed I could get on a plane to New York and fix her problems for her. Just like that, as though they were asking me to pass the salt at dinner. Thank you, they'd say, and think no more about it. And Julia hadn't even stayed behind to help me with this, she hadn't even tried. She had just gone away, given up, because it hurt. But I was still here, and now I was cursed to see that what I did in the world mattered.

No. Tammy's mistake, her mess to clean up.

But, Please, she had said, Get that man for me, and she couldn't do it for herself. But she had tried to manipulate me. She had slid her warm, smooth body on top of mine, belly between my legs, and her eyes had been wide, watching as the flush hit my cheeks, smiling as her pulse and mine ratcheted up and synchronized, as we came within a hairsbreadth of moving together in a dance that meant nothing to her, nothing. So close. But it had meant something to her. Her smell, the slipperiness between her legs, the way her nipples puckered and grew. Unmistakable. Her smell was on my fingers, mine on her belly.

She had wanted sex, maybe even needed it, and I'd said no. It would have cost me nothing to pretend, to give her, as she said, half an hour of my life.

I imagined how it might have been, to bend and kiss her, to feel the flutter of the pulse at her throat, to make her croon with her eyes closed, to lay myself slowly, ah, inch by inch along her length, mouth to mouth, lips like plums, breast to breast, belly to belly, thigh to thigh. Wet pubic hair would tangle together, and her breath would shudder, her eyes would flick open, stare into mine, blue, like still-wet-from-the-dye denim—

Tammy's eyes were brown. Brown. It was Julia's eyes that were blue, Julia whose lips were like plums. It was Julia's scent I imagined, Julia huffing down her nose, Julia's hands holding my cheeks, grinding me into her, pulling me down hard enough that her long fingers would leave bruises. But my palms tingled with the memory of Tammy's breast, Tammy's skin. Help me, she had said. They had both said.

I sat up. *Julia?* No response. *Should I do this?* There were always consequences. There always would be. Perhaps it was a bit late to think about that now. *Julia?* Nothing.

I put the light on again, made the seven strides to Tammy's bed. She lay on her side, back to me, very tense. "Tammy." She turned, slowly. "Tell me everything you know about Karp. What he looks like. His routines, his friends, his work. Everything."

"Are you going to kill him?"

"He's not worth killing. But I'll get the tape."

CHAPTER SEVEN

The red-breasted grosbeaks lifted from the clearing just after dawn. Three hours later, I lifted from Asheville regional airport, on my way to New York. I'd left Tammy with the truck, a brand-new cell phone, and a list of things she could attend to in the cabin and clearing, if she felt confident to do so. "I should be back tomorrow or the day after, but I'll call."

The flight was uneventful, and this time when I checked in at the Hilton I remembered to ask for a king-size bed. King beds are often put in corner rooms so that any noise the occupants might make is less likely to disturb other guests; the greater distance from the elevator means less foot traffic, and so more peace and less danger. They are also very handy to the emergency exits. This time, too, I remembered to bring underwear. Unpacking took longer.

At four in the afternoon, the hotel's corner coffee lounge was largely deserted—just me, the baby grand in the corner that looked as though it hadn't been played for months, and the solitary customer who sat with his back to huge windows onto Sixth and stared morosely at a legal pad covered in scribbled figures. I took a seat in the corner, facing out, where I could watch both the room and the three pigeons strutting in and out of the shadow on Fifty-third Street. In the sun their neck feathers shone green and purple, in the shade their tiny eyes glowed brilliant orange. Eventually a server in black trousers and white shirt came over to find out what I wanted. I ordered a latte. He ambled off.

Tammy had given me Karp's cell phone number. "He always answers it, if he's at home. If he's working, or with a client, he keeps it switched to voice mail."

"Always?"

"I was with him for nearly four months, I never saw an exception. He takes that phone with him to the bathroom, the bedroom, when he's emptying the garbage. He has four batteries: it's always on. It's the only phone he uses."

"What about when he's out, but not at work?"

She had frowned as she thought back. "I'm not sure. I don't remember it ringing when we were out eating dinner or at a movie or anything."

I took my own cell phone from my pocket and dialed his number. It went straight to voice mail. "This is Geordie Karp. Leave a message." He was working—but where, and for how long? A lot of the initial work on any project would be informal, she said. He would sit and watch for hours, not even taking notes, then he would talk to the client—again, usually informally; he liked cafés and food courts and bistros. It was only after that that he made detailed notes, and set up his cameras to record data. Then he analyzed the video data and drew up recommendations. He could be anywhere, at any stage in the process.

My latte arrived. It tasted like Starbucks; not a patch on Dornan's. Two of the three pigeons took flight and landed on the verdigrised metal sculpture at the corner, on Sixth. I had no idea what it was meant to be, but from the back it looked like an enormous green dildo. Perhaps the artist had been making some kind of statement about prostituting her art. I tried to estimate its size, ran through scale comparisons in my head: it would have to be wielded by a person about the same height as the Hilton. Assuming that person was having sex with someone of the same proportions, and that they were enjoying themselves and thrashed about a bit, they'd do more damage to Manhattan than Godzilla. For a while I had fun with film titles: *Attack of the Fifty-Foot Couple. Dyke! They Came from Bikini Atoll . . .* The body doubles would have a hard time of it, take after take rolling naked on tiny model buildings. Perhaps they would be paid time and a half, to make up for all the bruising.

It took me a while to realize Julia had not appeared to join in the fun. I tried not to think about it.

Karp liked to eat out, he liked to party, and when he had the choice he rose late and worked late. I could either check out his favorite haunts, one by one, or I could relax until tomorrow; he would be in or out of the loft at some point and I could track him from there.

I walked south under an early evening sky: violet and strawberry and peaches-and-cream, like some fanciful layer cake. I ate at a restaurant in the MetLife Building, where the haricot soup was better than mediocre, the service impeccable, and the highly polished marble floor slippery. One old man with frail skull and wrist but strong chin, too proud to use a cane although it was clear he needed one, nearly fell three times just getting to the bathroom. Perhaps the food was so expensive because of all the lawsuits.

It was still early, so I walked the fifteen blocks to the hotel. It was about nine when I got back, and the downstairs bar was filling up. I found a seat near the stone sphinx and snagged a harassed-looking server. I'd been drinking Syrah with dinner, but here they didn't have anything decent by the glass. I asked for brandy instead, and it arrived at the right temperature, and more swiftly than my afternoon latte.

When I brought the glass to my mouth, the fumes punched right into my hindbrain and the memories there: sitting in the restaurant in Oslo, stomach full of good food, sipping Armagnac while Julia leaned across the table and put her hand on my arm, her lovely hair swinging across her jaw, smoky sable in the low lighting. She wore the gorget I'd just given her, and her smile was lopsided, patient, because she knew I'd bought the gift because I loved her; it was just that I didn't know that yet, and she would have to wait a little longer for me to work it out.

I sipped, and the hot liquor eased the pain in the center of my chest, warmed the unfallen tears, made me long to bury my face in a woman's hair. In Julia's hair. I sipped again, and breathed more easily, and knew I wouldn't curl up and weep in the bar of the Hilton.

The bar was almost full, but the conventioneers—the Sixth Annual National Minority Business Conference—were easy to spot. They sat in tight groups of three or four, mostly men, mostly in black or charcoal suits with pin-striped shirts and silk ties. It was clear from the volume that most were meeting for the first time: as strangers, they didn't know who was the most important, so they had to seem comfortable, to take up space physically and verbally; they were defining their places in the hierarchy. Laughter and booming voices rose and fell in unpredictable patterns, accompanied by lots of backslapping and gaze-meeting. The occasional woman in these groups showed the same affinity for solid primary colors—sky blue, bright red—as women in politics used to.

A young Japanese woman stood as three sober-suited Japanese men approached her table. She bowed quickly, a test bow, to which they bowed in fast response, but a fraction more deeply, and now they had each other's mettle. She held a business card in both hands and bowed again deeply, committed, and they followed suit. Bow, bow deeper, straighten, bow more deeply still, back and forth. Inverse hierarchy: allow me the privilege of abasing myself more than your most illustrious self!

The conventioneers laughed loudly in their corner. I wondered how each group would manage in the other's culture.

The Japanese eventually sorted themselves out, and I judged by the body language that the woman was some lower-level employee pitching something to three superiors. She did not seem to be having much success. Somewhere in the back of the room, someone lit a joint. No one would call the police; the charge wouldn't be worth the negative publicity. An extra loud burst of raucous laughter rolled over the room from the front, followed by a higher-pitched but longer-lasting version from the back, where the joint was being smoked. It would just get worse. Time for bed.

I woke, slick with sweat, at four in the morning. "Julia?" She had never been gone so long. I sat up. "I'm sorry," I said, "I didn't mean it." But I had, I'd wanted her to shut up, just for a moment, and now it seemed she had shut up forever. "Julia?" I listened, but all I could hear were sirens in the street below, the hum of the fan, and the churning of blood through my veins.

Sitting at the table by the window with my tea and toast the next morning, I found it hard to believe that it was autumn. It seemed more like spring: puffy white clouds scudding by, sunshine, spits of rain. Even shackled by miles of road and pinned by monstrous glass and concrete towers, nature was exuberant. Karp, assuming he was tucked up in his windowless loft, would be missing it.

I finished my breakfast, wiped my mouth, and called him. He picked up after five rings. He sounded annoyed that the caller wouldn't respond, or maybe by the lack of Caller ID. I folded the phone. Time to hunt.

• • •

SoHo's huge, cast-iron-framed buildings were originally erected in the middle of the nineteenth century to house companies such as Tiffany's and Lord & Taylor; the lower floors were designed as display windows, perfect for the art galleries and boutiques and upscale stores of today. Across the narrow cobbled street from the building that housed Karp's loft were two cafés, a gallery, and a bar. Surveillance here would be easy and comfortable. Although Tammy had told me Karp never, ever left before eleven in the morning, I took a window seat in the first café at ten-thirty. The place was empty, and seemed likely to stay that way until lunchtime. I hung my jacket over the back of the chair, ordered mineral water, and opened the paperback I'd bought at the hotel—a best-seller, nothing too engrossing. If the elevator doors across the street opened, I wanted to be able to catch it with my peripheral vision. Good surveillance and good books don't mix.

It was eleven forty-five and I'd reached page 182 by the time the café began to fill up and the server started asking me every two minutes if I wanted to order anything else. She was new at her job, reluctant to push me, but an older woman at the counter kept punting her back in my direction. There was nothing on the menu that appealed, so I left her a twenty-dollar bill—about a four hundred percent tip—and walked over to the next café. They didn't have a table by the window, so I moved on to the gallery. Which was a mistake.

Like most galleries, most of the time, it was empty except for the owner in a tiny, glass-walled office that was really no more than a cubicle. He gave me about forty seconds on my own with the installation closest to the window—what looked like a rag doll impaled on a tripod with a nearby video projector beaming a moving face onto its cloth head—before he couldn't stand it any longer and came beetling over the Swedish finished maple floor, smile glued on, opening his hands and mouth, about to launch into some gushing praise of the art, and I felt reality shudder and stretch, and a stream of alternate worlds purled forth from this one, like soap bubbles when you blow through the filmy circle on the plastic wand. In one bubble world, Julia was still alive, and might be entering this gallery to talk to this man about buying the art on display for some corporate investment team. In another, she had never discovered corporate art investment and was running the place herself, and it was she who stood before me, looking me up and down, trying to judge whether I was good for the outrageous prices she was asking, tilting her head to listen, then tossing it back to swing her hair out of the way, smiling at something I said—because I would say something to make her smile, to see those indigo eyes glow and flicker like night-lights—checking my hand for a wedding ring. In yet another, we walked in together, trading a knowing look, having made a bet on how long the owner of *this* gallery would give us before rushing over. Then the owner spoke, and the words clapped like quick, vicious hands on every bubble until it was just a second-rate gallery in SoHo, empty of Julia.

I have no idea what that man said to me, or I to him, but eventually he went back to his box and I closed my eyes. Years, Dornan had said. Dear god.

Sometime later, the owner cleared his throat behind me and I realized I'd been standing, eyes closed, for a while. I walked onto the street. Rain spat cold on my face. I looked at my watch. Ten minutes. I fumbled out my phone, hit the redial button, and only had to listen to it ring three times before Karp snapped "Yes!" He must be waking up.

The second café now had a window table vacant. I tripped in the doorway, caught my elbow on the chair sitting down, and when I tried to make sense of the menu, found I was holding it upside down. Once I had it the right way up, I ordered a lamb and leek sandwich with mesclun in balsamic vinaigrette. I tried to breathe evenly, tried to remember to watch Karp's door, tried to remember why it was important.

But then my sandwich came, and the act of reaching out

and picking up the sturdy bread and thick meat, and lifting it to my mouth, all in logical sequence, helped the world make sense again.

I ate the sandwich methodically, followed by every leaf on the plate, then returned to the paperback. It took forty minutes to get through the next hundred pages, forty minutes of ridiculous plot culminating in two wet-behind-the-ears lawyers scooting on skis through snow-paralyzed city streets being shot at while their boss digs with her hands like a dog in the sand at some beach house location. By two o'clock I'd finished it and was leafing through the beginning again, marveling that any editor would countenance such stuff or that so many readers would buy it. Then again, I had.

The elevator doors opened.

Without taking my eyes off the elevator, I put the book and a twenty-dollar bill on the table, and stood.

"Hey, you forgot your book," my server said. I ignored her.

Tammy had described Karp as tall, about six-two, and the man walking north up West Broadway was six feet at most. But it was Karp. The hair was the same, reddish gold in boyish curls, as was his walk, eager and on his toes, almost bouncy, a walk much younger than his age, which Tammy had told me was late forties. The clothes were younger, too, sharply cut khakis, leather jacket, boots, shirt, saddle-stitched laptop case, the *Details* magazine look of a twenty-five-year-old making real money for the first time. I kept to the opposite side of the street, about thirty feet behind. We walked along at a brisk pace through streets full of that mix of tourist and resident which, along with the flowers and iron railings and small shops, reminded me of Knightsbridge.

Every now and again he stopped and looked in a shop window to check his reflection in the glass, but he never ran his hand through the curl that fell just so over his forehead, or tugged at the waistband of his trousers to look thinner. Odd. He walked for three blocks before turning right on Prince and buying coffee from an espresso stand. His manner with the stand owner was easy and confident. They both smiled. His smile switched off abruptly as soon as he was out of the owner's sight. Two empty cabs cruised by as he passed the mural at Prince and Greene. He walked on, sipping every now and again, avoiding pedestrians with relaxed, easy steps, frowning at a woman carrying two bags who bumped his laptop as she passed. The frown, too, was gone an instant later. Another empty cab going in his direction. He was walking all the way, then. I walked behind him, on the same side now, still thirty feet away, loose-muscled and relaxed, watching, assessing.

When he turned onto Broadway proper, which seethed with pedestrians, I shortened the distance to fifteen feet. His boots, brown nubuck, either were brand new or lavished with extraordinary care; his jacket was still uncreased; his hair bounced gently and shone whenever the sun poured out from behind the clouds. No rings on his hands, which were strong and well manicured and quite hairless. Half a block from a large store with a checked flag hanging outside, he stopped dead on the sidewalk and just stood there. There didn't seem to be anything to see except for the people and traffic. I stepped into the doorway of an antique shop until he nodded to himself, and walked on. I was still twenty-five feet behind him when he turned into the store with the flag. I followed him in.

Cheap striplights, huge floor space, a jumble of racks, plain-looking signs advertising jeans, army-navy clothes, and club gear: nothing like the upscale emporiums Tammy said he usually patronized or consulted for. At any other SoHo store I would have waited by the door, but there were several levels here, and probably more than one exit. I'd have to follow him. This was not easy; I couldn't stay in his blind spot, because I couldn't predict where his gaze might fall. One minute he'd be walking along slowly, looking at the floor, the next he'd stop and turn and watch the tourists goggling at vinyl fetish clubwear; then he'd go stand in a corner by the sports jackets and look up at the ceiling, at the pillars with their mirrors, at the mannequins in their cargo shorts and caps. After a while I decided he was calculating camera angles and placement, studying pedestrian traffic patterns, gauging penetration zones, and it became obvious that he didn't see people as people at all, that I could smile and wave at him every time he looked my way, and he wouldn't notice me. I would be just another data point, part of a flow pattern, a consumer unit. I stayed about twenty feet back and watched.

His face while he worked was empty, removed, like that of an Olympic springboard diver as he sets his toes on the edge, spreads his arms, and begins the bouncing jump. When he stood still, his body canted slightly to the left, with his head tilted to the right in compensation. He kept his hands clasped behind him, like male members of the British royal family, and I doubted—even if he had not had to carry his laptop—that he would ever put them in his pockets. Judging by his posture and musculature, he was not a physical person; there were no laugh or frown lines on his boyish face. A man who lived in his head, or in the heads of others.

Around me, shoppers moved in miniature flocks of four or five, doing a lot of looking and talking, in German and Japanese and Portuguese, but not much buying. No doubt Karp had been called in to remedy that.

He spent hours inside the store, watching, listening, absorbing. I followed him from floor to floor. At some point he decided he was done: his face tightened, then curved in a practiced smile which made his eyes twinkle, and he walked purposefully to the second floor, and across to the far wall, where he talked to a woman behind a counter. She obviously did not respond as quickly as he felt was his due, because he put his bag on the counter, leaned forward, and spoke forcefully, until she picked up the phone. Less than a minute later, a door marked PRIVATE opened, Karp shook hands with a young man wearing jeans and a hundred-dollar haircut, and they went through the door, shutting it behind them. The room was built against a sidewall; it was unlikely that it led to another exit. I settled myself behind a row of mesh T-shirts to wait.

When he emerged half an hour later, he was still smiling, still twinkling—at least until the door closed behind him, when his face smoothed. I followed him onto the street, with its rush-hour traffic of frowning pedestrians and honking cabs, where he stepped behind a lamppost, put his laptop between his feet, and pulled out a phone. I moved closer.

"—about, oh," he looked at his watch, "an hour? Two? Okay, eight o'clock. Yeah, yeah, or we can order in at my place if that's what— Sure. We can decide later." Not a business call.

He went back to his loft, walking briskly. This time I watched from the bar, drinking mineral water. He came out after only ten minutes, minus the laptop, wearing corduroy trousers and a sweater under his leather jacket. I followed him two blocks to Greene Street, and a restaurant and cocktail lounge paneled in dark wood, where he sat at the bar and nodded to one of the bartenders but didn't speak. I took a table against the wall right behind him where he wouldn't see me. A margarita appeared on the bar in front of him. He came in here a lot, then. It hadn't been on the American Express bill. He sipped, smiled appreciatively—the same curving, twinkling smile I'd seen him assume at the store—and said something to the bartender, who laughed. The other bartender, this one a man, came over and said something. They all laughed. Lots of exaggerated head tilting, smiling, hand movements: flirting body language.

I ordered a Heineken.

For the next hour and a half I watched him flirt indiscriminately with men and women, couples and groups and singles, flashing out that smile, hooking them in, dismissing them after a sentence or two when it became clear he could have them if he wanted. Geordie Karp did not add up.

The first eighteen months I worked for the Atlanta police force it was as an ordinary patrol officer. One of the most frequent calls my partner Frank and I'd get would be domestic violence. The abusers came in every size and shape and color, every background and political stripe, but the vast majority had this in common: somewhere inside, they were afraid. The bigger and louder and richer they were, the easier it was to overlook that fear, but in the habitual abuser—cases where a onetime psychosis or injury or other unusual circumstance was not to blame—it was always there. It might be fear of losing control, or of not being loved, of being ridiculed, or separated, or of being less somehow, but you could see it. Something in the way they held themselves, in the way they tried to fast-talk the officers who arrived, even, sometimes, in their misplaced pride.

Geordie Karp did not add up as an abuser. I could see no fear in him; I could see no genuine emotion at all. Everything, the smiles, the flirting, the frowns when he had been bumped into on the street, the peremptory attitude towards the woman behind the counter in the store, was fake: gone the second he no longer needed it. Learned behavior. I went through all the things Tammy had told me: the good sex, the confusing signals—treated as an equal one minute and raped the next—and his rapid, all-too-plausible explanations. There had been no putting Tammy on a pedestal, no overly fast discussion, when they first met, of them marrying or spending their lives together—none of the classic profile pointers of abuse. Tammy had been an experiment, an amusement, one of many, most probably.

The SoHo bar was overlaid with an image of a bar I had gone to many times with Frank. He would hitch his gun belt to a more comfortable position, order a draft and a bowl of pretzels, and expound upon the three kinds of crazy. "There's your basic loser, some guy whose wife maybe tells him his dick's too short so he goes on a toot and picks the wrong pansy to beat on. There's your psychos and sickos—oh, excuse me for breathing, your *sociopaths*—who are screwed up from crap in their childhoods. That looniness goes way deep, they're just fucked. And then there's your As-Ifs, what they call borderline personality disorders, and these guys aren't human. They look normal, but they don't feel a goddamn thing, don't know happy from sad from a hole in the ground. They walk around smiling and frowning and pretending to feel shit, and think everyone else out there is pretending too. No one's real to these guys, you know what I mean? I don't mind telling you, Torvingen, they scare the crap out of me."

Geordie Karp hurt people and manipulated them because they weren't real to him. He acted as if he were human, but he was a monster.

While I watched, he stood to greet a woman with long hair and long nails whose floor-length leather coat had what looked like solid silver buttons, to match her silver jewelry. It was plain, from the way their bodies asked before touching—a pause, a raised eyebrow, a you-first gesture—that they were almost strangers. What plans did he have for her? Would she let him? It didn't really matter. She was young and strong and capable of walking away if she didn't like it, as Tammy should have done. I was more interested in their plans for dinner. They ordered cocktails, then asked for menus. They examined the menus half-heartedly and I thought for a moment they might swallow their drinks and leave, go back to his loft, and get something delivered, but then the woman shrugged, and Karp nodded, and I heard them place their order: salad and entrée, and a bottle of merlot. They would be here at least another hour. I paid and left.

Elevator locks are a more difficult breed to replace than common dead bolts, and Karp had had no reason to bother once Tammy's key was returned to him. I slid the copied key into the lock and turned. It worked.

On the way up, I unclipped the panel covering the light in the ceiling and looked for a camera. Nothing. When the doors opened I stepped out and sent the elevator back down.

The loft was as I remembered—rich carpet, polished floors,

and stark brick support pillars all brilliantly lit, even with no one at home—only now wherever I looked I saw that unfeeling mind at work, controlling, manipulating, hiding.

I started in the most obvious place: the office. Karp's laptop was out of its leather bag and connected to the printer. I turned it on, but got a password screen. Passwords take time. I could come back to it. The bag held nothing but pens, a notepad, and two cell phone batteries. No interesting papers left in the photocopier. I turned to the stacks of videotapes labeled *Gateways Mall, Champaign, IL, cam. #22, 3/27/98* or *Courvoisier St., Mobile, AL, cam. #07, 8/19/00.* Ran a few at random. All what they purported to be. No surprise: the one I was after would be hidden somewhere more personal, like the bedroom. Nonetheless, I checked every drawer and cupboard before moving on.

Finding the camera was easy. It was behind the mirror on the wall at the foot of the bed, and hooked up to a sophisticated editing deck. Sophisticated for analog. I checked camera and deck: no tape. I moved on. Nothing in the drawers, or bedside cabinets, or closets. Nothing under the bed or between the mattresses. Nothing between the curtains and the blank, silvered windows. Eyes and souls and windows. Fifteen minutes gone. No tapes or camera in the linen cupboard or medicine cabinet or behind the toilet, nothing in the shower. I would have moved faster but it was not part of my plan for Karp to know anyone had been here. In the living room I peered behind books, lifted paintings from the wall, pulled aside rugs: no cutout boards, no hidden safes. The bronzes were too heavy to move; the mirrors were all one-way glass with nothing lurking beneath. On to the kitchen, where I found nothing in the freezer, or rice and flour bins, or even the garbage. Twenty-five minutes gone, and my heart was pumping easily and my breath coming smooth as cream. I stopped, and straightened, and stood by a support pillar in the center of the huge loft, thinking.

I slid the VCR from its shelf beneath the TV in the living room and traced the cables: no satellite, cable, antenna, or computer connections. I found the electrical box in the hallway by the elevator and flipped the breakers one by one. No circuits running power to any unexplained outlets. Unless he had a camera and recorder running on battery power, there were no more recording devices hooked up. Just the tape, then. Or tapes. It seemed unlikely that there would be only one.

According to Tammy, the loft was his private haven; no casual friends or business associates were ever invited over. So the tapes wouldn't have to be secure, merely concealed. He probably used them in the same way he used his tapes of shoppers: to study, over and over, and learn from. They would be readily accessible. The hiding place would be obvious, if you knew what to look for.

I closed my eyes and pictured the floor plan, placing the furniture, the lights, the rugs and art, then examined the picture slowly and methodically from every angle. Nothing unusual. I imagined the loft as a whole, its proportions, the roof with its exposed iron girders, its brick-clothed support pillars—and smiled. I laid my hands on the pillar in front of me. Why would he have covered a cast-iron support in brick when he'd left the girders exposed?

I got a ladle from the kitchen and began banging the pillars one by one, and found the hollow one on my third try. I popped open the false front.

There were five shelves. Only the bottom three were filled: a small, matte-black box, a slim sheaf of papers in a file folder, and two rows of tapes. Like his work tapes, these were neatly labeled: *Anthony, April, Cody, Fiona* . . . Alphabetical order. No *Strange Woman Who Took Tammy Away,* no *Unidentified Blond Intruder.* I found *Tammy* and took it to the office, where I turned on the video unit, put the tape in, and hesitated.

Have you ever seen yourself having sex? You don't look human. You are a thing . . . But I wouldn't put it past Karp to have one last joke on anyone who found these tapes, and I had to be sure. I pressed PLAY.

If I hadn't known what to expect, it would have taken me a moment to work out what I was seeing because the body, naked and bound and writhing, and observed close-up, does not move in familiar ways. He must have had remote control on the camera, because the focus zoomed in and out; one minute it was a close-up of a belly and right thigh, slippery with sweat and other things, looking white and enormous and inhuman, the next she was hanging there, about eight feet away. I fast-forwarded until the hanging, writhing figure moved its head and I saw its face. It was Tammy.

My hand shook slightly when I pulled the tape out and put it in my jacket pocket. No one but a lover should ever see such an expression, and then only fleetingly, yet here it was, captured forever.

I went back into the living room. Twenty-two tapes. I carried them eleven at a time into the kitchen. Only six would fit in the microwave at once. I tried the first batch on thirty seconds, picked one at random, *Jean*—who were you? what dreams of yours did he destroy?—and trotted it through to the office, where I played it. Nothing but a snowstorm. Perfect. Back in the kitchen I did the same for the other three batches, then carried them all to the living room and put them back on the shelves in the right order.

Forty-five minutes gone.

The box was made of steel, and locked. I tilted it gently and recognized the sliding thump. A handgun. I put it back. Then I took out the papers.

A seven-year-old girl with soft, toffee brown eyes and sharp baby teeth beamed at me from the head-and-shoulders photo. Her hair, cut just longer than her ears, was the color of rich, fertile mud, the kind you can't help plunging your hands in. I turned it over. The next sheet was typed. It had a bar code label at top right, a miniature black-and-white version of the bigger color photo on the left, and a large, florid signature at the bottom. It was written in Spanish, a medical report of a seven-year-old girl, one Luz Bexar, healthy and reasonably nourished, good teeth, good eyes, virgo intacta, no intestinal parasites, small scar above right elbow, vaccinations given on the following dates. Behind that, with the same bar code at the top right, was an adoption certificate, again in Spanish, with two signatures: the rounded, laborious letters of someone who doesn't write very often, and George G. Karp, of New York, New York. There was a catalogue of foster families in various parts of the country, followed by a receipt acknowledging Karp's payment and confirming his choice of the Carpenter residence in the town of Plaume City, Arkansas. After that there were progress reports dated at six-monthly intervals. I learned that she now spoke English fluently, had an excellent memory for rote learning as evidenced by progress with the Bible, was nimble—enclosed one embroidery sample—modest, demure, and clean. A medical update was stapled to the latest report: she was now well nourished, and still virgo intacta. The picture on the Mexican passport was the same one on the medical report; the visitor's visa to the United States had long since expired. There were two more pictures, one taken a year ago, one about three months ago. In the first, her hair had grown and lay about her shoulders in a wild swirl, her baby teeth were gone, and the light in her eyes did not fit with "demure" or "modest." My hand was now shaking so much that I had to lay the second photo on the floor: her hair was neat and her eyes wary. I didn't read the rest.

What I'd told Tammy was true. I was not in the revenge business; I was not the universal protector of the weak. I was only here to get the tape.

Fifty minutes gone. I put everything back in the folder, put the folder back on the shelf, closed the false front, turned away, then turned back and opened it again. What Geordie did to adults who knew the ways of the world was one thing, but this was another.

While I fed Luz's documents into Karp's photocopier one sheet at a time, a process made slow and clumsy by my gloves, I listened for the elevator. Six months ago I wouldn't have worried: if Karp had returned before I was done, it would have been a simple matter to disable him—a palm strike to the forehead would knock him unconscious for thirty seconds and leave very little in the way of a bruise—and depart before the police arrived. There would be no fingerprints through which I could be traced, and my description would mean nothing to New York police. The upright and outraged citizen—who might be famous in his own field but almost certainly was unknown outside it—wouldn't even have a bruise to point to, no sign of forced entry, and nothing disturbed; they would write him off as a kook. Until six months ago, everything had always gone the way I wanted it to; anything that hadn't, I had fixed, or walked away from with a shrug, and if anyone had had a few bones broken as a result, what of it?

Violence is usually a tool, like any other, but occasionally it is much more. Occasionally it takes me to a place where time and light seem to stretch, and the air is tinged with blue. In that blue place the test of bone and muscle becomes a pavane where everyone but me is locked into preordained steps while I dance lightly, mind clean as a razor: faster, denser, more alive. There I exist wholly as myself, wholly outside the rules, and the world is stripped to its essence: clean and clear and simple.

But I don't go to the blue place now. I avoid every temptation. Last time I had forgotten I had a gun: the mistake that got Julia killed.

I wanted to be out before Karp came back. I put the warm photocopies in my inside pocket with the tape, and the original papers back on the shelves. The false front clicked shut, and everything was as it had been. I took the ladle back to the kitchen and opened the drawer from which I'd taken it—and was almost overwhelmed by the urge to smash every glass and plate I could find. I shook with it. I wanted to tear the doors from the cupboards and break them over my knee, wanted to feel the heft of that cleaver and swing it hugely at the antique dresser in the bedroom, wanted to punch my fist through the screen of his monitor, to throw the copier against the fake brick support columns until the place was reduced to shards and splinters, and torn fabric glittering with scattered glass.

I used the elevator key, flattened myself against the wall to one side, and waited, the plaster cool and hard at the back of my head. The elevator rose slowly, stopped. I stepped away from the wall: empty.

I got in. Breathed. My hands uncurled. The cage lurched slightly as it descended, and the muscles wrapped around my femur and spine flexed. I breathed, in and out, and gradually my muscles relaxed. Everything had gone well, I told myself. There would be time to pack, get to the airport, and have a drink while I waited for the last plane to North Carolina. Everything had gone well. My blood pulsed evenly, and every joint felt oiled and smooth.

When the elevator opened, the only people on the street were two men entering the café where I'd eaten earlier: one of those strange city moments where, for an instant, it seems as though humanity has been swept from the earth. I stood for a moment, to adjust to the dark and the now-definite autumn chill, then turned to walk north up West Broadway, and had taken perhaps ten steps when behind me I heard the laughter of a woman and the answering "Yes, on this block" of a man as they came around the corner from Broome Street. I shouldn't have turned, but, oh, I did, and the streetlight caught on the reddish gold of Karp's hair as he leaned in towards the woman, and the light slid across her hair, too, as she tossed her head and the soft brown wing of it swang past her cheek, just as Julia's had, and I saw the way he looked at her, and wondered if, in some alternate world, I would stand by and do nothing while another Julia talked and laughed and trusted this man—wondering if maybe she loved him and whether he would take care of her—while silently he calculated and jeered and rubbed his hands as she let down her guard, little by little. And then my muscles moved and I was upon them, and "Run!" I spat between bared teeth to the woman, and she did, and I turned to Karp.

This is not the blue place. It is a rough roar in my ears, the need to damage this man heaving like volcanic mud in my belly, swelling through my veins until I shake all over—the long, rolling shudders of the ground before it splits open. I hit him across the throat, and with a small cough he can no longer breathe. I pull him into the elevator and throw him against the metai wall, and he starts slipping to the floor only half conscious but I hold him up with one hand while the doors close. If I had a good knife I would hang him up by the ankles and gralloch him, slit him from throat to pubis and watch his guts fall out in a soft heap. I would wipe my left cheek then my right with the flat of the bloody knife, and begin. I don't have a knife. I have my hands; they are very strong.

I growl as I hurt him; the noise spills from me as harsh and hot as gravel shoveled from a furnace. By contrast, the noise bone and flesh makes is mundane, dull and sullen as an uncooked roast thrown on the chopping board. Even when teeth break, their sharp snap is muted by the gush of blood—the same blood splashed on my face and coating my own teeth. A human arm coming free of its socket makes a deep creak, more like a wooden trestle under the weight of a train than a chicken wing being twisted off.

It is a few minutes after the doors open in the loft that I drag him out onto the polished floor. He slides easily in his own blood. I am covered in blood, and slick with spittle. He mews a little, then is quiet. I try to think but my brain is still thick and hot and swollen. I rub my forehead, then see my bloody footprints.

I take my shoes off and step onto a rug. That's better, but I'm not sure why. I stare at the red tracks. Tracks. Hunters.

I strip naked, except for my gloves. I drop my clothes on the bare floor by the body and walk to the bathroom. The shower fitments are sleek and modern, the water pressure strong. I wash carefully, thoroughly; the leather gloves feel odd on my skin; even after I'm clean I keep the water running a long time. I pick a couple of stray hairs from the plughole, get out without turning the water off. In the kitchen I find scissors and plastic grocery bags; I cut the labels off my clothes and put the clothes in the bags and the labels in a little heap on the floor. I have to take my jacket out again to get the tape and photocopies. Photocopies. It takes a moment to open the false front and find the original file, which I put by the cutoff labels, next to the tape and the copies. I line them all up carefully, edge to edge, then find there is a red glove print on the folder. It puzzles me: I can't make it line up with the tape or the photocopies. I put the photocopies inside the folder and the tape on top. Better. The scissors go back in the kitchen, and I bring back sponges and a towel. I wipe away my footprints, and dry the floor. I go back to the kitchen for a mop and bucket. The walls of the elevator glisten, and the air is thick with the sweet coppery stench of the abattoir: blood, marrow, intestines. I begin to clean it up, then vomit, then have to clean that up, too. I rinse the mop and sponges in the shower, leave it running while I take the mop and sponges back to the kitchen.

I don't want to stand naked in Karp's bedroom. I have seen the pictures of the women and men who have done so. There is no choice.

His clothes fit me surprisingly well, but his shoes are a little big. I add another pair of socks and tie the shoelaces tightly.

My gloves are shrinking and uncomfortable. I take a look around the loft—if only I hadn't taken the time to do this before, I would already have—

No. I didn't have time for that.

I put the bagged clothes in two more bags, stepped over the bloody thing in the hallway into the elevator, and turned the key. My heart thumped lumpily and I couldn't breathe quite right. The woman. She had seen me. But she had run, and she hadn't known where Karp lived: "Yes, on this block," he'd said, as they turned the corner. If I could take a cab without being seen, I would be safe.

The elevator doors opened and every muscle in my body clamped down hard on the nearest bone: the street heaved with people. A man lay dead or dying twenty feet above my head, and here I was, displayed like a vase in a museum. I couldn't move. A group of twenty-somethings walked past. One turned to look. His face stretched in shock.

Blood smeared on the elevator wall? Teeth on the floor? If I'd missed something on my cleanup, there was nothing I could do about it now. I jerked one leg forward, then the other, and walked right at him, and his little group burst apart like a school of minnows, and I was through. Three feet past, six.

"Hey!" Twelve feet. "You!" Thirty feet. More shouts. The cutoff whoop of a police siren stopping just as it was about to start; a car braking. Fifty feet. Never run from a scene, never. It's the first thing they look for. Walk. Eat the ground with your stride, but walk.

"Here!" A woman's voice. "Over here!" But I didn't stop, didn't look back. I moved past people as though they weren't there, not thinking or planning, just moving. Between one stride and the next, everything changed: unrelated pedestrians suddenly focused, sharpened, tightened into a crowd. Heads turned and mouths opened, and a hundred hands lifted to point. My mind did a terrifying thing: it shut down. I bolted.

Lights. People. Air harsh, like sand in my lungs. Fingers curled around plastic bag handles. Pavement hard hard hard under my feet. More lights. Darker alley. Fewer people. Breath tearing in and out, in and out. Another street. More people. Yellow. Open, in, red upholstery.

"Where to?"

A cab. I was in a cab. "Drive."

"That's what I do. But where to, lady?"

I couldn't think. "That way." I pointed at random. He drove. The bags were heavy in my hand. Wet and heavy. "Let me out."

I gave him a ten and climbed out, walked. Kept walking, mindlessly. Passed a street sign. King Street. I stopped at a traffic light. A cab stopped at the same time. I looked inside. The driver raised his eyebrows. I nodded, or my head jerked, and I climbed in. "East," I said, then, "That way."

"Not good that way," he said. "Trouble. Police trouble."

I was remembering the voice, earlier, shouting "Here! Over here!" A woman's voice. The woman who had been with Geordie? But she'd said "Here," not "There." Then the sound of a police car, the cutoff whoop—not a chasing-the-perp whoop, more a clear-the-crowd-from-the-scene whoop, one I'd heard a hundred times. She had called them, then. It would take a few minutes for them to understand what was going on, to put it all together with whatever that crowd had seen in the elevator. Had she described me? Had that group outside the elevator?

A street sign said West Houston. I knew where I was. "Go north. Tompkins Square Park."

I could do this. Dump the clothes at the park, take another cab to the hotel. Change. Catch the plane. Yes. I could do this.

T W O

pupa (from *pūpa,* L. for girl, or doll)

1. an insect in the third stage of homometabolous metamorphosis

... the development from pupa to imago often involves considerable destruction of larval tissue ...

p
u
p
a

CHAPTER EIGHT

It was four in the morning when I pulled into the clearing, set the hand brake, and climbed out of the rented Neon. Strange, to stand on grass again. In the starlight, the Neon's paintwork glistened, like mercury. The cold autumn air smelled different; it belonged to the world of someone I no longer knew.

A light flicked on in the trailer—yellow light, only a low-watt lamp, but I turned away. I couldn't see the trees, but I could hear them: papery and tired in the softly stirring air.

After a minute brighter light spilled from the doorway, casting my shadow ten feet long into the dark.

"Aud?" I kept my back to her. "Aud?" Closer now. "Did you get it?"

I turned, and Tammy, in half-buttoned shirt, jeans, and no shoes, stopped dead. "You're wearing his pants."

It took a great effort to speak. "Did you ever mention me—my name, what I looked like, anything—to him?"

She shook her head.

"You're sure?"

"I'm sure." She folded her arms against the cold. "Why are you wearing his clothes?"

I didn't have the strength to speak.

"Did you get the tape?"

I reached into the car, to the tape on the top of the folder of original and photocopied documents, and tossed it to her. She unfolded her arms at the last moment to catch it, looked at the label, at me.

"Did you . . . ?"

"It's the right tape."

She cradled it in her folded arms, holding it, protecting herself from it at the same time. She took another step towards me, peering at my sweater. "That's not his. He never wore black. And it's all wet, what—" She jerked back. "It stinks."

I said nothing.

"It's cold out here. Aud? Are you coming inside?"

I shook my head.

Lying naked and cold beneath the perfect, whispering dark, I imagined I could feel the curve of the earth under my back, that I circled the whole planet, so that my soles touched the top of my head and I blended with the dirt.

Dirt. Skin of the world, amalgam of eroded mineral and all things animal and vegetable, from tiny aphid to redwood giant. A burial ground or refuge; home for animal and insect, seed and spore. A place to rest, to hide, to grow secretly in the dark. A floor on which to stand. Alive and dead at the same time, fecund and rotten. Worm excrement. When dirt is disturbed, it becomes unpredictable: perhaps when turned and tilled it grows fertile and lush; perhaps erosion sets in and the whole turns to sand. Some soil is never meant to be turned; it's best left frozen and hard-packed. Sometimes it can be hard to tell until you try.

The blood and tears on my cheeks and chest and shoulders had tightened as they dried, my skin grown thick with cold. My throat hurt. There was no difference in light levels when I opened and closed my eyes. Perhaps I was already dead. Perhaps

I had never really been alive, and if I lay here without moving, my bones would fall into dust and be blown away with a hiss by the wind. Perhaps that had been true, once, before I met Julia, with her soft skin and bright eyes, her warm hands that reached right through my layers of permafrost. And now I had torn and beaten a man to the brink of death when I had been in no danger, when there had been no need. Every other time, even after she died, I had had no choice: it had been strike or die. Every other time I had come back to myself feeling washed in brilliance and huge with life, like a god, untouchable. Now I felt soiled and outcast, like oxygen once floating free above the atmosphere and now trapped in the ocean and bound in dirt; like the peptides that had skimmed through space only to fall to earth and be harnessed to carbon dioxide and form life; like Lucifer—

"A little grandiose, even for you."

I sat up and smacked my face into an unseen branch. "Julia?"

"Who else. Is that more tears, or are you bleeding again?"

The stuff running down my cheek was too warm and thick to be tears. I scrubbed it away impatiently and looked around, but it was so dark I could see nothing, not even the branch. "Where have you been?"

She ignored that. "Where are your clothes?" Judging from her voice, she was sitting on the ground by my knees.

I touched my throat. "I don't remember."

"Naked in the woods, at night, in late October. Do you remember how to get back?"

I didn't say anything.

"Oh, Aud." She sounded sad. "Don't do this to yourself. Karp was a monster. You said so yourself."

"He didn't deserve to die."

"Does anybody? Besides, you don't know for sure that he is dead. And even if he is, he wouldn't be the first."

"This is different."

"How?"

I didn't answer.

"Let me ask you something else, then. Think about Geordie Karp for a moment: smart, well-connected, cold, and manipulative. Forget the borderline thing for a moment. Who did he remind you of? And Aud"—she moved closer, until her voice was a caress—"please, get yourself back to the trailer and get warm." And she was gone.

Forget the borderline thing? I didn't understand. I did understand the last part: get yourself back to the trailer and get warm. And she'd said please. I sighed.

I tried to get to my hands and knees but my left knee wouldn't work. I felt it; there was no obvious cut. Bruised, maybe. Hard to tell because my hands were so cold. What time was it? I couldn't remember how long I'd been here, which direction I'd come from. No point trying to find the clothes now. No point trying to walk back to the clearing in total darkness. More blood ran down my chin and smeared stickily under my hand. I felt about me, patting. Not enough leaves. I rolled onto my belly, pulled myself forward a yard or so, and waved my hands to and fro, feeling for the branch. In woods this thick, a branch should not be so low to the ground.

Who did he remind you of?

I dragged myself another yard. There. Thick and sturdy, and growing upwards, from a point somewhere ahead of me. A fallen tree, with a small drift of dry leaves. I rolled onto my side, swept the leaves up around me. They'd keep me warm enough until dawn.

Who did he remind you of?

My knee began to ache. I must have twisted it somehow, earlier. I couldn't remember. Too stubborn to go mad, Dornan had said. It wouldn't be the first time he'd been wrong. My feet hurt, too, but I didn't want to reach through the leaves to feel them and disturb the warming air pockets.

Then there was nothing to do but wait for dawn, nothing to do but sit still before Julia's question.

It took two hours to cover what should have taken fifteen minutes, and well after the sun had risen I limped into the clearing, leaning heavily on a broken branch, sick, tired, and empty. I hobbled to the fire pit and lowered myself slowly onto the log. There was no sign of Tammy, and I didn't have the energy to call out. The rental Neon glowed zealous green in the early morning light.

"Aud!"

I was too tired to look up.

"Aud?" Somehow she was in front of me, kneeling on the grass, the way Julia had when Dornan was here, not that long ago, but oh, in what seemed like another lifetime . . . She was saying something else, about my clothes, but I didn't pay attention, until she put her hand on my calf, gently, and I flinched.

"I said, is this your blood?"

It was spattered on my chest, smeared on my stomach and thighs and neck, on my hands and feet. How had it got on my feet?

"Aud? Is it your blood?"

"This time."

"Can you walk to the car?"

I finally lifted my head and stared at her.

"I'll drive you into Asheville. You need to see a doctor."

I started to shake my head and the world slipped sideways.

"Whoa!" Strong arm around my shoulders. Her fingers brushed my bare breast and shifted instantly.

I looked at the grass until it stopped moving. "It's nothing. Cuts and bruises. I can do it, clean it up."

A long pause, then: "Can you stand?"

My knee was about twice its usual size and I'd lost some

blood, but I'd been hurt much worse than this in the past and still managed. Today, for some reason, I just couldn't seem to move.

"Okay." Her grip around my shoulders shifted to my waist. "I'm going to haul and you can lean on your stick, branch, whatever. On the count of three. One, two, three."

I tried, then, but it was as though someone had stolen the marrow from my bones and filled them with lead, heavy and soft, and I managed only an inch or two before I sank back on the log. How odd to be so helpless.

"Fuck," Tammy said under her breath. Then, more loudly, "I guess we'll just try again." She got behind me this time, put both arms round my waist, face pressed against my bare back. Her hair tickled. "Okay. And this time you're going to make it. On three. One, two, three."

I rose slowly on one leg and hovered for a moment, knee bent, precarious as a kite deciding whether to catch the wind, then I was up, clutching my branch with one hand, the other arm over Tammy's bowed shoulders.

"All right! Right leg first, okay, good. Now the left leg, I'll take your weight." Her voice was muffled: her cheek was crushed under my left breast. "Left leg, no, left leg. Good, good. Right leg. Okay. Let's just stand here for a second and catch our breath. No, Jesus, Aud, don't you give up. You have to help me. I'm— It's not far. You have to help."

She bullied, she panicked, she wheedled, and one step at a time I crept closer to the trailer, and after about five days I was there, swaying in front of the three metal steps.

"Fuck," she said.

"I can do it," I said, because she sounded near to tears.

"Yeah, right. Look, you sit on the edge of this step—"

"No."

"Jesus, Aud, you have—"

"Won't get up again."

"Oh. Okay. Well, how about if you lean here for a minute—

can you do that?—and I'll get inside first and try to drag you up the steps from behind."

"Move the steps."

"Move . . . ? Right." It took her a couple of shoves because she had to keep one arm around my waist, but they folded away underneath the rig eventually. She squeezed past me, climbed into the rig, and maneuvered me until my bottom rested against the cold sill. Then she squatted, put her arms under mine, and clasped them beneath my breasts.

"Now, when I say, you push off with your good leg and I'll pull. You can do this, okay? Ready? On three. One, two, three!"

I hopped and she hauled and we shot backwards into the trailer alongside the recliners, heads pointing at her bed, me lying on top, faceup, her hands on my breasts. She levered me away from her and scrambled up. I just lay there, looking up at her upside-down face.

"My bed's closest. You're almost done."

A confusion of trying to stand, pushing and being pulled, prodded, shouted at, until I found myself lying on her pullout and she was sitting next to me, water steaming in a bowl by her side. Where had that come from?

"Your throat's stopped bleeding. I wrapped it. It was already crusting up." I touched what felt like a towel around my neck. "Don't mess with it. You've lost enough blood. And you've got a scrape across your forehead and nose that I still have to clean. I already did your feet." They were wrapped bulkily in white bandage. When did she do that? "Full of dirt, but you didn't seem to feel me scrubbing away." She lifted the bottle of hydrogen peroxide. "This'll sting. Might have been better if you'd stayed passed out—"

Peroxide. Bleach. Pierced people with bleached hair and writhing tattoos. At night Tompkins Square Park was full of them. They hung out by the fountain that has been dry for years, on the side opposite the gay boys with their squat, muscular little dogs wearing bandannas. I didn't want those dogs getting a scent of blood-drenched clothes.

I stepped off the path. It felt wrong walking on grass in Karp's shoes. Light and sound faded until there was nothing but my breath and the rustle of plastic bags. I stopped, listened. Silence. And under the scent of green growing things, the smell of urine-stained clothes and unwashed hair.

I dumped one bag—the underwear, the shoes, the jacket—behind a tree. Someone would find it within half an hour, someone who wasn't particular about bloodstains, and who wouldn't talk to the police. I walked on a little.

The park bench was made of concrete, still almost whole, and in the dark you couldn't see the graffiti. I went down on one knee to shove the second bag—the trousers and tunic—beneath it and was about to stand when the razor touched my throat.

"My bench, bitch. What you doing to my bench?"

The concrete smelled of mold and cold stone. My knee, to which I had transferred all my weight as I was about to get up, hurt. The arm around my throat, the one holding the straight razor, was thin and scabbed.

"Gonna cut you good." A young voice, very young.

With a straight razor held firmly against your carotid, there's very little you can do. If you kick out backwards, the person holding it goes backwards, dragging their arm and the blade with it. You wouldn't feel much but you'd be unconscious in thirty seconds and dead in two minutes. If you turn to your left, it pulls across your trachea. You wouldn't bleed too much, but you'd be getting no oxygen. Turn to the right and the blade slices into your jugular as well as the carotid. Move downward and it takes the artery where it eases past your jawbone. Try to pull the blade down and it opens the blood vessels where they dive under the collarbone.

Neither of us moved. I couldn't think of a single thing to do or say that would save my life.

"What you say, bitch? Fucking with my bench."

This is how it would end, then, killed by a barely teenage junkie in a squalid little park in a city I hated.

The arm under my chin tightened. A thin trickle of blood ran down the neck of my borrowed shirt. Dying in someone else's clothes, with a pornographic tape in my pocket, dying as the kind of person who could disassemble a man with her bare hands for no particular reason and who hadn't even thought to check whether he was still alive.

"You think I'm shitting you? You think I won't do it?"

What did it matter? "Actually, I'm thinking of an afternoon a year or two ago, in my garden in Atlanta." I closed my eyes, remembering. "It was sunny and warm. I have a lot of trees: oak and pecan and beech—"

The arm jerked. "Shut up." This time the blood flowed smoothly, no little trickle.

"—and jays, a lot of blue jays. Noisy birds. But smart. They band together when there's danger. So one day I was outside—"

"Shut the fuck up!" The hand was trembling.

"—and these jays were all screeching around the big oak tree, then diving at it. There's this peregrine falcon perched on the end of a branch, about twenty feet up. It's ignoring the jays and watching this hole halfway up the trunk of the beech tree where chickadees liked to nest. Then I noticed that all the little birds, the finches and sparrows and tits, had gone."

The trembling against my throat grew worse and the razor shifted slightly as the wielder moved restlessly. In my peripheral vision I saw red sneakers. Small red sneakers. Razorboy was wired, needing a hit so badly that probably none of my words made sense. But the story wasn't for him.

"The falcon was so sure there was nothing in the garden to hurt it that it didn't see what I saw. A cat, skinning up the trunk of that oak, quiet as a snake. The jays were screeching even more: now there were two predators on their turf. The cat inched belly down along the branch until it was about three feet away. Its tail lashed back and forth, and it gathered its back feet, but just as it jumped, the hawk dived. It nearly hit the ground but just managed to swoop back up. It was so—"

The arm spasmed and the razor jerked, hard, and one of the red sneakers kicked out involuntarily, and the razor fell and clattered cheaply against the concrete bench. I stared at it. Blinked. Stood up.

He, or perhaps it was a she, it was too dark and he was too thin and too young for me to be sure, backed up a step. I picked up the razor, hefted it, looked at his oversize turtleneck and flapping khakis. He was shaking so badly he wouldn't get more than two steps before I'd be on him. He knew that, too.

I moved the razor back and forth, thinking, and took a step towards him. "—the hawk was so flustered the jays managed to drive it off. But do you know what the best part was? The cat. It was a long branch that the hawk had been on, and where the cat was now it was so narrow that it couldn't turn around. It was stuck. And that's when all the little birds, the finches and sparrows and tits, came out to play. They flew to the twigs and branches nearby and sang at the cat, and flicked their tails at it. The cat couldn't do a thing. Take off your sweater."

He was so far gone, arms and legs jerking so badly, that it took him almost a minute to get it over his head.

"Throw it to me." He tried, but it dropped at his feet. I advanced. He backed away. I bent, picked it up. Black, thick, filthy. "There are clothes in the bag under the bench." I lifted the razor and took another step towards him. He watched, dead-eyed. I folded the blade.

"So the cat had to jump." I threw him the razor and walked away.

The world jerked, like a badly edited film, and I was lying down with something taped to my face. I blinked. Tammy rose from one of the recliners.

"Hey," she said.

My knee seemed to be clamped between two blocks. I tried to move the cover to look, but Tammy leaned forward and lifted it for me.

"I iced it, then bandaged it and stuck a bag of ice on each side. I gave you some Vicodin for the pain, but you should really take ibuprofen or something too. Shouldn't you?"

I reached up and touched my face. Gauze.

"I cleaned it."

"Peroxide," I said, remembering. I hoped she hadn't used it on my neck. "Ice. Move the ice. And put some—"

The airport felt larger than it should but perhaps it was just because it was so late and there were fewer people. The black turtleneck was sodden with blood but it hid my throat. My scheduled flight was long gone. There was one more plane flying to North Carolina, to Charlotte, just before midnight.

"They'll be starting preboarding about now," the counter clerk said, trying not to be obvious about glancing from side to side to see if there was anyone within calling distance.

I started to walk. Nothing sounded right. I kept clutching for bags that weren't there. The concourse was hard hard hard beneath my feet. I was alive. I was alive because the damaged child who had wanted to kill me hadn't had the physical strength to hold a blade at my throat for three minutes. My pulse fluttered fast and light and sweat filmed my forehead.

I barely made it to the bathroom.

I vomited several times, resting in between with my head against the steel pedestal. It was warm against my skin and I longed for porcelain, white and cold. The whole airport was too warm; my feet sweltered in two pairs of socks. I retched again, and blood trickled over my collarbone.

• • •

Another bad edit, and Tammy stood in front of me, holding out pills and water. My arms would hardly move. She sighed, put the glass down, helped me sit up, and with one arm still around my shoulders handed me the pills, then held the water to my mouth. I spilled half of it down my front, which was more or less clean.

"Yeah, I sponged you down. Mud and blood. How come you were naked? What did you do with his—with the clothes?"

"She wanted to know that, too."

"Who did?"

But I was remembering the blood pouring down the drain of Karp's shower.

"Aud? Are you going to puke again? Aud? Jesus, I've just about fucking had it—" She was crying.

"Down."

She lowered me back down. "Don't fucking puke, just don't you dare."

If you button the jacket so all they see of the filthy sweater is an inch of turtleneck beneath obviously high-quality clothes, if your haircut is expensive and your teeth white and even, if you keep your voice pleasant, and if they find your money to be good and your ID valid, they will doubt the evidence of their senses. Smell is hard to document: impossible to photograph, difficult to describe. Move with assurance, act as though there is absolutely nothing wrong and—if the plane is half empty and you're flying first class—they will make no comment about your smell as they take your ticket; they will process your car rental in Charlotte without demur. Act as though there is nothing wrong and you can make it true, for a while.

Late afternoon. I hurt all over. The blocks were gone from around my knee. Tammy was reading at the table. I managed to sit up, but it left me panting. Tammy looked up; her eyes were red. "You look a little better."

"Yes."

"You scared the shit out of me."

I touched the bandage around my neck.

"You should see a doctor."

"I'll be fine." My mouth felt as though it belonged to someone else. "What pills?"

"Vicodin—"

Vicodin. Funny word. After a moment I realized she was still talking, repeating something. "What?"

"What did you mean, earlier, when I asked you about his—the clothes. You said, 'She wanted to know that, too.' Was there someone else in the woods?"

"Yes. No. Sort of."

"Well, that's clear. Is there someone or not? I mean, should I be worried about some crazy running around in the woods?"

"No." I felt myself drifting again.

"Okay. So where *did* your clothes go? Stolen by the wood ghost?"

I shut my eyes to the tears, but they leaked out. Who did he remind you of? Is that how she really saw me?

It's how you wanted me to see you, she said from beside me. I tried to turn without twisting my neck too much. "But you loved me anyway."

"Aud?"

She'll think you're crazy.

"Aren't I?"

Julia smiled, blew me a kiss, mouthed, *I'm glad you're safe,* and disappeared.

"Aud? Do you think there's someone there?"

"Not anymore." My eyes leaked again.

"But—"

"I'm tired."

"Jesus," she said in an after-all-I've-done-for-you tone, but when I didn't respond she changed tack. "You should eat before you go back to sleep. Unless you think you'll get sick again?"

I tried to say, I never get sick, but what came out of my mouth didn't make sense even to me.

She thumped about in the kitchen while I lay there, eyes still closed. Then she was carrying a tray with two bowls of soup and some bread. "You'll have to sit up. Here. There's no point hassling with a napkin, I'm going to have to wash the sheets anyhow—I was more worried about getting your cuts clean than the rest of you, so there's probably still a bunch of mud and leaves in the bed. You should see a doctor." I said nothing. "Well, it's your body. Here. Just say something if you think you're going to throw up, okay?"

Campbell's split pea soup. I only managed a few spoonfuls, then I slept.

The trailer lights were off, and firelight danced on the wall opposite the window. A stink. Burning plastic. I sat up with an effort, swang my legs slowly over the side of the bed, and panted against the pain. The wrapping on my knee was a big ball of bandage and tape. I tried to pick at the tape, but I was too weak and my right wrist and knuckles hurt. I flexed them. Hitting bone with bone. Stupid.

The door opened and Tammy and more of that stink wafted in with the breeze. She looked different: taller, denser, more substantial. "Don't like my bandaging?"

"Too tight."

"Here, lie back, I'll do it."

No, I thought, I was the one who was supposed to cope, the one people asked for help. But my eyes were stinging and I found myself lying down while she loosened the bandage.

"Jesus. It's black."

I managed to lift my head: puffy, puce mottled with blue-black. I flexed it, very slightly, and hissed.

"Jesus, don't *do* that."

I panted again for a minute, then did it again, just to be sure. "S'okay." The kneecap wasn't detached.

"I still think you should get it looked at, not that you ever listen to me." She stood up. "More painkillers will help. It's been a few hours." She brought me Vicodin and ibuprofen, which I swallowed obediently. "So. How did you do it—your leg?"

"I don't know."

"While running around with the clothes-stealing ghost?"

"Don't. Please."

"Jesus, just asking."

She went into the bathroom for a while, then fussed with something in the kitchen. The fire outside still burned, and I watched the changing light on the ceiling while the Vicodin eased molecule by molecule into my bloodstream.

"Look," Tammy said awkwardly, suddenly by my side again. "You know what you said to me a few days ago, about New York? About how I could talk about it if I wanted? Well, you could. If you wanted. I mean, you listened to me."

"This is different."

"So?"

She said it just the way Dornan had said, That's how it works.

"What?" she said.

"I used to think I knew how the world works." I gestured vaguely between us. I could feel the Vicodin rising like a tide.

"Does that mean you're going to talk about it?"

Her face seemed a long way off. "Was it the tape you were burning?"

She flushed and nodded. "Did you— I watched it again, to be sure. It made me feel . . . I hate him."

"He had a lot of tapes. He was a monster, I think." My thoughts were bumping together like moored boats.

"If he was here, I'd shoot him like a dog." Her voice was low and dark and vicious.

"I killed him." It just slid out.

She stilled. Her face went white, then slowly pink again. "You . . . killed him?"

I nodded.

"You mean you really . . . You killed him? Like, he's dead?"

"I think so." Slippery words, like eels.

"You're not sure?" She was looking at me, fascinated, the way you'd look at a just-born freak: should you strangle it before it draws its first breath, or raise it for the geek show. "Did he—Did it hurt?"

"Yes."

She licked her lips. "You killed him for me."

"No."

"No?"

"No."

She stood up, "I just have to—" and left the trailer abruptly. Images sloshed back and forth in my rocking brain: breaking teeth, sirens, the creak of his shoulder joint, blood-slicked hands . . .

The trailer door banged open. Tammy, nodding. Maybe I'd dozed off again. "So that's why you asked if I'd ever told him anything about you," she said. "Because of the police."

The fire outside set light dancing around her head, like one of those lurid saint's pictures. "I would have phoned the police from the airport. I would. But they were already there at—"

"The police were at the airport?"

"—Karp's apartment and why did I care anyway, that's something else that was different. I don't—"

"Wait. I'm lost. What was different?"

"—understand why I cared about whether or not he died. I never did before, they try to hurt me and I hurt them first and no second thoughts, like in Norway, they were going to hurt

Julia, and I just do it, I don't feel bad afterwards, I don't feel like this—"

"What? Stop. Stop. You went to Norway?"

"—do you know how blood sounds when it drips on ice, it's like. Nothing you. Ever . . ." And my brain lurched, turned turtle, and sank.

THREE

imago (from *imāgo,* L. for representation, natural shape)

1. in Jungian psychoanalysis, the subjective image of someone else (usually a parent) which a person has subconsciously formed and which continues to influence her attitudes and behavior

2. in entomology, the adult or perfect form

. . . metamorphosis is complicated by the fact that the rigid cuticle covering the body is very restrictive . . .

i
m
a
g
o

CHAPTER NINE

Fever is a fairground, full of garish colors and grotesque rides and the sense that the fun will turn to terror any moment. I whirled brightly from one amusement to another. Julia, sitting on my lap, smiling at me while she nodded and talked on the phone. Diving into a glacier lake as a man lifted a rifle to his shoulder. Tammy, feeling my forehead and shouting at me. The sickening creak of Karp's shoulder joint. Steel at my throat. Julia lying in a pool of blood on an Oslo street. Tammy saying, "Aud? Aud? Can you hear me? You have to take these." Julia lying in a white-tiled room on a white hospital bed hooked up to white machines. Her mother sitting there, cradling her hand, cradling her with love. My mother sitting by my bed, telling me the story of how trolls always win. A terrible thumping and grinding in my head. Swallowing shiny beetles, purple and green. Back at the glacier again, choking as the lake closed over my head, except somehow I was in a bed at the same time and some woman was trying to drown me in a glass of water. Crawling: crawling on grass, on leaves, on a hard road, underwater, crawling away. Trying to hide. But bright light followed me everywhere, into every corner, under every bed, hunting, until it pinned me down and I opened my eyes. Daylight.

"Open," Tammy said, as though I were a baby, and pushed something between my lips. I struggled weakly. Her grip on the back of my neck tightened. "Nice pills. Make you feel better. Come on, open up, just one." I let her get it between my lips, then spat it onto the bed. She sighed wearily. "Your mother must have had fun when you were sick."

The only time I remembered my mother being with me when I was ill was when I was seven or eight. I had tonsillitis. She told me the story about trolls; the only story, ever.

She picked up the pill. It was purple and green.

"What are you feeding me?" It sounded querulous.

"Aud?"

"Yes," I said, cross. "What's the pill?"

She sat on the bed, studied me a moment, then pulled a pill bottle from her jeans pocket. "You've been out of your mind with fever. I found these with your other first aid stuff." She handed them to me. "They seem to work. Your fever's down, anyway."

I squinted at the bottle. Augmentin: antibiotics. "I should have thought of that."

She snatched the bottle back. "Gee thanks, Tammy, for probably saving my life. Hey, Aud, no problem: I get such a kick out of nursing crazy people with a death wish who threaten to kill me every five minutes."

"To kill you?"

"Well, hey Tammy, sorry for any inconvenience, sorry for scaring the shit out of you." She turned away and wiped at her cheeks with the heel of her hand. "Ungrateful asshole."

I was too tired for this. "Tammy." She wouldn't turn around. "I'm sorry." I looked out of the window. Early afternoon. But what day? "I really said I'd kill you?"

She turned round. "A hundred times. You never shut up."

"What did I say?"

"A lot of things. To do with the girl, mostly."

"Julia's not a girl."

"Not Julia, the kid. The girl."

At my blank look, she slid off the bed, and retrieved a folder from the table. She wore a thick cable-knit sweater, blue: mine. I realized it was cold in the trailer. She held out the folder. Bloody glove print on the cover.

"Luz. Her. It was in the car."

I touched it with a fingertip but didn't take it. Nine years old and being trained like a dog. "I'll have to do something about her."

Tammy dropped the folder back on the table. "Like what?"

I hadn't meant to speak aloud. "I don't know." Nine years old. No one to love her. "What else did I say?"

"Bunch of stuff about glaciers and hospitals. Didn't make much sense. You cried a lot. And sort of snarled like you were fighting someone. And at me when I said I was calling 911. 'White!' you shouted. 'White!' And you got out of bed and started to crawl to the door. I had to practically swear on the Bible I wouldn't call a doctor before I could get you back to bed. But by then the antibiotics had started to work, anyhow. And then you started snarling again, only this time it was different. It— Is that what you're like when— Was what you said before true? Did you kill him?"

"I don't know." I would have to do something about that, too.

When I woke, it was late afternoon.

"How are you feeling?"

"Better." The fever was more or less gone. My neck and knee hurt, I was thirsty. The folder was still on the table. Nine years old. I sat up. It was still cold. "Give me the phone."

"Who are you calling?"

I just looked at her. She gave me the phone.

My head ached, and I couldn't remember Eddie's number at the *Atlanta Journal-Constitution,* so I had to scroll through the names menu. When it rang, the man who answered was not Eddie. After a moment's confusion, I discovered Eddie had been promoted to late-shift manager of the weekend edition. I was put through.

"Aud!" His voice was textured and rich, like nineteenth-century brocade. "Delightful to hear from you, as always. Where have you been?"

I've been up to London to visit the queen. "Renovating an old cabin in the woods. I need a favor."

"But of course. Though you and your latest client's expense account still owe me a dinner at the Horseradish Grill."

"I'll buy you two, just as soon as I'm back in town. But if you could get on the wires for me and find out if a man called George Karp was hurt or killed in New York, SoHo, three or four days ago, I'd be grateful."

"And I suppose you need this information yesterday?" I could hear him clicking on the keyboard as we spoke.

"Even the day before."

"Well. I seem to recall that last time I looked someone up for you, he turned up dead a month or so later, in a public bathroom."

"Nothing to do with me."

"On this particular occasion, I believe you. Ah ha. Here we go. George Karp, white male, assaulted by unknown assailants inside his own home, a fashionable loft in— How much detail do you want?"

"The extent of his injuries, whether or not he's dead."

"As good as, according to this. 'Deep coma.' Somebody really did a number on him. Cervical vertebrae fractured in two places, spinal cord disrupted. Left eye ruptured—associated orbital fractures. Both shoulders dislocated, some muscles torn out. Ruptured spleen, both kidneys severely damaged. Ribs splintered, which probably caused the pneumothorax and liver laceration. Jaw broken, and teeth. Legs more or less untouched, strangely enough. Cranial fracture—that's what did the damage, they think, although it's possible that the injury to the larynx, and one to the spinal cord, led to oxygen deprivation before the head trauma. Police are looking for two assailants, white male and white female. From the descriptions you'd think they were brother and sister. Description one is from a group of young men and women passing the loft just after the incident: male, six-two, blond hair, possibly something wrong with his eyes. Description two is from a woman who was apparently accompanying Karp home from a restaurant, who says the attacker was female—still tall, though, another six-footer, and blond hair again, very pale blue . . ." His voice trailed off. "Aud, is there something you're not telling me?"

"Always," I said lightly. It was an effort. "Any other details?"

Click click click. "Ah. Now this is interesting. Tabloid stuff, though. Want to hear it?"

"Yes."

"After the news hit the real papers—apparently this Karp is some kind of minor celebrity in the retail universe—a woman talked to the *Daily Post,* said Karp abused her so much he drove her insane and she ended up in a psychiatric facility. She says, and I quote, 'He's a perv and a wacko.' " The colloquialisms sounded alien in his smooth diction. "Though, of course, she herself is certifiably insane, so it's a case of the pot calling the kettle black." He clicked away. "Lurid tale of kink and coercion follows. According to the tabloid, her statement is corroborated by videotapes found in Karp's apartment. Although they were all erased somehow, the labeling is apparently suggestive. The tabloid hints that the police now believe this to be some kind of revenge attack." More tapping. "Officially, the police will say only that they're pursuing leads."

"No mention of anything missing?"

"Not that I can see, although a few items of obvious value were left untouched." A few more clicks. "No. Nothing. Anything else I can do for you?"

A sudden picture of Eddie in his cubicle, smiling down the phone, relaxed and calm, made my eyes smart. "Just keep being yourself."

There was a startled pause. "Is everything all right with you?"

"Fine. And thank you. I'll buy you that dinner very soon."

I folded the phone and dropped it on the bed. Tammy put it on the table with the folder.

"He's still alive, isn't he?"

"In a coma. A deep coma. He's not going to recover."

"He would hate that," she said, "lying there totally helpless," and her whole face curved in a predatory smile: the old Tammy coming out to play.

I pushed away the blanket and swang my legs off the couch bed. Instead of lead, my bones felt filled with polystyrene.

"*Now* what are you doing?" she said.

"There's still Luz to take care of."

She stood in front of me. "You're joking, right?"

I stood on the second try, and shivered. It was definitely cold in the trailer, and I was still naked.

"Jesus, you're not, are you?" I ignored her and concentrated on moving. Styrofoam was not reliable construction material. "What are you going to do? You can't even drive with that knee."

Seven feet from the foldout bed, I couldn't seem to move anymore. I leaned dizzily against the kitchen counter.

"You've still got some fever," Tammy said from behind me. "You haven't really eaten for a couple of days. You've lost blood."

I tried to straighten up and the pain in my knee bloomed like a fireball. I didn't dare let go of the counter. If someone knows you need them, it gives them a weapon to hurt you over and over again. But the counter began to tilt and slide. "Help me."

I thought for a moment she was going to fold her arms and say, Pretty please, but her response was a neutral "Back to bed?"

"Bathroom first."

She took my arm and some of my weight. "You really are a stubborn asshole," but the hard look had faded, and while I was balancing carefully on the toilet she went and got me one of the oversize T-shirts she slept in. It wasn't easy to get it over the bandages on my head and neck.

By the time I got back to bed my knee felt as though someone had poured molten tin in the joint.

"You shouldn't have gotten up," Tammy said as she lifted my leg onto the bed for me.

"No."

"Probably needs more ice."

"Heat would be better," I said. "There's a hot pack in one of the storage bays. Stick it in the microwave." She pulled the blanket up to my chest. "Why is it so cold in here?"

"Because there's not a lot of propane left, and I didn't know how long you were going to be sick."

"What about the solar panels?"

She just gestured at the window: heavy overcast.

I nodded. "When you get the hot pack, bring the first aid kit, too. Please."

She raised her eyebrows at the "Please," but brought the kit back with the hot pack. "I turned the heat up." We unbandaged the knee. "Looks painful."

"It is," I said shortly, then swore as she nudged it positioning the hot pack.

"You hold it, then." I did. She brought me a glass of water and two pills.

"No more Vicodin."

"They'll help with the pain."

"I don't *want* any more Vicodin." Pain reduces everyone to childishness. It reduces, full stop.

She put pills and glass on the table and gave me a look that said, You're crazy.

"I do want to take a look at my throat, though."

I told her what I needed, and when she had the warm water and Band-Aids and mirror assembled, I put the hot pack aside and unwrapped the thin towel around my neck.

The cut was about three inches long, not deep, but wide. When I turned my head this way and that, it gaped and seeped at the center. I set about the grim business of cleaning it.

"Are you going to leave it unwrapped like that?"

"I'm letting the skin around it dry so I can put some Band-Aids on." Steri-Strips would have been better, but I didn't have any. I picked up the scissors and cut chunks out of two sides of a Band-Aid so that what was left looked a bit like a very short dumbbell. I peeled away the sterile backing and put it over the slash in my neck so that the edges of the cut were pulled together. Instant butterfly suture. I did it all twice more. It shouldn't scar too badly. Then I smeared antibiotic ointment over the seam and dabbed some on my face, and the backs of my hands.

"I don't see why you don't just go to the doctor."

"Hospitals are . . . they have bad associations for me."

She gave me a jaded look. "Like they don't for everyone else?"

After a moment I said, "I didn't take that last antibiotic you were trying to give me, did I?"

"No." She brought the glass of water back and pulled the bottle out of her pocket again. "How did you get all this stuff, anyway?"

"I asked my doctor."

"You said, 'Hey, doc, I kill people for a living and sometimes they fight back, so can I have pills and stuff, in case?' "

"I don't, and he didn't. Fight back."

"Then—"

"It was later. I got careless." Which wouldn't happen when I went to Arkansas for the girl. That trip would be planned down to the last detail, no more mistakes. No one would ever know I'd been there, until the girl went missing. I wrapped my neck again.

"So? How did you get her to give you the drugs?"

"Him."

"Whatever."

"I travel all over, sometimes to remote areas. If you're somewhere like Kamchatka and get a compound fracture, you can't just phone a pharmacy. There might not be a doctor for several hundred miles. He gives me prescriptions so I'll always have antibiotics, and morphine, and a few other things."

"You've got morphine in there?"

"I used it up, in Norway."

"Norway again."

I blinked. Pain might chew away at your defenses until you said whatever came into your head, but obviously the narcotic-based Vicodin had been worse. "Pass the heating pad, please." She did.

"Doesn't look like it's helping much."

It wasn't.

"Changed your mind about the Vicodin?"

I started to shake my head, hissed as my neck pulled and the throbbing in my scalp started up again.

"Right, what was I thinking? Of *course* it's better to grind your teeth and make the veins in your forehead stick out in pain than to take a couple of pills. Great. Fantastic. Especially the part where you start to get mean and shout at me again. Can't wait."

I didn't want to babble my head off again about Julia. Julia was mine. Had been mine. *Julia?*

Tammy stood up. "I'll make us something to eat."

Julia?

Tammy banged and clattered resentfully in the kitchen. The pain in my knee slid like a superficial warm layer over the terrible ache deep in a part of me I couldn't reach, couldn't even name.

"Listen," I said.

Bang, clatter.

"Tammy—"

She turned, snapped "I'm doing soup," and went back to stirring.

"Listen. I need you to listen. We met in Atlanta. They were trying to kill her but I said I'd keep her safe. She was paying me to help her find out who killed her friend. But that wasn't why I was doing it, although I didn't know that. Well, I did, but I'd never loved anyone before. We went to Norway—"

Tammy looked up from her soup. "Norway?"

"—I thought it would be safer there." Home was supposed to be safe. "She had business in Oslo, but when we went to Lustrafjord, it wasn't business anymore."

Tammy left her soup and sat on the foot of the bed.

I tried to explain how I'd shown Julia who I was by taking her to the *seter,* the farm where I'd spent my childhood summers, but it came out sounding like a bad romance: boats on the fjord, sun on the water, flowers on the *fjell.* "She went back to Oslo for a meeting. One of the killers came for me by the glacier lake. He shot me."

I rolled up the left sleeve of my T-shirt. The bullet had hit my shoulder blade, bounced a bit, and traveled down the underside of my arm. The scar was pink and puckered, no longer an ugly purple red.

She looked at it. "You could have that fixed."

"He shot me, so I broke his legs and left him to die. There was no choice because I couldn't call the police to help him, or to help Julia, because if they found him they'd detain me, stop me from helping her." I'll protect you, I'd said. "So I did it, left him without a second thought."

But I didn't help her. I went to the blue place, forgot that it wasn't just me against them. Forgot that Julia was in the middle.

"I killed the ones in Oslo, too. They weren't real people. No one is. Was. So I killed them, but not before they— Anyway, she died. And I haven't thought about them, the killers that I killed, not really." I ran my fingers down the bullet track. Physical pain was easy to deal with. "The people I've killed were just objects, things to be removed. They only mattered as far as how they affected me. Everything, everyone used to be like that. Not anymore. Do you understand?"

She shook her head.

"She opened me, and now it's all different. I feel different. I do things differently, like with Karp."

"You still haven't told me about that."

"I don't understand why I did it. I don't understand it at all. Rage. I've never felt it before, not really."

She looked skeptical.

"Mostly I would feel a kind of disgust, and irritation. I would look at them and think, You're in my way, and I'd move them aside. Like moving a chair." I thought about it. "Or like twisting the barrel of a rifle, breaking it so it can't be used against you. I felt some annoyance, maybe. Not rage. People weren't worth getting angry about."

Neither of us said anything for a minute. It should have been getting warmer by now.

"You're not wearing your watch," I said.

She glanced at the pale band around her wrist. "No." Silence. "So I still don't know what happened with Karp."

"It was Julia. A woman who looked like her. Except she didn't, not really. It just— I was thinking about her, then I came out of his loft, and there they were. She ran. I hit him so he couldn't breathe, took all the fight from him, then dragged him into the elevator and hit him again. Beat him. Hands, elbows, knees, feet." My bones began to fill with lead again. I felt heavy enough to sink through the bed, through the floor of the trailer, into the dirt.

After a moment she said, "Did it hurt him?"

"Yes." My knee hurt so much I couldn't think. "Something's burning."

She jumped up, ran into the kitchen. "Shit." She turned off the stove and came and sat down again. "That's it for the soup."

"I'm not hungry."

"Knee?"

"Yes."

"There's always the Vicodin."

I was talking anyway. I nodded tiredly. The bed shifted as she leaned, handed me pills and glass.

The water was cold, and ached all the way down my gullet. "She loved me. She wouldn't now, not like this."

"Like what?"

"Like *this*." I thumped the mattress. "If she were here she'd say he was a monster who would have just kept hurting people, and that he deserved what he got. She'd probably even try to believe it, but—" If I wanted, I could remember every creak and pop and spatter.

"So now you're saying he wasn't a monster?"

"No, he was. Is."

"Okay. Then you think he wouldn't have kept hurting people?"

"Of course he would have kept doing it!"

"Don't yell. I told you you'd get mean if you didn't take those pills. I'm just trying to figure this out. Geordie Karp was a sick son of a bitch and I'm glad you hurt him. He probably deserved everything he got."

"Yes, but how do you stand it, every day, not being sure? Even you're saying 'probably.' I never used to feel this way."

"Let me see if I've got this straight. You used to kill people and not care about it much one way or another. But you're upset about Geordie—even though he's not dead, and even though you hurt him for a good reason. Yes? You're upset that you *feel* when you practically kill someone?" She waited for my nod. "You don't think that's an improvement?"

"She said that I was like Karp." That I used to be. That I pretended to be.

"She said—?" She cleared her throat. "So she died, when?"

"Five months and four days ago." And a few hours: it had been midafternoon.

"And you saw Geordie for the first time in New York just this week."

I nodded, shivered.

"But you said she told you— That she said you were like Geordie." I shook my head. "Someone else said that?"

"No. She just asked me who he reminded me of."

"And that was . . . when?"

"Three days ago." Or two, or four, or whenever I'd been under the trees.

"That's who was in the woods, wasn't it? You see Julia."

"Yes."

Silence. Then she said, "What's that like?" and my muscles locked up. Nothing worked, except my eyes. I wept soundlessly. I couldn't even turn away.

She got up, sat down again, stared some more, and after a while hitched herself closer and pulled me awkwardly to her chest. She didn't say anything, just stroked my head. The touch of her hand was like someone taking an axe to a dam; I wrapped my arms around her waist and keened. I hated her for not being Julia, but I couldn't let go, and I couldn't stop. Her hand went on stroking my head, and I wanted to shout, Stop! No! This is mine!, but that touch just kept widening the breach.

"She'll never see this place," I said. "You have, but she never will. I've never seen her grave. I should have stayed, in Atlanta. Should have helped her mother. Seen to her things." Her clothes still lying on the floor in front of my washing machine.

It was getting dark out, and quiet. Tammy shifted, the couch creaked; her shoulders looked tight and tired. I wiped my face with the back of my hand, smearing the ointment. I didn't want to talk anymore.

"I think I can make it to my own bed, if you help. The bathroom first."

I used the toilet again, brushed my teeth, paused in the middle of wiping my mouth with the towel. It wasn't my face anymore. It wasn't just the smudges under my eyes, the smears of antibiotic, the scab. The muscles moved differently, as though someone else's bones were trying to emerge.

CHAPTER TEN

Morning. I hobbled out of bed, made coffee, took it and the blood-stained folder to the table. Tammy was still asleep. I leafed through the documents. The pictures. The medical evaluation. The passport, the birth certificate and certificate of adoption. Karp was the legal adoptive father. No mention of permanent residency application, and the visitor's visa had expired. I had no idea what the INS would make of that. No mention of the Arkansas couple on any official paperwork, though I found check stubs I had missed the first time around, records of bimonthly payments to J. Carpenter. There was no photo of either Jud or Adeline Carpenter, no hint of their age or anything but the fact that they were "good Christians who believed in old-fashioned family values," and some details about the congregation they belonged to. What would they do now that Karp was permanently out of the picture and the money supply dried up? What would happen to the child?

I pushed it all to one side, took my coffee to the door, and opened it. It was a bright, cold morning. The season had shifted. The vibrant color of a week ago had faded and everywhere I looked bare branches poked through the threadbare tapestry.

Careful of my strapped and swollen knee, I propped myself more securely against the doorframe. My coffee and breath steamed. During the night, fog had frozen on the fallen leaves and spiky turf, riming the world in sparkling hoarfrost. Something small had left tracks across the gray carpet, and while I watched the tracks expanded as the sun warmed the ground. Where a bird had hopped about on the hood of the rented Neon, bright green showed through.

"How's your knee?"

I turned awkwardly. Tammy looked tired and frowsy in her pile of blankets.

"It'll take my weight. But I'll have to keep it strapped for a while. Coffee's hot."

"What I really liked about you being away was being able to sleep past dawn."

We silently contemplated everything that had happened since I left: Tammy writhing on tape; my hands red and dripping; telling her what I'd told no one about Julia; asking for help—and getting it from a most unlikely and mostly unliked person.

"Stay in bed," I said. "I'll bring you a cup." I closed the door, stumped into the galley, poured and stirred, and stumped more slowly back.

She nodded her thanks. I took my coffee back to the table and sat. Neither of us said anything for a while.

"So," she said. "What do we do now?"

"I don't know." It would take some time to understand the shape of the change between us, so I ignored it for now. "I have to make some phone calls. You may as well stay in bed and enjoy your coffee."

The first person I called was my lawyer. Her personal assistant picked up.

"Ms. Torvingen! Ms. Fleishman's been trying to get in touch

with you for a couple of weeks now. Hold just one moment and I'll get her on the line." A click, followed by Bette Fleishman's velvety, young-sounding voice. A great voice, especially if you were really sixty-two and as brittle as a praying mantis. "Aud Torvingen, the original mysterious disappearing woman. How are you, girl? I've been calling your machine and leaving messages for a month it feels like. There's some few year-end matters that need to be taken care of before—"

"Are they urgent?"

"If you mean urgent as in life-or-death, hell no, but they might save you a dime or two if you could get them tidied up before the end of the tax year."

"Just use your best judgment, Bette. I'll be in before the end of the year to sign anything you think I should. But for now I need some information about adoption and immigration law."

"Outside my area of competence."

"Yes, but—"

"But if you let me finish my thought, I know just the person you should talk to. Great guy, crackerjack, a real immigration hotshot." I imagined Bette flipping through her Rolodex, which she swore was faster and more reliable than a computer. "Name of Solomon C. Poorway. Believe he goes by Chuck." She gave me the number. "Make sure he knows I sent you. And Aud, I know you're in a hellfire rush, but don't forget about coming in before year-end."

I dialed the number she'd given me and was soon speaking to a contained, careful-sounding man. I outlined Luz's situation: her age, visa status, the fact that she was in private, unofficial foster care and her adoptive parent was dead—or as good as. Poorway asked me a few questions about nationality, date of entry, and so forth. "Not an ideal situation," he said, with lawyerly understatement. "With the visitor's visa expired, adoptive father dead, and no permanent residency applied for, she is technically an illegal alien. If her existence is called to the attention of the INS, they'll deport her."

"Any suggestions?"

"She needs to be adopted by someone else. Then have the adoptive parents and child live together for two years, after which you can apply for permanent residency—the green card—and social security number."

"How do I do that if she's an illegal alien?"

"That will take some thinking about."

Tammy got up and headed for the shower.

"What about citizenship?" I asked him.

"Once the child has permanent residency, the adoptive adult can apply for naturalization."

"So what you're saying is we really have to find a way to get her adopted."

"Essentially, yes."

I had the original adoption certificate. A template. I knew some creative people. "And how carefully is such documentation scrutinized?"

A pause. A long pause. "It's not so much the physical documentation as the electronic trail." A diplomatic way of saying that forging the certificate won't do you much good unless you can hack State Department computers.

Perhaps the problem could be tackled from the other end. "Suppose the adoptive parent had applied for the green card for the child before he died. What would happen to the application then?"

"There's no reason for it not to go through if all other conditions have been met. Especially if the adoptive parent had also left a will specifying legal guardianship for the child in the interim."

"Mr. Poorway, will you take me as a client?"

Another of those long pauses. "I'm assuming we're now speaking to the issue of client-attorney privilege?"

"Yes."

"Give me your number, please, and I'll call you back in a few minutes." I agreed, gave him the number, and folded the phone. It wasn't hard to guess who he'd be calling now.

Tammy wandered through wrapped in a towel, drying her hair. "Done already?"

"Waiting for him to call back."

"How about waiting somewhere else?" She gestured at her near-nakedness.

I hauled myself up the two steps to my bed. I'd lost count of the times I'd seen Tammy naked, both live and on tape. I wasn't the only one pretending the last few days had never happened.

The phone rang. "Yes, I'll take you as a client," Solomon Poorway said. Bette Fleishman must have persuaded him I wasn't a mass murderer. I smiled bleakly. "Ms. Torvingen?"

"Aud," I said.

"Very well, Aud." No offer to be called Chuck. "Our conversation is now privileged. However, I would prefer that you not test my ethics too severely."

"Thank you for your candor. Here's another hypothetical question. If the INS should receive a packet dated before the adoptive father died, a signed and dated application for permanent residence, and if there was an addendum to his will giving, say, me guardianship, then I would be her legal guardian until she became a legal resident, yes? Then once she got her green card, I could get her a social security number, and apply for citizenship on her behalf?"

"Yes." He didn't sound happy about it.

"And it wouldn't be necessary for the child to live with the legal guardian." I would send checks. I didn't particularly want to meet her, but I could at least make sure she had warm clothes, enough to eat, and someone to look after the basics.

"No."

I wanted to ask what kind of wording would be necessary on the addendum about guardianship, but no doubt that would be pushing his ethics too far, so I thanked him and hung up. Tammy was now dressed. I limped back down to the table and reopened the folder.

"You want breakfast?" Tammy asked.

"Um."

"Well, don't jump up and down with gratitude or anything."

I looked up. Not pretending quite everything away, then. "Jumping up and down would be a bit tricky at the moment."

"Is that a joke, Aud Torvingen?"

The old Tammy had not been pleasant, but this new one was unfathomable. I turned back to the folder and riffled through its contents, thinking. I spread out the information on the Carpenters, including the black-and-white photograph of a house, surrounded by farmland; it looked fairly isolated. I picked up the fact sheet again, read it more carefully. Church of Christ. New Testament literalists. Not technophobic, exactly, but disapproving of frivolity; a phone would be fine, and a car, but definitely no music—apart from the human voice in praise to His glory; modern medicine would be acceptable, as long as it was absolutely necessary—no antidepressants, no Valium, no sleeping pills. Nothing about dancing, one way or the other. Jud Carpenter was a deacon of the Plaume City Church of Christ congregation. I found an atlas, and paper and pencil, and took notes.

Tammy made toast and eggs and tea. I ate the eggs, crunched my way through the half-burnt bread, sipped at the overbrewed tea, still thinking. It might work, but I'd have to check a few details. No carelessness this time. I touched my neck.

"Hurt?"

"Um? No."

"Good. So, you decided how to handle it?"

I had never talked to anyone about my methods before. Julia had never had the chance to see me work.

"They live in an isolated house in the middle of Nowhere,

Arkansas," I said. "Which is good, in the sense that I should be able to snoop about unseen because there'll be hardly anyone around. But it's bad because if there is anyone about, I'll stick out like a sore thumb. But the best thing is, they're big-time churchgoers."

"Sunday," she said, nodding. "The whole family." Smarter than she looked. "All day. All that preaching and singing. Hours and hours to get into their house and take a look around." She grinned at me, then remembered and turned away.

I turned on my laptop and while it warmed up Tammy pulled on a sweatshirt and went outside. I hooked up my cell phone, got online and started searching the web. After a few minutes, I heard the chunk-and-scatter of wood being chopped into kindling. For the next hour, I clicked my way through web pages, and Tammy got a real rhythm going with the hatchet; she had peeled down to her T-shirt and the wood was piling up. We didn't need it. I watched for a while, then picked up the phone book and turned to electronics suppliers.

Tammy came back in just as I finished organizing my notes. The exercise had done her good; she looked bigger, stronger, more relaxed.

"Tea?"

"Thank you," she said, and smiled tentatively. "It's great out there, real fresh and clean-smelling." I smiled back, then got up to fill the kettle. Tammy looked at my neat pile of notes. "You look all set."

"I've worked out a beginning. But there's nothing I can do for a while." In New York both knees had been whole, and I'd still had my throat slit by a scarecrow with a razor.

A house is more likely to be inhabitable in the long term if you approach it as a spaceship. Think of the walls and roof and windows as hull integrity; electrical, heating, and sewage systems as life support; floors and interior walls as decorated bulkheads. I had walls and a roof but would need to get the windows glazed before there was perfect hull integrity. I'd dug and installed the septic system months ago, but still needed to install toilet, bath, sinks, and shower. The electrical system could wait. Heating couldn't. I needed glass, I needed a wood-burning stove, and I needed to check and repoint the chimney and flue. We would have to go to town for the glass and the stove, which for now left the chimney and flue.

The cabin smelled of cold stone and raw wood, and my breath steamed. I stood in the middle of the unfinished floor and studied the massive fieldstone fireplace.

"How are you with heights?" I asked Tammy.

"Depends," she said warily. "What did you have in mind?"

It seemed that Tammy could climb a ladder up to the roof and the chimney, but not let go of it once she was there, which made the whole exercise rather pointless. I would have to wait a few days before I could get up a ladder and do the chimney repairs myself. Meanwhile, I took a look at the flue and inside stonework. Apart from a few minor repairs, the flue looked solid and well designed, and we didn't need ladders for the first stage of interior pointwork.

Under my direction, Tammy carried the bags of cement and buckets of water and mixed the two in the right proportions until I was satisfied. Then I showed her how to slap the mortar between the stone with an upward stroke, slice the excess off with the downstroke, and shape what was left with a fast right-to-left horizontal swipe.

"The trick is to not get mortar all over the face of the stone because then you have to chip it off bit by bit when it's dry, which is tedious and time-consuming."

Slap, chop, scrape. Slap, chop, scrape. Stretch, bend, sigh. Mindless rhythm of stone and mortar and steel, dusty scent of mortar and wet mixing board. It was probably not much over fifty degrees outside, and a breeze blew through the open door, but Tammy's face grew lightly sheened with sweat, and my knee ached.

I woke in the early hours. I took the phone outside and called Eddie's number at the *Journal-Constitution.* I had to leave a message.

"It's me. I need follow-up on that George Karp story, whatever comes over the wires: new leads, witness statements, police activity, Karp's condition. I'm particularly interested in what evidence the police think they have. You've got my number."

The first two days, we worked only until lunch because I was still too tired to do a full day. When my knee got strong enough to lighten the strapping, and limber enough to climb cautiously up the ladder to repoint the chimney, I spent an hour every afternoon in the woods. There wouldn't be many of these days left, and it gave me time to think about Karp and what might happen if he woke up and gave the police a good description; what might happen if the police took that description to the local cafés, talked to the waitress in the second café, where I'd left the book. I tried to think about moving money to a Swiss account and how I could build a new identity, but each time found myself wondering instead how I could make sure nothing went wrong in Arkansas, or contemplating what still had to be done at the cabin.

Tammy and I didn't speak much during the day, but at night, over food and coffee, we talked of this and that. I told her about Dree, the hairdresser, about Asheville, what I could remember of the history of the place. She told me of her undergraduate years at the University of Georgia, the friends she had lost touch with. We didn't drink. We didn't read. We would climb into our respective beds and sleep like stones, or at least Tammy did. I woke up suddenly, at all hours, thinking of Karp—I should have killed him, should have made sure; I shouldn't have hurt him in the first place—wondering what was wrong with me, why I wasn't already running, and where a nine-year-old girl might go to hide, if she could.

One morning I woke before dawn. The air was still and cool and humid, the way it gets in an airtight metal box, no matter how nicely you disguise the interior with leather upholstery and good carpets, and I wanted to walk. I dressed quietly and crept out into the clearing. My breath bloomed before me like the thought balloon of an empty-headed cartoon character. There were no tracks in the hoarfrost. The predawn sky was like lead, with barely enough light to see. I was glad of my thick jacket.

Amid the trees, leaves fell, gray and silent, like something filmed in the early days of cinema. The air was crisp enough to slice at the warm mucus membranes of my nose and throat, and smelled of iron. Autumn. This is where new life begins, with the seed falling on hard ground, being buried by dead leaves. The old life had to die first.

Tammy was dressed and on what looked like her third cup of coffee by the time I got back. The bright interior of the trailer seemed garish after the cold clarity of the woods.

"I was trying not to get worried," she said.

"I woke up this morning and it occurred to me that I hadn't seen or heard a groundhog in days, that they've begun to hibernate, and I went out into the woods and saw the first gouged tree of the season—from deer, rubbing the velvet off their new antlers—and I realized it's November."

"Okay. Let's pretend I don't understand what you're talking about and need a few hints."

"Today is the second of November. My birthday."

"Your birth—"

"And I was thinking, there are a few things we need, and I should return that Neon."

"Wait. Back up. How old are you?"

"Thirty-two. And you were saying only yesterday that your hair needs cutting. We could go into Asheville. Maybe have something to eat, something to drink."

She blinked. Maybe it was her first cup of coffee after all. Then she smiled. "When do you want to leave, birthday girl?"

We dropped the Neon off first, then I drove the truck to the salon, where there were already two people waiting; I stayed long enough to say hello to Dree and tell Tammy that if I wasn't back by the time she was done I'd meet her in the café next door.

On Church Street, I hesitated, engine running, outside the Asheville Savings Bank, while I thought, I can't, I'm not ready, but had no idea what I meant. Eventually I parked.

The manager's office, white shelves holding books and plants surrounding her door, light wood desk, medium window, was as relaxed as she was. At my suggestion, she called Lawrence, my banker in Atlanta, and decided as a result that she would be very happy to attend to my every need as far as local business dealings were concerned. She came round to my side of the desk, shook hands, and prepared to escort me back into the public space and the care of a trusted teller.

By the door, I noticed the bonsai tree. A perfect oak, ancient and stately, and only six inches high.

"Eighty years old," she said. "It was an anniversary present from my husband. Beautiful, isn't it? It came with a book—"

When I had tried to talk to her about setting up a Swiss account, my mouth had dried up, and I imagined a nine-year-old in a foreign country, with no love, no one to rely on. I don't care, I told myself, I've never even met her—and what use would I be to her in jail? But I still hadn't opened my mouth.

"—torture it: prune the roots, clip out new limb growth, and wire the branches to achieve the desired shape. Sometimes I wonder what would happen if I just let it grow."

The manager shook herself from contemplation of the tree and asked if, apart from facilitating an immediate account, there was anything else she could do to help.

She gave me directions to Architectural Glass, two different hardware stores, and a place called Bathed in Light.

Bathed in Light had exactly what I needed. I arranged to go back later that afternoon to pick up the bathtub, sinks, and other fixtures I had picked out. Thoughts of Karp and fingerprints got muddled up with stainless steel faucets and brass-accented showerheads.

Architectural Glass was harder to find and there was nowhere nearby to park—unusual in Asheville. The woman who tried to answer my questions was one of those transplants from the Northeast who believe they are far, far better than anyone who has ever lived in any of the southern states. She smiled patronizingly while I explained what I wanted, then explained to me why that wouldn't be possible. I asked to see the manager. She told me she hardly thought that would be necessary. I told her she was right, she hardly thought, which was why I wanted to see the manager. Now. It turned out I couldn't have the glass until the day after tomorrow.

By the time I got back in the truck, I'd been gone from Dree's for two and a half hours. The hardware store and Radio Shack would have to wait. I parked outside the café and went in. No Tammy.

"Aud!" she said from Dree's station as I pushed open the door of the salon, "we were just wondering where you'd got to! Sorry it's taking so long but Dree had three people in front of me." She pointed at three bags lined up in the waiting area. "I even had time to do some shopping." But then she turned around to the mirror again and she and Dree went back to talking a mile a minute about Dree's mother, who according to Dree seemed to be getting weird in her old age, I mean like *different,* and Tammy totally agreed: that seemed to happen to moms at a certain age, they forgot they were *old.* It amazed me how people could bring out different facets of each other's personalities. It looked as though they would be a while.

"I'll be next door, in the café, if—"

"Oh, I'll be through in just a minute," Dree sang. "Why don't you wait?"

So I sighed and stayed and watched as the damp tangle around Tammy's ears turned into beautifully shaped hair, and they talked about some upcoming party or other. Then they were both standing, swatting chunks of hair off the nylon robe, dusting at Tammy's neck, admiring Dree's handiwork in the mirror.

"Tammy's been telling me all about your cabin!" Dree said. "You didn't tell me you were doing the work yourself."

"No. It's—"

"That's thirty-five dollars," she said to Tammy, then back at me, "Your cut's holding up well, but don't leave it more than another two weeks before you come in again."

"All my cash is gone," Tammy said. It had been my cash to start with. I handed over two twenties and two ones.

Dree put them in the till, then said, "Why don't you come tonight, too? It's your birthday after all, right?"

I stared at Tammy, but she didn't even look apologetic. "Dree's mother is having a party tonight. Dree wanted to know if I'd go with her."

"Yeah," Dree said, "everyone else will be fifty."

You don't know us, I wanted to say, What would your mother think? But then I remembered her mother was an ex-hippie woman-on-the-land feminist who had named her daughter after some Hindu earth mother figure, and it seemed clear that Tammy really wanted to go, and it was one way to not think about the New York police gathering clues, or a nine-year-old girl lying in bed alone at night wondering why no one loved her.

"It's just outside town," Tammy said. "Closer to the cabin."

"Come about seven," Dree said.

"What should we bring?" I asked her.

"Something to drink?" She didn't sound too sure.

"Perhaps if I knew what the party's for . . ."

"Well, you know. To have fun?"

"It's something they do every year," Tammy said. "Dree's mother and her old friends—about forty. Some bring guests, some don't. They like meeting new people, right Dree?"

Dree looked amazed at Tammy's summary, but I should have trusted Tammy to know everything she needed in order to bring, wear, and talk about the appropriate things.

"About seven then?" Tammy said to Dree. "And thanks for the cut."

She didn't thank me for paying for it, just picked up two of the bags and left the third for me to carry. It was the heavy one.

Tammy dropped the high school senior act as soon as we'd stowed the bags and entered the café. "What's good here?"

"I have no idea." But the chili and corn bread looked worth trying. Tammy decided on Caribbean quesadillas with avocado and pineapple.

I told her about the glass showroom, that we wouldn't be able to fit the windows for at least two days, and then tried to describe the bathroom fixtures I'd chosen. I found I wasn't very good at it. In the end, I got up and brought the catalogue from the truck.

"Very you," she said as she looked over the simple, turn-of-the-nineteenth-century reproductions, the lever taps with white porcelain handles, the deep, claw-footed tub, the wide, white-enameled kitchen sink. "Modern faucets for the kitchen, though, right?"

I nodded. "You can take authenticity too far."

We talked about bathrooms, how as a child she had longed for one like a pink palace, pink quartz floor, red gold taps with ruby inserts, pink fur rugs . . . "I'm not sure when the pink thing faded. A couple of years ago I wanted one of those industrial-looking places, you know: all steel and glass and straight lines. Black floor tiles, white porcelain."

Like a hospital room.

"Now I'm thinking something warmer: terra-cotta tile, plants, big old tub."

"Did you and Dornan . . ." I didn't finish the question. I had no idea why I'd begun it.

"Talk about setting up house? No. He wanted to but he never brought it up. I'd have run a mile. Did you and Julia?"

"No. It . . ." I shook my head. "No. It seemed so obvious we'd spend the rest of our lives together that we didn't even discuss it."

"So, you would have got back from Norway and argued about bathroom furniture."

I picked up the catalogue and traced the picture of the tub with my finger. "She might not have liked this."

"Who would have won?" Tammy was smiling, and just for a moment my memories of Julia were happy ones—watching her face in the Oslo art gallery as she explained Norwegian neo-Romanticism; pulling her to me when I was in the tub; frying freshly caught fish—free of a hovering sense of doom, free of guilt, free of anything but happiness, and I was able to smile back.

"She would."

"You want more coffee?"

I didn't, there was still the hardware store and Radio Shack to visit and the fixtures to load, but the sense of lightness and gladness, of being able to remember Julia without guilt, persisted, on and off, all afternoon: the perfect birthday gift.

I took another sip of the Woodward Canyon Reserve chardonnay—Tammy's choice; mine was rioja—and its smoky oak flavor distracted me for a minute from what the man standing opposite me near the fireplace was saying. His name was Henry something or other, an old-fashioned name for a man wearing aggressively fashionable glasses, slits that didn't seem big enough to see through.

". . . those days, not like Adrian"—Dree's mother—"and the rest of us."

"How long have you been here?"

"Not as long as the women's land collective. I came in '79. We started with nothing, not even common sense." He smiled as if to say, You know what it's like to be young and foolish, and I realized that I had not thought about Karp or New York for at least an hour.

"So how do you know Adrian?"

"Oh, I've known *of* her for about twenty years, but she and the others were rabid lesbian separatists until the mid-eighties." He gave the woman sitting on the tapestried couch on the other side of the room an affectionate look. Adrian was in her mid-fifties; her hand rested on the thigh of a man who appeared to be ten years her junior, and the looks they exchanged were frankly sexual. Now I understood Dree thinking her mother was getting, like, weird. "She's changed a lot then?"

"We all have."

There were about fifty people at the party, ranging in age from early sixties to early twenties, the older crowd's children. The atmosphere was one of village get-together: people who had known each other for decades, and been through economic, political, and emotional change. I tried to imagine them in tie-dye and beards, or working naked on the land, getting stoned and talking about the power of the patriarchal military-industrial complex, but all I could see were accountants and psychotherapists, the sons and daughters of middle America finally leading the kind of lives their parents would at least have understood, if not wholly approved. For that there would have to have been more wedding rings, more socks, and some meat among the Brie and smoked salmon and vegetable dip in the dining room.

I excused myself, and refilled my glass. Tammy stood to the right of Adrian's couch, talking to a man and woman in their twenties who were hand in hand. The man's blue eyes seemed vaguely familiar. I watched Tammy for a while; she wasn't touching the man on the arm, or giving him extra big smiles, or arching her back so that her breasts pressed against her thin sweater; she wasn't canting her hips and shoulders so that the woman was cut out of the conversation; she wasn't just a couple of inches too close. I stepped forward and she saw me.

"Aud!" She opened the circle. "This is Shari, and Ken, Dree's brother." That explained the eyes. I swapped my wine to my left hand and we exchanged handshakes and pleased-to-meet-you's. "Ken works for a construction company—"

"McCann, right?"

He smiled. "How did you know that?"

I pointed to my haircut. "Dree."

He smiled some more, but I saw how his hand stiffened in Shari's and thought he must get tired of Dree talking about him and his affairs to all and sundry.

"Like I was saying, Ken works for a construction company. I told him about the cabin and what kind of stove we were looking for, and he thinks he knows where we can find one. I told him we'd already tried that place on Merrimon."

Since when had there been a *we*?

"Tammy tells us you want something you can cook with," Shari said. She had long, honey-colored hair and beautifully shaped nails. "Maybe a wood-burning range is the way to go."

"Just a plain stove," I said. "Something along the lines of an old Intrepid, that'll heat the cabin—"

"—and boil a pan of water if necessary." Now Ken's smile was real. "We had one of those our first couple years up the mountain. That's *all* we had. Wonderful thing. Dree was just starting to crawl. I was seven. It was my job, while Mom was in endless collective meetings, to make sure Dree didn't stick her hand on it. Those puppies get *hot* when they're going! Wonder what happened to it." He literally shook himself, like a dog trying to get dry. "There are a couple places along Emma Road you might try. They supply me when I do independent contracting. Tell them I sent you and they might give you a discount."

"I will. But I don't know your last name."

"Johnson."

Son of John. "Bet Adrian didn't like that."

He grinned. "She changed our names to Moon for a while after she left Dad and dragged us up here, but never got around to making it legal, so at school Dree and I were always Johnson, and it just crept back. How about you? You sound British."

"Norwegian. Aud Torvingen."

Shari's mother, it turned out, was originally from Denmark. Shari had visited Copenhagen for the first time last year. Wonderful city. Did I know it?

At midnight, we were the only vehicle on the road.

"I liked that," Tammy said.

"Good."

"Did you?"

I thought about it. "Yes."

"I liked it a lot," she said. "I liked the people, the way it felt. It must be cool to live with people you've known for twenty or thirty years, to work in the same town where people went to school with your parents. Wonder what that feels like."

Stifling, probably.

She said wistfully, "They seemed like a real community."

"I didn't know you yearned for community."

"It just seemed . . . I don't know. Nice. Like they were really in each other's lives. It wasn't just that they all belonged to the same gym or something. They've got history together. These people know each other: they remember when which kid had what illness, when who split up with who in junior high and why. Ken told me stories about how they had to share everything the first few years. How they still do, sort of. They grew up together. I can't even remember the names of people I went to college with."

A community of necessity and proximity would probably drive her screaming into the sunset. "Most real community comes from shared hardship."

"Still. I think I could live here."

If it hadn't been such a narrow road, and dark, I would have turned to look at her. "I wouldn't have thought there were a lot of business development opportunities here."

"Now that's where you're wrong. Asheville is hot. Did you meet Jonas? Tall guy, gangly, beaky nose? He's a VP at Sonopress, and he was saying that the company gives money to the town, for stuff like the annual Bele Chere festival, and WCQS, and the local Arts Alliance, but that they want to do more, give the company a higher profile in the community. It sounds like a job I could do: get to know people, find out what people want, find a way to give it to them so everyone's happy."

"Yes. You'd be good at that."

"And"—she sounded as though she were smiling—"Sonopress is part of Bertelsmann."

"So if you get bored you can move up the parental corporate chain?" It began to make a bit more sense.

"Right. But it's not just that. I could really do that job, and I'd like it. I could get them to expand the community liaison stuff to other things—getting some of the bands whose CDs they press, or stars whose movies they put on DVD, to come to the festivals, maybe persuading some of the software writers to donate time to local schools. Whatever. It wouldn't be just about money."

"But meeting all those big names would be fun."

"Fun is good." Definitely smiling. "And it would be fun to get to know people who live here. Business development is lots of smiles and promises, but when you've got them to sign that deal, phht, that's it, you fly to another city and smile at someone else. This would be different, it would be the same people over and over. I'd be part of something. Yes"—out of the corner of my eye I saw her nodding to herself—"yes, I could live here."

Could I? Even if the police let me? I made the turn onto the ungraded mountain track. Stay in the world, Aud, she had said, and I had promised. I just wasn't sure which part.

CHAPTER ELEVEN

The rain beat steadily on the new windows and washed in a sheet over the handmade glass. Wavy water on wavy glass.

"Makes me seasick to watch it," Tammy said. "I still don't see why you paid so much money for bad glass."

We'd been over it; I wanted the cabin to be as close as possible to the way it might originally have been built, using handmade materials where possible. But glass had improved in the last ninety years, and I was beginning to think she might be right. At least we were weathertight.

"We should light a fire," I said.

"We don't have the stove yet."

"It would test the chimney."

While I built the fire Tammy watched, standing by the long counter and dry sink of what at some point would become the kitchen. The tub and pedestal sink leaned against the wall of what would be the bathroom, once I'd installed a pump house and a combination of solar panels and generator to power it. If Eddie didn't call. If Karp didn't wake up.

Smoke eeled up the chimney and disappeared satisfactorily. I added more kindling to the ancient cast-iron grate, waited for it to catch, and began to lay on logs. Four walls, a roof, sturdy door, glazed windows, and now heat. Almost livable. The flames grew, turned from blue to red at their center.

"It works."

I nodded. So far.

"Hey, we could eat here tonight, instead of the trailer. I'll go see what there is to cook."

The door squeaked as she closed it behind her. It might be that the hinges were slightly out of true, or just that they needed oiling, and at some point I would have to fix it, but at this moment I was more interested in the fire; I wanted it to be perfect: symmetrical, lively, just the right shape and color.

Tammy came back carrying the laundry basket; it was full of sacks of flour, and butter, some milk and bread and wine and what looked like my two cast-iron frying pans.

"It's a surprise," she said. She set to work, flouring the kitchen counter, pouring and measuring and kneading.

The fire roared. I used the tongs to unfold the iron bar hinged to the sidewall of the fireplace, and pulled it out across the flames. Like the fire, it gave me deep satisfaction. It had been a tricky bit of mortaring but now it was positioned just right to hang a pot or kettle over the flames—not that I'd need it once the kitchen had a range, or even when the stove was in place.

Tammy seemed to be making some kind of flat cake. "How much longer until the coals are hot enough to cook with?"

"Half an hour."

Runnel of rain on the roof, pop and hiss of green wood on the fire, slap and whisper of dough. I stretched out on the unfinished floor and let myself drift for a while. Noises from the kitchen counter changed: Tammy had half a dozen cakes lined up and had moved on to wrapping a variety of vegetables in aluminum foil.

Hot yellow nuggets piled above and below the grate. I raked a few onto the front hearth. They began to cool to orange and go gray around the edges. I raked them back. "Ready when you are."

The vegetables went in first. She held up the silvery packages one by one, "Corn, onions, butternut squash, sweet peppers," and put them in the fire. She got up again and brought back one of the skillets, covered with a wet cloth.

"That's my pillowcase."

"I had to get creative. I needed wet cloth."

Get creative. I could find out which hospital Karp was in. Go make sure he wouldn't wake up.

Tammy wrapped the cakes in the pillowcase, put them in the skillet, put the skillet to one side in the hearth, then raked a handful of coals and ash over the lot, just like something out of a Foxfire book.

"The cakes and the vegetables should cook a bit before the bacon goes on," she said. "I thought we'd have some wine."

I got up and found the bottle and glasses and corkscrew and brought them back to the fireplace. It was a good rioja. Tammy had been paying attention; it no longer surprised me.

The smell of applewood and roasting corn mingled with red wine as I poured. I handed Tammy her glass.

"To your cabin," she said. "May you have many dinners in front of this fire, with people you care for."

I couldn't see it, but I raised my glass, and drank.

She pushed up the sleeves of her sweater. "It got warm fast."

"Wood's a good insulator." Now that the windows were glazed and the fire working, the place was more or less livable as it stood. Hook up the toilet to the septic system, flush it using buckets filled at the pump outside. You'd have to leave before the snows, though, or stay until spring . . .

Karp's hospital room might be guarded.

"Tell me about those cakes you're cooking."

"Ash cakes. Ken was telling me about them at the party.

Some old toothless woman showed Adrian how, and Adrian showed Ken as soon as he could be trusted not to set the house on fire. That was when he was eight, he said. Or maybe nine. Anyhow, they're supposed to taste good—if they don't burn to a crisp. Which is where the wet pillowcase comes in. It sort of steams them at the same time, he said. Poor old Ken, keeping house at eight."

There were worse things. "What were you doing at that age?"

"Eight? Eight was when I learned to ride a bike. And how to fall off a pony." She laughed. "God, I wanted a pony so bad. Then my father took me to this riding school, where I found out that horses are big scary animals that stink and won't do as they're told, and it's a long way down if you fall off." She sighed. "I was Daddy's princess. That's what he called me, his princess. I think he liked it that I couldn't ride. It kept me his on some level. What about you?"

Self-analysis from Tammy. "I learned to ride when I was nine. In England. With the daughter of one of my mother's friends." Galloping over the Yorkshire moors, wild as a lynx, with Christie Horley. Another life I had left.

"You looked quite nostalgic for a while there."

"Nine is a good age," I said. By then I had realized that although my mother behaved as if she loved me, and maybe even wished that she did, she didn't. My father had been in Chicago that summer.

Tammy was studying me.

"What?"

"You used to scare me. You always scared me, even when Dornan was there. Always judging, and usually not in other people's favor. Not in mine, anyhow. But since you got back from—Since you got back, you've been different. That night, when—" She squirmed and glanced away. "It was a pretty sad seduction attempt, I know, totally embarrassing, but the way you reacted . . . I thought you were going to strangle me. You looked crazy. Not the kind of person you could ever imagine being nine years old. You seem more human now. And now I've embarrassed myself again. Jesus, it's hot in here." She put her glass down and pulled off her sweater. When she picked up her glass again, the wine was a rich red against the cream of her bodysuit—which, like the sweater and the wine, she had bought that morning in Asheville. It was strange, seeing her in clothes I had not bought or lent her, drinking wine she had selected without my advice, without needing me there.

"You're different, too."

"Yep. Since I— Well, I've learned plenty. The world can be big, and stink, and it hurts if you fall off, but hey, it's worth trying, mostly, and what doesn't kill you . . . Well, it doesn't kill you." She lifted her glass. "To learning experiences, even though they suck."

"To not being nine years old and at the mercy of the world." Like Luz.

She got up, came back with the second skillet. "Time to fry that bacon."

The bacon hissed and shrank and turned translucent, and when it browned we filled our plates with it, and corn and squash and onion, and the doughy-looking things that were the ash cakes. I tried one. It tasted of cinders. "It's good," I said. It's easy to lie to people you're leaving.

I ate deliberately: onion sweet and smoky and soft, corn bursting rich and yellow under my teeth, and the bacon melting in places but chewy in others. And then the plate was clean.

It didn't matter about Luz. She was nothing to do with me. Sending money was as much as I needed to do. More. I hadn't put her with the foster parents in Arkansas. I didn't have to help her, or any of the others—because, oh, suddenly it was so clear that there were others. Many, many others.

I stood up. "Wait there," I told Tammy.

Outside it was raining harder than ever, thick drops the size of raisins, but cold and hard, and it was quite dark. On the way back, I stuck the file in my shirt to keep it dry.

"You're dripping," she said when I returned.

I sat closer to the fire and pulled out the folder. She recognized it, but made no comment.

I opened it. "They've been very careful."

"Who?"

"The agency who handled all this." I fanned the sheaf of papers on the floor. "Not one mention of the agency name, not a single letter or fax or printed e-mail with a person's signature."

"Then how do you know there's an agency involved?"

"The bar code. The brochure. They're professionals. Someone is doing this a lot."

"They could be, you know, just a regular adoption agency."

"Adoption agencies don't usually farm out the adopted to foster parents."

"Jesus." She stared at the documents. "How many kids do you suppose there are?"

"I don't know." Dozens? Hundreds? Thousands?

I looked at the photograph. Only nine, learning that there was no love in the world. By now the agency might have heard about Karp. It's likely they would hand the girl over to some other pervert, for more money. That or leave her with the foster parents, who would dump her on social services once the regular checks dried up. All about money.

Tammy poured us both more wine. "So what are you going to do?"

"I don't know."

The wine was warm now from being by the fire, its taste as rounded and familiar as the roof of my mouth. It would be very easy to just finish this bottle, then start another, sleep soundly, and get up in the morning and go about my business, rebuilding this cabin, pretending to turn it into a home. Why had I hurt

Karp? Why wouldn't he just die? I laughed. I couldn't even make up my mind about that.

"I don't think it's funny," she said.

I didn't really care what she thought. I drained my glass and filled it with what was left in the bottle, ignoring her glass. I looked around at the cabin: the fire without its stove, the unconnected toilet, the dry kitchen. "We have to speed up the work here. I'll be taking the truck and trailer. If you want to stay out here, you'll need this place to be livable."

"What are you going to do? You don't have to rush. You can't. What about your knee?"

"My knee will be fine." I shoved the poker in the fire, stirred it about. Put the poker down. Picked it up again.

"I don't want to be here alone. I want you to stay."

"People don't stay just because you want them to." They never stayed.

"And why are you in such a rush anyhow? You could wait until spring. Why do you want to do it now?"

"I don't want to do it at all." I stood up, paced restlessly to the sink, the fireplace, back to the sink. "She's just some nine-year-old. Why should I care?" Back and forth. Back and forth. I stopped, standing over her. "Why the fuck should I care?"

She flinched, then glared at me. "So if you don't care, why are you shouting? Why don't you just run off in your trailer someplace and live happily ever after?"

"I can't."

"Why?"

Because running would mean closing up seamlessly, leaving everything behind, again. It would mean breaking my promise, acting as though Julia had never existed. I sat down hard, scrubbed my forehead with the heel of my hand.

"I'm sorry," I said. "I shouldn't have shouted."

"You keep saying you're sorry and you keep shouting at me."

I stared into the fire. Stay in the world, she had said, and this was the world I had made.

"Aud?" She touched my hand to make me look up. "I'm sorry I got you into all this."

"You didn't," I said tiredly. "Dornan did. Or Julia did, by dying. Or maybe I did, by loving her. It's all connected." Irony is rarely amusing. "Just one big happy human ecosystem, like the woods, with some trees trying to grow too fast and smother the rest."

"And you're the axe," she said.

The fire popped. An axe, cold and unlovely. "Is that really how you see me?"

The old Tammy would have smiled and said, No, of course not! and tried to reassure me, soothe my ruffled feathers, but though a fleeting regret showed in her sigh, she nodded. "You can use an axe to bang in nails, but that doesn't make it a hammer. It's still an axe. Cutting is still what it's made for."

The rain washed down the windows in an undulating sheet.

"Remember when you asked me why I didn't hit Geordie? It was because I don't know how. That little girl in Arkansas doesn't, either. You do. I know that. But do you have to go yourself? Or if there's no one else to send, do you have to go now? You could wait until I—"

She wrestled the old Tammy to silence. "I guess you want to leave as soon as you can."

Tammy had just gone into the bathroom to brush her teeth and I was already in bed when my phone rang.

"Congratulations," Eddie said. "Your boy's case has made it to the front page. Give me your number and I'll fax it."

"Just read it out."

"Very well. It's the usual tabloid banner—"

"Tabloid?"

"Just so. Not at all the sort of thing a respectable paper

would lead with. Did I misunderstand your request for follow-up?"

"No. What's the headline?"

" 'Avenger Twins Out For Blood,' with a crime scene photo filling the remainder of the page."

They wouldn't print a picture of Karp in that state. What had I left? "Describe it."

"Bloody handprints in a nice arc up the wall, body draped in a stained sheet and half covered in videocassettes, some of which are rather artistically unspooled over the victim's eyes."

A mock-up.

"The story itself is quite delightful. Another interview with the unbalanced young woman who claims to have been abused by the victim, this time with some interesting detail. Let's see. They're now calling Karp a serial abuser. Quotes from anonymous victims. A sick man, says one. An evil psychopath, says another. All very breathless. The real focus of the piece, however, seems to be these twins. At least on first pass. There's a sidebar—two sidebars. One headed 'Angels of Vengeance?' and the other 'Well-Versed Agents.' Two rather unattractive artists' impressions."

"What do they look like?"

"Sweet but moronic thugs: corn-fed football players who have found god."

"Even the woman?"

"Especially the woman."

"Police comment?"

"Just the official statement: 'We continue to pursue a variety of leads with all due diligence.' However, reading between the lines I'd say the *Daily Post* has an unofficially sanctioned source inside the department. They have a lot of hard information disguised as tabloidese. In sidebar one, that's the angel argument, if one can dignify such sloppy prose with that label, we're told that all the tapes have been wiped clean, as though by a powerful magnetic source 'not unlike that which could be produced by the healing auras said to emanate from saints.' There is said to be no sign of a struggle, and no blood visible to the naked eye except on the victim and his immediate surroundings. It contradicts the crime scene photo, of course, but no doubt they're assuming their readers have the average IQ of a second grader. But that's a very specific qualification, 'visible to the naked eye.' The kind of phrasing used by a careful police press liaison."

Or a prosecuting attorney.

"The second sidebar is equally informative. No fingerprints, they say, or, rather, four or five different sets, but none bloodstained."

I'd worn gloves every time.

"No sign of forced entry. Evidence of information theft: the photocopier was on, and when the police arrived, the laptop—which is supposed to switch to sleep mode after sixty minutes' nonuse—was fully powered." I'd missed that. "Evidence, too, of prior surveillance of the victim—a café waitress and a gallery owner apparently remember someone who could fit the description. There is some speculation—"

"When was the suspect seen in the café?"

"The day of the assault, apparently. The morning. Ah, now this is interesting, fuel for the angel argument, perhaps—no earthly sustenance, and so on. According to the witness, she drank only water."

I closed my eyes for a moment. Not the café where I had left the book, then, the book with the shiny cover that would hold fingerprints so well. "You were saying something about speculation."

"Indeed. Professionals, they think: the surveillance, the wiped tapes, no fingerprints, and the laptop. 'Sensitive documents,' they say darkly. In other words, industrial espionage."

Industrial espionage. That wouldn't make any difference one way or the other to the official NYPD investigation. It might involve some of Karp's corporate clients who would be anxious to discover whether confidential information about their retail operations had been leaked to the big wide world. A corporate security team would have more money and more time.

The toilet flushed. I didn't really want to talk about this in front of Tammy.

"I don't see what the *Post*'s interest is in all this." There were literally dozens of more sensational stories in New York every week.

"Do you remember the original witness, the woman who was with the victim?"

"I remember that there was one." And the shine and swing of her hair.

"Her name rang a bell, so I ran a search."

I waited grimly. There was no point trying to hurry Eddie when he was in this kind of mood.

"She's the daughter of the GOP's next senatorial candidate for the state of New York."

He paused, so I obliged. "And what's the *Post*'s editorial stance?"

"Oh, very good. As yet uncommitted."

"I see."

"Precisely. One suspects the entire story—espionage flim-flam, avenging angels, juicy hints of sexual perversion and all—is being built to keep reader interest alive, without annoying either the Democrats or Republicans, until the *Post*'s publisher makes up his mind which way to jump—that is, until he can work out which party could do him more favors on the Hill. Was she consorting with an evil abuser, and therefore probably a pervert herself, in which case what does that say about her father? Or was she an innocent involved with a sweet man who—"

Politics. Nothing to do with me.

"—all vastly entertaining."

Unless, of course, the police had evidence they weren't talking about: if they had found the book, or Karp had woken up.

"Any information on a change in Karp's—the victim's—condition?"

"I don't— Ah, here we go. He is now in a persistent vegetative state, which they helpfully translate for the reader as 'a permanent vegetable.' The patient's doctors won't comment on his condition in any detail, but 'a consultant hired by the paper' to review information already in the public domain says he would be surprised if the man lived another week, even with all the artificial assistance, which in his view is a needless waste of . . . yadda yadda yadda . . . oh, and he seems to think that as soon as the hospital finds a relative they'll see if they can get permission to switch him off. He won't survive that, the expert says, and even if he does, and I quote—where do they come up with these people?—he'd have the mental capacity of a Twinkie."

Another metal bed in another white room.

We drove to Asheville the next morning, Tammy chattering, me answering in monosyllables.

I bought bedding, and a bed, plus armoire and dresser, and a couch, and mirror, shelving, a garbage can, and half a hundred other items.

"You don't have to do this just for me," she said, not meaning a word of it, but they were all things I'd need to get at some point.

On the way back we stopped at a car rental place, where I suggested something with four-wheel drive, enough horsepower to carry her up and down the mountain roads, and the weight to keep her safe if the snow came early.

"Why, how long do you think you'll be gone?"

"I don't know. A week or two. It's hard to say." Hard to say because apart from the fact that I would drive to Arkansas and learn how the girl was being treated, I had no idea what I was going to do. Tammy said nothing but she got that pinched look that meant she was afraid.

"You know people here now," I reminded her. "Now, how about a Subaru wagon?"

The bed and chest went up into the loft easily enough, but the armoire took some maneuvering up the narrow stairs. Tammy grunted in satisfaction when we lifted it into place. "I've never been so strong." She flexed her right biceps, then looked around. "Needs a rug."

We stayed up late that night, Coleman lamps burning, while Tammy hammered up shelves and I hooked up the toilet and stove. By the time I carried in a bucket of water and flushed the toilet successfully, Tammy was wiping down the shelves and arranging food and crockery to her satisfaction. The bears would be hibernating about now and wouldn't cause any trouble.

Dinner was canned split pea soup heated on the stove, and crookedly cut bread. Tammy had a way to go before becoming a domestic goddess. We opened the stove door and pulled the couch up to dine in comfort. We ate silently until Tammy was wiping the inside of her bowl with a hunk of bread. She wouldn't have been caught dead doing that six months ago. A new Tammy, the tentative beginnings of a new life. But there were still a few threads from the old that needed to be dealt with.

"You'll have to call Dornan sooner or later," I said. "You should have called him days ago."

"I know."

"What will you tell him?"

"What will *you* tell him?"

"That I found you in SoHo and brought you back. Anything else is up to you."

She nodded, and we watched the tiny, captive flames.

It's a thousand-mile drive from Asheville to the Arkansas River Valley; I would have liked an early start, but I slept like the dead in the prewinter quiet and woke late, and then it took three hours to make the trailer ready for a long drive. And when all that was done, I found myself still unwilling to leave.

"If you decide to go," I said to Tammy over one last cup of coffee in the cabin, "make sure the place is clean, and leave a note so I know where you've gone, and when." I didn't want to be worrying that she had got herself into trouble again.

"Or I could just call," she said.

"Yes," I agreed, but I knew she wouldn't. Notes left to be discovered were easier. She shivered. "And don't stint yourself on firewood. There's plenty. And if you need anything else, I've left some money—"

"In the top drawer of the dresser. I know."

Then there was nothing to do but wash the coffee mugs and climb into the truck. As before, Tammy directed me out so I didn't end up in the ditch. The truck pointed down the track, the trailer was straight behind me, Tammy waved. I waved back, then leaned out of the window.

"Call him, Tammy." She nodded noncommittally. I wound the window up and put the truck in gear.

CHAPTER TWELVE

I headed west on I-40 at a steady sixty-five miles an hour, through the rounded hills of Tennessee, and the town names tolled in my head—Knoxville, Crossville, Cookeville. Before I got to the country-western smugness of Nashville I began to wonder if *-ville* was a not-so-secret indicator of poverty and a particular lack of taste, or at least zoning control, as evidenced by billboards crowded up against the interstate like long-legged cockroaches swarming a line of molasses.

"Ah, Tennessee, it never changes," Julia said from the passenger seat. She looked around, shook her head, faced me. "So, what's the plan?"

I squeezed the steering wheel. "Just like that, what's the plan?"

She tilted her head. "You sound angry."

"Yes." And I was, and it frightened me, because I was angry with her. "You left me. And when you come back, instead of helping me, you say I'm a borderline, not a real person inside."

"I didn't call you a borderline—"

" 'Who does he remind you of?' you said."

"—I asked you to ask yourself, honestly, how you used to see yourself, before you met me."

"Before you came along and worked your magic and turned me into a real human being?" It came out sounding half angry, half desperate.

"You know better than that."

"I don't know what I know anymore. I'm so . . . Everything's changed."

"You've changed. That's what I wanted you to realize the other night."

"What if I want to change back?"

Her smile was sad. "Doesn't work that way."

She reached out as if to touch me, and for a second I thought I felt her fingers on my cheek, then realized I was crying. "It's so hard, without you." Help me, I wanted to say, stop this terrible ache.

"Road," she said, and nodded at the CAUTION signs and the grooved road where the surface had been ripped off to prepare for a new layer of asphalt. Tires roared over the striations. I had to concentrate to keep the trailer in its lane.

"Why did you bring that thing, anyway?" she said.

"Cheaper than motels."

"Since when have you worried about money?"

I just shook my head. The roadworks ended and we were now on velvety new blacktop. The wheel noise faded to a smooth hum.

"So," she said. "Tell me what the plan is when you get to Arkansas."

"I won't know. Not until I see how they—the Carpenters—are treating her." I made an effort. "As far as I know, she's not on anyone's radar. No one is looking for her, no one even knows she exists, except the Carpenters and whoever placed her with them. If I decide to take her out of there, no one will complain."

"So what will you do with her, if you take her?"

I hadn't the faintest idea.

"Would you keep her?"

"What for, target practice?" Silence. "No, I wouldn't keep her. Not even if she was a normal, well-adjusted child—and what she's been through has probably left her essentially broken. Broken people, as we both know, don't mend."

She studied me for a moment. "Pull over. There's a rest stop ahead."

When the engine was quiet I rolled down the window; it was cold. A hardy chickadee sang from the pines alongside the rest stop. The place smelled of freshly sawn wood. She swiveled to face me.

"Self-pity doesn't suit you."

"No?"

"You are not broken."

"Normal people don't hurt others in elevat—"

"Let me finish. You're not broken, you're grieving. You're grieving because you can feel. No, your mother didn't love you, and yes, you pretended you didn't care, but pretending doesn't make it true."

"Then—"

"Don't be dense. You were protecting yourself. You wrapped yourself in armor and pretended to be invulnerable. Growing up inside that armor twisted you a bit out of true, but it doesn't matter. The essentials are all there."

She searched my face.

"The armor's getting too small, Aud. You have to choose."

Tennessee had not exactly oozed wealth, but when I pulled off the interstate west of the river for something to eat, eastern Arkansas under the winter-pale late afternoon sun—the gas stations, the shacks with TV antennae, other vehicles on the road, even the dirt—sighed tiredly with poverty, worn and faded as though it had been through too many summers without shade, too many growing seasons without replenishment, too great a workload with no relief. Perhaps it was my mood, but I felt heavier just driving through it.

Once I was back on the interstate, the road became bland and boring. Towns like truckstops punctuated some fallow farmland and a few plowed fields. A hundred miles west of Memphis, the towns gave way to the river valley. I left I-40 twenty-five miles past Little Rock and wound west through backcountry roads, where settlement grew a little less dense and the countryside hillier, shrouded here and there with clumps of pine. For a seven-year-old fresh from the color and noise of Mexico City, it must have looked bleak.

But seven-year-olds are plastic, almost endlessly adaptable. Perhaps Luz no longer remembered much about Mexico; perhaps she no longer spoke Spanish; perhaps she was dull and content to follow her fate. Perhaps I should have stayed in North Carolina instead of driving out here in what was probably a hopeless cause.

The yellow lines slipping beneath my wheels dimmed to lemon, then dust, then disappeared altogether. The wheels hissed on loose gravel, and something in the trailer began to rattle rhythmically. Should have run, should have run, should have run. After an hour the pine and white oak grew thick and I was in the corner of a state park. I turned onto the first track I saw, and bumped along at twenty miles an hour until it grew dark enough to need headlights. Then I pulled over and turned the engine off.

The forest was still and quiet and smelled of pine needles. My breath sounded soft and even. I had the overwhelming urge to put my head on my arms and sleep. It wouldn't solve anything but it would make the questions go away for a while.

Who had the right to choose for a nine-year-old girl? Her parents? There had been no mention of a father, and her mother had already lost her, in all probability had given her away, exchanged her for money—even assuming she was still alive. Her adoptive father? He had forfeited any rights he might have had. Her foster parents? They were doing it for money. The state? They could offer nothing but deportation or a children's home, and I had seen jails and psychiatric units and emergency rooms full of the product of the latter. And the girl herself? I had no idea.

I had to go see for myself. And if I saw she was being mistreated, I would not be able to simply turn around and leave and pretend none of this had ever happened. I would always wonder what I could have done, and inevitably I'd imagine Karp on his hospital bed and remember all those things I didn't want to ever have to think about again.

Luz existed, a responsibility I didn't want, resulting directly from my own actions. Perhaps my mother had felt the same way. I imagined a little brown-haired girl skipping along the pavement, holding the hands of her parents: me on one side, Geordie Karp on the other.

On the way to the Carpenters' address, I passed two other vehicles, both full-size pickups. Both drivers stared for a moment, then raised an index finger from the steering wheel in acknowledgment. Big rigs were probably common in this part of the world. I could have been coming from anywhere, heading for anywhere else; I wasn't worried. The road, graded and graveled by the county, wound through low hills. I saw no more vehicles. The turnoff to the Carpenter place was nothing but a dirt road, marked by a wooden board—their name and an arrow—that looked freshly repainted. I drove past and up a rise, and pulled into a stand of trees.

Some of the Carpenters' fields lay bare, but judging from the neat rows of stubble, they were hayfields, bales long since sold. Clover and redtop stippled the field nearest the house, which looked tidy and cared for. It was painted light tan, probably three or four bedrooms, the kind of thing families had begun in the twenties and added to when time and money allowed.

From around the side three people—one large and two small, carrying bundles—came into view and climbed into the cab of a pale blue pickup. A Ford. I lifted a pair of field glasses and watched them jounce down the dirt track towards the county road. One adult and two children, all on the bench seat in the front. The early morning sun slanting in from the east and south turned their windscreen to fire, making it hard to be sure, but as they came over the slight rise I thought the one in the middle might be Luz. Yes. She was smiling while the boy on her right, whose face was lower down than hers, talked a mile a minute. It was a good smile.

I couldn't get in the house because Adeline Carpenter was still there, and you can't tail a vehicle when you're towing several tons of fifth-wheel, but tomorrow was Sunday.

The next morning I left the trailer at a campsite and drove back to the Carpenters', where I parked my truck off the road, just below the rise, invisible from the house. I put what I needed in a pack and climbed the hill. It was a mild day for November, in the high fifties. I unrolled my camping mat, poured tea from the thermos, and opened a Sara Wheeler book about Antarctica. Read, relax, and wait. Everything was planned, every eventuality taken into consideration; I had nothing to worry about. After a while I closed the book and watched the sky.

The sound of a truck engine blew like dust into my daydream of mariachi bands and black-haired, snapping-eyed Mexican girls parading their finery in the town square. I rolled onto my stomach. The field glasses showed four people on the bench seat of the Carpenters' pickup. Five minutes after they drove by, I was pulling up on the bare dirt in front of their house. Up close, I saw that although the siding wasn't exactly peeling, it wouldn't hurt to retouch the paint, at least on the southern side. Pink chrysanthemums brightened the doorstep in tubs to either side. I put on my new gloves; they smelled of leather.

No dogs. I called out, waited. Nothing. The first farm I'd ever been to without animals. The lock took less than a minute. I took my pack inside.

The hallway was wide and warm. An embroidery sampler hung behind glass on the wall opposite the stairs. *Do unto others . . .* The colors on the lower left had faded, as though it had once hung in strong sunlight. There was no scriptural attribution—something I would have expected in a fundamentalist household—and the unfinished phrase seemed sinister. The kitchen was in the back. Watery winter sunlight glittered on the still-wet white enamel sink; the last time I'd seen one of those had been more than twenty years ago, in a poor town in Yorkshire. Beef and vegetable stew with dumplings simmered in a crock pot next to the stove. A bright red coffee mug stood half full on a large sixties dining table that was topped with yellow-and-blue Formica. It was the kind of kitchen where a lot of family conversations happen. I stuck the first receiver to the underside of the table.

Upstairs, there were four bedrooms, one large and one small on each side of the hallway. In the large one on the front side of the house, a sewing table and Singer were pushed up against the wall under the window. Someone was making a pair of child-sized pajamas from blue-and-white-checked flannel. A long, plain table with two wooden chairs faced another, smaller table and single chair. Home schooling. A map of the world, still depicting the USSR and Ceylon, hung behind the teacher's chair, and the rest of the walls were covered in bright children's pictures. Some were huge, incomprehensible splashes of orange and brown and yellow, but many were careful pencil drawings—a house with a picket fence, a church, a lopsided rose, a cat, a cow—and still others neat, geometric patterns drawn in felt-tip pen, painstakingly colored between the lines. Which were done by which child? There was one painting in the same careful style as the pencil drawings: a river with bright birds in stiff-looking trees and hills with tiny buildings in the background. One of the buildings had the arched windows and big doors, the sloping roof of a Catholic church. So. A bookcase contained several versions of the Bible, and a variety of children's Christian books. *The Young Lady's Guide to House and Home. What God Hath Wrought,* which seemed to be an earnest explanation of the Creation. There were also reading primers, and several fiction books with Plaume City Library stamps, such as volumes two and three of the Narnia series. C. S. Lewis seemed a bit exotic for a Church of Christ household. On a high shelf, out of a child's reach, sat a set of Collier's encyclopediae. I checked the copyright date: 1961. The first volume seemed to be missing. A small cupboard next to the sewing machine was locked.

Down the hall, with a view of fields, I was greeted in the smaller room by a wallful of cheerful young-boy motifs: cartoon steam trains and cowboys and Indians. The bedside lamp could not be reached from the bed, and a small wire cage made it impossible to tug the plug from the socket. Not the usual precautions for a seven- or eight-year-old. The armchair next to the single bed looked old and well used. The drawers did not spill clothes; no toys or gadgets cluttered the floor; no stacked music system or computer sat on shelves against the wall. Poverty, or perhaps just an empty mind. Next door, the parents' room held a double bed with a mattress that should have been replaced years ago, and an unremarkable, cheap dresser. Like the boy's room, it was clean and neat, with one of every necessity, but everything was worn, or old-fashioned, and the only luxury was a silver-backed dresser set of hairbrush, comb, and mirror, whose perfect centering before the mirror made them treasured possessions. The design was something from the seventies, perhaps a wedding present. The rag rug was relatively new: handmade. I imagined Adeline Carpenter sitting in front of the mirror, brushing out her hair before bed, talking, and I put the second receiver under the lip of the dresser.

Luz had a tiny room, with a narrow bed that faced the window with its view of scrubby Arkansas countryside and minor road. No chair here for a mother sitting in the dark, watching over her child. On the bedside table sat the fourth Narnia book. The lamp next to them worked. The long nightdress folded neatly on the pillow was made of the same blue-and-white check I'd seen in the schoolroom. The foster daughter may have got the worst room, but she had the first nightclothes. Interesting. I put the third receiver behind the headboard; maybe Luz sometimes talked to herself.

I found the missing encyclopedia under the mattress. A scrap of paper divided *atlatl* (an implement used for hurling spear or lance) from *atmosphere* (the gaseous envelope surrounding the earth). I thought of all the households in this country that would rejoice at a child's ferocious need to learn, of the fact that this book had been hidden away, and wanted to push Adeline Carpenter's face into the stew to boil along with her dumplings.

The booster transceiver went in the pot of chrysanthemums by the front door. On the way back to the trailer, I threw the barbiturate-saturated hamburger into a convenience store Dumpster.

According to the Arkansas Church of Christ's website, Sunday services in Plaume City ran from ten-thirty to one. It seemed like a long time to expect children to sit still, but it gave me the opportunity to change and drive the twelve miles to the church well before the end of services. Small communities tend to be suspicious of outsiders, and while my conservative clothes might escape casual attention while I was on church property, a woman on her own driving such a truck would not. Once everything was in place, it wouldn't matter; until then, I couldn't be too careful. I parked half a mile down the deserted road and walked the rest of the way with my oversize gas can and plastic tubing. If I saw anyone, they might assume I'd run out of gas and was walking to the nearest service station.

I have lived more than a third of my life in this country, but still, to me, the word "church" conjures images of tenth-century Norwegian stave churches, taller than they are long, or the Gothic cathedrals of England and France with their soaring stone buttresses and tall, slitted windows, and naves echoing with history. The red-brick, one-story Plaume City Church of Christ stood by the side of a road running from nowhere to nowhere, and, with its square windows and orderly parking lot, looked more like a library or care facility for the elderly than a church.

The parking lot was half full: as many midsize American sedans as pickups. I found the Carpenters' pale blue Ford and left the gas can and tubing in its cargo bed.

The congregation was singing a cappella, but they stopped just before I reached the entrance. The main doors stood wide, so did the inner doors, probably because of the overefficient heating system: even in the vestibule it was too hot. It looked like a full house, eighty or ninety people in their Sunday best, nodding every now and again, with the occasional "Amen!" or "Yes, Lord!" when the preacher hammered on his lectern for emphasis.

He was on a roll, voice following the rise-and-fall, call-and-response cadence first brought to this country by Africans torn from their homeland and now used by fundamentalists of all colors. It wasn't easy to follow, but after a while, amid the litany of biblical references, I found that he was preaching a modern version of the Good Samaritan, only in his version it seemed that the Good Lord saw nothing wrong in the Samaritan getting paid for his kindness. "Now when the Lord says 'Do unto others as you would be done by,' He's not sayin' you should give away your pension, He's not sayin' take that money you saved to help out your son's new wife who is in the family way and hand it over to some homeless person, no, He's sayin' play nicely with the other folks. You have to use your judgment, your God-given wisdom. Maybe that man is homeless for a reason, maybe it's a punishment from God. Maybe he has some lessons to learn. And charity begins at home, with your own flesh and blood."

I looked at the congregation, the nodding heads with their careful parts and poverty-dulled hair, and doubted more than five percent had the kind of job that came with a pension. It seemed more likely that the preacher was trying to convince himself; maybe when he counted up the takings every Sunday his conscience bothered him.

But I'd seen all I needed to see. If they were only as far along as the sermon, they would be there at least another thirty minutes. I only needed ten.

The Carpenters' pickup was fifteen years old, made long before Detroit started building in all the electronic antitheft details that make modern vehicles a challenge to break into. It took less than ten seconds to pop the door, then the gas tank, and another five to feed in the thin hose. I always forgot how long it takes to suck, suck, suck on the tube and get the gas moving. At least with the clear plastic you could see the gas when it welled up; if you were quick and skilled, you didn't get that stinging mouthful. While the can filled, I looked through the pickup's cab and the toolbox in the bed: all my preparation would come to nothing if Jud had a can full of gas stowed away.

I'd brought a seven-gallon container but the gas kept coming. It crept past the three-quarters mark. I didn't want to leave any in the tank, but I couldn't just let it spill on the asphalt because the Carpenters would smell it, and the first thing they'd do was check the fuel gauge. I had begun to wonder if I'd have to break into the tan Chrysler next to the pickup and siphon the remaining gas into that tank when the flow stopped with an inch or two to spare. I moved the tube around a bit in the tank, just in case it sloped, and sucked again, but it was more or less dry.

The old Fords were gas-guzzlers. The Carpenters wouldn't get more than three or four miles before the engine gave out.

The full can probably weighed about forty pounds. I lugged it around the back of the church and hid it and the tubing by the Dumpster, where it was sure to be found in a day or so. By the time I was done, my knee had begun to ache.

I touched my throat through its concealing scarf. This was not New York. Everything would go smoothly, according to plan.

The blue pickup made it further than I'd expected before it sputtered and jerked and died: nearly five miles. A minor detail. I watched through the field glasses as Jud unscrewed the cap to the gas tank and peered in. Then he walked the two hundred yards they'd just covered, and back again, looking at the road. Then he got down on his hands and knees and peered up at the undercarriage. He did that for a long time. By the time he had the hood up, I was pulling in beside them and rolling down my window.

"Afternoon," I said.

His face looked like a piece of old hardwood left too long in the sun, his eyes pools of baked tar. His suit was at least ten years old, and made for a wider man.

"Looks like you might be having a problem. Anything I can help with?"

Perhaps he found it hard to talk up to a woman in a big truck.

"Gas," he said, eventually.

I climbed down, careful to let my legs bend a little to minimize my height. I nodded at Adeline and the two children, who peered at me from the truck. Luz, in a dark green dress that didn't suit her, watched me steadily, but the boy's eyes wandered after a moment. "Lonely out here. Not the best place to get stranded with your family."

Adeline stuck her head out of the window. "He filled the tank just yesterday," she said.

"I could run you or your wife to the nearest gas station, if that would help." Jud looked at me with his dark, sticky eyes. "Or if you live nearby I could drive you home. If that would be easier." If I read him right, he didn't want his wife to be alone with a stranger, or to leave his family stranded in the middle of nowhere. But he didn't say anything. Us standing in the middle of the road staring at each other was not part of the plan.

Adeline got out. "Luz, stay in the truck with Button." She stepped between me and her husband. Like her husband's, her clothes were old-fashioned, a matching dress and shoes in aquamarine: bought years ago, rarely worn, and looked after with care. Her bright red lipstick couldn't hide the fatigue in her smile. "We live six, seven miles north and west of here, off of Route 10. We would be sorely grateful if you would give us all a ride back."

"I'd be more than happy."

She smiled again briefly. "Luz, bring my purse. Button, come on out. Into the nice lady's truck. No, in the back, scoot up, leave room for me. Your daddy will sit in the front."

Jud, moving very deliberately, dropped the hood, retrieved the ignition key, shut but didn't lock the pickup doors, and got in next to me. I started the truck.

"Mile down the road," he said. "Then take a right." He laid both hands palm down on his thighs and stared steadily ahead, like the seated pharaonic statues at Luxor. His hands were tan on the back, with the flat tendons and knobbed joints of hard physical labor, and there was a trace of oil under two of his fingernails. When I glanced down again, he had put them in his lap, right hand uppermost; the knuckle on the third finger was crushed, long ago by the looks of it—the kind of thing that happens if you punch someone in the head, or hit a wall with your bare fist.

I drove. Two minutes later Jud said, "Here," and we made

the turn. I couldn't think of a single thing to say. Nor, it seemed, could anyone else. The next ten minutes passed in silence, until I pulled up in front of their house. I turned the engine off.

"Obliged," Jud said, and got out, and went into the house without another word.

Adeline paused, half out of her door. "It's just his way," she said, apologetic. "I hope you'll still be willing to give him a ride to a gas station."

"I'd be happy to."

She hesitated, and I thought she was about to introduce herself, but then she said, "He might be a minute or two. Would the wait be too much trouble? You've been so kind."

"It's a nice enough day and I can't say I'm in a hurry." And the Good Samaritan will demand payment.

She got out and the children scrambled after her. "You go change your clothes and play in back," she told them, and went into the house. But the boy seemed unable to tear himself away from the truck. He patted the paintwork, then squatted down to look at something. Luz hung back, not wanting to get too close to me, unwilling to leave Button alone.

I got out and stretched. The boy was unscrewing the dust caps from my tires.

"I'm Button," he said in a shiny voice, looking up at me. "What are these for?"

"Pleased to make your acquaintance, Button." His teeth looked huge, adult teeth in a child-sized mouth. Just like any seven-year-old. "They're to stop dust from getting in the air valve and clogging it up. I'll need them back." But he wasn't listening; his eyes were wandering again, gaze alighting on this, flitting to that. "Button—"

"That's not his real name." I turned to the girl with the quiet, precise voice. "His real name is Burton, only he can't say it right, so now we call him Button. He's eight. Nearly nine," she said carefully, waiting to see how I'd react: a nine-year-old should be able to say Burton.

"I'm surprised," I said. She turned her head slightly, to examine me out of each eye, as though each saw a different world but only one could be trusted. Her straight, shoulder-length hair was a dense, matte chocolate brown, and would have looked better without the amateur cut. Delicate bones contrasted with the stance; she stood the way a Theban might at Thermopylae. Nine years old. "I'm pleased to make your acquaintance also," I told her, "though I don't know your name."

"I'm Luz. It's Spanish. It's not short for Lucy."

"My name is Aud, rhymes with loud. It's Norwegian. It's not short for Audrey."

"Aud," she said, trying it out. I blinked at the perfect Norwegian pronunciation. "Aud."

"You say it very well."

She accepted the praise as her due, and opened her mouth to say something, but shut it when the front door opened.

Adeline had wiped away her lipstick and swapped her pumps for tennis shoes. An apron covered the dress. Judging by her hair—blond going gray, and pulled back in a short but thick tail—and the smile lines around mouth and eyes, other lines in neck and forehead, she was in her early fifties. Her eyes were not strange, but she was recognizably Button's mother. Or grandmother. "Button, in the house." Button wasn't listening. "Luz, take Button in and get yourselves changed."

"Yes, Aba."

We both watched them go inside. "Now," she said, turning to me. I got the impression she had spent some time thinking about what to say. "My husband is getting out of his Sunday clothes and will be back down directly. It's his way to be a bit wary of strangers, but he would be most obliged for a ride to a gas station. I can't tell you how thankful we are for your kindness. The name's Carpenter. Adeline and Jud." She held out her hand. Plain, thin wedding ring; straight-edged nails with no polish. Hardworking hands, but not overworked.

"Aud," I said, giving it a deliberate American pronunciation:

sounds like god. I took off my gloves. "Aud Thomas." We shook hands. I put the gloves in my pocket.

"Now, Aud Thomas, although men make fun of us women and the time it takes to change, I think my husband might be a minute or two." She patted the pocket of her apron nervously. "Is there something I can bring out for you meanwhile?"

Being parked on the doorstep was not what I had planned.

"If I'm to wait a minute or two, I'd like to borrow the use of your facilities if I may."

Natural suspicion warred with Christian charity. She patted her pocket again. A weapon? It would have to be a small one. I shivered a little. That and the morning's sermon turned the tide. She stood to one side and motioned me across the threshold. "Upstairs, first on your right." Then, in a rush of overcompensation, "When you're done I'm in the kitchen. In back."

The bathroom was what I think of as southern feminine: clean, decorated in pastels, and with a shower curtain depicting sunrise over a perfect valley, complete with Bambi look-alike and rabbits. I used the toilet, washed my hands, and ran my fingers through my hair. What did someone like Adeline Carpenter see when she looked at me? No way to know, just as I didn't know why I had used my real name with Luz.

I turned away, then back again, and opened the bathroom cabinet. On the top shelf lay the explanation for the lack of pets: asthma medication. Pills, and two kinds of inhaler. Adeline's.

I used a towel to wipe down everything I'd touched.

"Poured you some coffee," Adeline said as I went into the kitchen. The same red mug, steaming now, stood at one end of the Formica table. At the other end, Luz and Button, now in identical worn corduroy pants, ate from already half-empty bowls of beef and vegetable stew. Adeline patted at her apron, utterly unconscious of the gesture. Asthma medication.

I sipped. "Tastes good." Luz looked up and studied me for a moment, then turned her attention back to her lunch.

"That's a big truck you've got there," Adeline Carpenter said.

"Only thing big enough to pull my trailer, a fifth-wheel. I'd planned to vacation up around Petit Jean, or maybe Lake Maumelle."

"Awful late for a vacation." Suspicion seemed to be winning again.

I touched my throat, just enough to show the healing gash, and then my waistband, which hung more loosely than it had. "I've . . . I spent some time this summer in the hospital." Poor pitiful Aud Thomas, probably has the cancer, yet she still takes time to play Good Samaritan to those in need.

The children finished their stew. Button wiggled in his chair, but Luz, although she looked down at a chip in the Formica as though it fascinated her, was listening to our conversation.

"Luz, take Button out back."

"Yes, Aba."

Aba. Some weird fundamentalist title? "Great kids," I said.

"Jud and I had Button late in life. He's . . . he's not quite right, but he's a blessing from the Lord."

"His sister, too."

Adeline Carpenter smiled. "She's as good as gold with that boy." She sounded proud, as if she really cared. If I hadn't known how she was being paid to train this girl, I might have believed her. Her smile disappeared suddenly as she remembered she was talking to a stranger. She drummed her fingers on the table, blushed when she caught me watching. Maybe that was something good Christian ladies weren't supposed to do. "Well, Miz Thomas, I don't know what's keeping my husband, but if you want to take your coffee outside and sit in the sun, I'll go see if I can find him."

I left by the front door, but walked around to the back. It must have been nearly sixty degrees outside, and the sunshine was a little bolder. The cabin in the clearing would be lit by sun, too, but probably fifteen or twenty degrees cooler. Be present.

Pay attention. I breathed deeply, exhaled, breathed in: Arkansas soil; the thin, crumbly smell of mold formed on hay stalks that have been sodden but are now dry; and, faint in the still air, the pine scent of the woods. Luz and Button were nowhere in sight.

The barn was big and old and the right-hand side was cluttered with farm machinery: half modern, half the broken, rusting remains of seventy years of automated progress. Sunlight streamed in through the open door and through chinks in the eaves. A child's steady voice, and another, interrupting, came from behind a truck of forties vintage. I moved closer. The truck had no wheels, and was filthy with rust and dirt and rodent droppings, but its headlights were intact, round and clean and shining. Luz spoke in Spanish.

"—y por eso la Virgen María fue una reina que vivía en una catedral. Ella fue la reina de cielo, y ella fue linda, con una vestimenta azul junto con diamantes en el dobladillo—"

And so the Virgin Mary was a queen who lived in a cathedral. She was the queen of heaven, and she was pretty, with a blue dress that had diamonds on the hem.

I moved quietly until I could see Button sitting with legs splayed before him, playing with something on the floor. The words meant nothing to him; perhaps he found the rhythm soothing. Luz's eyes seemed far away, but every now and again she glanced at the boy to make sure he was close by.

"It's a horse!" Button said, holding up what looked like an ancient threaded bolt.

"Yes," Luz said in English, and patted him on the head. He went back to playing. She resumed her tale. "Y la virgen reina escucha en caso que rezas. Y cuando mueras vas a su palacio en cielo, que tiene tantos colores lindas y lo huele a . . . a flores. Y cirios se quemarsen en grutes, y huelen bien también."

And the virgin queen listens if you pray. And when you die you go to her palace in heaven, which is such pretty colors, and smells like flowers. And there are candles in grottoes, and they smell good too.

It was a six- or seven-year-old's vocabulary, apart from *grotto.* Her native tongue. I couldn't understand how she had retained so much. Adeline Carpenter would not approve of the Virgin Mary being called the queen of heaven, nor of any talk of cathedrals and incense and diamonds.

"El palacio es— Button, put that down." She sounded so much older speaking English. Button had found something on the floor he liked. He stood up and carried it into the closest column of sunlight. It glittered. "That's very pretty. Let me see." She held out her hand. He handed it over reluctantly. A piece of old bottle glass. She sighed, just like Adeline. "Glass, Button. Glass. What did Aba tell you about glass? It might hurt you. If you see it on the floor, don't pick it up."

"Glass," he muttered, unconvinced, but then something else caught his eye, and Luz sighed again.

"Fue un relato agradable," I said—it was a nice story—and her head whipped round. "You don't need to be afraid."

"I don't understand you," she said in English.

"Yes you do," I said, still in Spanish. "I won't tell anyone. I promise. Not even Aba."

She opened her mouth, then thought better of it and shut it again. Her eyes narrowed. I'd seen that look on a hundred suspects' faces: I would get nothing from her.

She was still studying me. "You talk different when no one else is around."

Careless again. The child was smart; pointless trying to lie to her now. "So do you."

"Why?"

"Why do you?"

I watched her work out that we both had things to hide. She decided she wanted to keep it that way. "Button!" she called. "How about we go indoors for some milk?"

"Milk?"

"Milk," she said firmly, with a look at me. I was briefly tempted to wring her neck.

"But I want to stay out here!" His face began to crumple. "Want to stay here!"

The next step would be a full-blown tantrum. I knew when I was beaten; there were other ways to get the information.

Jud and Adeline found me sitting on the front step. I stood, drained the last of the coffee, and handed the mug to Adeline. It would be washed and free of fingerprints in minutes. "Perfect timing," I said. I put my gloves back on.

"Thank you again," she said. "The gas station's just two miles north on 10, then it'll be a four-, five-mile drive back to the truck."

Jud said nothing at all.

"Shall we?" I gestured at the truck. He nodded.

He sat as before, though this time his hands rested on dark blue denim, and his shoes were sturdy work boots. Perhaps it was my imagination but he seemed a little less stiff.

At the gas station, the attendant seemed to know who Jud was and filled a cheap plastic gas can without comment. I went in and bought myself coffee in a go cup. Jud settled his bill in cash. He counted his change so carefully that I felt guilty about the ten dollars' worth of gas I'd siphoned off earlier. I shook my head as we walked separately back to the truck. These people were profiting from the abuse of a young child. I wasn't here to feel sorry for them.

We drove to the stranded pickup without exchanging a word. He climbed out, then leaned forward to speak through the open window. "Wife tells me you've been sick."

"Yes."

"You'll be in our prayers." And he nodded once again, and walked away.

I parked in what was by now the familiar off-road spot behind the rise and took my mat, field glasses, receiver, and go cup to the top of the hill. No movement outside. I extended the receiver's aerial, plugged in the headphones, and put them on. I had to take my gloves off for fine-tuning the receiver, but then I had it: running water, dishes banging, a drawer opening and shutting. From only three or four hundred yards, there was little distortion. I made a slow sweep with the field glasses. Inside the house a door opened, then closed. Then nothing.

I sipped at the coffee. All I had achieved with my visit so far was the discovery that the situation was complicated. I wondered what Tammy was doing, whether she had called Dornan yet, and what would happen then: to her, to Dornan. To me.

Adeline started to hum. It wasn't a hymn but an old show tune. Fringed buckskin, white teeth, blond hair . . . and then I had it: Doris Day in *Calamity Jane,* singing about the windy city. When her husband wasn't around, did Adeline dream of being transformed by a big-city suitor?

After a while I heard Jud's pickup. I wondered what had taken him so long. Maybe he'd been giving thanks for the gas. He drove round the back of the house. Two minutes later, the back door slammed.

"Sit," came Adeline's voice, loud and tinny from the receiver. "We'll eat."

Scraping of a chair, chink of cutlery on crockery. Scrape of another chair. Moment's silence. Then, "Dear Lord, we're thankful for this food. Amen." Jud's voice. "Amen," Adeline's voice. Food sounds: lighter *tink* of spoons on bowls.

Adeline's voice: "Truck all right?"

Pause, while I imagined Jud nodding. "Drove her to the gas station, had John put her up on the blocks. No leak as I could see." Eating noises. Pause. "Gas come to near nineteen dollars." Audible sigh: Adeline. "Children fine?" Jud asked.

"Out back. Right as rain." Which was more than Adeline sounded. "Jud?" Eating noises. "Jud, why haven't we heard?"

"Couldn't say."

"We should have heard by now. How can we manage without that money?"

"We'll hear soon enough." Definite tones in his voice of I-don't-want-to-think-about-it-right-now.

"Maybe I shouldn't have written to Miz Goulay, maybe it'll make him mad. But that check should've come a week ago, more. He's never missed before. We need that money."

Chair scraping. "Tractor needs work," Jud said. The door closed behind him. Adeline sighed and started collecting the dishes, then stopped, and it took me a moment to identify the strange sounds: she was crying.

CHAPTER THIRTEEN

I had finished the coffee and refilled the cup with lukewarm tea from my flask when I saw movement in my peripheral vision: a car moving down the road to the Carpenters' house. I put down the cup and focused the field glasses. My adrenal system switched from standby to power mode. A dark gray Maxima, a man driving and a woman in the back. Not the configuration for a social call.

The Maxima parked three or four yards from the Carpenters' front door, and the man took just long enough to remove the keys and open his door to tell me the car was probably a rental. He climbed out, looked around. Sloppy training. He should have looked around before he parked, and again before he left the car. He should have familiarized himself with his vehicle. He should have looked up. He closed his door, checked around one more time before opening the woman's door.

The woman who got out of the car wore expensive, beautifully draped trousers, handmade boots, and a cashmere twinset under a camel-hair overcoat. Gold earrings gleamed below her short blond hair. Subtle cosmetics; a touch of color on a strong, straight mouth. No purse. One in the car? Even royalty must show ID to board a scheduled flight. Her clothes were good, but not private plane level.

They approached the door, him walking a yard ahead and a little to her left. Small steps, and slightly pigeon-toed, like an amateur weight lifter or college football player. Haircut from somewhere north and east of Arkansas. Gray suit, from one of the better department stores by its looks, and cleverly tailored around the shoulders and chest. The cleverness was wasted: the swing of his left arm was a little careful, a little self-conscious. Not a cop, though. Cops have to carry their guns all the time.

My heart began to hum like a turbine.

He knocked on the door, then stepped aside for the woman. I measured him against the doorframe: an inch or two taller than me and much, much wider. Not a good idea to get within closing distance of those arms. But maybe this had nothing to do with Luz. I finished my tea, crumpled the cup one-handed.

The door opened. From the expression on Adeline Carpenter's face it was plain that her visitors were not strangers but that their arrival was a surprise, and worrying.

Adeline said something. The woman said something. Adeline stepped to one side and the woman, then the man, went in. The door closed. Muffled noise from the kitchen transmitter. Maybe they were talking in the hall. More noise. Definitely voices. I should have thought to put a bug in the hallway. Or the living room. It had seemed unused, not a good choice for my limited resources, but it was just the place Adeline would take guests, especially well-dressed ones. I flexed my knee, scanned the windows. Nothing.

But then the kitchen door creaked, and Adeline's voice came clearly.

"—in the oven. Please, take a seat."

"You don't seem pleased to see us, Adeline." The woman's voice was smooth and light, but with the occasional metallic Boston vowel.

"I thought maybe you would write. Or call."

"Yes, well, I have the kind of news best delivered in person. I'm sorry to tell you that Mr. Karp is dead." My hands tightened on the field glasses and I lost the focus for a moment. "—sending any more checks."

"Dead?"

"At least so far as the courts would see it. He's in a coma that he won't be coming back out of. A vegetable. I can make up this month's arrears from my own account, that's only fair. But I have to tell you there won't be any more to come."

"But I need . . ." The rest of Adeline's soft voice was lost. Or maybe she just trailed off. She cleared her throat. "Hay prices were down this fall. With two children we depend on that money."

"Which is why I've come to take Luz off your hands."

Three hundred yards. With this knee it would take at least two minutes to get down there. Another two to disable the car. Two more to get back out of sight. I scanned for hiding places closer to the house.

Someone shifted noisily in their chair. Probably the man. "Take Luz?" Adeline sounded bewildered.

"It's for the best," the woman said. "Her sponsor can't help her anymore, and there's no provision in his will for her maintenance." She couldn't know that; he wasn't dead yet.

"But what—"

"We've found another sponsor."

The hum in my chest climbed a note.

"We could—"

"He wants Luz to be fostered closer to his residence. Now, Adeline, I know you and Jud have done a fine job, and I'm prepared to offer you a bonus, something to help you redecorate her room, perhaps, after she's gone. Where is the child?"

"She's out back." Her voice got stronger. "On the land. Might not be back till suppertime."

"Then you'd better start looking for her now. Mike here would be glad to help. These things are best done quickly."

"But her things . . ."

"Not necessary. Her new sponsor will see to it that she has everything she—"

A crash. The stew dishes? The hum in my chest rose to a whine. Someone was saying something quietly, over and over again, softly at first, but then loud enough for me to hear. ". . . not right. That's not right." Adeline. Her voice grew thick and stubborn. "We've cared for that child for close on two years, me and Jud. She's like our—"

The woman talked right over her. "But she's not. She's your paying guest, no more. And now I think we've wasted enough time on this. Any more argument and you won't get that check I mentioned. Mike, go find the girl."

Scrape of chair. Creak and soft slam of door. I waited, but there was no shriek of pain as Adeline threw her boiling stew in the woman's face, no solid crack of plate on self-satisfied Boston skull, nothing but silence. Adeline would do nothing to stop this woman bundling Luz into the rented Maxima and driving away. Because I don't know how, Tammy had said.

My breath poured in and out, in and out.

Choose, Julia had said.

I swore viciously, rolled up the mat around my gear, picked it up with one hand, and ran for the truck.

I drove fast, yanking the truck through the turns. The man and woman would be leaving soon, with the girl. The man had a gun and I did not. I would need a diversion. On the way to the trailer I watched for turnoffs and side roads, looking for hedges or trees or other potential screens for a roadblock. Nothing big enough.

I slammed into the campground in a cloud of dust. The trailer wasn't hooked up to power or sewage, but it still took precious minutes to get it hitched to the truck. There was no time for precautions; anything loose would just have to break. Halfway down the dirt road, I braked hard, found the thermos, and got out. I kicked a hole in the dirt with my heel, poured in the tea, and scrabbled it about with a stick until it was mud. I picked up a double handful: one went on the truck's front license plate, the other on the trailer's. It would dry on the way.

Driving more than sixty on a narrow Arkansas road while pulling six and a half tons of trailer behind you is not fun but I was all out of options. When the familiar rise came into view I didn't slow: six hundred yards, five hundred, four, and at three hundred yards I stood on the brakes and pulled a long, curving skid, fighting the wheel, feeling the trailer begin to catch up with the truck, easing the brakes and goosing the engine just enough to stay ahead of a disastrous jackknife, hanging on, braking again, until I heard a sharp crack and the rig juddered to a halt, slewed right across both lanes, blocking them. I jumped down from the cab, swore at the spike of pain in my knee. The rubber burn was long, and stank of danger only just averted. It looked convincing, at least at first glance, which was all I'd need.

But that crack had not been part of the plan. A quick look under the chassis showed no ominous leaking of fluid. I couldn't see anything when I walked around the trailer and truck. Could be the hitch. But this wasn't the time to find out. I got back in the cab, made sure the truck would still start, turned it off, and climbed out again with the field glasses. I hurried, but with my knee it took nearly two minutes to work myself around the rise without the possibility of being seen from the house. The car was still there. I lay on my belly and focused on the front door.

The door opened. Mike came out first, carrying a child's suitcase. Luz's. She'd get to take some of her things after all. It looked ridiculously small and light, or perhaps Mike just made it seem so. He put the case in the trunk of the car. He turned, and even from this distance I saw his surprise. I pulled back on the focus: Jud stood immobile and as far as I could see unspeaking on the far right of the house. Then he walked off around the back. Mike shrugged to himself, then leaned against the car, legs crossed at the ankles, arms folded, lifting his face to the weak afternoon sunlight. I focused back in. He stood up and unfolded his arms when the woman stepped through the door, her hand on Luz's shoulder. Luz's face was very pale. She kept twisting her head to look back, and now Adeline appeared in the doorway. Adult and child stretched their hands to each other. I couldn't imagine what Adeline was saying. They didn't touch. Adeline followed Luz and the woman to the Maxima. Mike lifted his hands and spread them as though he was about to step in front of Adeline and take her by the arms, stop her from going any further, when suddenly everything changed. They were all looking to the right. I pulled out again: Jud stood by the side of the house, a shotgun at his shoulder. His cheeks glittered in the sun.

Nobody moved for two or three seconds, then Mike lifted both hands as if to say, Hey, I'm harmless, and Adeline stepped in front of her husband. She touched Jud's cheek, said something. Not this way, maybe. Or perhaps, It's not worth it. Or even, I don't want to lose you, too. Whatever it was, it worked. He lowered the gun. Mike started forward, but the woman said something and he stopped. The woman spoke again, and he opened the back door of the car. The woman put one hand on the handle and gestured to Luz with the other: Get in. Luz shook her head, and looked at Adeline. Adeline tried to smile, tried to blow a kiss to Luz, but her mouth wouldn't shape it properly. Instead she nodded. Luz climbed in. The woman slammed the door. She smiled pleasantly at the Carpenters, then walked around to the other side of the car. Mike started the engine. The woman got in the back and closed the door, and the car pulled onto the road.

Watching in dumb show and from a distance made the whole thing look like some strange puppet performance, utterly divorced from me and my life.

When the car came over the rise, I was standing between truck and trailer, looking in fake feminine annoyance at the hitch. Mike braked, and I prayed that Luz was either too smart or too much in shock to speak. I waved in that awkward, windscreen wiper way people with no physical coordination do, and smiled, and then threw my hands up as if to say, It just broke! Mike looked back at the woman and said something. She nodded. He climbed out of the car, already wearing that tolerant, capable-urban-man-approaching-silly-rural-woman expression I had counted on.

"I am so glad to see you!" I said. "If this just doesn't beat all. I had to put the brake on so hard I thought that was it, time to visit Jesus. You're just the man I want to see. See here? Around this side?" I walked around the truck so that the hitch was between us. He followed. We were now out of the woman's line of sight. "I'm just not strong enough to lift this thingie back on."

I pointed, and when he leaned forward I stepped behind him, shoved him against the side of the truck bed, and yanked his belt up with my right hand so his pants crushed his scrotum. While he concentrated on not fainting I slipped my left hand inside his jacket and slid out the gun. A Glock with the seventeen-shot magazine. Oversize, like his muscles. I thumbed off the safety and pressed the snout under his left ear. "Take out your wallet."

"I don't have much—"

A hard upward yank cut him off mid-sentence. "Now." Didn't he understand it would be easier to just shoot him, then shoot the woman and drive away?

He reached behind him and lifted it from his back right-hand pocket. He didn't try to drop it. Good. Still in the first phase of shock.

I'd left my gloves in the truck.

"Open it."

His hands shook as he unfolded it.

"Not the money. Your driver's license and insurance card. Put them on the bed so I can see them." He did. It had been about fifteen seconds. He would start to recover his wits very soon. "Don't even think about trying anything."

I scanned the cards over his shoulder. Michael Turner, a White Plains, New York, address. Social security number on the insurance card.

"Tip out the rest of the wallet. Spread it all apart."

American Express, MasterCard, debit card, frequent flyer cards, AAA card, an emergency contact number card.

His muscles tensed but I dropped his belt, punched him irritably over the right kidney, and had hold of the leather again before he could translate thought to action. He went limp and the rhythm of his breathing broke. No concealed weapons permit for this or any other state. No private investigator license.

"I know your name, address, and social security number." I glanced at the emergency contact card: the name Nicki Taormino, the designation fiancée, and a phone number in the person-to-be-contacted slot. "And I have your girlfriend's number. Do exactly as I tell you and I won't ever have to use any of that information. Upset me and I'll shoot you in the gut. Walk two paces to your left and kneel down."

I let go of his belt and he did as he was told.

I made sure he could see the gun trained on him. "Do you have a handkerchief? Good. Throw it to me." He tossed me a clean, folded square, still warm from his pocket. "And your tie." He obeyed silently. I put the tie and hankie on the truck bed with his wallet. "Now take off your belt." He took off the belt. "Make a big loop." It took him a moment to understand that I wanted him to thread the tongue through the buckle. The brain does not work well when the system is adrenaline-charged. "Hold it in your left hand, put that hand behind you." His reaction time was getting slower as his system began to shut down. In three or four minutes it would rev back up, but by then he'd be helpless. "Now the right hand. Wrists together."

I stepped behind him and yanked the loop tight.

"Lean back, as though you're reaching for your heels."

Good thing his waist was so big; there was enough leather

to wrap around his ankles, tuck under the loop, pull tight, then knot.

"I'm going to tip you over." I gave him a second to brace himself, then pushed one shoulder with my foot. I stepped over him to the truck bed, retrieved the hankie and tie. "Open your mouth." He knew what was coming and began to thrash. I racked the slide on the Glock, pointed the muzzle at his stomach. "Gag or gun." He opened his mouth. I stuffed the hankie in, then pulled the tie over his mouth to keep the gag in place and knotted it behind his head. He'd probably be able to work it loose in an hour or so, but I wouldn't take nearly that long. I went back to the truck, fished the driver's license and insurance card from the pile, and slipped them in my pocket. I needed a minute to stop, to think, but I didn't have a minute.

I slid the safety back on, tucked the gun in the back of my waistband, and stepped into view of the Maxima. When the woman saw me I waved, opened my mouth to speak, then shut it again with an apologetic smile, as though remembering it wasn't ladylike to shout.

The woman watched me calmly as I approached, though her shoulders and back looked tight. Her window slid down, but instead of speaking to her I leaned in the driver's side and took the keys. That bothered her. I smiled at Luz and shook my head slightly, hoping she would understand. She didn't smile back, just watched me the way you'd watch a rabid dog.

"Step out of the car please, ma'am," I said to the woman, and the tension in her spine eased a little: law enforcement generally pay attention to well-paid lawyers. Hijackers and thugs don't. She got out of the car.

I closed her door and window, then used the master control on the driver's side to lock the car up. I didn't want Luz running off.

"Well, officer," she said, "or is it agent? I'd say prior knowledge of my travel plans means some kind of wiretap, which rules out local involvement." She didn't look worried. "FBI or INS? Not that it matters. I've been through this before. It's a waste of my time and yours. You have nothing in the way of documentation."

My eyes felt hot and a little too big for their sockets. This was all her fault. "I don't need proof."

She raised her eyebrows. "Since when—" Then she got it. She took a step back. "Where's my driver? What do you want?"

"Your purse."

Like Mike Turner, she immediately assumed I wanted to rob her and turned to the car with relief, but unlike him, she realized within a second or two that no one would go to such trouble for a few bucks and a handful of credit cards, and her hand dropped before it touched the handle. "Who are you?"

I got out the gun and pointed it at her. "Someone who is getting more irritated every second." There was no one here to stop me. Aud rhymes with allowed. I used the key remote and her door lock thunked open. I nodded at the car. "Your purse."

Luz suddenly wriggled out of her seat belt and lunged to the front of the car, reaching for the horn. She managed to hit it once, just enough for a light *pap* that no one would hear, before I got the door open and yanked her out with one arm.

I stood her up on the pavement. "Don't." I switched to Spanish. "Estoy salvando te de esta mujer. En unos minutos, te devolvere a . . . a Aba." And in the middle of explaining to her I was rescuing her, that I would take her back to Adeline, she gave me that bird-eyed look again, and I understood, then, why I recognized it. I had looked at my own mother the same way all those times she had said, Yes, Aud, this time I *will* be there for the school sports day, or, Of course I don't have to work on your birthday.

The woman was edging towards the car. I pointed the gun again until she stopped, then turned back to Luz. "I will explain very soon, but I need you to be very quiet and very still, just for five minutes. No one will hurt you. Do you understand?" She nodded, amenable but uncommitted. "Get back in the car."

She shook her head.

There was no time to argue. "Then stand right here, next to me, and don't move."

She crept to my side.

I turned back to the woman. "Su bolso."

"Ella no comprende," Luz said.

"Your purse," I said again, in English.

"I could get it," Luz said. If you please Mummy, she might do as she promised. And I wanted to pistol-whip this smug woman, this panderer of children, until her blood seeped into the Arkansas dirt.

Luz climbed into the backseat, felt around the floor, and emerged with the purse. "It's heavy," she said, and held it out to me.

I made myself breathe. In and out. "Find her wallet," I said. I locked the car again and put the key in my pocket.

Luz rooted around and came up with a slim, calfskin billfold.

"Open it. I want her driver's license and insurance card. Read them to me."

Luz did. Jean Goulay, an address in upstate New York.

"Any business cards in there?"

"What's a business card?"

I didn't take my eyes off Goulay. Any minute now she was going to realize she was in even deeper trouble than she thought. People don't avoid leaving their fingerprints if they mean you well. "Tip the purse out onto the road." Luz did, and looked at me nervously. I forced what I hoped was an encouraging smile. "There, those pieces of cardboard with phone numbers and e-mail addresses." Maybe she didn't know what an e-mail address was, either. "Lift one up so I can read it." I read it aloud. "Goulay Adoption Agency: specializing in difficult cases. Discreet. Established in 1987." Nineteen eighty-seven. Fifteen years of processing children like imported grain. Some of them would be old enough to already be married.

"This will stop," I said to Goulay. Terrible heat was building in my bones and it was hard to get the words out; the hinges of my jaw felt dry and swollen. I put the gun back in my waistband.

"Nothing I've done is illegal." Perhaps it was seeing me put the gun away, but Goulay had relaxed again, on surer ground. She looked almost smug.

My stomach squeezed. I took a step towards her. She would break so easily under my hands. " 'Illegal' doesn't interest me. If you import one more child, I will hurt you."

"What is it to you? They're better off here. They're well fed and well taken care of. Over there this girl would be a prostitute, like her mother. She'd probably be dead by now; her sister is. Her brother already has AIDS."

Well fed. Well taken care of. It wasn't enough. I took half a step towards her.

"You can't touch me. You think I run a business like this without the best lawyers money can buy?"

My arm came up, and as she realized her lawyers couldn't stop me smashing my fist into her well-bred face her mouth fell open and her pupils dilated, and it reminded me of Karp's fear; I remembered the animal noises I had made, and the vomit, and I didn't want to do that, didn't want to be that anymore. I lowered my hand, and the way the color rushed back into her face and the sweat started at her hairline made me think of one of those dolls that cry or wet their underwear when you press a button, and I laughed. My laughter made her change color again, which was even funnier.

Eventually I sobered. "As of today, you are out of business." I nodded at her purse. "I have your name and social security number. I know your face and where you live. You, on the other hand, know nothing about me. Not my name, not where I'm from, not even how I found out about you. If you do this again, even once, I'll find out, and I'll come for you, and you will spend the rest of your life in pain. Now put your belongings back in your purse and get back in the car."

And that's when everything went wrong, when Goulay smiled instead of looking scared, and bent to pick up her purse.

It's heavy . . .

I understood why at the same moment I understood that I could not move in two directions at once, and that, here, Luz was the point, just as in Norway Julia had been the point, only I had forgotten.

When Goulay straightened with the purse in one hand—gaping as though disemboweled where the previously concealed compartment now lay open—and a nickel-plated Ruger .38 five-shot in the other, I was standing in front of the child. Luz inhaled sharply. The hand holding the Ruger didn't waver.

All the heat had burned from my bones, leaving them light and strong. A fly hummed a few feet from Luz's head. I felt dense and supple and utterly relaxed. "Luz." I reached behind me, put a hand on her shoulder. "Está bien."

She had been so brave all this time, but now I felt the tremble deep in her little bones.

"It's all right," I said again.

"Child, get the car keys and bring them to me."

"They're in my right-hand pocket," I told Luz, not taking my eyes off Goulay. The child was the point. This time I would not forget.

Luz groped in my pocket for a moment and came out with the keys. The Glock hung in my waistband, but there would be no time to use it.

"Bring them here." Goulay held out her left hand, the gun in her right still trained on my stomach. The gun's vanity plating meant it was probably the cheap model Ruger had taken off the market a few years ago, because there wasn't much demand for a pretty weapon with a stiff trigger. And it wasn't cocked.

My head filled with humming. It wasn't the fly. I breathed in, deep and slow, until the world took on a dreamy blue edge. All the time in the world. Luz moved in slow motion towards Goulay with the small unsteady steps of a terrified nine-year-old. One step. Two. On three her hand lifted and dropped the keys into Goulay's palm.

The human body is densely studded with nerve endings which constantly send information to both our conscious and subconscious minds. Generally the brain does a superb job of traffic control, and training can improve this, but an untrained person cannot focus on two important and unfamiliar things at once. When those keys touched the sensitive skin of Goulay's hand, for a split second her attention was divided: her right arm still pointed at me, her index finger still rested on the trigger, but for that moment, just a hitch in time—the space between a breath, the time it takes for an electrical impulse to leap a nerve synapse—her body knew more about her left hand than her right. And it takes more pressure than the untrained realize to pull the trigger of an uncocked gun.

Remember the child. Oh yes. This is who I am. This is what I do.

I took one sliding step with my right leg, slapped the gun away with my left hand, and hit her neatly under the ear with my right elbow. She folded without a sound. I smiled at Luz, picked up the gun, broke open the cylinder, and tipped out the bullets. Dry-fired it. Just as I thought. Stiff. Cheap. I wiped the gun clean on my sweatshirt and dropped it into Goulay's coat pocket. The bullets went in mine. Luz stared at me, lips pale.

"She'll be fine," I said. "Can you be brave just a bit longer?"

She nodded jerkily.

"Good. I'm going to need your help to tidy up a bit." I bent and plucked the keys from Goulay's white hand. "If you open the back door, I'll put her inside where she'll be more comfortable until she wakes up." My knee flared when I bent to pick up Goulay. Pain is just a message, information about an injury. If the structural damage isn't enough to stop you, the message can be ignored. Goulay was heavier than she looked and it took me a while to make sure all her flopping limbs were safely inside before I could slam the door. "We have to move the rig, too." I pointed at the trailer and truck.

"Where's the man?"

Mike. Right. "He's . . . You'll have to help me with him, too. He's tied up behind the truck, but he's not unconscious, so we'll have to bring the car to him to make it easier to get inside. Okay? Come on. You can sit in the front."

Like all rental cars, the Maxima smelled new and unblemished. The tank was still two-thirds full. I drove the few feet to the rig so that the back door was as close as possible. "Open the door. I'll go get him." She slid out and went to the back door. I left the engine running.

Mike's face was livid. He writhed as much as he was able and grunted explosively as I pulled out his gun.

"Two choices. One, I drag you to the car, face down, which will rip your skin up quite a bit, might even damage your eyes. Two, I untie your feet and you get into the car without a struggle. If you struggle, I shoot you. Dead people are just as easy to move." Easier. But it would probably upset Luz. "Should I untie you?"

More grunts.

"Should I untie you?" I asked again, patiently.

He nodded.

I loosened the belt so he could free his feet but pulled it back tight on his hands. "Stand—"

Luz's scream sliced my sentence in half. I whipped around just in time to see Goulay, now in the front seat, one arm around Luz's neck, her own head craning to see behind her, before the car screeched away in reverse. I lifted the Glock, and that's when Mike hit me on the back of the neck with his clubbed fists.

How did he do that? I thought stupidly, as the strength

drained from my legs and my hands went numb. I staggered, the Glock fell from my fingers, and Mike hurled himself at me. I went down face first, him on top. One of my ribs popped with the long, leisurely sound a cork makes coming out of a particularly anticipated bottle of port. The gravel under my cheek should have felt cold but didn't, though the metal at the corner of my eye did. Somewhere a child was screaming. Someone grabbed my right wrist and pinned it to the road by my head, so that I pointed after the reversing car, which was only a few yards away and moving terribly slowly. Dust and that scream hung in the air as though someone had stopped the world.

The man on top of me shifted, dropping his whole weight down and forward on his hands to pin me more securely. My cheek tore on gravel as I smiled. Give me a long enough lever and I will move the world.

The child had stopped screaming. I put it from my mind.

For the Chinese, it is the source of chi, for the Japanese, ki, for dancers and gymnasts, it is the center of gravity: the fulcrum around which the body moves. Shift your balance, and everything changes. Balance is also psychological. If your opponent expects you to pull in one direction, he sets his muscles to resist. Mike had put all his weight over my wrist: he was balancing on it; he expected me to pull my hand in instinctively and protect my torso. So I did, but slowly, so he had time to resist, and when he began to push the other way—which pleased me so much I laughed, which startled him, which made it even easier—I thrust both hands up over my head, simple as stretching. His balance followed my wrists, sliding as smoothly as the bubble in a tilting spirit level, and as he fell forward, I pulled both legs under me and bucked. Thigh muscles are enormously powerful. He soared, upturned face comical, and I was scrambling after him on all fours like a strange, bloodied train, Glock in hand—where had that come from?—before he hit the ground. He was lovely and fast, already up on one knee before I pistoned right elbow into his neck, left fist into his solar plexus, and arced the Glock into the back of his skull. He collapsed. I smiled, and stood. Staggered. Pain is just a message.

The Maxima was now forty yards away, veering wildly, jerking, driving again, still in reverse. I wiped the blood from my face, squinted. The child had stopped screaming because she had her teeth buried in the woman's wrist. I lurched forward. My knee buckled and I almost went down again. Just a message. I ran. In another fifty yards, the Maxima would reach the crossroads where there would be room to turn around. Once it was out of reverse, I'd have no hope of catching it.

The woman slapped the child. The child hung on. The car slowed almost to a stop. I ran. Thirty yards. The woman hit the child again. Twenty-five yards. The child let go. Twenty yards. Now or never. I lifted the Glock, sighted, breathed out, held it, and shot out the left front tire. I moved the gun slightly, sighted on the woman's chest. Neither of us moved. Slowly, she raised both hands.

I limped as fast as I could to the car. "Out," I said to the woman. "Now." Even in rural Arkansas a shot might not go unnoticed. She climbed out warily. There was blood on her right wrist. I could smell her fear. "Turn around. Hands on the roof of the car." Before she'd even turned around properly I whipped the Glock across the back of her head. I caught her before she fell.

The child had squeezed herself up against the passenger door, as far away from me as she could get. "Open the back door," I said. She didn't move. I ignored my knee, ignored the terrible need to hurry, and dredged up her name. "Luz. I need you to open the back door." She stared at the gun, then my face. The gun, my face. I couldn't put the gun down without letting go of the woman. Another child . . . shiny eyes . . . "Button needs you," I said. "We have to hurry." There was no more time. I slung the woman as best I could over my left arm and tucked the Glock back in my waistband out of sight. That's when I remembered the noise my rib cage had made. I cursed softly, then put that message aside, too. I could just reach the door handle. I got it open and stuffed the woman in. She left a smear of blood on the upholstery. I slammed the door, got in the driver's seat.

Luz still hadn't moved or spoken. I picked her up bodily—she was practically catatonic—put her in her seat, and pulled the seat belt round her. The pain was making it hard to breathe.

The tire rim ground on the gravel as I drove the hundred yards back to the rig and the sprawled lump in the road.

Out of the car, open the back door, drag the man to the car, lift and prop, fold and push him on top of the woman. Close rear door. Use remote to lock all four doors. Open door of truck, sigh, walk back to car, open passenger door. "I'm going to move the rig—the truck and trailer—so we can drive past. I'm coming back." I'm going to pass out. "Stay there." This time she nodded cautiously.

I got in the truck, turned it on. I could just drive away and never come back. I checked my throat in the mirror: red, but not reopened.

It took four minutes of slow and careful backing and filling before I had the rig on the side of the road, pointing south. Each time I twisted, each time I moved my right arm to change gear, I thought I might throw up. Just a message. The hitch didn't feel right, but there wasn't time to check it properly. Somewhere a sharp-eared neighbor might be dialing the sheriff. I turned off the engine, climbed down, went back to the car. The child was so quiet I could hear the two in the back breathing slowly but steadily. The child—Luz, her name is Luz—had unfastened her seat belt.

"Fasten it back up."

Luz looked at me. "Button?"

"We have a short drive to make first."

She looked over her shoulder at the woman Goulay and

Mike, but didn't speak. Probably thought I'd shoot her if she did.

I had to slow for every curve. With that tire gone, the car tilted to one side and the front wheels had a tendency to skate. I checked the rearview mirror often. No pursuing traffic. "How far can you walk?"

Now the look I got was full of incomprehension, as though I were speaking Urdu. How many nine-year-olds would know how far they could walk? She could probably manage three or four miles without any lasting damage, and I could always carry her. "There's a map in the glove compartment," I said. "Pass it to me please." I slowed, one hand on the wheel, the other tracing tiny lines. Brink Creek campground was about four miles. The woods there would be dense enough to confuse most city people, and there wouldn't be much traffic. I handed the map back to Luz, who refolded it and put it back in the glove compartment without being asked. Remarkable adaptation to circumstances. Her early life must have been interesting. Or perhaps all nine-year-olds were this resilient.

The campground was empty. I pulled in under the trees, parked, and pocketed the keys. Luz seemed to listen to the silence.

"Now you have to help me wipe the car down." I eased Goulay's heavy coat off her shoulders and ripped away one of her cardigan sleeves. "Take this and rub it all around the steering wheel. It's very important that you rub every single bit of the surface."

"Why?"

It wasn't her fault the Carpenters didn't have a television. I forced myself to breathe through the pain in ribs and knee, and managed to speak without growling. "Fingerprints."

While she scrubbed industriously at the wheel and gear stick I tore off the other sleeve and wiped at the doors and roof where I might have touched the metal inadvertently. Then I tackled the shiny vinyl on the backs of the seats and inside windows.

I remembered the belt and wiped that down, too—after I'd retied it around Mike's ankles. He must be more supple than I'd thought. Just as I was finishing that, he woke. "Don't," I said in his ear. "Keep still and you'll be fine. She'll wake up in a few hours and untie you." It would be dark and cold by then. I tucked Goulay's arms back into her coat.

I motioned Luz away from the car, gave the wheel and stick a quick wipe myself, then threw the ragged sleeve on the front seat.

"Now we walk back to the trailer. It's a long way." She didn't move. "What?"

"My stuff."

The suitcase, in the trunk.

At first she insisted on carrying the case herself. She carried it two-handed, in front of her, bumping her knees. I tried not to wince.

"When you get tired, let me know."

I matched my pace to hers, but even at two miles an hour my knee burned. The back of my neck throbbed and every now and then my hands tingled. Some kind of nerve bruise. I felt at my ribs gently as I walked; no obvious splintering. Cracked, perhaps, or maybe just soft-tissue injury at the sternum. Cartilage probably.

I had no idea what to do with this child. I had seen the look on her face as Goulay tried to take her away from the Carpenters. But a dog will bond even with a cruel owner, one who beats it and starves it.

We walked on. Luz began to lag. I slowed even more. She hung on to the case with grim determination. I had no idea what nine-year-olds talked about.

"What's in there, then? Gold and jewels?"

"Stuff."

"We can buy you more stuff. More clothes."

"Not just clothes."

Of course. Books. "You know what one of my favorite books used to be? *The Lion, the Witch and the Wardrobe.* Have you read that?"

On an adult, her expression would have meant, Don't tell me you love me if you don't mean it. I plowed on, glad I didn't have to lie. "I've read all of them."

"There are seven!"

"Yes. I've read them all. But I think *The Lion, the Witch and the Wardrobe* is my favorite. Or maybe *Prince Caspian.*" A bloody thirty-two-year-old Norwegian discussing 1950s English novels with a nine-year-old Mexican girl in backwoods Arkansas.

The absurdity of the situation didn't seem to bother her. "I like it best when they have supper with Mr. and Mrs. Beaver," she said. Safety, warmth, food. Tenderness. Every child should have them. "And I like it when Edmund is in the sleigh in the snow with the White Witch eating Turkish delight." She swang the suitcase to one hand, then changed her mind and tried the other.

"You want me to carry that for a bit?"

"Okay. Just for a bit."

All her worldly possessions. It weighed about eight pounds. Not much, but eight pounds more than I wanted to carry.

"I like it too that Edmund was good in the end and that his sisters and brother were nice to him." She frowned. "But I don't know what Turkish delight is. Aba doesn't know, either. She said maybe it's kind of like chocolate."

"Real Turkish delight is soft and squashy and sweet. It comes in round boxes. The pieces are pale yellow or pink cubes, and all dusted with powdered sugar."

"Is it nice?"

Being in the rig, being out of sight, and getting my ribs

taped would be nice. "It's a bit perfumey, like eating roses. Sickly. I'll buy you some if you like, then you can tell me."

"Aba doesn't like me to eat sweet things." A slitted, sideways glance.

Aud Torvingen, White Witch. "Did you know that they made a film based on *The Lion, the Witch and the Wardrobe*?"

She gave me that look that said I was speaking Urdu again, and I remembered she didn't go to school, where children are exposed to other children talking about cartoons and movies and gross-out videos.

"So what books do you have in here?" She shook her head and flushed, which I hadn't seen her do before. "Must be a heavy one."

She actually hung her head. I imagined her poring over a book of knowledge in tiny type with black-and-white illustrations that was forty years out of date and smelled of mildew, imagined her agony of indecision when it came time to pack her things: she would have wanted it so, but known it was stealing.

"I could buy you encyclopedias, too. New ones."

"Why?"

"Because they're better." But that wasn't what she meant. She stumbled, but pulled away when I tried to help her.

"How far is it?"

"Another two miles."

She nodded wearily.

"I could carry you, if you like." Even if she didn't like. We were already conspicuous; I wanted to be back at the trailer before dark.

"Like a baby!" Enough energy for scorn.

"Aslan carried Lucy."

"You're not a lion."

"No, but I can talk, not like a horse or a car."

She considered that. "Okay. But piggyback."

"Of course." I shifted the Glock to the front of my waistband and squatted. My knee was visibly swollen. She climbed onto my back. "Wrap your legs tightly because I need one hand for— No!" I pulled her legs down a little. "No," I said again, more softly, "not there."

We set off again, her arms around my neck tightly enough to choke. If Mike's weight hadn't reopened the wound, hers probably wouldn't. After a while she relaxed. A little while after that, the pain in my knee notched up from burning to searing.

Now that she wasn't walking, Luz was more talkative. She talked about Button a lot.

"He's okay. Not as smart as me but he's good, I mean he's good when he can be. When Aba tells him, Don't leave the yard, he doesn't leave the yard on purpose, he just forgets. So it's my job to remind him."

"But he has tantrums." I was getting very thirsty.

"When he's upset. Because he doesn't always understand things."

"Does he ever hit you?"

"On purpose? No! But once when I was little he was wiggling about and I tried to hold his hands and he knocked one of my teeth out. But it was just a baby tooth so it was okay. It was falling out already."

"Does anyone else ever hit you?"

"Like who?"

"Like anyone. Like Aba, or Mr. Carpenter."

"Why would they hit me?"

"Sometimes adults hit children when they're not good."

"I'm always good."

"Always?"

She squirmed. "Mostly."

"And what do they do when they find out you haven't been good?"

She squirmed again. "Make me say more prayers."

"Prayers are boring," I said.

"Sometimes."

"Always."

"No, sometimes they're nice. They make me feel . . ." Her arms tightened a bit while she thought about it. "Like someone's looking after me the same way I look after Button."

"Don't Aba and Mr. Carpenter look after you?"

"Aba does. Mr. Carpenter . . ." I felt her shrug. "He does things like drive the truck and cut the wood and do the farm stuff, and he takes us swimming sometimes, and Aba leans on his arm when we go to church. But . . ."

She didn't have the vocabulary, in Spanish or English, to talk about the inability to deal with the outside world, with strangers and hard moral choices. Jud Carpenter seemed like a good man who belonged in a simpler time. "But he didn't stop that woman from taking you away."

"He wanted to. Aba stopped him. But I'm going back, aren't I, so I guess Brother Jerry was right. God works in mysterious ways." Brother Jerry? "What's wrong?"

"Nothing. It's not far now."

My neck hurt, my ribs hurt, I was beginning to imagine I could hear the bones in my knee grinding together, but more than that I didn't want to see her face when we got in the rig and I drove her away. I walked on, right foot left foot.

"Aud." That perfect pronunciation. "Aud? There is something wrong, isn't there? Am I too heavy? We could leave my stuff here and get Mr. Carpenter to come back for it in the truck, later."

"Luz, would you like to live somewhere else? I mean, live in a big city where you could have everything you wanted, watch TV and read books and talk Spanish and play with other girls?" Would I have left the care of my mother, such as it was, if a stranger had asked?

"Could Button and Aba come, too?"

"Luz, do you remember your life before Aba, when you lived in another country?"

"No."

"You don't remember a big church with pretty-colored

glass, or your mother and brother and sister? Where everyone talked Spanish?"

"No." Her voice had an edge to it.

"You were telling Button about it."

"That was just a story." Loudly now.

"But if the story were real, about a real place and a real time, would you like to go back there?"

"No! It was a story! I want to go home. I don't want Turkish delight or cyclopedias, I want to go home to Aba and Button and Mr. Carpenter!"

I gritted my teeth and kept walking. How do you persuade the beaten dog it would be better off with someone else? Perhaps you couldn't. Perhaps it wouldn't.

It was about six o'clock by the time we saw the truck and trailer. "I can walk now," Luz said. I didn't say anything. "Let me down, Aud."

Stay in the world, Julia had said, but there were so many different worlds. There was one where I put Luz in my truck and we drove off to Little Rock, where I placed her with social services. There was one where I took her to Atlanta and she lived with me. There was one where we stopped by the truck and I got in and she kept walking, back to Jud and Adeline.

I set Luz down. "You can walk to the truck."

"I don't want to get in the truck. I want to go home."

"I'm very tired, and I don't want to leave the truck out here. If you get in, I'll turn it round and take you home."

"Swear on the Holy Bible?"

"I don't have a Bible." I switched to Spanish. "But I swear on my own name that if you get in this truck, I will drive you home to Aba." Aud rhymes with vowed. Another promise hanging around my neck.

"Today?" English. The language of mistrust.

"Right now."

"And you won't lock the doors?"

I should never have offered to buy her Turkish delight. "No. No one is going to lock a door on you ever again."

As soon as we pulled up outside the farmhouse, she tore into the house and slammed the door behind her. I switched off the headlights and the engine, turned on the dome light. It seemed very bright. I pulled the Glock from my waistband and put it in the glove compartment. After a while I opened the glove compartment again and took out a folder and my phone. I looked at the phone. There was no one to call. The engine ticked.

The front door opened again. Adeline Carpenter. She took one step out and stopped. I turned the light off, put the phone back, picked up the folder, and climbed down. The pain was constant now. I could hang on perhaps another hour.

"Luz says . . . well, I can't make head nor tail of it, but she's here, and you're here . . ." She waved vaguely with her left hand, and her eyes were brilliant and glassy. "And your face . . ." She pulled an inhaler from her apron pocket and sucked hard. I thought for a moment she might pass out.

"Mrs. Carpenter, may I come in? We have a lot to talk about."

CHAPTER FOURTEEN

We sat at the kitchen table, on our third cup of coffee. The same stew still simmered by the stove but the room looked flatter and harsher in electric light. Luz was with Button, watching Jud work on the truck. Adeline had watched while I cleaned the grit and blood from my face and smeared the graze with antibiotic ointment. She gave me ibuprofen for the pain. Her breathing improved as I washed away the evidence of violence. I hadn't mentioned my knee or ribs.

I had given Adeline an edited version of what had happened, up to the point where Luz and I walked back from the woods, and her confusion was mounting.

"So Miz Goulay's in a car in the woods?"

"Yes."

"And she's not coming back?"

"When she wakes up, she'll untie Mike, and they'll both spend a fair amount of time searching for the car keys, which they won't find, after which they'll have to walk out. They might walk the wrong way, but it shouldn't be cold enough tonight to do them any harm."

"But she won't . . ." She took a moment to breathe. "She won't be coming back after Luz?"

"No."

"And . . ." She used her inhaler again. Breathed. Another snort. The color came back to her face. "She won't go to the police?"

"No. If the police were called, she would have a lot of explaining to do." The list of charges a good lawyer could level at Goulay would be long, beginning with kidnap of a minor, trafficking in illegal immigrants, carrying a concealed weapon without a permit . . . "Jean Goulay will never bother you again. Luz will stay here, with you and your husband and Button. If that's what you want."

"Yes! And her . . . Mr. Karp?"

"He's in a persistent vegetative state, the kind of coma from which you never wake. He'll get weaker and weaker and then die."

"She told the truth about that, then."

I opened the folder, spread out Luz's birth and adoption certificates, her passport and medical reports. "The only people on this earth now responsible for Luz are you and your husband. And me."

She frowned. "Where did you get those?"

"From George Karp's apartment."

She reached out and touched the birth certificate with a fingertip. "In New York. Miz Goulay said he was beaten half to death, but she didn't say who by."

"George Karp was not a good man."

She nodded, but I wasn't sure if she was agreeing or simply acknowledging what I'd said. "You weren't here on vacation, were you?" she said.

"No."

"And it wasn't just chance that you came by when we ran out of gas." She was breathing fast, but this time it wasn't asthma. "You told a pack of lies to get into my house."

"I had good reason."

"You lied, just like that Goulay woman. You even lied about having cancer."

"I never said I had cancer."

"Don't you get clever with me! You know what you meant for me to think."

"Listen to—"

"No, Miz Aud Thomas or whoever the heck you are, I've had my fill today of being bullied and lied to. You're sitting in my kitchen. I don't have to listen to one word you say." She folded her arms and leaned back in her chair. Adeline discovers strength through righteous anger. Shame she hadn't been able to break free of the Kind Christian Lady persona a little earlier.

The stew simmered peacefully for a while. The dishes on display were a willow pattern; one had a carefully mended crack. Under the table, my knee was swelling.

Eventually she couldn't stand it. "Just what is it you want with us?"

"A bargain. You don't want Luz to go, and Luz doesn't want to go, but you can't afford to keep her. I can help."

"Why would you want to do that? What's Luz to you?"

"My motives have no bearing on the matter."

"They do for me."

If I sat here another hour, I wouldn't be able to drive. "Did you know that the legal age for marriage is fourteen in Georgia, and just twelve in Delaware?" She kept her arms folded, but now she looked uncomfortable. "Wasn't too hard to put two and two together, was it? Don't get righteous with me. You have no moral leg to stand on."

Another pause. "What do you mean, help?"

"Luz stays here. I pay you and untangle the immigration situation. When she's eighteen she gets to choose her own life."

She half unfolded her arms, bewildered now. "But why?"

I ignored that. "We'll come to an agreement, write a contract, a covenant. For the money I send I'll expect certain things."

"Why should I trust you? I don't know you. I don't even like you." Heady stuff, freedom. But her timing was inconvenient.

"You don't have to like me. I don't have to like you. We simply have to abide by an agreement. For example, one of my conditions would be that she goes to school. A good school."

A long, cautious pause. "She's got to attend church."

"Fine. On the condition that when I set up health and other insurance, you take her in for regular checkups—physical, dental, optical—to medical professionals we agree on beforehand." She did not say yes or no to that. "If you break the terms of the agreement, I come and take Luz away. If I break them, I give you the documents." It would be easy enough to take them back again. "All we have to do is make the agreement, and all communication between us will thereafter be through my lawyer, who will hold the documents until Luz is eighteen. Agreed?"

"If you tell me who you are, and why you're doing this."

"No."

"Then we're done talking."

"You don't need my name."

"I might not be Miss College Mouth Audrey Thomas or whoever the hell you are, but I know a woman who's hiding something pretty big when I see her. Checks and insurance and doctors. We aren't talking pin money here. So I want to know who you are and what Luz is to you."

The key to negotiation lies in ensuring the other party needs to reach an agreement more than you do, my mother told me once when I was twelve. *If you're willing to walk away, you will win.* When I asked her what to do if it was something you really, really wanted, she said, *If you have a personal stake, get someone else to negotiate on your behalf.* That only works if you have someone else.

If you're willing to walk away . . . But, Choose, Julia had said, and she had loved me. "I won't tell you my name."

"Then—"

"But I will tell you this. I used to be something like that man, like Geordie Karp, but I've changed. I've— I've seen the error of my ways." I remembered the sampler. "Now I want to do unto others as I would be done by. I want to atone for the past. Helping Luz, helping you all—Luz and you and your husband, and Button—is the only way I know to make it even partway right."

Long silence. "I met that man but once," Adeline said meditatively, "and I didn't like him. Not one bit. He wasn't the kind to give anyone anything—especially not something like this." She leaned forward and tapped Luz's documents. "So I reckon you took them, or maybe made him give you them. So I'm thinking that maybe it's not a coincidence that he's in the hospital mostly dead and you're sitting here talking to me about his daughter. No, close your mouth, I haven't finished. You had something to do with his hurt. It might be that you hired some roughnecks to settle his hash. It might be that you had good reason. But I don't much care. He was a bad man. A very bad man. You say you used to be like him. Now, you don't seem that way to me, except for all your lying, but how can I tell for sure? The way it looks to me, Miss Walk-in-Here-with-a-Big-Checkbook, is that I could be getting myself into just the same mess I got myself into before. There's a lot I don't understand and don't know, and that means maybe one day someone, maybe you, could show up at my door and take Luz, take my child away. And she is mine. She may not have come from my loins in blood and sweat and tears like Button did, but she's in here." She thumped her breastbone. "And I need something—some kind of guarantee that's more than a lawyer's paper—and I reckon that's your name."

I was sipping air carefully, trying to protect my ribs. "What will you give me in return?"

"The time of day." She folded her arms again.

I stared past her for almost a minute, then reached into my pocket for my wallet. Moving, even my right arm, was getting harder. I pulled out my license and stared at it. The face in the picture seemed naked and defenseless.

"I'll show you this license on two conditions. One, that you never write my name down anywhere, ever. Two, that you tell no one what it is, not even Jud." And that you treat her like a daughter. That you love her, because she's only nine years old.

She considered, nodded, and held out her hand. I gave her the license.

"Aud Torvingen. What kind of name is that?"

"Norwegian."

She nodded again, mouthed the name to herself a couple of times, and handed it back.

Now she had my name. And a woman in New York had seen my face. One chance phone call could put them together.

"Aud? Miz Torvingen?"

I wrenched my attention back to the table. "Yes."

"Your color isn't so good." Kind Christian Lady returns, magnanimous in victory.

"I'm fine."

"Yes, well." She picked up her coffee mug. "Get you a refill?"

I shook my head, paid scant attention as she got up and poured for herself. What was it like to care so fiercely for a scrap of humanity you could carry as easily as a small sack of potatoes? What was it like to be the one so cared for? "Why does Luz call you Aba?"

She cleared her throat and made a production of adding sugar and cream. She cleared her throat again. "She called me that from the beginning. Two years now. It's from Abuela, Spanish for grandmother. I looked it up," she added defiantly.

"That's not all you taught her that you weren't supposed to, is it?"

"No."

"I'd like to hear about it, about Luz. Will you tell me?"

She turned and sat. "She was such a sad little thing, always weeping and talking in Spanish. Wouldn't eat, wouldn't talk English, wouldn't take any comfort. I didn't know what to do, until one day I took Jud's truck to the library and borrowed a cassette and a book. Had to buy a cassette player too. Had to hide it from Jud. But, oh, you should have seen her sweet face when I put that tape on!" She wiped absently at her eyes. "A flood of words! What with the book and everything, I learned to say Hello and Eat this, and after an hour or two, she was eating pretty as you please and calling me Aba."

"And you two talk Spanish to each other."

"God gave her her own language and I don't see anything wrong in having it spoken in this house."

"Mrs.— Adeline, I'm not criticizing. Just the opposite. But there's more, isn't there?"

She twisted her wedding ring. "Math. She could add and subtract if she did it in Spanish, so I didn't see the harm of showing her how in English. And you can't get much done in the house if you don't know how to multiply and divide. And then . . . Well, you've talked to her, she's a curious little thing. Once she had the bit between her teeth she had to know more. So I bought some encyclopedias at a yard sale and I taught her, and after a while I started sneaking to the library for extra books when Jud had them both off swimming or suchlike. He doesn't know. I thought it best."

"How much of an obstacle is he likely to be?"

"Mostly I worried, before, about following the agreement we had with Miz Goulay. Jud's stubborn about such things. A man's word is his bond." She gave me a complicit woman-to-woman smile that congealed suddenly: no doubt remembering I was nothing like a good Christian wife and mother.

"Perhaps it would be best for you to speak to him privately."

"I can speak of it some," she said slowly. "You'll have to do the money talk."

"Yes. But perhaps you could give me an idea of what he might think was fair." I gathered the documents. "How much did Karp send you a month?"

"Five hundred dollars."

According to his records, it had been four hundred. "And do you think that's fair? Take a moment to think it through."

"Six hundred?" she hazarded.

"Let's begin with seven-fifty, and review the situation after three months." By my estimate, they would need at least fifteen hundred a month to give Luz what I thought she needed, but for the Carpenters, especially Jud, that might be an immoral sum, easily confused with a temptation of Mammon.

"We could manage with that." She got a determined look on her face. "There's her food, and clothes, and things for her room, not to mention all the extra trouble of teaching her good English. It won't be long before she's a teen, eating us out of house and home, growing out of all her clothes. Then there's the books . . ."

She was rehearsing her argument for Jud. I felt around under the table until I found the transmitter. It peeled off easily and dropped into my hand.

". . . thousand and one other things a man doesn't pay any attention to . . ."

Once they were used to the arrangement, I would buy items such as a television and computer and music system. I'd provide the money for private tuition so Luz could catch up on those subjects Adeline might not have covered. I'd pay to send her to interesting places on vacation, make—

All money and no love. The way my mother had been with me.

No. It wasn't the same. It wasn't. I wasn't Luz's mother—she already had one, or at least someone who loved her.

I stood carefully. "You'll talk to Jud tonight? Then I'll take my leave. I'll talk to my lawyer and get a preliminary agreement drafted. I'll come back tomorrow. Afternoon." I was sweating; the bug cut into my palm.

There was still the booster unit in the tub of flowers by the door, which would be easy enough to retrieve on my way out, and the transmitters upstairs.

"If I may, I'll go up and use your facilities before I leave."

I used both hands on the stair rail, and counted backwards from two thousand in sevens as I climbed. Pain is just a message.

In the Carpenters' room, the back window was open. Faint voices—Button chattering, Jud answering, one short phrase from Luz, an acknowledgment from Jud—drifted up on the night air. The bug was exactly where I'd left it.

Luz's room looked different without the books on the bedside table. Maybe the suitcase was still downstairs. My heart felt too big for my rib cage, and my lungs too small. I had to sit on the bed for a minute before I could lean forward and reach for the transmitter. When I stood, my face felt cold. The door seemed a million miles away.

I dragged myself to the bathroom, telling myself I did not have concussion, that if I could just drink some water, splash some on my face, I'd be all right, but when I got there my good leg started to fold under me, and I half fell, half sat on the toilet. I shivered, swallowed. I just needed a few minutes, and some water.

A child thundered up the stairs. The bathroom door slammed all the way open. Luz. She stared.

"I have to use the bathroom," she said.

I didn't move.

"What are you doing?"

"I was going to get some water," I said. She looked at the sink, then at me. "My leg hurts."

She absorbed that. "Would you like me to bring you some?"

"Yes. Please."

She tipped the toothbrushes out of a glass, rinsed it, and filled it to the brim. She carried it from the sink with great deliberation. When I reached for it, she said, "Use both hands. If you spill it, it'll make the floor slippery."

I sipped. "Thank you." My breathing steadied.

"What did you do to your leg? Did you fall down?"

"I hurt my knee."

"Aba helps me if I hurt myself, she helps Mr. Carpenter, too. But most people don't have an Aba. Most people have a mom."

"Mine is a long, long way away."

She nodded, unsurprised. "What about your brother?"

"I don't have one."

"Button's not really my brother. Mr. Carpenter isn't really my daddy, either. My daddy's dead."

A child skipping along the pavement, holding my hand on one side, Karp's on the other. "Mine too."

She looked worried. "Then who's going to kiss you better?"

The bathroom walls wavered. A little hand took the glass from mine.

"Don't cry," she said. "I can do it. See?" She kissed my cheek, light as a cricket. "There. All better. Only I hope it works. I don't think you're supposed to be older than me."

Her tenderness was unbearable. She was nine years old. She knew how to kiss me better: a simple thing, but one I could never have taught her. And I had come here to save her.

"Aud? I have to go to the bathroom now."

"Yes," I said, "of course," and hauled myself to my feet.

She closed the door behind me.

On the way down the stairs, climbing into the truck, putting the engine in gear, I kept feeling that cricket kiss on my cheek.

Back in the park, I managed to get out of the truck and into the trailer. The dizziness was passing; probably more long-delayed shock than concussion. I stripped, and probed at my ribs cautiously. There was no way to be sure without an X ray but I didn't think anything was broken. I strapped myself up as well as I could, took more ibuprofen and some Vicodin—not much left—and forced down an apple, half a can of tuna, and two glasses of water. I propped myself on the couch with a bag of ice on either side of my knee. It hurt too much to lie down.

I dozed for a while.

When I woke, I felt shaky, but I could think. I forced myself to my feet, found a flashlight. My phone was in the truck. Might as well take a look at the hitch while I was out there.

The lever that unclamped the tongue had snapped off. Not dangerous, just a nuisance: I'd have to drag the trailer behind me for the rest of my stay in Arkansas because getting the hitch off would destroy it.

Back inside, I called Bette's emergency number. It was an hour later in Atlanta, and she usually retired before nine, but she answered on the third ring and didn't ask questions, just let me outline what I needed. I spelled out the exact terms: money, school attendance, home access to information, penalty for breaking the agreement. "Please e-mail me a draft as soon as you can."

"Shouldn't take long. Basically we're talking about customizing a general child custody agreement. Do you want any visitation rights—her coming to you, you going to her? Vacations, weekends?"

I touched my cheek.

"Aud? Hello?"

When I had gone back to Norway as a child, speaking English with more fluency than Norwegian, my great-aunt Hjordis gave me books and helped me with the words I didn't understand. When my mother was busy and my father out of town, she had wrapped me in a warm coat, taken me by the mittened hand, and walked with me through the city, pointing out the different buildings, telling me their history, funny stories about people who had lived there that weren't written on the plaques or in books. She had helped me belong.

"Are you still there? Hello? Goddamn these cellular—"

"Sorry, Bette. Yes. Visitation rights. I don't know yet. Can you keep the door open?"

"I could write a general clause about unsupervised access, to be mutually determined at some unspecified later date, permission not to be unreasonably withheld, etc. etc. Would that suit?"

"Yes."

"I'll get right on it." She hung up.

Bette loved the unusual, the unexpected. She loved her

work. I could see her pulling on her robe, walking barefoot down the carpeted hallway to her home office, sitting down, rubbing her hands. I'd have the draft within the hour.

There were other things to do, but I felt restless and unsettled, as though my skin didn't fit. I managed half a bottle of beer and no food at all. Towards midnight I left the trailer and stood in the dark under the trees.

The afternoon sky above the Carpenters' house was an ominous yellow gray and the air smelled metallic. If the temperature fell a few more degrees it would snow. Maybe not today, maybe not tomorrow, but soon. I transferred the briefcase to my left hand and knocked. Adeline answered the door in a daffodil yellow apron, wiping flour from her hands. Julia and I had eaten homemade food once. It was at Aunt Hjordis's house in Oslo. "A fine morning," she said. Her faded blue eyes looked ten years younger. "Jud will be just a while." She glanced at the briefcase.

"How long a while?"

"Oh, not long. An hour? He's just . . . well, you know how he is. He's just running through things in his mind, getting it all to hand, so to speak." She looked past me. "I see you've brought that trailer again."

"The hitch is broken."

"Yes, well. Still, it's a piece of good fortune. Button has been talking about nothing else since yesterday. Jud took them up to Conway for swimming first thing but the boy just won't be distracted. He'd dearly love to see inside. I'll send them out to you, shall I?" She smiled brightly, back to the Kind Christian Lady mode of getting her own way.

Aud rhymes with cowed.

"Luz!" Adeline called as she headed back into the house, "Button! Miz Thomas is here, and she says you can play in her trailer!"

• • •

I had barely dropped the briefcase on one of the recliners before Button was picking up the grapefruit knife I'd left in the drainer that morning. I took it away from him and asked Luz to sit for a moment while I made sure there was nothing else sharp lying within reach. She seemed fascinated by the luxury of the leather recliners; as I put away a bottle opener, I saw her furtively stroking the leather of her shoes and then the chairs, as if wondering how both could be the skin of an animal. She eyed the briefcase. My knee was less swollen today, but the pain was worse, as was the pain in my ribs. Stretching up to the higher cupboards hurt.

Eventually everything harmful was out of reach. Button found a paper clip and became absorbed in its shape, so I left him to it. I moved the briefcase from the chair opposite Luz and sat. My heart was beating faster than it should have been, and my mouth was dry. Perhaps it was a blood sugar problem.

"Is your knee better?" she said.

"Yes, thank you. The, ah, the kiss worked. For my knee."

She nodded solemnly. "Aba always puts a Band-Aid on mine."

"Good," I said. Gentian violet. That's what Hjordis had used on my cuts and scrapes.

I looked at Luz, she looked at me. She had seen me bludgeon two adults half to death with a gun. I had no idea how to begin, or even what I wanted to begin.

"How are you?" I said.

She shrugged. Her eyes were clear, no sign of a sleepless night, but it would come: the nightmares, the sweating, the fear that nothing around you is safe. Payment always came due.

"If you have bad dreams, you can talk to me. If you want."

She shrugged again. I looked around the trailer. Maybe my mother hadn't known what to do with a little girl, either.

"Would you like to see my computer?"

She didn't say no, so I got out the laptop. The case was soft black leather. While I booted up and acted busy with screen and keyboard, she pulled the case onto her lap and stroked it with the back of her hand.

I swiveled the whole thing around on my knee so she could see the SimCity screen. "This is a game where you can build your own city."

She gave me an uncertain look.

"Here," I said. "Let's put it back in the case, keep it safe while we play." She handed over the case unwillingly, but once the laptop was snugged in place with the screen still up, I put it back on her lap, and now she paid attention. I couldn't kneel, so I squatted next to her to type. Her hair smelled faintly of chlorine. "See, I can make factories, and parks, and farms."

"Can you make churches?"

"Yes," I lied, and put in a hotel.

"It doesn't look like a church."

"No," I agreed. "It's not a very good program."

"Program," she repeated under her breath.

"We could see if we can draw a better church." She looked around, as if expecting crayons and paper to appear from thin air. "No, look, here." I pulled up Photoshop. "This, here, works like a paintbrush, and this a bit like a spray can." I sketched an outline of a cathedral. It looked like a derelict shed. She smiled politely. I erased it. "Or we could borrow someone else's picture. From the web." For once the connection worked first time. I went to the Library of Congress image database. And then I knew exactly what I wanted.

I worked quickly. It didn't take long. "There," I said, and sat back. It was the Mexico City cathedral. She was riveted. "If you like, we can copy that over, use the image, the picture, for cathedrals in the game."

She nodded mutely. I kept a small window open in the top left of the screen for her to look at while I got back to SimCity.

"Now, see, we paste this into here, and look, there it is." A tiny cathedral in the middle of downtown SimCity.

"Not there. Here," she pointed to a park. Quick look to see what Button was up to. He had abandoned the paper clip and was examining the hinge on a cabinet door. "It should go there, on this side. And there should be government *edificios* on the other side."

Just like Mexico City, where the Catholic cathedral, built on the ruins of an Aztec temple, faced government buildings across a huge plaza. Maybe one day I'd tell her about Montezuma's palace.

"You do it," I said. I showed her how to work the touch pad. Her fingers weren't used to machine ways, but after a while she got the hang of it. She moved the cathedral.

Button was trying to dismantle the stove, but I had disconnected the propane before leaving North Carolina, so I didn't worry.

"How do I make buildings?"

"You have to pay for them." I showed her how, and she set to work with a curiously bland face, no frowns of concentration or lip caught in her teeth.

Button started in on the fridge. I distracted him with the remote for the TV, and while he sat, fascinated with the changing pictures, Luz played god, or at least mayor.

"What are taxes?" she asked after a while.

I thought for a minute. "The government's tithe."

"Oh." Ten minutes' silence while she put in too many parks, stroked the leather carrying case absently, hummed tonelessly under her breath, checked once or twice to make sure Button was still amused by his own toy, and finally turned to me for help. "There's no money left."

"You'll have to demolish some of those parks."

She frowned. "Parks are nice."

"Yes. But there's no point having them if everyone's leaving."

Fidget. Check on Button again. Sideways look. I just waited. "So what should I do?"

"Hard choice. Demolish the parks or have an empty city." I knew which I'd choose.

"No."

"They're your only choices."

"No."

"No?"

"No."

"Well then, you'll have to cheat."

Consternation. Cheating was probably not much encouraged by the Plaume City Church of Christ congregation. Aud as devil's advocate.

"You don't like that idea?"

She shook her head.

"Why not?"

"Cheating's bad."

"Who says?"

"God."

"Where does it say that in the Bible?"

Thoughtful look.

"Is there a commandment against it?"

She ran through the commandments in her head. "Thou shalt not bear false witness?"

"You don't actually have to lie. You just sort of step around what everyone expects. It depends, of course, on what you want from the game."

"People *and* parks."

"Yes, but do the ends justify the means?" Incomprehension. How old did children have to be before you could talk to them as real human beings? I tried again. "Sometimes people play this game to test how clever they are: to see how many people and parks they can make without cheating. And sometimes people use it to just play, to have fun, not as any kind of test: just to build things, to see how they look." All about perspective.

"People *and* parks," she said again.

"Then watch." I tapped in *call cousin vinnie.* "Now, you see that window—that man offering free money if you'll just sign his petition?" She nodded. "If you go ahead and take that money, it's yours, no strings attached."

"For nothing?" Not so much a question as an expression of skepticism.

"Yes and no. Now watch, see what happens if you don't take the money and type in this extra code."

I entered *zyxwvu.*

"Oh!" she said as the beautiful SimCity castle appeared.

"That boosts land prices, which—"

The trailer filled with the blatting of a sell-sell-sell commercial for cheap furniture: Button had discovered the volume control. I had to get up to turn it down manually. I swapped to a channel with strangely colored cartoon characters running about doing impossible things, and recorded three minutes of it. Then I showed him how to play back: freeze frame, slow motion forwards, backwards, jump back to real time. He loved that, making the characters go backwards and forwards, backwards and forwards. He giggled: a strange, grown-up sound.

Luz was looking fixedly at the screen again. "What's that?" She pointed to a farm on the outside of her city.

"Ah. Crop circles."

Before I had to try explain to a nine-year-old Christian fundamentalist some computer geek's in joke about alien visitors and crop circles, Adeline knocked on the trailer wall and called, "Miz Thomas? If you'd send the children out, then step into the house when convenient, I'd be grateful."

Hjordis's house in Oslo is filled in the afternoons with sunlight. In the evenings and during winter, she burns a score of candles to soften and lift the dark that flattens even the best artificial light. Her living room feels alive; it seems to dance. By contrast the Carpenters' front room, with its thick brown curtains, umber wool rug, and heavy furniture, felt stiff and formal, but Hjordis would have understood immediately the ritual aspects of the gathering: to the right of the fireplace, Jud sat in a wingbacked chair turned slightly to face the upholstered sofa, where I sat in a carefully nonconfrontational pose, briefcase tucked out of sight. Adeline's chair faced Jud's across the fire, turned to give him all her support.

Jud wore his Sunday best for a second day in a row. I don't know what Adeline had told him about me and my reasons for wanting to give them money every month, but he treated me as though I were the nineteenth-century son of his employer, come to ask for the hand of his daughter in marriage. He was not in a position to say no, but the forms must be observed.

He cleared his throat. "Miz Thomas," then stopped. I could feel Adeline willing him on. "Be obliged if you would listen." I nodded. He took a handwritten document from his inside breast pocket and stood, and began to read, as though it were a church lesson: seven hundred and fifty dollars a month, payable to J. Carpenter, in advance, on the first of every month; a day school to be agreed upon, Luz to attend, extra items such as uniforms and school equipment to be paid for by me; Luz to be kept clean, well fed and clothed, and happy, "loved as best we're able, as if she were family." Luz's legal documents to be kept by my lawyer, and a letter received from said lawyer confirming that fact. Luz to remain with the Carpenters while she was a minor. If my payments were more than thirty days late, the Carpenters were to receive the legal documents, and the agreement was rendered void. If they broke the agreement, they would surrender Luz.

He sat down, still holding the paper in both hands.

In my briefcase I had a sheaf of crisp photocopies and printouts, and Bette's impregnable legal draft. None mentioned love or family or happiness.

"May I see the paper?" I said.

He stood, handed it to me, sat.

There were several blank spaces I was obviously meant to complete, and a place to sign at the bottom. Under name, "Aud Thomas" had already been filled in. It was a feminine hand, Adeline's, though she was acting as if she had nothing to do with the proceedings, resolutely refusing to catch my eye when I looked at her. There was nothing about visitation rights, or lack of them.

"I agree with all these terms," I said. He took a pen from his pocket, handed it to me. It was an old transparent Bic ballpoint. "However, before I sign, I'd like to discuss one more matter." Adeline shifted but said nothing. Jud gestured for me to continue. "Your reassurance that I'm keeping my side of the bargain will come every month, with the money, but we haven't talked about my reassurance. Mr. Karp received written reports, but I would prefer a more personal arrangement. I'd like to talk to Luz myself every now and again, in person or by phone."

Adeline stared at her tightly clasped hands.

"You can't take her from this house," Jud said.

"Certainly not from the neighborhood," I said. Not until she was older.

After a long pause, he nodded. His word is his bond, Adeline had said. I nodded back. I filled in the name of my lawyer, along with her address and phone number, signed, and returned the paper to him.

He put his signature under mine. He hesitated a moment, then stood and offered me his hand. I stood, too, and we shook. He seemed momentarily confused as his hard, dry palm encountered mine.

I sat, opened the briefcase, and took out the papers. I separated Bette's draft, put it back in the case, and tapped the rest into a tidy pile. "These are copies of Luz's documentation. Birth certificate, adoption, passport, and so on. You'll need them to register her at school." I laid them next to me on the sofa. "There's also the matter of the first payment. In future months, of course, the funds can be wired directly to your account—

though I will need the number of that account." Adeline was trying to communicate something to Jud with her expression. "I have enough cash with me to cover the first payment, but as your cash flow has been interrupted recently you might well prefer to begin with a larger sum, say, three months' worth. I could get that to you by tomorrow morning." Hopefully he would prefer nice crisp greenbacks to a personal check, which, with all its personal information, was out of the question.

He cleared his throat. "Appears acceptable." More frantic expression from Adeline. "The three-month sum. One month's money now." Adeline relaxed. "Rest tomorrow."

I stood, he followed suit, and I counted out seven hundred-dollar bills, two twenties, and a ten—slowly, so he could watch, and not have to appear untrusting by counting it afterwards. I handed him the stack. He seemed unsure what to do with it. Adeline rose and crossed to his side.

"The coffee will be ready about now. Should I take that to the accounts, then fetch it here for you while you finish up with Miz Thomas?" Jud handed her the money gratefully. She scooped the photocopies from the sofa. "Now you two sit. I'll be but a moment."

So we had to sit. Jud laid his hands on his knees, nodded at me, as solemnly as if we were sitting on pews.

The silence was complete. No ticking of a clock on the mantel. "Mrs. Carpenter tells me the crop wasn't too good this year," I said.

"Been worse."

"Yes," I said. "Still, I'm sorry for it. Perhaps next year will be better."

"Up to the good Lord."

"As is everything." I longed for the scent of rain-wet North Carolina dirt, of leaves slowly mulching beneath sturdy trunks. Or perhaps it would be snowing up there already. "But as my father used to say, God helps those who help themselves. And I think—"

Adeline came in with the coffee: not mugs this time but white china cups and matching saucers, decorated with tiny red roses, and a silver-plate set of pot, creamer, and sugar bowl. The teaspoons did not match. She poured, handed out the cups carefully. Once everyone was settled again, I went on.

"Mrs. Carpenter, I was just about to say to your husband that I think Luz is going to need your help. Yesterday was a very hard day. For you and Mr. Carpenter, yes, and Button, but especially for Luz."

"Yes," Adeline said, "but she does seem to have come through it nicely. She's a hardy little thing."

"She is," I said. Jud turned his sticky eyes to mine. "But I think in a little while—maybe a few days, maybe as long as a few weeks or even months—she won't be so fine."

"Nightmares," he said. "Had them when she first come."

"Miz Thomas, there aren't so many childish fears that a good hugging and a bit of prayer can't fix."

"Her fears aren't so childish. A lot happened yesterday that she won't have had time to tell you about yet." I looked from her to Jud. "When she's afraid, let her tell you what she's afraid of. And don't tell her it can't happen because some of the things that will be in her nightmares *have* happened." I would probably star in a few of those nightmares.

"They won't happen again," Jud said with certainty.

Adeline shook her head vehemently. "Not while there's breath in our bodies."

"No." I sipped my coffee. "It might help, when she's scared, to tell her that she's very brave. She was very brave—very resourceful. There aren't many children her age who would try to defend themselves against an adult."

"Brother Jerry," Jud said, nodding.

"Luz mentioned a Brother Jerry yesterday," I said. "Apparently he told her that god works in mysterious ways."

"Brother Jerry was in the army or the marines or some such—" Adeline began.

"Navy SEAL," Jud said. "Doesn't much hold with the notion of turning the other cheek. Mite troubling to begin with."

After a startled pause, Adeline continued. "As my husband says, the elders didn't share Brother Jerry's point of view at first, but then after a lot of soul-searching, it was decided that Brother Jerry might have a point. Man, after all, only has two cheeks, and once you've turned both of them, it might be reasonable to fight back. So since September, the church has been sponsoring a self-defense class for the children. They seem to like it. I went to the old back field to watch once, lots of healthy yelling and kicking. Brother Jerry does nothing but good for those youngsters."

"When he doesn't try to teach scripture," Jud said.

"Brother Jerry seems to believe that 'Do unto others . . .' means do unto others before they can do unto you," Adeline explained. "More coffee?"

Early morning frost smells different in Arkansas: like cold straw. With Adeline's permission, I invited the children to eat breakfast with me in the trailer before I left.

They arrived, brushed and scrubbed to within an inch of their lives. Luz seemed different. Not exactly hostile, but wary. When they were seated, I put the kedgeree on the table. She sniffed at her plate suspiciously.

"What is it?"

"Breakfast." She stared at me, I stared back. "It's kedgeree. Smoked fish and rice all mixed together," and boiled egg and nutmeg, but she didn't need to know that.

"Fish," she said. Button was already tucking into his. She shook her head.

"Try it."

She put a tiny amount on her fork and ate it. "It doesn't taste like fish."

It certainly didn't taste like fish sticks. "That's because it's smoked. Try some more." She did, a bigger portion this time. Button munched happily. Luz took another forkful.

When I put three mugs of Irish breakfast tea on the table, Luz looked but was too proud to ask. I let her suffer. It's important to learn that if you want information you have to ask for it. I turned back to the bowl on the kitchen counter. I had made a fruit salad, but I could see how that would be received. I filled a plate for myself and sat down.

This time she couldn't resist. "What's all that?"

"This is papaya, this is litchi." She watched each spoonful, from my plate to my mouth and back. "Do you want some?" She shook her head. "There's also apple, and orange, and banana."

"Banana!" said Button.

"Would you like some banana?"

"Banana!"

Luz smiled at him indulgently. "He likes banana."

I got up again and chopped some banana into chunks and slid the plate in front of Button.

"Have you ever seen papaya before?"

She shook her head.

"You could look it up in your encyclopedia. But that wouldn't tell you how it tastes." I got up again and filled a small glass plate with fruit salad, which I put next to her bowl. "Just in case you want to try a bit."

Button took a piece of banana in one hand and squashed it with the other, slowly, almost experimentally, and when it was mashed to pulp, he examined it with great deliberation and then licked it off. "Banana," he decided, and calmly put another piece in his mouth. He chewed and nodded. "Banana."

"Yes," I said. "It tastes the same no matter what shape it is." Luz gave me that birdlike look from one eye, then the other. I sipped my tea and applied myself to the fruit salad.

When everyone had eaten as much as they were going to, I stood to clear the table. Luz automatically picked up some dishes. "Thank you. I'll do the rest."

"Thank you for the breakfast it was very nice," she said in one breath. "Please may we be excused?"

"No. I have a present for you, and for Button."

"A present?" More wary than excited.

I had no idea what she was thinking. "Yes." She perched on a recliner while I got the presents. The TV blared and chopped from one station to another: Button had found the remote again.

I'd bought four of the boxes in Little Rock yesterday morning; one, wrapped in heavy silver paper, I'd had shipped from San Francisco via Delta DASH at a cost that would have made Adeline pass out. One large box, two medium, and two small.

"This big one for Button first," I said.

Luz and I watched while he ripped his open and pulled forth a scale model of a fire engine, with working ladder, unspoolable hose, and flashing light. "This," I said, pointing to the tiny manual pump, "will actually suck up water and squirt it out here." He seemed not to hear me, but I was beginning to suspect that Button heard and understood a lot more than I had at first thought. He touched everything methodically, and found that all the firefighters came off, too. It would keep him happy for a while.

I passed her a medium box. "This one's for you."

Although she opened the wrapping carefully along the seams, her chest was beginning to rise and fall more quickly. She lifted the lid. It was a cell phone and charger. "Oh," she said, in the same tone she'd said "Fish."

"This is a serious present, Luz."

"It's a phone. A funny phone."

"Yes. But there's something else in the box."

She lifted out the phone and charger, and when she saw

what lay beneath, her eyes positively glistened. A beautiful calf-skin pouch, in natural brown, and a belt to go with it.

"It's to hold the phone. You slide the belt through those slits at the back, and put the phone . . ." But she was already threading everything together, sliding the belt around the waist of her corduroys, closing and snapping open the pouch with an almost voluptuous satisfaction. "Don't forget the phone."

I showed her how to slide the battery in until it clicked, how to put the phone in the charger. She listened with half an ear while running her fingers back and forth on the smooth belt and kicking idly at the recliner.

"Pay attention. I want you to carry it with you everywhere." I handed it to her.

"Even when I go swimming?"

"Not in the water, no. But everywhere else. Put it in the pouch."

She slid it in, appeared to be delighted with the fit.

"And there's a present that goes with it." I gave her one of the small boxes.

She opened it and lifted out a thick metal bangle. She weighed it expertly on her palm and frowned at its heft. "Is it silver?"

"No. Look on the inside."

"There's some numbers."

"They are secret numbers, just for you and me. Not even for Aba." I would just have to hope. "That's my cell phone number." I pulled my phone from my pocket and flipped it open, turned it on, and showed her. "I carry it everywhere." Or I would from now on. It beeped: three missed calls and one voice message. All from Dornan. Her wary look was back. Dornan could wait. "I want you to keep that bangle on your wrist, and the phone at your belt or in your pocket, and I want you to call me anytime you need me."

"So you won't get lonely," she said.

"Yes. Yes, that's right." I recovered myself. "You can call me in the middle of the night or first thing in the morning, anytime, I won't get— I'd like it."

She was watching Button with his toy.

"Luz?"

"Is that why you want to be my *tía,* so you won't be lonely?"

"Tía?"

"Aba says you're going to be my auntie."

"I— Ah, well—"

"Are you Button's *tía,* too?" She still wasn't looking at me. "I've never had an auntie before."

And then I understood: she was afraid. For her, gaining a relative had always led to terrible change.

"I have an aunt," I said. "Her name is Hjordis. She talks to me on the phone and sometimes buys me presents. That's what aunts do."

"She didn't take you away, even when she was lonely?"

"Never." I took her chin in my hand, turned her head so she was looking at me. "Luz, I'm going home today but you'll stay here. A few things will be different—you'll go to school, a nice school where you'll make friends—but every day you'll come home to Aba and Mr. Carpenter and Button. No one is ever going to take you away. I might talk to you on the phone sometimes, when . . . when I wish there was someone to kiss me better, and you can call me. If you don't know what a word means, or if you get lost, or you think something Aba or Mr. Carpenter wants you to do is wrong, call that number. I'll always answer and I'll always listen. That's what aunts do. Do you understand?"

She nodded, eyes enormous.

"Now I want you to take out the phone and learn how to use it."

She put the bangle on the carpet and took the phone out of its pouch. It was as big as her nine-year-old hand.

"Open it up. That little button there, the round one, turns it on, you have to press that first. Then you dial the number." She nodded. "Do it now. Dial my number."

She read the number from the bangle, dialed it. "It's not ringing."

"When you dial the number, you have to press Send, the green one." My phone shrilled. I flipped it open, put it to my ear. Luz lifted hers.

She blushed, hesitated. "Aud," she said.

"Anytime," I said into the phone, then closed it up. "You end the call by pressing that button, the red one."

She pushed the button solemnly, put the phone back in its soft leather pouch, and picked up the bangle again. The fear seemed to be gone. "There's two numbers."

"The other one is my lawyer. If ever I don't answer, if my phone breaks or something"—if I'm lying dead in a park with my throat cut—"you can call her and leave a message. She's very nice. Keep the bangle safe, wear that all the time, even in the pool if you want. It's white gold."

Her expression didn't change but she slid the bangle onto her left wrist and admired it for a while.

I pushed the phone box over to her. "There's an instruction book in there. It's a bit hard to figure out, but eventually you'll be able to program those numbers into the phone for speed dial."

She mouthed speed dial to herself and looked determined. I filed that response away for future use. While she experimented with the pouch, sliding it back and forth until she found the most comfortable position, I opened the other small box.

"And this one's for you, Button."

"Button." Luz tapped him on the hand until he looked up from his mostly dismantled fire engine. "Another present."

I fastened the stainless steel ID bracelet around his right wrist. He looked at it, took it off, put it back on again, then went back to his engine.

"That has his name and address and phone number on it," I said, and Luz nodded. She had her eyes on the last box, the silver one. "And this is a special present. I hope you like it."

It was heavy for a nine-year-old, but she didn't ask for help so I didn't offer it. After a bit of a struggle—she refused to tear the paper—she had it unwrapped. She folded the paper with great care: putting off disappointment as long as possible. Eventually she contemplated the hinged wooden box.

"There's a latch at the side," I said.

She looked at me, looked at the box. I nodded. She lifted the lid. It opened like a book. Nested on green velvet were seven volumes bound in brown leather, each stamped in gold on the spine with the name C. S. Lewis and the title.

"For when you have to take the others back to the library," I said. She was hardly breathing. "Take one out."

"Which one?"

"Your favorite."

"But I haven't read them all."

"Then my favorite, *The Lion, the Witch and the Wardrobe.*"

She lifted it reverently. Traced the lettering on the cover, turned it over. Opened it. Rubbed the maroon silk bookmark between her fingers, touched the gold-edged pages.

"There are illustrations," I said.

She turned a few pages, studied the first picture. Turned another page and, two minutes later, another. She was reading.

I opened my phone quietly, dialed, and listened to Dornan's message. "Aud? What's happening? You said you'd call. Turn your bloody phone on! Call me." He sounded angry and anxious, but not as though anything bad had happened. I closed the phone.

Luz read on, head bent. Her scalp gleamed at the part, very white, very vulnerable. So young. So much she didn't know.

"Luz." She looked up. The open inquiry in her toffee-colored eyes stopped me cold.

I cleared my throat. "When you've read them all, I want you to call me, tell me what you think. Which one's your favorite. Will you do that?"

She nodded. Her eyes flicked back to the page for a moment. I leaned down so she had to focus on me.

"Do you promise?"

"I promise."

They all stood in front of the house to wave me goodbye. Jud stood as though in church. Button moved restlessly, head turning this way and that. Adeline had one arm tight around his shoulders but her eyes rested on Luz. Mine, her gaze said, My girl. Lucky woman: to believe she'd lost her girl and to then get her back. She had never even said thank you.

Driving across the Mississippi, I was nearly blinded by the sun glinting off the buildings in downtown Memphis. Once on the other side, I hit drive-time traffic, so I found a strip mall with big parking lots, parked the rig, and went into a bar. It was small and long, just a dark oily bar down one side and a jukebox, currently silent, at the back, opposite the toilets. I took a seat on a stool with ripped red vinyl and asked the thin, balding bartender what they had in the way of imported beer on draft, which turned out to be Bass ale, chilled until flat and practically frozen when it should have been room temperature and aromatic.

At some point Luz would wonder who I was and why I paid for everything. I'd seen how stubborn she was; one day I might have to give her some answers.

I sipped my beer.

My mother had never given me any answers. Then again, I hadn't asked her any questions, once I understood that the answers wouldn't come from the place I wanted them to. Asking questions made you vulnerable. But I wasn't Luz's mother. I was a banker with the honorary title of aunt.

A woman with dyed black hair slid onto the stool next to

me. "Fucking kids," she said. "Fuckers took all my money, said they wanted some food for a change. Food my ass. Drugs. Only in seventh and eighth grade and already probably smoking and snorting and sticking it in their arm. Yo, Jim Beam here, Barney! Fuckers." She turned to me. "You got kids?"

"I'm not sure."

"What kind of answer is that? Do you got kids or don't you?"

"Beats me." My phone rang. "That's probably her now." But it was Dornan.

"Aud, where are you?"

"In a nasty little bar in Memphis drinking nasty beer."

"Do you have Tammy with you?"

"No."

"Only I'm here, in the clearing—"

"You were supposed to stay in Atlanta."

"She didn't call. You didn't call. So I came out here, and the trailer's gone, and there's no sign of Tammy."

"I see."

"You see? What do you mean, you see? Where is she?"

"I don't know."

"Christ. So she's done another disappearing act?"

"She was fine when I saw her a few days ago."

"If that bloody Karp—"

"She was fine. And Geordie Karp isn't in any position to do anything anymore. She might only be gone for a few hours."

"When are you coming back?"

"Day after tomorrow."

"What are you doing in Memphis?" I didn't respond. "I'll see you up at the cabin day after tomorrow then?"

"Yes." He hung up.

"Yours sounds bad," the woman with the Jim Beam said. "Fuckers. Here's to kids." We clinked glasses, I drained my beer, and left.

• • •

I was forty miles outside of Memphis when my phone rang again. I answered it cautiously.

"Hello?"

"Aud? Eddie." The muscles in my belly went rigid. "The story has taken an amusing turn. In just the last week, apparently, our twin avenging angels have been spotted in two other states outside—"

This is what happened when you walked away from your armor. All it took was one phone call.

"—sylvania. It seems—"

"Where?"

"Two incidents in West Virginia and one in Pennsylvania. Is this not a very good line? Should I call you back?"

"No. I'm sorry. Go on."

"It seems that the credulous readers have taken our entirely imaginary twin angels to heart. Apparently they have stricken a wife beater with terminal cancer and terrified the life half out of three seventh-grade bullies in the schoolyard at Chester Junior High, both up near Clarksburg. And in Sunbury, Pennsylvania, they appeared in the middle of the road and made a truck run off the pavement, killing the driver and one passenger. Another passenger survived. The two victims, according to the surviving witness—who, incidentally, on seeing the terrible twins glowing with wrath, has changed his evil ways forever—ran a dogfighting ring that local authorities have been trying to shut—"

West Virginia and Pennsylvania. Not Arkansas. Not Tennessee.

"—*Post* has substituted color paintings of the angel twins for last issue's quick pencil sketches. Offhand I'd say that they intend to play this one for a while."

"No police comment?"

"Oh, this story has moved way beyond the realm of such

mundane concerns. Knowing of your interest, however, I did take the liberty of contacting the NYPD and asking for a quote on their progress with the Karp assault."

"And?"

" 'No progress at this time.' They made some noise about being happy to talk to any member of the public who wants to come forward with evidence, from any state, but they didn't offer me an 800 number."

"They've stopped looking, then."

"I would agree. Unless, of course, a miracle happens." He giggled at his own wit. "Oh, and Karp? They found some family. Cousins, I believe. The *Post* describes them as 'estranged.' They say, and I quote, 'If his insurance won't pay, turn him off. He's not our problem.' "

I drove through the night.

An angel and aunt. Banker and devil's advocate. Aud rhymes with crowd. My name is Legion.

CHAPTER FIFTEEN

Powdery snow dusted the road up the mountain but it was thin and would probably melt off by midafternoon. I would have been able to get the trailer up, after all. Tracks of two different vehicles striped the snow, one set very fresh.

Dornan's Isuzu stood in the clearing, and thin gray smoke drifted from the cabin chimney. When I climbed down from the cab, my breath steamed, even though it was after midday, and the carrier bags I held in each hand crackled in the cold. The trees stood gaunt and bare against a gray sky streaked with blue. Winter had been late in coming this year, very late, but it had finally arrived.

My boots crunched on the frozen turf, and when I reached the cabin I paused to tap my heels on the stoop to knock away snow, making a mental note to buy a real doormat, before I opened the door.

Dornan sat on his heels by the hearth, poking at the logs in the stove. He spoke without looking up. "It's different, trying to make a fire inside something."

"You seem to be doing well enough." I put down my bags,

pulled off my jacket, and hung it on the banister. His lay over the couch in front of the fireplace.

He looked up. "Your face. And you're limping."

"Superficial. It'll heal. I'll make some tea." He nodded, more to himself than me.

I carried the bags to the kitchen, filled a kettle, and brought it out to put on the stove. It would be a while. Back in the kitchen, I busied myself with pot and mugs, milk, sugar for Dornan, and the shortbread biscuits I'd bought in Asheville. I brought everything on a tray which I put on the hearth, and then I sat on the couch and Dornan stayed on the floor, and we watched the flames in silence, waiting for the kettle, and the tea, before he said what he had come to say.

The flames grew and rubbed like cats against the cold iron, which ticked and creaked as it expanded. After a few minutes, I heard the first rumble of water warming. I ate a piece of shortbread. It dissolved, rich and buttery, on my tongue.

At the first quavering whistle, I lifted the kettle from the stove using the front of my sweater as an oven mitt, and poured the water and curling steam into the pot. Heavier steam curled back out and I sniffed it. Aromatic.

"You always do that."

"I know."

I stirred deliberately, put the lid on the pot, and waited. After three minutes, I poured. Perfect color, like dark oak. I handed a mug to Dornan. He stood, added sugar, and sat again, cross-legged, facing me. His face was tired, but very still. When the worst has happened, there is a certain peace for a while.

"She came back, and now she's gone again. She told me some of it." He tasted his tea, added more sugar, stirred, sipped again, and added, "I'm glad you hurt him."

I nodded but my heart squeezed. Annie had said almost the same thing while Julia lay fighting for her life: I'm glad you killed them.

Dornan stared at his tea. "Now we've both lost them."

There didn't seem much more to say.

After a while, I made more tea and Dornan added more wood to the stove. The cabin grew warm. The sun managed to break through the cloud and stream through the front windows. I watched the flickering flames and thought of nothing in particular. Eventually Dornan stirred.

"The forecast is for snow tonight, and I have to be in Atlanta by midmorning. I should start back now."

"Dornan—"

"No. I'll be all right. The sun won't be down for another two hours and I'll be safely onto the interstate by then."

"That's not what I was going to say."

"I know." He smiled sadly. "But I don't want to hear anything else. She's gone. She said she's sorry, that she always liked me, but that she should never have agreed to marry me in the first place." He stuck his hand in his pocket and pulled something out. He opened his hand: Tammy's engagement ring.

"I'm sorry."

"Not your fault. I know, that's not what you meant, either." He stood, reached for his jacket. "I just stayed to tell you. And to thank you. For everything. For finding her and bringing her back, in more ways than one."

He pulled on his jacket, a cheerful magenta-and-black waterproof, probably picked for him by Tammy, and moved towards the door. I put down my mug and followed him. When he put his hand on the latch, he smiled again. "We hung a good door, didn't we?"

"We did." He didn't move. "I can show you my workshop, if you like, when I get back to Atlanta."

"You're coming back then?"

"Yes."

"When?"

"Soon. Very soon. A day or two."

"Good. Being out here alone is not good for a person. Grief, I find, is . . ." He shook his head. "Listen to me, talking as though I know it all." He laughed shakily. "I thought it would be easier this time." He looked so small and wounded in his bright jacket that I opened my arms and pulled him in. He wrapped his hands over my hips, leaned his forehead on my breastbone, and wept. He smelled of woodsmoke and tea.

Eventually he stopped. He tried to wipe his face on his jacket sleeve. I brought him a box of tissues. "As you said, every modern convenience, even in the middle of nowhere."

A smile tried to break through his grief, but unlike the sun, it failed. He mopped and snorted for a minute or two, but turned down my offer of more tea. "I really have to get back, to stay busy. At least for a while. No," he said as he opened the door, "don't come out with me. Stay where it's warm. I'll be seeing you in a day or two." He stepped onto the stoop, then turned and took my hand. Either his was very warm, or mine cold. "Friends help. Don't forget that." He patted my hand, then walked with that quick step of his over to his Isuzu, opened the door, slid in, turned on the engine and lights, and pulled away.

I carried the rest of my things from the truck—a few clothes, two folders of documents, some toiletries—to the cabin and took them upstairs. The bed was stripped, everything neatly washed and folded. I sniffed the linens: clean, but no longer smelling of laundry soap. It had been at least three days, then.

The weather forecast was wrong; the snow did not come. A little before nine that night I bundled up in jacket, hat, and gloves and went outside to stand under the cold magic of stars and listen to the huge attentiveness of dark. I stood for a long time.

An owl flew across the moon and from half a mile away the sound of a Subaru engine drifted up the mountain. It grew louder, and five minutes later Tammy pulled into the clearing.

When she climbed out of the car, I saw the difference, the

sleekness, her buttocks ripe as mangoes, her arms and legs plump and muscled.

"What are you doing standing out here in the cold?"

"Looking at the stars. Thinking of Thomas Wolfe's description of the night."

"Oh. Right. Where's the trailer?"

"In storage in Asheville. I thought there would be snow and I wouldn't be able to get it up the track."

We went inside. I lit two lamps, then sat on the couch. Tammy went straight to the stove and opened it so she could rub her hands in front of the naked flames. "Forgot my gloves. I forgot to *buy* gloves I've been so busy."

That was my cue to ask what she'd been doing, but I felt out of sorts, grumpy on Dornan's behalf, even though, rationally, I knew none of it was really her fault; it was just that she looked so good and he looked so bad.

"You don't seem exactly thrilled to see me."

"I'm not too happy with the world in general. Everything is so . . . complicated."

"Things didn't go so well in Arkansas, huh?"

"No. Well, yes, sort of."

"Well, that's clear." Déjà vu. She shut the stove door. "Have you eaten? One thing I learned while you were gone: you can cook a whole meal in one pan if you just fry everything. How about steak, eggs, and fried potatoes? And then you can tell me all about it."

She cooked. We drank coffee with our meal. In the mixed lamp- and firelight, Tammy's rounded cheeks glowed like those of an ancient, burnished idol.

"You look good," I said. She raised her eyebrows. "The mix of softness and strength suits you."

"I feel pretty good. More at home with myself, you know what I mean?"

"Yes." At least sometimes.

"So now I want to hear about Arkansas."

I told her about the Carpenters, of Luz and her Spanish and Adeline's covert fostering of it. Of Jud and his discomfort with strangers, of Button and his odd eyes. Of Goulay, and Mike.

"You tied him up like a pretzel?"

"He looked more like a pool triangle, actually."

"I don't get how he got his hands loose to hit you."

"I was careless. I made an assumption—that he wouldn't be flexible enough to step backwards through the belt and get his hands to the front."

"Well, hey, you won in the end, even if you did get a few more dings to add to your collection. But the letting-them-go part doesn't seem too smart."

"I couldn't turn them over to the police, because then I would have had to explain how I'd come by my information." She gave me a crooked smile, and eventually I nodded. "Killing them would have upset Luz."

"They might come and find you."

"They can't, and they won't. They're going to be only too glad to forget I exist."

She gave me a look. "Oh, right. You said you'd be shutting down their business. *That's* pretty easy to forget."

"True. Except it'll be my lawyer doing the watching." Bette already had the preliminary information, and was busily amassing more. When we had sufficient hard evidence, she would—without using my name or Luz's details—bring in the child welfare agencies, charities, and news organizations, the crusaders and rights groups, and INS. There had to be a way of helping these children without wholesale deportation. Meanwhile, if Goulay broke or even bent so much as a traffic ordinance, Bette would tie her up in knots.

Then I told Tammy about Luz. "So Adeline has told her I'm an honorary aunt. But I don't know if I'm doing the right thing, if I should have left her or taken her away. How can you tell if a child is getting what she needs?"

"Jesus, if you could answer that one you'd be pulling down the big bucks as a parenting guru." She grinned. "Imagine the Oprah show: 'Well, Oprah, you tell them what to do, and if they don't, you kill them and buy another.' No," she said hastily, seeing the look on my face, "you'll figure it out after a while. It's like anything else: you get better with practice."

"Do you think I'll do a good job?"

She looked at me, fascinated. "Are you asking me for reassurance?"

Being vulnerable got easier with practice, too. "I suppose I am."

"This has got to be a first. Okay. Well, you're stubborn and smart, and you like to be the best, so whether you end up being Fairy Godmother or the Wicked Witch to that little girl, you'll find a way to make sure she gets a good life." She grinned again. "As long as you don't fuck it up. Or as long as she doesn't. It takes two, you know."

It takes two. "Tell me what you've been up to."

"I took that job at Sonopress—start Monday. I found an apartment in Asheville, it's small but it'll work for a while. I got the utilities turned on day before yesterday and the phone went in today."

"I guessed. All your things were gone." I paused. "Dornan was here. He told me you talked."

"How is he?"

"About as you'd expect. Sad. But no blame."

"I'm not sure I deserved him."

"People aren't merit badges." Which is a good thing because I had never deserved Julia. People just . . . choose, and then leave, one way or another.

Tammy got up, went to her jacket, and pulled out her cell phone. "I don't need this now."

"Keep it, just transfer the account to your name."

She nodded. Thanks would have been ridiculous. "I'm taking the car back tomorrow. I'll make sure they run it on my plastic, now that I've got an address to bill things to. Here's the new address and phone number."

A three-by-five card with that strong black lettering I'd first noticed weeks ago when I had searched through her papers. I put the card in my pocket.

"Dree said she'll introduce me around, and I'll meet people just doing my job. It'll be cool not being in the city for a while. You're going back, aren't you?"

"Yes."

"Why?"

I was quiet for a few minutes. A year ago, Tammy would have been unable to bear the silence. Now she just got up and brought the coffeepot to give us both a refill, and settled back comfortably, happy to wait. "I don't know. To be in the world. It's home."

My muscles lay lazy and loose on my bones, the food sat well in my stomach, the mug warmed my hand. I sighed and leaned back. Tammy's weight shifted slightly with the couch cushion, touching me now at hip and thigh. As we breathed her jeans rubbed against mine, seam to seam, but there was no question being asked, and no answer needed. The tension was gone.

She kept her T-shirt on and climbed under the covers, and when I came to bed she took me in her arms and I rested my face on her breast, and we lay like that for half an hour, not talking, not moving, just holding and being held, until our hearts slowed, and our breathing softened, and we slept.

I didn't wake in the middle of the night; I had no bad dreams; I slept, neither protector nor protected, just one human being next to another, mending.

When we woke, I made breakfast, and she left at first light.

• • •

By midday the yellow snow clouds began dropping their load and fat flakes sifted down in silence. The Subaru tracks were invisible within ten minutes. I packed the truck bed carefully, snow boots and shovel on top, just in case. The woodworking tools were well oiled and wrapped in tarps, the hogpen securely locked. I'd drained the pump so freezing water didn't split the pipe while I was away, and the cabin, ashes raked, flue shut, food removed, and bed stripped once more, was as winterproof as I could make it. I had built well. It was sturdy. It would be here when I came back in spring.

I changed my mind about the snow shovel and boots, and threw them in the backseat instead.

I made one last circuit of the clearing, beginning with the cabin, checking the door and windows, then moving on to the heath bald at the south end. The trees would soon be hidden with snow folded down on the branches like meringue. If I stood here a month from now, all would be white, with nothing but animal tracks to indicate the massive fecundity beneath. It has been here two hundred million years, a climax forest, very stable, not changing, not in the middle of turning into anything. I envied it.

A wren flittered onto the boulder I had used as a seat a few weeks ago: a tiny mouthful of a bird, fluffed against the cold like a Viennese truffle. It tilted one bright eye at me, then another, just like Luz, and flew on over the snow. Six months from now, it would have three cheeping fledglings running it ragged.

"I'll be back," I told it, and crunched my way to the truck.

It started with a low rumble that suited the wintry quiet, like a bear grumbling in its sleep, but once I was at the top of the track I turned off the engine, took my foot off the brake, and coasted down the road in silence.

"Lovely," said Julia. "Like Narnia. You mustn't forget to send that child her Turkish delight."

"What do you think of her?"

"She's nine. It's hard to tell. But she'll probably grow up to be a Bible-spouting evangelist who thinks you're Satan incarnate by the time she's twenty. At least she'll be a Bible-spouting evangelist who won't be pushed around. Not if you have anything to do with it."

"I'll teach her how to fight."

"You taught Ms. Tammy a thing or two, certainly." She smiled privately. Snow began to build up on the windscreen. "You should probably turn the engine on now and get those windshield wipers going, or we'll end up nose to nose with a tree."

I did.

"If you teach her to fight, don't be surprised if she fights you. Once she's grown she might just leave."

"People always leave."

"Often. Not always." I felt a ghostly touch just beneath my right eye. "Is that a tear?"

"Will you leave me eventually?"

She laughed, a round rich laugh full of good humor. "Aud. Look at me. Stop the car and look at me." I braked and stopped but did not turn off the engine. I looked at her. "Reach out and touch me."

"No."

"No. Because you can't. Because I'm dead. I can't leave you, Aud, because I come from you. I am you. You know that."

Tips of manicured but winter-pale Bermuda grass glittered in the frost under a hard blue sky and stinging lemon sun. Everyone wore sunglasses. Atlanta. I turned right off McClendon, and right again, and parked on the street. For some reason I was surprised to find the maple on my front lawn bare of leaves. I was even more surprised by the rose bushes, which had not been here in May, when I left. I got out of the truck and stretched.

Someone had cut the grass and cleared the leaves. I walked down the driveway, through the double gate, and into the back.

No flowers now, in November, but the mystery gardener had been at work here, too: shrubs trimmed, grass neat, flower beds turned. I peered through the garage window. The Saab was still there.

My key still fit the front door. I closed it behind me. The soaring living room felt enormous after the cabin. The floors gleamed. I sniffed: Murphy's wood soap, and recently split kindling. Someone had laid the fireplace. In the middle of the dining room table stood a vase of freshly cut carnations. And a note, on yellow, lined paper.

> *Somebody called Beatriz has been taking care of the garden since you've been gone. She says you know who she is. Annie came into the coffeehouse the other day and said if you were coming back she wanted the key to the house because she wanted it to be nice when you got back—but she said she'd call you. I told her to leave the key in the mailbox. Don't blame me if she didn't! Welcome home.*
>
> *Dornan*

Still holding the note, I walked back outside to the mailbox. The brass key was there. No mail. No doubt yet another uninvited guest had brought that in and put it somewhere.

A dinged-up old VW Rabbit pulled up outside the house opposite and a man with a scraggly goatee and bright yellow fleece jacket got out and climbed the steps. No sudden barking. He let himself in. New neighbor. Deirdre and her two massive dogs must have moved. At least he didn't seem interested in my business. I put the key and the note in my pocket and went back in.

The phone machine blinked green. Next to it lay a sheaf of carefully transcribed messages, all in Dornan's hand. I read the top one, dated five months ago, at the end of May. *Atlanta police: routine call (but isn't that what they always say?) about some arson murder last week*. I flipped forward a few pages—one from Philippe at the Spanish consulate, wanting me to take on another bodyguarding job—and a few more, then back two. June 14th. *Else Torvingen (your mum?), wanting to know if your friend was all right.* Another caught my eye. *Señor SomebodyorOther (heavy accent) saying something about how you owe Them (definitely capital T) a Favor (ditto) and they're going to Collect. Some job or other they want you to do. You're supposed to call.* A Tijuana number. I went through the rest, page by page, dozens of them, until I came across another message from my mother, this one dated on my birthday. *Else Torvingen again, sounding frosty. Something along the lines of "Hey, you didn't call me back (you ungrateful cow), maybe you've gone off somewhere again without telling me, but Happy Birthday anyway."* I glanced absently at the rest.

Sometimes it takes two.

One new message. I pressed PLAY.

"Aud, it's Annie. I have been so *worried* about you. Why didn't you tell me where you'd gone? I finally managed to track down that nice young man who runs the coffeehouses and he was kind enough to lend me your key"—not even a Sherman tank would deter Mrs. Miclasz when she had decided on something—"so that I could make the house a bit more welcoming for you when you got back. There are some bits and bobs of food in the fridge, and I tidied up a little. Aud, don't disappear again. I know you feel alone, but there are people here who love you. Call me."

I walked numbly to the fridge: milk, bread, cheese, eggs, apples, pâté. Even beer.

People here who love me. I had helped Beatriz last year, and seen her blossom. I had forgotten she was coming back from Spain to work in a downtown advertising agency. Annie, whose daughter I had killed. People here who love me. Whether I liked it or not.

I wandered into my workroom. The chair I had been working on before Julia's death gleamed. I pushed it with a fingertip and it rocked back and forth on its runners, wood against wood. In the bedroom there were more flowers, and the bed was freshly made. I stroked the silky antique quilt. I imagined Julia's mother smoothing it with her hands. Julia had never seen it.

And then I couldn't avoid it any longer: the laundry room, where I would find my clothes and Julia's still on the floor where I had dropped them months ago, the day I got back from Norway. The clothes that still smelled of Julia.

I closed the bedroom door, trod through the kitchen, and stopped at the door. I smoothed back my hair, took a deep breath, and went in.

The clothes were gone.

I tidied up a little. Freshly laundered sheets . . .

I ran into the bathroom and yanked open the linen cupboard. No neatly folded clothes. Into the bedroom. Nothing in the closet. I jerked the top drawer of the dresser so hard it flew out, dumping underwear on the carpet. Nothing, nor in the second drawer, or the third. Nothing.

I ran into the living room, the dining room, the kitchen. Nothing. Nothing. She was really gone.

And then I laughed, and walked back to the laundry room, and to the dirty linen basket, and lifted the lid. There they were. I reached for the blue shirt but didn't pull it out immediately, just ran my hand over it, touched the buttons, rubbed the cuff between my thumb and forefinger. Then I lifted it to my face and breathed.

Sunshine and musk and dusty violets, but so faint. I breathed again: her rich skin, and her hair, oh dear god her hair . . . Tears ran down my face, my neck, dripped on my hands, onto her shirt. All I had left of her. So faint. So very very faint.

ACKNOWLEDGMENTS

The texts at the beginning of each section, while inspired by the *Oxford English Dictionary* and the *Encyclopaedia Britannica,* are faithful to neither.

I'm grateful to Timmi Duchamp, Steve Swartz, Holly Wade Matter, Mark Tiedemann, Vonda McIntyre, Ed Hall, and—particularly—Cindy Ward for their many useful comments; to Marcus Eubanks, M.D., who helped with the medical details; to Carolyn Soloway, immigration attorney, who has now helped me twice—with information for this novel and in real life; to John Swartz, for sending a box of leaflets, directories, and maps; to Brooks Caruthers, for Arkansas details; to my editor Sean McDonald, for prodding me relentlessly in the right direction; to Colleen Lindsay; and to my agents, Shawna McCarthy, Danny Baror, and Jane Bradish-Ellames.

A NOTE ABOUT THE TYPE

The text of *Stay* is set in Monotype Garamond. Variations of Garamond have been a standard among book designers and printers for four centuries; nearly every manufacturer of type or typesetting equipment has produced at least one version of Garamond in the past eighty years. The name is attributed to sixteenth-century printer and type designer Claude Garamond. However, there is evidence tracing the design to a version cut by Jean Jannon in 1615. Monotype Garamond was designed in 1924 by F. W. Goudy.

Akzidenz Grotesk Berthold, the display face in this book, was designed by German designer Günter Gerhard Lange for the H. Berthold type foundry in Berlin. Born on April 12, 1921, in Frankfurt-an-der-Oder, Germany, Lange was a painter and graphic artist and had studied calligraphy, typesetting, and printing. He began his association with H. Berthold in the 1950s and was appointed artistic director in 1961.